RITES OF PASSAGE

RITES OF PASSAGE

JOY N. HENSLEY

HARPER TEEN
An Imprint of HarperCollins*Publishers*

HarperTeen is an imprint of HarperCollins Publishers.

Rites of Passage

www.epicreads.com

Library of Congress Cataloging-in-Publication Data

Hensley, Joy N.

Rites of passage / Joy N. Hensley. — First edition.

pages cm

Summary: "Sixteen-year-old Sam McKenna discovers that becoming one of the first girls to attend the revered Denmark Military Academy means living with a target on her back"— Provided by publisher.

ISBN 978-0-06-229519-4 (hardback)

[1. Military training—Fiction. 2. Sex role—Fiction. 3. Bullying—Fiction. 4. Schools—Fiction. 5. Secret societies—Fiction. 6. Blue Ridge Mountains—Fiction.] I. Title.

PZ7.H39835Rit 2014 2014010022

[Fic]—dc23 CIP

AC

Typography by Torborg Davern

14 15 16 17 18 CG/RRDH 10 9 8 7 6 5 4 3 2 1

❖

First Edition

To our servicemen and -women, and all those who protect—because everyone deserves a fighting chance

and

to those who try and fall down and try again. Nothing is impossible.

Also, to Dr. Randy Oakes—I miss you and wish you were around to see this. You were the best writing teacher a girl could have. I hope that, wherever you are, you're saying a "poor thing" or two for Sam. She needs 'em. I wrote her just for you.

RITES OF PASSAGE

ONE

I'M PHYSICALLY INCAPABLE OF SAYING NO TO A DARE—I'VE got the scars and broken bone count to prove it. And that fatal flaw, Bad Habit #1, is the reason I'm sitting in the car with my parents right now, listening to some small-town radio DJ talk smack about me.

"So, stop me if you've heard this one: You know Lieutenant Colonel McKenna, right? Well, in case you've been living under a rock all summer, here's a refresher: Commander of the Third Special Forces Group based out of Fort Bragg, North Carolina. One son was a Ranger; the other is the cadet colonel at our very own Denmark Military Academy this year. Well, now the McKenna family is taking their patriotism one step further."

"Turn it off, Topher," Mom pleads, waving her hand half-heartedly at the center console. I'm surprised she even came along. Since my oldest brother, Amos, died last year, she hasn't done much of anything except pop pills. And, for someone who married into the service and has two kids who bleed camouflage, she hates the military with a fiery passion that rivals an inferno.

Dad sucks in air through his teeth, but otherwise says nothing; he doesn't need to because the radio DJ continues. "That's right. The Light Bird's daughter, *Sam*, is set to start at the DMA today. Who knows? McKenna could very well ruin the finest military high school in this country with his own hands."

My eyes jerk to see Dad's reaction to his rank being disrespected like that. His jaw clenches. The Light Bird is *not* happy.

"That's right. She's joining four others to be the first class of females determined to do what only young men have done in the last hundred and twenty years: graduate from the Academy." The DJ's laugh is scratchy, like he's smoked about fifty too many packs of cigarettes. "Hey, Sam!" The DJ yells into the car and I close my eyes, waiting. "It's great that women can fight on the front lines now. If you want to go to the Middle East and get your head blown off, I won't stop you. Equal rights and all that. But no one wants you here. Go back to Fayetteville and stay the hell out of our school!"

In the backseat, I shake my head. The DJ couldn't be more condescending if he tried. But I've heard it all before. Emails and calls came all summer long from alumni, current students, and those too scared to give their names. All of them said the same thing: we're not wanted at the DMA, and there will be trouble if we show up.

I shift my weight and stare out the car window, at the

mountains that I'll be calling home for the next three years. I've seen bigger, especially when we were stationed in Germany, but the Blue Ridge is still pretty impressive. The rolling hills go on for waves and waves of blue, stretching from here to the north. The Appalachians rise up to my left far into West Virginia.

Mom turns from staring at her own reflection in the visor mirror to peer into the backseat at me. Big watery tears fill her eyes and she begs. "You don't have to do this, you know. I know you think you do, but you don't."

I thought maybe she'd finally given up, and I'm glad I'm sitting on my hands so she can't see my fingernails—or lack thereof, thanks to Bad Habit #2. "Please. Can we *not* start this again?"

She doesn't know about the dare, of course. After the epic hitchhike-to-Turkey dare three summers ago when we had to get a military escort back to Berlin with the Funkhauser boys, dares of any kind are strictly verboten in our house. No, the only "win" for her is if no one in our family ever has anything to do with the military again. After Amos, the last thing she wants to see is a uniform on any of us.

"I mean," Mom continues, her words slow, "what will kids say to your children? They'll get teased! 'Your mom wears combat boots!'" She ends in the voice I used to use when I picked on Amos.

I let out a burst of air. "Is that really all you have left in the way of arguments?"

"Samantha Jane," Dad barks. "You will not speak to your mother like that. Apologize now."

"Yes, sir." I cross my arms as the car creeps forward another inch. "Sorry, Momma."

Mom gazes out the window. "Do you think we'll see Jonathan when we get on campus?" She picks at her fingernails. The *tick tick tick* is enough to make me want to jump out of the car.

The line of traffic stretches up to the gates and inside the DMA, but we're not even close. Do they plan this—the long wait to get checked in—to let the anticipation build and build? I wonder if anyone drops out before they even get inside the gates.

"Even if we do see Jonathan, you and Sam are not to say a word to him," Dad orders.

I resist the urge to salute. I got the same speech at breakfast this morning. No talking to Jonathan. No looking at Jonathan. No thinking about Jonathan. Definitely no embarrassing hugs for Jonathan.

Jonathan is the cadet colonel. You can't be all female *around him.* As if being *female* is somehow a sickness Mom and I can get over.

Not like he'd give me a hug even if I begged for one.

"Now, Sam," Dad says, eyeing me in the rearview mirror. "I made sure Reverend Cook is your faculty mentor. He and I go way back. He lives off campus, but he's at the chapel every day. You'll meet with him weekly, at first, to make sure you're assimilating well. Then the meetings will spread out."

"I know, Dad." I try to keep the annoyance out of my voice—it'll only make things worse—but he's told me this three times today already.

"You promised me she'd be fine." Mom sounds like one of those little cartoon chipmunks. I wonder if they have medics on campus to resuscitate her if she keels over. "She's not a delinquent like most of the kids here. She also doesn't need to be an ROTC cadet like your *sons*, either. And she shouldn't *have* to go through training since she's not a freshman."

"She's a McKenna. That name comes with certain privileges around here. But she'll go through hell just like all the others. Every new student goes through freshman training, even if they are a year older. And it's not like they're going to let a female skip out on all the rites of passage. It's not going to be easy. It's not *meant* to be easy."

"Well, then maybe you should tell her not to do it. She's only doing this because of you. You can be proud of her even if she doesn't wear camouflage."

Dad's eyes get dark. Mom never pushes back, especially not where I'm concerned. Not anymore. I push open the car door. "I'm going to walk. I can't have this argument again. I'll see you guys at the gate." I slam the door shut before the commander of Platoon McKenna can order me back.

The humidity of Virginia in August has me sweating before I take five steps. I might as well be swimming up to the gate with the air as thick as it is here. I glance into cars as I pass wide-eyed freshmen dressed in what we all have to report in—khaki pants, white button-down, black tie. Yes, a tie, even for the females. No special treatment for the first girls at the DMA.

I don't know the four other females who signed up to do this with me. We're either incredibly brave, or stupid. "Stupid," I say to myself. "Definitely stupid."

If Amos hadn't used my weakness of needing to please Dad to goad me into the dare, I wouldn't be here. I could have easily enlisted after high school just like he did. I kick a rock as I move toward the entrance to campus. Thinking about Amos through this whole process is not going to help at all.

The DMA sits on top of a hill overlooking the town. The walls are tall, making the campus look like a castle or a prison, depending on the reason you're there. It's weird that it's here, in Middle of Nowhere, Virginia, but if I get the chance to stay in the same place for three whole years and make an actual home for myself, I'll take it. Bed, place to eat, place to shower—that's all a home is to any military brat. It would be nice to add friends into the mix for once.

At the gate, a tanned and toned upperclassman sneers at me, but I don't miss how his eyes slide down to my chest and linger just a second too long. I haven't been issued a name tag yet, so he can't know I'm a McKenna or the sister of his cadet leader. I give him my sweetest smile when he slowly brings his gaze back up to my face.

"Can I help you, miss?"

I let my eyes slide suggestively down. He's got incorrect folds in the front, probably a loose shirt stay. Wrinkles in the trousers. Shoe shine needs a bit of work. It's like a disease. I couldn't turn off my military bearing if I wanted. That's what you get when you're raised by Lieutenant Colonel McKenna and live in a house full of military-obsessed males. Once I've taken it all in, including the last name on his uniform, I meet his gaze straight on. "Not at all, Cadet Evers. Just waiting for my dad to come check me in."

Beads of sweat line his forehead under his garrison cover and he wipes at it. "You're with the incoming class?" He takes a step toward me, a little too close for comfort.

I know the type—I've dealt with them my whole life. He thinks he's hot in the uniform and any girl will melt into a puddle at his feet. But not me. I laugh instead. "No, I just wear this outfit because I think it makes me look good."

He glares and turns away to help the next car in line.

But I've got to watch it. No matter what I think of this cadet, I've got to keep my mouth in check. Who knows who this guy might end up being? If he's my drill sergeant—the drill sergeants here are always juniors, always seventeen—I'm in trouble already and Hell Week hasn't even started.

Two cadets pass to my left and Evers brings his hand up to his eyes, saluting. "Good afternoon, Colonel."

"What's up, Evers?"

I'd know that cocky-ass voice anywhere, but I turn toward Cadet Colonel McKenna anyway. My brother doesn't even bother glancing in my direction.

"Just guarding the gate, passing the time 'til we get to see what these Worms are made of."

The other cadet with my brother looks my way, and then whispers something in Jonathan's ear. They crack up and a trio of birds startles in the nearest tree. The other cadet is Lyons, Jonathan's second in command. I've never met him, but I've seen pictures and heard lots of stories.

"Stop by after the Worms meet their cadre tonight, okay?" Jonathan says to Evers. "We're having a party."

"I'll be there. Thank you, sir," Evers says, bumping fists with Jonathan.

Lyons is already a few steps ahead. Jonathan moves on, ignoring me like he has all summer. It wasn't always this way. Back in Germany we'd been thick as thieves—the three McKenna amigos. But all that changed when Amos hung himself and I decided to come here.

It's another ten minutes of awkward silence with Evers until Dad's car pulls up.

"Can I help you, sir?" Cadet Evers's voice pulls me back to the here and now. "Oh, Colonel. I didn't realize. It's an honor to meet you, sir." He brings his hand eye-level and salutes my father. "I'm a friend of your son."

Dad salutes back. "Well, then, the colonel should have taught you how to dress your shirt properly and iron your trousers. You're representing your school today, Cadet Evers." Dad looks my way. "Get in, Sam."

Evers's eyes get just a hint wider as he realizes who I am. There's no way to miss the embarrassment and anger on his face. He quickly fixes his shirt, though it's still not up to regs, and checks his clipboard. Then he looks at me once more before turning toward Dad. "Pull on through, sir. You'll want Stonewall Hall, third building on your right. Cadets will meet you there with further instructions."

Dad nods but doesn't take his foot off the brake yet. "When you get a break, take a rag over those shoes, too. I should be able to see myself in them."

"Yes, sir." On his walkie-talkie before we've even pulled

through the gate, Evers is probably telling someone at Stonewall Hall to roll out the red carpet.

I can't help grinning as we pass by.

The rest of the day is exactly what Dad warned me about: a lot of boring standing around doing nothing. Cadets carry my footlocker up to the top deck of the barracks and even put it in my room for me. Dad helps me unpack undershirts and underwear, rolling them to regulation length and putting them into drawers, and we hang up the few white shirts I've brought along. There's nothing else to set up; we're not allowed to have TVs, phones, or anything, really.

The cadets make friendly—or at least not awkward—conversation with Dad as we walk around campus, but they don't even glance at me. Once I passed through those gates I became nothing. Less than nothing. I'm a recruit—a Worm (the "friendly" word recruits are known as until we're recognized as cadets sometime around Christmas) at the DMA. That's it.

We find the laundry and get my standard issue uniforms to carry back to the barracks. At least I don't have to walk in the gutters yet. It's the only place recruits are allowed to walk on campus, right where the rain washes away into the drains, where the leaves will collect when the seasons start to change. Walking on the sidewalk is something to be earned, like everything else around here. Like getting to live on the first floor of a building, being able to walk across the grass or leave campus whenever we want, having a television in our room, and wearing civilian clothes. Everything's earned here. And I'm determined to get every little privilege I can.

The whole time, Mom stays in the car.

"Attention, recruits." The voice over the loudspeaker echoes across the parade ground. "You have five minutes to say good-bye to your families. When your time is up, you are officially recruits at the DMA and you must abide by all rules forthwith. Any recruit caught not walking in the gutters will be given demerits. Any recruit caught not saluting or properly addressing members of the Corps of Cadets will receive demerits. Dinner will commence at seventeen hundred hours. There will be no talking in the mess hall, in accordance with Fourth Class rules and regulations. After mess, you are to report to the armory for your swearing in."

There is a pause before the voice continues, giving some of the less focused recruits a chance to freak out. "You now have three minutes. Family members, we look forward to seeing you during Parents' Weekend in October. Thank you for coming."

I turn to Dad, ignoring the stinging in my eyes. My arms ache to reach out and hug him, to feel his arms around me, supportive and loving. But he's in uniform. You don't hug the LTC when he's in uniform. "Tell Mom bye for me. Tell her I love her."

Dad looks at me, lips tight, sizing me up. Then he nods. "Make me proud, Sam."

He's said it now. The one thing I've been telling myself it's not about since I agreed to this stupid dare in the first place.

Because of course this is for him.

It's always for him.

After all, when you're a girl and your dad's pretty much the most badass lieutenant colonel there ever was, there's no way you're ever going to be able to make him proud.

Unless you do something stupid.

Like agree to be one of the first girls to enroll at a previously all-boys military academy.

TWO

AT THIRD MESS, THE THREE OTHER FEMALES WHO'VE ARRIVED and I get through the line quickly and sit at the first table designated for Alpha Company—the group of recruits I'll eat, drill, and sleep with the whole year. We've got three assigned tables and the boys choose to fill up the rest of them before even beginning to sit at ours. Even then, they leave an obvious no-man's-zone between us and them. The barrier of empty seats tells me everything I need to know about my "brothers."

All five of the incoming females have been assigned to the same squad—for ease, I guess. That way only one company has to have female bathrooms and go through special assimilation training. We're still missing one, but while I eat, I size up the others.

Directly across from me sits someone who should be a runway

model, not a cadet. She's wearing the same clothes as the rest of us, but she owns those clothes. There's not one stray blonde hair out of place. Pearl earrings and makeup complete the picture. Not quite your average camouflage and push-up kind of recruit. She's the girl my mom probably wishes had been her daughter. The one next to her doesn't look like she weighs more than a hundred pounds soaking wet. Tears sit in her eyes, waiting to spill over. Her hand shakes so much that the fork she holds clatters against her plate. I can't see her lasting the week.

Beside me sits the only one I think might make it through the year with me. Her brown hair is cut super-short already and she looks like she's got some muscle to back her up. Maybe she's planning on trying out for the rugby team.

The guys are easier to figure out, in my opinion. After living with Jonathan and Amos and dealing with their stupid friends, I call 'em like I see 'em. The ones who are ready for this already have military haircuts—shaved at the sides and buzzed on top—a "high and tight." It's the only haircut I've ever seen on Dad.

The ones who aren't going to make it are easy to spot. Their eyes bug out and scan the room like they're looking for the quickest escape. Maybe it was a scholarship that brought them here. Maybe, like me, they're part of a military family. Some have been court-ordered here because they can't go back to public schools. But whatever the reason, they're not going to make it. I've picked out two so far, and I'm on the fence about three others. I kind of feel sorry for them, but right now they're not my problem.

The guy who will definitely survive sits closest to us. He's got light brown hair and a spray of freckles across his nose, and winks at me, his teal eyes sparkling with mischief. I try not to return the smile. But it's hard. If I lose my concentration here for even a second, the upperclassmen will sense blood like sharks in the water.

I eat slowly, knowing that nothing bad will happen until after the swearing in. When Jonathan went through recruitdom he emailed me every week, giving me a blow-by-blow account of what happened. That was when there was no chance I'd be able to be a recruit myself. Now he refuses to talk about the DMA—like it's some kind of state secret. I wish Amos had been in the car this morning to bring me here, to say good-bye to me. I wish he'd said good-bye at all.

"Good evening, recruits. I'm Cadet Colonel McKenna, your leader here at the DMA." Thankfully, Jonathan's voice over the intercom interrupts my train of thought before it goes to all the bad places. "You have fifteen minutes to finish dinner and meet me in the armory. I look forward to starting you down a path of success here at the Academy."

I swallow the last of my water and walk my tray up to dump it.

The model follows along with me. "Do you know where the armory is?"

Against my better judgment, I whisper, "Yes. When we leave, just follow me." I send a prayer to whoever is listening to make her *not* be my roommate. It may not seem like a big deal to talk, but we've already been ordered not to. I scan the room, looking for any sign of upperclassmen or that someone's watching to report the first females at the DMA already breaking rules.

"I'm so turned around I don't even remember where our barracks are."

She's not going to need to know if she keeps on like this. Only thing she's going to need to remember is the way out the front gate.

The armory is only a five-minute walk, but with seventy-five kids in the incoming class, it takes a little longer before everyone is seated. Upperclassmen stand on a running track suspended from the ceiling, whispering and pointing at various recruits, mostly me and the three other girls. We're sitting another twenty minutes in near-silence, getting fidgety, when Jonathan finally shows. He enters from the back, staring straight ahead. He was born for this. I straighten my back as he marches past me toward the stage.

"Good evening." His voice booms around the armory. He doesn't even need a microphone.

One of the upperclassmen above us uses the ring I'll wear someday to create a ping against the metal railing. First that solitary ring taps the handrail. Then another. Soon, all the upperclassmen join in, the air filled with the metallic pings. The clink of metal on metal makes me shiver. Not one of them is smiling.

"You are freshman class number one hundred twenty-seven at Denmark Military Academy. It is an honor and a privilege to act as your cadet colonel during the course of this school year. I promise to uphold the Cadet Creed and the standards set by my predecessors at the DMA, a long line of honorable graduates who have gone on to do heroic deeds."

He lists the names of some former graduates, our father included. Names that are burned into my brain—heroes of my father, and other men who have been legends to me since I was old enough to start hearing war stories. I can't help but smile, wondering where I'll fit in this list after a few years in the service.

"I look around and see some scared faces. I see the faces of our female recruits—one of whom may be the first female graduate of the DMA." His eyes skim over the four of us, but he doesn't meet my gaze.

Someone hisses behind me. A "boo" echoes off the polished wooden floor. My face warms under the scrutiny. Jonathan ignores it all and continues. "Before me are future military leaders, future Army Rangers, future Marines. Whatever path you choose, we are here to start you out on it. To give you a strong foundation of military readiness and preparation. It is what you learn within the boundaries of Denmark Military Academy that will help you to rise to the top in whatever career you choose upon graduation. The network of DMA grads helps one another in every way possible and you are about to join a brotherhood like no other."

Recruits shuffle around me, but I keep my eyes on Jonathan.

"Now I invite you to stand and take the oath to the DMA that thousands of cadets have taken before you."

The chairs around me scrape on the gym floor. I glance to the left. The model's eyes are wide, like she's finally realizing the magnitude of what we're about to do. The tears that were threatening to fall from the mousy recruit at dinner are finally rolling down her cheeks. She dabs her eyes, her hands still shaking. The future rugby star just grins. I smile back, my heart racing.

"Do not say these words lightly. When you swear this oath, you will be held to the same standard as every other cadet at Denmark Military Academy. You are starting a career as an upstanding citizen of this country and swearing loyalty to the land on which you stand. If you are unsure, you may walk out those doors and no one will think less of you. But once these words are uttered, you are at the mercy of your peers and the DMA Code of Conduct. Take a moment to understand the sheer awesomeness of what you are about to do. If you are not ready, leave now."

The doors through which we entered clang open. Freedom is only fifteen steps away. The theatrics are ridiculous, just made to intimidate, but there is movement to my left and first one, then two, and a third recruit—all guys—walk quickly out into the fading light. We've already lasted longer than some.

Once the doors are closed again and we are trapped inside, Jonathan continues. "Now, hold up your right hand and repeat after me." My brother's words boom out across the armory. Goose bumps cover my arms and I can't keep the smile off my face. Military bearing be damned. My heart pounds as I finally begin the dare that has consumed my thoughts for the past year. The last dare Amos gave me. The one I can't lose.

"I, Samantha McKenna, understand and will uphold the Denmark Military Academy Code of Conduct. I will not lie, cheat, or steal, or tolerate those who do. As a recruit, I am duty bound to uphold the laws of society, to respect those entrusted over me, to uphold the traditions of the Corps and to carry out my responsibilities as a citizen of the United States of America."

The voices of my fellow recruits fade around me and in the moment of silence that follows, the energy is electric. It pulses through the room and I can barely keep still. Then the ring tapping starts again. I scan the upperclassmen above us. When I meet Cadet Evers's gaze, something twists in my stomach. I can't look away until, like magic, the tapping stops. When I turn back to Jonathan, his hand is raised to silence the room.

"Welcome to the Corps of Cadets, recruits!"

A cheer rises up around me. That, and the clink of metal on metal, fills the air, almost deafening. While we celebrate, though, the upperclassmen are stone-faced and staring. Not one of them smiles.

Model Recruit leans over, her eyes scanning the upperclassmen. "This is so exciting!" she squeals.

We weren't given permission to talk, so I smile back but don't respond. No need to break the "no talking" rule twice on the first day.

"Now, recruits," Jonathan says, trying to get our attention again. Slowly the celebrations die down and we all still, waiting for him to continue. "My first order of business is to allow you the opportunity to meet your cadre. These carefully selected sophomores and juniors will be responsible for your military training during the school year. They have survived the rigors of the Fourth Class system and they have been entrusted with your upbringing. There may be times you don't like them, but they've earned the right to your respect, and you will give it to them." Jonathan pauses dramatically again and I almost roll my eyes. Where does he come up with this stuff? "When you are dismissed, walk with your fellow recruits back to barracks and form up. Your cadre are waiting. Recruits, dismissed!"

Some of the guys almost fall over each other in their eagerness to get out the door. The boy with freckles from dinner waits for us, though, and without talking, takes the lead as we leave the armory, the last five to go.

Freckles, the other girls, and I follow the long line of recruits up the hill to the parade ground, a big, open, grassy field where we'll spend much of our training time throughout the year. The ceremony has taken over an hour and the sun is gone by the time we get outside. It's not dark, though. Stadium lighting shines around the edges of the parade ground, putting only the corners in darkness. The upperclassmen who were on the track before now hang from windows, calling out and yelling to each other across the green lawn. There's only a handful here—the rest will come back next weekend, just in time for classes to start.

In front of Stonewall Hall, we shuffle into a sad semblance of rows and columns with the rest of the members of Alpha Company, but I don't worry about it. The cadre will sort us out soon enough. For now, we're all equally ignorant of what is expected. We're all first-time recruits, in this together. For better or worse, or something like that.

The silence on the hill gives me the jitters.

Jonathan and the commandant of the DMA stand in the middle of the parade ground, talking to another man in uniform. Two cadets stand near a cannon, looking for all the world like they're about to light a fuse and start a battle.

Where the hell is the cadre?

I swallow hard, wondering where they'll come from, how they'll introduce themselves. I know it's not boot camp or anything, but I'm sure, just like everything else here, this will be done in some dramatic fashion.

The urge to move, to be familiar with my surroundings and know where danger could come from, is overwhelming. But before I break my bearing and look around for some hint of what's going to happen, the lights go out, and we're plunged into darkness.

THREE

THE GUY ON MY LEFT STARTS GIGGLING LIKE A LITTLE GIRL.

"Shut the hell up," I hiss, squinting into the darkness, trying to see something. Anything.

"This is so gay," he says.

But he doesn't know. Doesn't feel it. Every inch of the darkness pulses with energy. Something's coming. I don't know from where. I don't know how long we'll have to wait. But something is coming and it's not going to be good.

I hear one tap first, then another. Suddenly the night is filled with the clinking of ring taps again. My heart thunders in my chest. Giggler continues giggling. Freckles, standing close on my right, shifts nervously. I stay still, balanced on the balls of my feet.

Waiting.

The tapping stops.

Silence.

Something that sounds like a church bell rings out in the darkness, echoes in the black, and gongs three more times, but the sound bounces off the barracks. There's no way to tell where it's coming from.

Then all hell breaks loose.

Lights come on and we are surrounded by people dressed in black with black face paint.

They start screaming, indecipherable sounds at first, but through the heavy guitar now playing along with the bells I start to make sense of things.

"Stand at attention!"

"Arms by your side! Hands in fists!"

"Backs straight!"

"My name is Corporal Matthews, your squad leader. You will address me as such at all times!"

"I'm Corporal Julius. So help me if any of you in my squad decides to screw up from this moment forward!"

I gather my wits and slide into the perfect attention stance Dad taught me as soon as I learned how to walk.

"What are you looking at? I know you don't have the balls to look at me, right? Right?" The cadet who is yelling stands in front of Giggler. I think it's Matthews, though it's hard to tell without looking, which I'm not allowed to do while standing like this.

Then, like a flash, the cadet is in front of me.

He's as tall as me, and fit, like the rest of the cadre, huge and imposing, like a pit bull on steroids. A sneer lights up his face and he's got dark eyes, but I can't study him any more than that. I stand at attention and stare straight ahead, reminding myself that he's my age—he's just a kid, too—and he's got nothing to yell at me for.

He steps closer, his breath hot on my face. "You shouldn't be here, McKenna. Pack up and go home now." His voice is quiet, but I don't miss the hatred in it.

How does he know who I am? There are three other females who could be the female McKenna. Without a name tag on, I should be anonymous. I grit my teeth but don't respond, wondering if the guys around me could hear what he said. I'm not eager for them to discover who I am. Something tells me it'll only get harder for me once they know.

Matthews takes another step toward me, his body pressed against mine—way too close for comfort. Where the hell are the adults who are supposed to be running this show? They need to call off their watchdog.

"We don't want you here. You're just going to slow us down, make us weak. Get out before we force you out." He steps back, looks me up and down, and then lunges forward. Something warm and wet hits my face. "Trust me. It'll be easier if you just give up."

Even though Matthews's spit oozes down my cheek, I don't move a muscle.

He's pissed but continues down the line, yelling at Freckles next.

The cadre come, one after another. They're the cadets who will train me, the people who will make me part of a unit with my other platoon members—sixteen- and seventeen-year-olds. And each and every one of them tells me to leave.

I stand still and take it. I don't flinch. I don't cry. They don't know it yet, but I can't quit. I've been a member of Platoon McKenna my entire life. The lieutenant colonel doesn't like quitters. And then there's Amos's dare. I couldn't quit even if I wanted to.

A guy in front of me throws up. Giggler dissolves into tears. I'm sure one of them will be gone by morning, maybe both. I take it all in, but I don't make a move.

When the next member of the cadre appears, though, everything changes. The guy who stands in front of me—I remind myself he's only seventeen, a year older than me; he's no one to be feared—wears a black drill sergeant cover pulled down low, his eyes shadowed beneath the bill, the black shirt of the cadre pulled tight across his chest. He's a good four inches taller than me and lean, not the G.I. Joe–shaped drill sergeant I expected.

"I'm Drill Sergeant Stamm." His voice is low, threaded with authority. I have no trouble hearing it, even with everything going on around me. He's got a leader's voice, just like my dad. Even the cadre stand at attention when he talks. "We're in a unique situation this year. We're the only company with females. Some of you may not like it. Some of you may hate it." He pauses. This guy doesn't even look like he knows how to smile and I wait for him to tell us to leave, too. "I don't give a shit. I'm here to lead you as a company, not as individuals. You are all equal in my eyes. Worms. The lowest of the low. My job is to make you into warriors." His eyes scan us as he gives his speech and I can't look away. His military presence alone makes him someone to be obeyed.

I stand a little taller when his gaze falls on me. I'd follow this guy into battle right now.

"Matthews, lead them out!"

"Yes, Drill Sergeant!" Matthews stands in front of my platoon and yells. "Right face!"

I make the turn without even thinking, standing at attention the second I've finished the movement. As far as I can tell, though, no one else budged. They don't even know what a right face is.

"What lazy sacks of shit you guys are. Take an eye up here."

I turn back to the front. Matthews demonstrates the right face maneuver twice. He calls out the order again and we all do it, some slower than others. At least we're all facing the right way now.

"When you march, you always start with your left foot. You remain directly behind the person in front, and in line with the people to either side. You move as a whole. From this moment on, you are *one*. When one of you screws up, you will all pay. Is that understood?"

"Corporal Matthews, yes, Corporal Matthews!" I scream out, but none of my other company members yell along with me.

"Oh, we've got a know-it-all, do we?" Matthews is in my face in a flash. "McKenna!" he shouts, and it's hard not to flinch. If my fellow recruits didn't know who I was before, they do now. "Of course you know what to do. Brother-dearest probably told you all the tricks. Or was it Daddy? Trying to give you a leg up?

Make things at the DMA a little easier on you?" He laughs. "Get a load of this, guys! Recruit McKenna thinks she knows what to do. Sandwiching names." The sneer on his face tells me I'm making a mistake—I know too much.

"You're supposed to work as a unit at the DMA. You're a family now." The other corporal stands next to Matthews, both so close I'm itching to take a step back.

"So what do you think we should do about it, McKenna? How can we make sure your company thinks you're with them, not that you're better than them?" Matthews yells over the sound of the music still blaring around the parade ground.

I want to close my eyes, to slink away and be invisible, but I can't show weakness. McKennas don't believe in weakness.

"Corporal Matthews," I manage to say without my voice shaking too much, "push-ups as a family would be very motivational, Corporal Matthews." I can feel the eyes of the other members of my company drilling into me, wondering what the hell is going on.

"Alpha Company! Drop and give me twenty!"

The adrenaline helps. I drop to the ground, muscles shaking and ready.

The corporal starts counting. "One, two, three!"

Down, up, down. "One!" I shout as I push back up. Of course we use military counting, where even though we count to twenty, we're actually doing forty.

"One, two, three!"

Down, up, down. "Two!"

One of my squad members drops to the ground after just two

reps. The cadre are on him like vultures to roadkill. What kind of kid comes here and can't even do push-ups? I want to scream at him. But he wasn't expecting this. None of them were.

None of them signed up to be in a company with the most infamous person on campus. Everything that happens to them from here on out is my fault.

FOUR

IT'S BEEN FOUR DAYS, AND EVERY MORNING THEY WAKE US up the same way. The music they pump into the hallway at 0515 starts with a soft chord or two. But no matter how nice it seems, in about three seconds it turns into some heavy-hitting hard rock/death metal mix that I'd never listen to of my own free will. My muscles tense and I wait.

"Wakey, wakey, recruits!"

Then they kick the doors—as if the music isn't enough to get us up and out of bed.

I'm already awake—the anticipation of the morning routine more than enough to keep me on edge. I swirl the polish cloth one more time on my combat boot and set it to the side. "Come on, Quinn. Time to get up." I'm paired with the crier from the first day. The tears stopped, but she's definitely not adjusting well.

“It can’t be.” She groans and rolls over in her bed, pulling the blanket up over her head when I turn on the light. Our door cracks as one of the corporals kicks at it again.

“On the wall now, Worms!” The words echo down the hallway.

“Matthews says otherwise. Hurry up.” I tuck my Knowledge Book in my sock, which we have to wear pulled up to mid-calf, check the laces on my tennis shoes, and hoist my DMA-issued backpack up on my shoulders before hurrying out the door. I stand next to Freckles, whose real last name is Kelly, against the wall, and give a quick tug on the Camelbak hose coming from my backpack to make sure I’ll be able to get a drink when we head out on our five-mile run.

“Where’s your roommate?” he whispers when Matthews’s back is turned. He’s been kind of a protector of ours for the last three days, making sure we’re all where we need to be and that we’re not the last ones to finish any of the drills. It might be cute. If we needed it.

“She’s coming. Just tying her shoes.” I hope it’s true. I definitely hope she gets out here before Matthews notices.

“Obstacle course today. Can’t wait!” His eyes are gleaming and I smile back. He may be a bit protective of us, but from what I can tell, his heart is in the right place, and we’ll take allies wherever we can get them.

“Anyone not out in thirty seconds will be the sole cause of Alpha Company doing an extra three miles before training this morning.” Matthews looks at his watch, and then scans the wall. When his eyes fall on the empty space next to me where

Quinn should be, I cringe. He takes two steps toward me, ready to pounce.

"Corporals, to me."

I sigh, glad that Drill Sergeant Stamm's chosen this exact second to show up on deck. Matthews veers away, falling in line in front of Drill. While they're talking, Quinn slips out on the wall next to me.

"What took you so long?" I whisper.

"I had to dig my KB out from the trash can."

I hide a smile. Knowledge Books are the bane of our existence here. A little book packed with information we have to read and memorize in our downtime—like we actually have any. Out in front of the mess hall, waiting for PT to start, or whenever the cadre want to see how tired we are. It's filled with everything a good recruit at the DMA should know: our Cadet Creed, dates, important people, uniforms, Standard Operating Procedures. We spend a lot of time ordered to stand with our arms held out, the book in front of our faces, memorizing and hoping we're not called on to spout off information we're too tired to really take in anyway.

Before I can say anything in response, though, Matthews is back, standing in front of me, Quinn, and the other two females—Short and Cross. The fifth one never showed. "Drill Sergeant Stamm wants to see you at the end of the hall," he says, disgust in his voice. "Hurry up or we'll miss our obstacle course time. We've got three extra miles to run because of you four this morning."

I keep the snide comments to myself—the hardest part about

Hell Week so far. "Corporal Matthews, yes, Corporal Matthews!" We sound off and run to the end of the hallway. No walking for us.

When Drill sees us come, he holds a hand up. "Just a second, Worms. Let the rest of the company clear out." He stands tall, his light blue eyes bright and alert. His blond hair is shaved to military regulations and, while there's no stubble on his face, there is a little nick near his ear. He's been a presence on deck every second of every day, but the corporals do most of the instruction. They've taught us how to march, how to hold a rifle, how to salute. This is the first time the females of Alpha Company have been in front of Drill and I'm hoping it's not because we screwed up somehow.

Quinn digs an elbow into my ribs and I force my eyes back where they're supposed to be—looking straight ahead at the cinderblock wall in front of me instead of on Drill. Once the thundering of twenty boys running down stairs recedes, he finally turns to us.

"At ease, Worms."

I slide my legs shoulder-width apart and hold my hands at the small of my back, daring to glance at Quinn. Her lips twitch in a smile. She must think I was checking Drill out. Crap. I'm never going to live that down.

"You've made it nearly four days and I'm proud of you. I just wanted to tell you that, personally. We've already lost four recruits, not to mention the female who didn't show. The other companies are about on par. You've lasted longer than others and you should take pride in that."

When he takes a deep breath, I resist the urge to fidget. His voice isn't hard and commanding like it was when we met him. He's talking like we're people and it's hard not to worry—the compliments are too good to be true.

"But if you thought these last few days were hard, you ain't seen nothin' yet." His jaw works back and forth and worry lines appear on his forehead. "I'm not going to lie. It's going to be a hard year for you four. I just wanted to take a sec before the Corps comes back to make sure you know a few things. First, you'll each be assigned a faculty mentor. Someone outside the Corps itself you can go to if you have questions or concerns. Questions?"

"Drill Sergeant Stamm, who are the mentors for these recruits, Drill Sergeant Stamm?" It's Short, the rugby wannabe, who asks the question. Talking in third person is second nature to us now. It's just another way for them to break us down, make us more Worm-like. Anytime we refer to ourselves as "I" or "me" we have to do push-ups. After the first day of a thousand, none of us make that mistake anymore.

"Yours is Professor Armind. Cross has Professor Williams, Quinn has the commandant, and McKenna's mentor is Reverend Cook. They are the most highly regarded faculty members. You're in good hands. You'll meet with them on Sunday for the first time and you may go to them whenever you need to. No one can stop you." He meets each of our eyes when he says this. "The second thing I want to make sure you all understand is the chain of command. Do any of you know what it is?"

"Drill Sergeant Stamm, this recruit does, Drill Sergeant Stamm," I say.

"Care to explain?" He smiles, more proud than impressed. It's one of the things I like about him. He never thinks we can't do anything. He expects us to push ourselves, to prove ourselves. He won't allow us to slack.

"Drill Sergeant Stamm, the chain of command means there is an order a recruit has to follow if the recruit wants to report something. This recruit would report the problem or incident to Corporal Matthews first, then to the drill sergeant if the solution isn't acceptable. Then on up the chain until getting to the cadet colonel, and the commandant himself."

He nods, then turns, meeting each of our gazes again as he speaks. "But I want you four to understand something. There are people who don't want you here—a lot of them. None of us are sure if the chain will hold up this year. We've been told to report any concerns you four have, but unless it's reported to me, I can't do anything about it."

I snort. "Like that'll ever happen." There's no way Matthews would ever take our complaints anywhere. He wants us out more than anyone, it seems.

Drill studies me for a second, his head tilted a little to the side.

With his eyes on me, I shift first to my left foot, then to my right, heat burning my face. "Drill Sergeant, this recruit—"

"I told you you're at ease, McKenna." He finally looks away, waving my concern aside. Matthews would have made me eat dirt or something equally disgusting for being so informal with him. But not Drill. It'd be easy to think he's on our side. And dangerous, too. "I've told your cadre that if you have concerns they are to report, with you, directly to me. If you feel uncomfortable speaking with your corporals, however, I am giving you orders to jump the chain. Is that understood?"

When his gaze stops on mine again, I'm suddenly more interested in my shoes and if I've tied them right. "Drill Sergeant Stamm, yes, Drill Sergeant Stamm."

"One last item, then we'll catch up with the company. The DMA has not had to deal with dating within its ranks before, but other military schools have come before us and we're going by their example. I want to be clear about my expectations in regards to relationships with other members of the Corps. This year, dating within the Corps is off-limits to you. That means there will be no fraternization above your rank—that's a rule in the military and we will follow that here as well. You are not allowed to date your recruit brothers, either. If you choose to go to dances, you will go alone or with boys from outside the DMA. Is that understood?"

I can't meet Drill's eyes because if there's anyone I'd be interested in, it'd be him. Maybe it's the way he expects things of me. Maybe it's the kindness he's showing right now. Or maybe it's just because he's off-limits.

"Drill Sergeant Stamm, yes, Drill Sergeant Stamm!" the four of us reply in unison.

"Remember: you can come to me whenever you have a concern or a problem. I mean it." He sounds so much older than seventeen. The responsibility in his voice is more than I've ever heard Jonathan have, and he's in charge of the whole Corps. "Now, we'd better catch up to the rest of the company. Recruits! Attention!"

I snap into position, my hands pressed tight against the legs of my sweatpants.

"Fall out!"

We run down the stairs as fast as we can, even though there's no way we'll beat Drill out onto the parade ground. He gets to walk out the front door on the second floor. We've got to go down one more flight of stairs to the basement, out the back of the barracks, and up the stairs at the side. Allowing Worms to use the front door of anything if there's a harder way to do it? Not likely.

By the time we get outside and fall into line on the PG, Drill's standing calmly, chatting to a guy I've seen around all week. He's definitely not a shining example of what a fit DMA cadet should look like. He's got a potbelly that stretches his PT shirt across his stomach and stubble has turned his jawline almost black.

"You joining Ranger PT this year, Huff?"

The heavier cadet laughs at Drill, a real belly-shaking laugh that makes me smile. "Do I look like I'm in line to be an Army Ranger? You, your corporal, and those two other cadets are the only ones insane enough to do that crap. I'll stick with my remedial PT and enjoy every second of it, thank you very much. Now," Huff says, looking at us, "don't you have a run to lead these Worms on?"

"Whatever you say, Huff. I'll get you in shape one of these days."

"Keep dreaming, Stamm!"

"All right, recruits, let's go." Drill takes off running, his pace fast, and he doesn't look back once. Cross—Model Recruit—and I take the lead. We've finished first in every run we've done as a company. Even still, we always run back and make sure the other girls finish strong. We've got to stick together or we're goners.

* * *

After our five-mile loop, we end up behind the barracks, on top of another hill on campus. The rest of the company waits for us. They're still breathing hard, though, so I know we're not too far behind, even after our chat with Drill.

I stop beside Kelly and bend over, my hands on my thighs, trying to catch my breath. I'm dripping with sweat. Even at 0630, it's already hot and humid.

"About time you got here, McKenna. What took so long?" Matthews asks even though he knows the answer.

I snap to attention. "Corporal Matthews, this recruit was in a meeting with Drill Sergeant Stamm and then—"

"Drop it, McKenna," Matthews says, and then turns to the rest of the company. "Alpha, listen up. Every year, each company competes against the others in a tradition that started with the founding of the school. Alpha Company has won the distinction of being the Company of the Year six years running."

He doesn't sound too happy about it. I wonder what his original company was last year.

"The obstacle course is part of the huge Worm Challenge at the end of the year that you will have to prove yourselves on if you have any hope of winning the competition. Other factors in the decision are room inspections, daily uniform inspections, Weekend Warrior competitions, various other Corps activities throughout the year, and your ability to motivate your upperclass Alpha and the commandant."

Corporal Julius, in charge of first platoon, picks it up. "Now, last year Charlie Company only lost by three points," he says, high-fiving Matthews as he goes. They must have been Worms together. "They're out for blood this year. So if you all have any hope of winning"—Julius lets his eyes slide over me and the other girls—"which I doubt, considering your company makeup, now's the time to start trying."

Designed to prepare us for combat situations later in life, the DMA obstacle course has twelve stations. We have to jump, crawl, balance, pull, and duck our way through each obstacle at a run to beat the course time.

The corporals show us how to maneuver each station to get the maximum points allowed. It's an individual test, but our totals are added together for a company score at the end, too.

"Any volunteers to go first?" Matthews asks when we're done with the introduction. He's staring straight at me and I take a small step back, trying to blend in with my recruit buddies.

Kelly, beside me, raises his hand. Matthews glances at a man standing at the edge of the course—during training we're never without an adult to watch over us. The man nods and Matthews scowls. "Fine, Kelly. Show them how it's done. You've got two minutes." Matthews barely gives him time to get into place before starting the stopwatch. "Go."

The company runs at the edge of the field, watching Kelly as he breezes through each of the obstacles. It takes him four minutes, thirty seconds, but he gets it done. Even Matthews has little he can say to critique him. For his first time through, completing all the obstacles, he did really well. I bet Drill's friend Huff, who's been here for years, still can't do it.

"You're up." Matthews is next to me, his breath hot on my ear.

"Show them how the McKenna family gets things done."

I take a step away, heart pounding. "Corporal Matthews, yes, Corporal Matthews." My voice isn't strong and I hate that.

I walk over and stand at the starting line. The first obstacle is an eight-foot-tall wall I have to jump up and over. The company moves over to stand near me. But Matthews doesn't tell me to go.

"All right, Alpha. The best time for this obstacle course is one minute, fifty-three seconds. It's something I'm expecting at least one of you to beat by the end of the year. But it's not going to be McKenna. Girls are slow. They're weak. They're scared. The best thing you can do is get them to give up before classes start. Then we can all go on with our merry lives."

I glance at Drill. His arms are folded across his chest, a scowl on his face, but he doesn't call Matthews off; he's been saying the same thing all week.

"So, show us how good you females are, McKenna." Julius laughs and crosses his arms, standing next to Matthews. "Go!" he yells when Matthews starts the clock.

Twelve steps and I'm at the wall. I jump, planting a foot halfway up, using the momentum to hook my elbows over the top, and then swing a leg over. I let myself fall to the ground and sprint to the stepping-stones—big wooden blocks spaced far enough apart that I've got to jump from one to another.

After that, it's over-unders—six metal bars that I have to alternately hoist myself above and crawl beneath. My chest burns, needing oxygen. The tunnel is easy and I drop to the ground, pulling myself through with my elbows.

Next I maneuver through the maze, weaving back and forth

to find my way out, and then I'm standing in front of the rope climb. I stumble as I run up to it and my first jump is feeble, barely getting a foot off the ground. Dropping back down, I take a few steps back and try again. Still pathetic.

Shit. Come on, Sam. It's just a freaking rope.

But all I can see is the blue color of Amos's skin when I found him hanging in his bedroom. My hands shake, but then Kelly's there, standing at the edge of the obstacle.

"Come on, Mac. You can do this. Five steps, jump, hook the rope around your leg. You've got this. You're doing great."

I shake my head, tears burning my eyes and making it impossible to tell which ropes are real and which are doubles.

"Yes, you can. You've done everything else that asshole's ordered you to do. You don't want him to win now, do you? Do it!" He stands there the whole time, cheering me on. The rope is hard and brittle in my hands, burning as I climb, but I'm climbing. I focus on the physical pain, the rope tearing at my skin. It's easier that way.

At the top I ring the bell and glance down at Kelly, who cheers and claps. I'm down on solid ground before I know it.

"You did it, Mac. Now bust butt and finish or we'll never hear the end of it!" Kelly runs back over to my recruit buddies and I move on to the next obstacle as fast as I can, eager to put it behind me and stop imagining what the rope around Amos's neck must have felt like.

FIVE

THREE DAYS AFTER THE OBSTACLE COURSE DEBACLE, THEY wake us up an hour earlier than normal, at 0430. I groan and roll over, dropping out of the top bunk. "Come on, Katie. Time to get up." She hates being called Quinn when we're alone. She wants to be normal, at least when we're in our room. "It's Declaration Day. Let's go."

I jerk my camo pants on, then the brown undershirt that goes under the camouflage button-down. I know it's going to take me a minute or two to lace up my boots. I'm not wasting any time.

Katie moves slow, like always.

"Get your lazy butts out here! It's a big day for you, Worms!" Matthews pounds on our door, then moves to the next one and bangs some more. "Declaration Day! The day you declare your intentions to stay here and become men, or go home and stay pussies."

I grit my teeth. It's only taken a week for Matthews to become my worst enemy. Every day he pushes me harder and harder, as if it's his personal mission to get me to quit. He leaves the other girls for the rest of the cadre to deal with. He hasn't spit on me since day one, but I expect it to happen again anytime now.

My fingers work quickly and I pull the laces tight and dress the ends of my pants so they rest at the top of the boots, mid-calf, like they're supposed to. I even take a second to brush a layer of polish on them, the acrid scent of the cream stinging my eyes.

Katie is just crawling out of bed. "Go on without me. I'll be there when I get there."

"If you make us late, we're all going to pay for it." But I've said it before. We're all tired, all exhausted. We haven't even had a chance to get to know each other because each time we get into our rooms we're asleep within seconds. Maybe after today I can figure out what motivates her.

I open the door and grab the bright orange baseball cap that I'm forced to wear with this uniform, designating me a Worm, and then rush out to stand, back straight, against the wall. I feel naked without my KB. Since the beginning of Hell Week I've had it with me at all times, but we're not allowed to have it on us today. It would just get ruined.

"Your roommate's not out here, McKenna. I see you're already leaving your battle buddies behind."

I stare straight ahead, even though Matthews is yelling at me from the side. If I look at him I'll just get yelled at more.

"Corporal Matthews, this recruit didn't want to be late for reveille, Corporal Matthews!" The yelling scratches my raw throat and I have to cough.

He rolls his eyes, snorting in disgust. I ball my hand into a fist at my side and hope he doesn't see the motion. Around me, the other recruits in my company are starting to line the walls, one arm straight down, the other out in front of us at a ninety-degree angle, gripping the bill of our orange hats like we've been ordered to all week.

"Get back in there and wait for her to come out! We don't leave anyone behind!"

"Corporal Matthews, yes, Corporal Matthews." I turn and head back into the room. "Hurry the hell up, Katie," I grumble through gritted teeth.

She's sitting on her bunk, tying her boots as slow as a zombie. I kneel down in front of her and pull the laces from her fingers.

"Not much of a morning person, are you?"

She utters something unintelligible as I finish and dress the top of her pants like mine. No time for a shine, though, so she's on her own.

"Leave your KB and grab your cover. Let's go."

"Thanks, Sam." She reaches for her orange hat before following.

I shrug it off and head back out to wait on the wall. We're the last ones, of course.

"Way to be late, ladies. Nice to know that if we're ever in a combat situation we'll be waiting for your lazy asses."

I don't bother responding to Matthews. There's no time,

anyway. After a rousing round of push-ups, flutter kicks, jumping jacks, and high knees, we run single file down the four flights of stairs and onto the parade ground.

Outside, the world erupts in a cacophony of yelling. Each company stands at attention in front of their barracks, corporals screaming orders nonstop. Just another fine day at the DMA. Adults stand in the center of the parade ground—professors and dorm monitors who keep an eye out for anything *unfavorable* that might happen to the recruits. The rising sun lights the horizon and already it's hot enough to make me sweat. It's going to be a long day.

I let the yelling go in one ear and out the other, my eyes focused on a tree at the opposite end of the parade ground. It's the easiest way I know of to cope. I hear the orders, fix my attention stance to their specifications, but other than that let the insults slide off me like water. When we get the order to go, for the first time we're moving as a battalion, all seventy DMA recruits stepping in sync toward part one of Declaration Day: the thirteen-mile march.

We've lost another recruit in our company before we even get to the top of House Mountain. That makes seven since we met the cadre a week ago. Quitting now, after everything we've been through? It seems like a waste.

"All right, Alpha Company. Take a few minutes to breathe, then we've got to get to work," Drill Sergeant Stamm orders, then heads away almost immediately, going to talk to the commandant.

Before I sit down, I check to see where Matthews is. He walks toward his buddies instead of yelling at us for a change. When I'm sure I'm safe, I flop down onto the grass between Katie and Kelly. Cross and Short rest across from us, both lying back and trying to use the break for all it's worth.

"You need to drink. Keep hydrated," I tell Katie.

"Mmph." But she doesn't even reach for her Camelbak.

The top of House Mountain is beautiful. I gulp water as I look around, enjoying the three-hundred-sixty-degree view of the mountain ranges and the little town, home to the DMA, below. I've got no idea what we're doing up here, but there certainly couldn't be a prettier place to do it.

"I never got to say thanks for the obstacle course." I keep my eyes on the mountain when I talk to Kelly. "I really appreciate it. I don't know if I could have done that without you."

"You don't have to thank me. We're recruit buddies. This is what it's all about, right? Becoming a family?"

If my family at home is the model the DMA goes by, I'm not sure I want another one. "I guess. Thanks anyway, though."

"You're doing okay, McKenna. Pretty impressive, really, despite the way Matthews keeps yelling at you."

I stop drinking and look at him. Throughout the week he's separated himself out as a leader, shining at anything the cadre ask us to do. I didn't expect that from him.

"Oh, I didn't mean"—his face flushes red—"I really meant you're doing a good job."

I let out a sigh. "Thanks, Kelly." I wonder, briefly, what his first name is, then decide it shouldn't matter. "You too."

"Can't believe I've made it this far, actually. No one in my family has ever done anything like this before."

"Really? I'd have thought your family was career military." I study the mountains again and hope my face isn't obviously red.

"Nah. My dad's a high school teacher. Mom works at the bank in town. My older brother has Down's so I thought I'd come here and get a scholarship to college." When he grins this time, one dimple shows itself on the left side of his face.

It's weird to talk so much after a week of not being able to. "So what do you want to do?"

He rips off the wrapper of an energy bar he'd hidden somewhere. My mouth waters at the sight. Breaking off a piece, he scoots a little closer and hands it to me. "College, Officer Candidate School, career in the military. What about you?"

While I finish chewing, I tell him, "The same. I'm a McKenna. My life's all mapped out."

His eyes, that teal color that I could get lost in if we were anywhere else, study me for a second longer.

"I kind of have dreams of following in Jonathan's footsteps, being the first female cadet colonel. Then college, OCS, and the Army, like normal."

"So, your hopes aren't set too high, then?" He rocks to the side, nudging me with his shoulder. My stomach does a little flip at the contact. "I think it's great that you want to do that, Mac." He looks like he wants to say something else but the cadre start yelling. He jumps up and reaches a hand down.

I grab my backpack and let him pull me up. "Thanks."

"Anytime," he says, giving me that wink again.

Drill's order to not get involved with any of the boys nudges at my brain.

"Form up, Alpha!" The order comes from Drill, standing across the field, giving me an excuse to not pay attention to my hand, where Kelly's had touched it just seconds ago. I help pull Katie up, then the three of us sprint over to where Drill is standing and get in line with our squad.

The second part of Declaration Day is a team-building exercise. We camouflage our faces and practice buddy carries across the field at the top of House Mountain. Katie and I pair up with the other females. Even if they want us gone, the DMA takes the threat of a lawsuit pretty seriously. They won't put us in a position where we could get sexually harassed.

Two hours of carrying each other across the field during a simulated battle leaves my arms and legs quivering. Even though I trained all summer, doing these intense workouts all day, every day for a week, has been rough on my muscles. And since I'm the only one strong enough to lift Short, there wasn't a chance of switching off partners. I'd kill for a chance to carry featherweight Katie across the field.

When they let us stop for lunch, we collapse again into the grass. Kelly sits next to me, grinning like a fool. Sweat has smeared the paint on his face and I reach out to wipe a smudge of it off his nose. "You've got a little . . ."

His eyes meet mine for a second before I jerk my hand away. He clears his throat and reaches for our meals. "Let's eat."

"I'm starving." My heart pounds and I focus on the food so I don't have to think about how I shouldn't have touched him.

Our lunch is in the form of plastic-wrapped, prepackaged food. MREs—Meals Ready to Eat—from the military give us a taste of what meals would be like in a combat zone. I chow down despite the cardboard texture and lack of flavor. We're allowed to talk, at ease up here, but I'm used to eating at attention, staring straight ahead, having to bring my fork to my mouth at a right angle and not talking to anyone. It's all I can do not to "square" my meals even up here.

"All right, Alpha Company, get your asses up," Matthews yells.

It's instinct by now, snapping to attention at any voice that yells at me. It's only a little better when it's Drill rather than one of the corporals.

"It's time for us to head down House Mountain," Drill says, his voice barking across the field, hoarse after giving commands and singing marching cadences all week.

I break my military bearing for just a second to glance at him. His eyes are shining and he smiles. I quickly move my gaze back where it's supposed to be.

"We're not going down the same way we came up, though. You've got an hour to get yourselves down to the bottom by rappel and then to the river entry point. Remember everything we've taught you this week. The ropes are secured over there. Understood?"

"Drill Sergeant Stamm, yes, Drill Sergeant Stamm!" we all yell at the top of our lungs. We hear the other recruits sounding off around the field.

"I expect to see all of you in formation below sooner rather than later, Alpha Company."

"Alpha leads the way!" we yell as one. Drill turns his back on us and walks away. He glances back once and I think he's looking at me, but Matthews and Julius start to yell and bark orders. They're just as hoarse as Drill, though, and we can barely hear them. My muscles protest, seizing up as I force them to move again, but there's no way I won't follow these directions. No way I'll let them know I'm so exhausted I could cry. At the end of this, school starts. Sometime soon, surely, there will be a chance for me to sleep more than four hours at a time. The thought spurs me on.

Checking to make sure the other girls are with us, I turn to the right and follow Kelly across the field and to the belay ropes, trying to remember everything I've learned about rappelling over the past few days.

We stop in front of a cliff, a drop-off that stretches at least a hundred feet below us, where, by the looks of it, we get to jump into a mud pond.

The first column in my company makes it over and down easily, just like we'd practiced during the week. Then suddenly it's my turn. My heart pounds in my chest and I refuse to look over the edge of the cliff.

"Ready, McKenna?" Kelly turns to me and holds out a harness. Another buddy, Nix, the giggler from the first night, grabs my arm to steady me. He's a typical ginger, head full of hair and pale skin constantly sunburned. I step in, pulling the nylon harness up over my BDUs—the camouflage uniforms soldiers wear into battle—and tightening the straps around my thighs and waist. Katie's supposed to go behind me so I swallow the fear and let Kelly hook the rope to my harness.

Blood roars in my ears and the ground spins below me. I grip the rope like we practiced and turn around, the heels of my combat boots lined up with the cliff edge. Kelly and Nix both smile. I fix my eyes on Kelly.

He nods encouragement. "You got this, Mac. Just like we practiced. Don't look down, keep your legs straight, and bend at the waist."

I nod back and keep my eyes focused on his face. Then the training takes over. My right arm stretches behind me, locking the rope in the "brake" position. I let just a bit slide through my hand and feel it give, letting me sit back out over the cliff. Taking a deep breath, I move one step, then another, sliding the rope ever so slowly through my hands as I lower myself.

"Good, McKenna. Good. Now, just pick up speed a little bit or we'll be here until we're recognized as cadets." Nix grins so the implication that I'll be here until Christmas doesn't hurt and when I take another step, I realize I *can* do this.

Three recruits are descending at the same time as me, and they disappear below quickly, pushing off against the rock face and bouncing out over the nothingness beneath us. I've done everything else they've asked of me this week. I'm not going to stop now.

I push off, releasing the brake position for a few seconds, my body freefalling through space, before pushing my arm behind me and locking it back into place. I quickly lose sight of Kelly and focus on the rocks in front of me instead.

I've gone twenty-five feet. Three more pushes like that and I'll be down. A grin tugs at my face through the paint that's setting up hard on my cheeks. I can totally do this.

"Atta girl, Mac!" Kelly's voice bounces off the rocks. "See you down below."

Three, two, one . . . my boots sink into the mud as I hit the ground. For a second I could have been flying. It felt awesome—definitely not the worst way to travel down at all, and the rush is enough to keep me moving.

"Hit the deck!" I hear someone yell as soon as I've gotten out of my harness. I press myself flat against the ground, mud and all.

In front of me stretches an oozing brown pit, surrounded by the rock wall I just descended on one side and a bank of trees on the other. Barbed wire stretches across the gap about a foot above my head. I hear the pop of weapons as people in the trees fire blanks at me and the other recruits slogging through the pit.

"Get some!" someone yells from above.

I keep my head down and start crawling, inch by inch, through the mud. It oozes in through my clothes and slides down the neck of my shirt. My hands and face are covered but I keep crawling, head down, just an inch above the mud. The bullets are blanks, but they're meant to sound real and right now that's all that really matters.

Another recruit pushes his way through the muck in front of me and I stall, having to wait before I can move again. Hair dangles in my face, coming loose from the mandatory bun I've got it in, and I blow with all my might to get it out of the way.

"Hurry up, recruit!" I yell at the guy in front of me, but he's going too slow. I glance behind and there's a line of Worms waiting. They're going to think it's all my fault. Is he hurt? Tired? Who the hell cares? "Whatever," I mutter and push myself up equal to him. "You okay?"

He glares at me, his eyes like moons in the darkness of his face. "Shut the hell up."

"You're keeping everyone back. There's a line of people behind you."

"Like I'm going to let some *girl* tell me what the hell to do. Just get back in line."

"No way. You want to take your sweet little time, that's fine. But you're not holding me back." I move my elbows, first one, then the other, and crawl past him. The bullets are coming with more frequency now and I really don't want to be the reason everyone "dies." I make my way past him and pick up speed. The path in front of me is clear. Easy going now, I crawl on, rocks scraping my stomach.

At the end of the mud pit I pull myself up and go to find Alpha. They're busy, picking up large stones and arranging them on the ground in the shape of an *A* for Alpha Company.

"Way to go, McKenna," Ritchie, Kelly's roommate, says. "Grab a rock and help out."

He's the only one who talks to me, but a few others smile and nod approval as I grab a rock so big I have to carry it with two hands. I place mine and when Short and Cross appear, I hand them each a huge rock of their own. They look exhausted as they put the last two in place, finishing the *A*. Then we take a few seconds to rest while watching the little camouflaged ants of the rest of the battalion make their way down the ravine, through the mud pit, and to their companies. Finally Kelly appears, high-fiving me and the other recruits, taking time to rally us, even though we're exhausted.

I high-five Cross and Short. "Way to go, guys. Almost done, huh?"

Cross couldn't smile any bigger if she tried. "In just a few hours we'll be official recruits. God, this has been intense."

"No kidding." I straighten the orange hat on my head. "I'm just asking for an hour of sleep."

"I want a shower. That's all I can think about." She glances at her roommate. "I gotta go cheer her up or something. She's dragging today."

Cross and Short move off to the side, now deep in conversation, oblivious to the team motivation that is going on right in front of them. But they stand and get ready to march when it's time to move out.

We're one recruit short, though. Katie is nowhere to be seen.

SIX

EVEN THOUGH IT'S BEEN OVER A HUNDRED DEGREES THE last five days, the water of the Maury River is still cool when we finally arrive after hiking seven miles from our rappelling site. It takes all I have in me not to squeal as the water reaches my neck.

Once in, we're ordered to run in the water together as a company, following Huffman, the upperclassman Drill talked to the morning of the five-mile run, and our blue-and-gold Alpha Company flag down the river. Thirty minutes. An hour. Ten hours. I can't tell how long we're in the water. At a shallow section, where the water splashes against our ankles, we drop to the ground. I can't feel my feet, and my fingers sting from the tiny cuts caused by doing push-ups in the river.

"Flutter kicks! Move!"

At this point, I would kill Matthews if it would put an end

to Declaration Day. I lie on my back, using my arms to keep my head propped above water. Still, we scissor our legs out in front of us, stirring up the river mud. Cold, gritty water fills my mouth and I sit up, coughing and spluttering. I try to squeeze air into my lungs but it won't come.

"Keep going, McKenna," Matthews says, although he's looking up the riverbank and farther up the hill rather than at me. "Don't slack off now."

I finally catch my breath and spit water from my mouth. I grit my teeth and lift my legs, moving them up and down to Drill's count. Every inch of me hurts but I do it—no way am I giving Matthews a reason to yell at me for holding everyone back or not pulling my weight.

Upperclassmen shoot blanks all around us, and yells echo up and down the river as companies get to each physical training portion of the river run. Of course at the DMA we can't have just a simple march through the river.

When we get the order to march, Cross stumbles and I reach out to grab her arm. Short is moving slowly, and because we're sticking together, we're at the back of the pack. Our recruit buddies are way up ahead.

"You okay?" I ask. Kelly leads the rest of the company around a curve in the river and we're alone in the water.

"Damn rock," Short says. "Slippery as hell. I rolled my ankle, but I'll be fine."

"You're doing really well," I say, once the last of our company is gone and the three of us are alone in this section. We haven't seen Katie since the rappel. Bravo is coming up fast behind us.

"I know I'm not the most obvious person to sign up for something like this. You must have it made, though, right?" Cross's words are a dig even though I don't think she means them to be.

"Matthews has been riding her harder than any of us, Bekah." Short walks slowly, pushing her legs through the water.

"She's the sister of the cadet colonel. I just figured once classes start he's not going to let anything happen to her."

It's what I've been scared of all along—anyone thinking I'm getting preferential treatment that lets me ease through the Corps without really completing Amos's dare. She doesn't know Jonathan, though. There's no way he's going to cut me any slack. "We need to hurry up," I say. "We're falling behind."

After just a few more minutes, though, Short speaks up. "I don't think I can do this anymore." It's the first time I've seen her doubt herself, but she's looking for all the world like she wants the river to swallow her up.

"Sure you can. It can't be much farther," I say, trying to sound encouraging. I think it just comes out sounding annoyed.

"How do you know?"

"I heard the cadre talking about it. They're tired, too, you know. We're almost done."

Short shakes her head, shivering in the river and not even moving. "With today, but not with the year. I want to go home."

"Come on, Short. We've talked about this in the room." Cross sounds annoyed. The fact that they've had this conversation before surprises me.

"I know." Her teeth chatter now, her eyes about to spill the tears that are gathered there. "But I don't have anything else to prove. I made it through Recruit Week. It's more than a lot of guys can say."

"Yeah, but—" I try to rally her, but she cuts me off.

"No. I'm done."

"That's right! Quit! No one wants you here!" A voice yells from the riverbank. They can't hear us over the roar, but it must be obvious what's happening. Boy or girl, quitters all look the same. "Get the hell out of our school. You sluts aren't even worth screwing!"

The pain of the words is obvious on her face. She's the last one of us I expected to quit. Strong, squared away. If she can't make it . . . but I can't let the doubt creep in.

"Ignore them," I say, looking around nervously. We've got to pick up the pace—the company's already too far ahead. "If you quit, that's it. You can't regret it and come back later."

"I know." Her teeth clack together. Then she decides. Her shoulders hunch over and she takes a step to the side. "Good luck, girls." When she turns away, she holds her hands up in surrender. Cadets cheer on the riverbank, and instantly I'm pissed. They treat us like we're no better than animals.

"We've got to get going." I glance at Short once more but she's made up her mind. Bravo Company's flag bearer leads the way and they're bearing down on us.

"So, let's move." Cross takes off, not bothering to give her roommate another glance, and suddenly it's me who's the last one.

Short has made it up the riverbank and is sitting there, head hung low, not even listening to the upperclassmen around her, laughing and jeering, happy they've broken her. I give her a small wave and then turn away and push on. I've got to catch up to Cross, then we've got to catch up to the rest of the company.

The water is waist high here, making it hard to move while dressed in full camouflage pants and combat boots. Every step uses energy my muscles just don't have. The only thing that saves me is that the freaking day is almost over. I can see the end up ahead: a giant DMA flag waving over the bridge that leads back into town. I keep pushing on and soon I've caught up, surrounded on every side by my recruit buddies. I can't even take a step without stumbling over them.

Matthews is helping my recruit brothers climb onto the riverbank and grabs Kelly's hand in front of me. "Great job, Kelly."

"Corporal Matthews, thank you, Corporal Matthews."

Once Kelly is out of the way, I reach up and Matthews grips my hand. Just as I'm starting to climb, though, he loosens his fingers and I fall into the water, a sharp rock digging into my elbow. Tears sting my eyes instantly, but Cross reaches for me and helps me stand up.

"Ignore him. Let's finish this." She's determined to finish strong. Kelly reaches a hand down. When I grab hold, he puts his other hand on my wrist and helps me climb up on the bank. We both hoist Cross up and just like that, we're done. We're officially recruits. Around us, Alpha Company cheers. We join in, for a moment free of any worry.

After high-fiving, Kelly leans in. "Are you okay?" he whispers, though I doubt anyone could hear him over the splashing water as Bravo reaches the bank.

"I'm fine."

"Your arm okay?"

"I said I'm fine." My elbow throbs a little, but it's not going to kill me.

He *humphs*. "Matthews is a dick."

"You aren't wrong." I grin, hoping he knows I'm not mad at him. Just tired. We're all so damn tired. But we did it. We survived Declaration Day.

"Alpha Company, fall in!" Drill yells. Once we're in position he continues. "Congratulations. You are now officially Worms of Denmark Military Academy." He pauses for a minute, our cheers too loud for him to continue. "At this time you will fall out to the barracks where you will shower and be at ease. Lights out at 2300 but you are not to square the halls or walk in the gutters the rest of the evening. Is that understood?"

"Drill Sergeant Stamm, yes, Drill Sergeant Stamm!" The reward we've been given for doing the impossible today doesn't seem like much, but the grins from my recruit buddies say it all—we've earned this.

"In your racks you'll find instructions on how to log in to your email as well as the rules for calling home. Five-minute limit on phone calls. You will line up outside Corporal Matthews's door to get the phone. Thirty-minute limit on the computers in the science building or in the library. Movies are available for your viewing pleasure in the library as well. You may not sleep in your racks until lights-out and as usual, doors must be propped open if you are in your rooms during the day. If you do leave, don't forget to sign out." He pauses, his eyes scanning the recruits and falling for a minute on me before moving on. "Good job, guys! Alpha company: fall out!"

The fallout is more of a fall over as we try to force our muscles to move once more.

Kelly waits for Cross and me before heading up to the barracks.

"Did you see Quinn after the rappel?" She's nowhere down here on the riverbank—we females are easy to spot.

He shakes his head. "I don't know if she made it down. She was still at the top when I went over the edge. Matthews stayed with her."

Not like that would have been encouraging at all. "If she didn't do the obstacle, would they have kept her out of the river part? Or do you think she quit?"

"She's your roommate. She say anything about quitting?"

"She was tired this morning, just like all of us." But then I think of Short, who I didn't ever expect to quit.

"We'll find her. Maybe she's at the infirmary," Cross chimes in.

"Great. That's the last thing we need to be seen doing—going to the infirmary." If upperclassmen see us walking in there, they'll think we're trying to get off easy.

"I'll go check on her," Kelly says. "Just let me get cleaned up first."

"Thanks." I'm with him—I can't wait to get clean.

"God, I need a shower," Cross says, picking up speed to a light jog. "See you guys back at the barracks."

“Hey! Don’t use all the hot water!” I run after her, and Kelly does, too.

I didn’t know it was possible to have so much mud on my skin and in my ears. But finally, after fifteen minutes, the scalding water runs clear into the drain. I dress in PT gear and stand in line to call Mom. When I approach, my recruit buddies stop whatever they were talking about. Wilson, a recruit from first platoon, glares at me.

“What’s your problem?” I’m too tired to sugarcoat anything. It’s going to take every ounce of strength I have just to ask Matthews to borrow his phone.

“You shouldn’t be here.”

“Oh, come up with that one on your own, did you? I’ve held up just fine this week.”

“You needed help on the rope climb. You couldn’t get out of the river on your own—” He sounds like a tiny little Matthews. “Girls shouldn’t be here. I didn’t sign up for a watered-down version of the DMA.”

“I’m pretty sure my time in the obstacle course beat yours, and I think I saw Matthews pull you out of the river, too, right?”

Nix, who just came up behind me, steps out of line and stands toe-to-toe with Wilson. “Back off, dude. She made it through just like the rest of us. She didn’t get anything easier than we did.”

“Whatever, man.” Wilson gives me one more look of disgust. “I’ll make my call later.” He turns and walks back down the hall.

"Next," Matthews yells as Ritchie leaves his room, wiping at tears on his face.

I look away from him quickly. My lip trembles. "Corporal Matthews, this recruit would like to call this recruit's mother, Corporal Matthews," I say when he asks who I'm calling.

"Well, isn't that sweet. Why don't you ask her to come get you now that you've made your point?"

He hands me the phone and I dial the number. She picks up on the third ring.

"Hey, Mom. It's me."

"Sam?" Her words are hesitant, like she doesn't believe I'm actually calling.

"Yeah. I just wanted to tell you I made it through Hell Week."

"You're okay?"

Matthews sits at his desk, arms across his chest. He's wearing camouflage pants with the brown undershirt. It's tight around his arms and he cracks his knuckles as he watches me.

I clear my throat. "I'm fine. Everything's fine."

There's a long pause and I hear her take a drink of something. "Well, that's just great, Sammy. Just great."

"Time's up, McKenna."

There's no way it's been five minutes, but it's not like I can argue. "I gotta go, Mom."

"Of course you do. Probably some formation you've got to get to."

"Right. So I'll see you at Parents' Weekend?"

"I'll have to see." She hangs up before I can even say "I love you."

"Well, sounds like your mom is real proud of you, McKenna." He laughs. "Now get the hell out of my room."

I slam the phone down and push my way out the door.

"See you in the library, Mac?" Nix asks.

"Sure. Nothing else to do." I say it quickly and move past him so he won't see the tears in my eyes.

While Alpha Company sits around a television watching an old VHS movie about kids at military school—because we need to watch others go through the same shit, apparently—I sit at the last computer in the back row. I hear the guys laughing and promise myself I'll join them in a minute.

I'm logged in to my school email in a matter of seconds. There's a note from Dad reminding me to talk with Rev and one from Jonathan setting up the weekly meeting Mom's forcing us to have in the chapel, plus a few general ones from school with headings like "Lunch Menu Update" and "Worm Outings in September." It only takes a second to respond to Dad, telling him I survived Hell Week and that I'll get a chance to meet with Rev tomorrow. I'll look at the school emails later, but there's one that catches my eye. The email glows blue on the computer screen, sent an hour ago. I click to open it.

To: smckenna@dma.edu

From: jaxhax@mail.com

Subject: Congrats

Congrats on surviving Hell Week. What you accomplished

was amazing. But you've proved enough for the first year. Why not just quit while you're still ahead and let someone else do the hard stuff?

Who the hell would send an email congratulating me and then telling me to leave? Probably some upperclassman's idea of a joke. I click "Delete" without even responding.

Over by the television, Kelly scoots down and makes room for me on the couch between him and Cross. "I checked on Quinn. Sprained ankle. She should be back in a day or two." He smiles. "So that's good, right?"

"That's great. Thanks."

He turns back to the screen.

I lean over and whisper, "I feel like all I do is thank you for helping me. The obstacle course, getting me out of the river, now this."

He smells like soap when he leans toward me. "Guess that means you owe me, huh?"

It takes me a second, but I lean away, getting comfortable on the couch and trying to breathe normally. It's hard to think, especially when he's sitting this close, his presence so comforting, but that would only lead down a road I can't travel. Drill made sure we knew dating anyone on campus is strictly forbidden and I certainly don't need to add a complication to the mix of recruitdom. According to the laws of the DMA, we're brothers and sisters—we can help each other and take care of each other, but hooking up would be just a little awkward.

Besides, I refuse to be *that* girl. The one who could've made it, and who gets booted over a stupid fling, a never-ending walk of shame. Everybody's out to get me, and to fail over something like that? No. I won't do it.

SEVEN

THANK GOD WE'VE GOT A FULL SUNDAY TO REST BEFORE classes start, even if we do have to be up and in uniform for reveille formation at 0700. After first mess, where I eat three plates of waffles, hash browns, and eggs, Cross and I run back to the barracks to sign out. SOP—Standard Operating Procedure—requires us all to sign out on the whiteboard outside our rooms every time we go somewhere without the company.

Now everyone knows when we've left, where we're going, and when we plan to return. That's not creepy at all.

The rest of the Alpha Company Worms are all in the library again, watching another military movie and staying out of the rain that's settled over the DMA. Their cinematic choices are going to get old really fast.

Cross and I begged off due to exhaustion and no one asked

any questions. It's not entirely a lie, but we didn't want anyone to follow us to the infirmary. They'll all wonder if we're weak. If we're cracking.

Outside, the rain drenches my camouflage, but at least my feet stay dry in combat boots as I walk through the gutters on the way there. We're moving slower than normal as we walk up the hill toward the edge of campus. My muscles scream from Declaration Day, and Cross doesn't seem to be doing much better.

The infirmary is a little white building across the street from the main part of the DMA. Before we go in I glance around. Hopefully, no one saw us come this way.

I open the door and we enter the small waiting room.

"Can I help you?" A small woman with whiteish-blue hair and a blue sweater—despite it being August in Virginia—sits behind a desk. Cross and I push our way through rows of chairs and tables piled high with magazines. Boxes are stacked to the ceiling along one wall, last names written on them.

The nurse puts her finger in the middle of a romance novel to hold her place. The man on the cover has no shirt on and his face bears a strange resemblance to Drill. She has to ask again before I remember why I'm here.

"We're looking for my roommate, Kaitlyn Quinn." I wait for her response, trying to keep my gaze off her book.

"Quinn," the woman says. "Room seven. Up the stairs, third door on the right."

"Thank you, ma'am."

I take the steps two at a time, the stairs shaking beneath me.

"Katie?" I say as I knock on her door. It's slightly open and I push it the rest of the way. When Cross gets in, she shuts the door behind us.

"What are you guys doing here?" She wipes at her eyes and pulls the blanket up around her shoulders.

"Are you okay? You just disappeared." Cross sits on the edge of the bed and I make my way to the chair next to the window. Outside, I can barely make out a cadet standing across the street looking at the infirmary. It's raining too hard to tell who is watching us and there aren't any blinds to pull down. I take a step away from the window.

"Twisted my ankle at the top of the rappel. I told Kelly yesterday."

"Who brought you here?"

"M . . . Matthews and another upperclassman."

"Matthews?"

"Yeah. You know how he was at the top of the rappel, making sure we all got down? When he saw me twist my ankle he was nice enough to bring me here."

She'd just been standing next to the tree when I went down the side of the mountain. How had she twisted her ankle doing nothing? "Matthews was nice? Right. There's no way I'm buying he played knight in shining armor."

"It's not like I could have finished the activities. My ankle was killing me." She glances at the window, then back at me. "Why are you here, Sam?" She sounds defensive.

"We were worried about you. Do you want help getting back to the barracks?" Cross asks.

"They told me to stay off it for a few days." Katie turns her head to look out the window again. Rain streams down the glass now, and the view that she would normally have of the DMA parade ground is completely obscured.

"So stay off it in the barracks. You're going to miss everything." It's not just that, though. If she stays here, she's showing them how weak she is.

"Look," Cross says. "I know it's hard, and it kind of sucks right now. But it's going to get better. You should just—"

"It's easier here. If I were there I'd feel like I had to do more than I should." It's a good excuse, almost solid.

"Short quit. Yesterday in the river. The cadets started calling us names and she just decided she couldn't take it," I say. "If you're going to try to finish out the year, you need to come back. We've got to stick together."

"I just need to rest my ankle for a day or so. I'll be back up there tomorrow when classes start, okay?" She's not budging. Her jaw is set firm and she's not changing her mind. Even though she'd hated Hell Week, she'd never once talked about not wanting to be there.

But Katie wouldn't last if Matthews started spitting on her or yelling at her like he did me. She'd crack. "Did Matthews threaten you or something?"

It's a small hesitation, but it's there just the same. "No . . . of course not."

"Matthews doesn't treat us as hard as he treats you, Sam. It's crazy how much pressure he puts on you," Cross says, sounding at least a little sympathetic, then turning to Katie. "But that's no excuse. We've got to work just as hard. Everyone's watching us this year and we can't slack off at all," she says, for the first time hinting that maybe Katie isn't pulling her weight.

"I can't help that I got hurt." Katie sits a little higher in the bed and winces.

"Just get better, okay? The sooner you're back, the sooner we can stick together."

"We'll see you at lunch tomorrow. Get back to the barracks as soon as they say it's okay," Cross says.

Katie crosses her arms and looks out the window. "Now, I think I really should rest while I have the chance. And I'm sure you guys want to get back to be part of the company."

I stand and look at Cross. There's no point in pushing anymore. "Ready?"

She nods. "See you, Quinn."

Katie doesn't say anything, though. She just keeps staring out the window. The conversation is over.

The rain turns to drizzle as we trudge back across campus, squaring corners, our eyes locked straight ahead. It may be a Sunday but we won't be at ease on campus until we're recognized as full-fledged members of the Corps. And that won't happen for at least a few months. When Cross heads to the library to meet up with the rest of the company, I give her a little nod. I've still got one more stop to make, so I continue around the PG, then down the hill toward the mess hall.

The chapel is a redbrick building with window frames, columns, and a steeple all painted a blinding white. Once the school year starts up, every Sunday we're allowed to come to a service if we want.

I open the heavy wooden door and walk in.

"Good morning, Miss McKenna."

The voice makes me jump, even though it's the quietest voice I've heard in days. The man who spoke is tall and portly, and has a mustache as thick as three fingers. He smiles through the 'stache, although I can't see his teeth behind the whiskers. He wears a long white robe with a red cross on the front and a rope belt tied at his waist—very Christ-like. I'm surprised he's not wearing sandals.

He's standing in a small open area in front of the sanctuary. "Why don't you come into my office?" He gestures to his left. Maroon carpet cushions my steps as I follow him through the open door.

I run a hand over my hair, trying to catch any stray drips, then shut the door behind me. A lamp on his desk lights the room with a warm orange glow. Every inch of the office and floor, other than a small walkway to get to the chair and the reverend's desk, is covered in stacks of papers and books. Pictures of Rev with cadets and soldiers, some on battlefields, some in dress blues with women in white dresses, cover all but a small portion of the walls. This is a man who clearly loves his job.

"Sir, thank you for meeting with this recruit, and for agreeing to be this recruit's mentor this year. It means a lot to this recruit's father, and to this recruit, sir."

He chuckles, his laugh warmer than any I've ever heard from Dad. "Sit, Sam, and please, drop all that recruit stuff while you're with me. I'm Rev, you're Sam, and if we're going to be spending the year together, we need to be as relaxed as we can."

"Yes, sir—I mean, Rev." Heat fills my face and I look away, focusing on the photographs on the wall. I'm standing before I even realize it, my hand reaching out to a picture of my father. "This is from a long time ago." He's just a lieutenant in this picture, standing next to Rev. They're geared up, desert camouflage on, helmets and radios in place. Dad looks happy, his eyes shining, no gray in his hair, even then buzzed short.

"Desert Storm. A lifetime ago." Rev leans back in his chair, linking his fingers and putting them behind his head. "We became really close during our tour."

"Dad says some friendships never die."

"He tells the truth. I'd do anything for him." He clears his throat, his voice heavy with memory. "Now, let's get down to business. Think nothing of me being your mentor. Even if your father wasn't who he is, I would have mentored a female cadet anyway."

"Thank you all the same."

He unlinks his hands long enough to wave my thanks away. "So, do you have any concerns right off the bat? Anything we need to take care of? Your company treating you okay?"

I bite my lip and glance at the open door.

"I'm not Catholic, but consider this a confessional. Unless what you tell me demands my interference because it could harm you or another cadet, it stays between us." His words hang in the air. Here, surrounded by cadets from years past as well as Rev's friends, and my father, the weight of what I'm doing slips off my shoulders. Rev, and the men on the walls, are men I've been around in some way or another my whole life. They are my father, my brothers, my friends.

"I'm tired. God, I'm so tired and it's only the first week."

Rev nods. "The first week is exhausting. You're learning, surviving on a lack of sleep, adrenaline fueling every move you make. Now you're crashing. It's definitely understandable. You aren't the only recruit going through this—trust me."

"And tomorrow is going to suck even more."

"Ah, yes. With the Corps coming back today, there will be a new level of exhaustion. You'll be on display—all eyes watching to see what the females of Alpha Company are able to accomplish."

"I know everyone's going to be watching me. I just . . ." The words won't come, though. How can you put words to something you are unable to fail at—no matter what? The ghost of Amos sits in this room with me and I won't let him down.

"May I tell you something your dad once told me?"

I sit a little straighter. "Of course." Dad never tells me anything of consequence unless it's how to be a better soldier. I definitely want to hear what he told Rev back in the day.

"I was a very green reverend back in Desert Storm. When soldiers would come in wounded or crying and I just got too overwhelmed—he would always tell me I was looking at the problem wrong. 'Rev,' he'd say"—Rev closes his eyes, a smile lighting up his face—"'I don't know who said this but I'm going to claim it until someone tells me otherwise. It goes: you are not a drop in the ocean. You are an entire ocean in a drop.'"

My forehead crinkles up and I give Rev the same look I gave Amos when he gave me this dare. My *Are you flipping crazy?* look.

Rev laughs, a big laugh that makes him bend over and try to catch his breath. "I never knew what the hell that meant. But I've come to figure it out while working here. Each of us is capable of amazing things, Sam, if we just believe in ourselves. The ocean may seem overwhelming if we're looking at it from the shore. But if we've got the ocean all bottled up inside us, all the power we need to succeed—nothing can stop us. That's my advice to you. The Corps may not think it's ready for females, but you and your companions have the power to change that if you'll just believe it."

We talk for a few more minutes, but my mind spins with words I can't believe my father ever said to anyone. Hard-ass Lieutenant Colonel McKenna being inspirational? Motivational? Philosophical, even? I won't believe it. Because if he was ever that way, why couldn't he be that way with me?

As I trudge toward the library to meet up with the rest of Alpha Company, the ghost of Amos and the shadow of my father lead the way, their big McKenna footsteps getting harder and harder to fill.

EIGHT

I'M NOT EVEN UP FOR GOING TO DINNER, THOUGH I'M NOT allowed to skip the march down to the mess hall. When the campus bell tower chimes five o'clock, I trudge out of my room and get into place beside Kelly nanoseconds before the cadre come on deck. He smiles and gives a little nod of hello.

"Good evening, recruits!"

A day of rest from yelling seems to have helped Drill's voice recover and I stand a little straighter just because, trying to get the book-cover image of a shirtless Drill from the infirmary out of my mind. If I thought finding Kelly attractive was bad, wanting Drill would be a nightmare. "Drill Sergeant Stamm, good evening, Drill Sergeant Stamm!"

"Looks like we've got a wet walk down to mess this evening, but it doesn't matter. This will be the first time the Corps of

Cadets sees you little Worms walking in formation so I expect eyes locked front, military bearing, and not one foot out of step. Is that understood?" He's walking as he says this, down the hall of the barracks, then back toward me.

"Drill Sergeant Stamm, yes, Drill Sergeant Stamm!" The shout bounces off the walls and echoes around us, driving into my skull where I don't need any more distractions at the moment.

"Let's move out. Form up downstairs!"

We turn to the left, boots snapping as one against the tile floor. Then we're running, jumping, and sliding down five flights of stairs to the basement. Out the back door, rain puddles on the sidewalk, just another thing to run through. Then we leap up the outside stairs to ground level.

I'm breathing hard and sweating by the time we're standing in formation. I hold my arm out to the front to judge my space, then out to the side, to make sure everyone is equal distance. I will not be the one to screw up when the Corps gets to see us for the first time.

Corporal Julius fine-tunes someone in his squad whose name I still don't know. They've organized us by skill level in each platoon, so when we right-face and prepare to march, I'm staring at the back of Kelly's neck.

Drill's voice echoes around us, singing cadence to keep in step. "We like it here!"

"We like it here," we yell back, though not nearly as nicely as Drill performs.

"We love it here!"

"We love it here!"

"We've finally found a home!"

It's then that I notice the crowd. It's hard not to when there are cadets everywhere. Some are in various stages of dress, standing on the grass despite the rain. Others are hanging out windows. I keep my eyes locked firmly to the front.

"A home!"

They can't be here just to watch a recruit parade down to dinner.

"A home!"

No. They're here to see Cross and me. The DMA females.

My hands in fists at my side brush the seam of my camouflage pants as I march in step with my company, eyes straight ahead, staring at the back of Kelly's perfectly shaped head. Drill is somewhere off to the left, marching beside us like he always does. The corporals are somewhere, too, watching for the slightest mistake to yell about.

"A home away from home!"

"Hey!"

Drill has timed it expertly, so that the last words of our cadence end right outside the mess hall. When we turn to face Drill, he's standing right in front of me, and while he's talking to all of us, his eyes are locked on mine. "Now, listen up, Alpha Company." Drill's voice demands we pay attention. "You are on show—and you will be for a while now, it seems, thanks to the infamy of being the first company with female recruits in the history of the DMA. But you're a damn good company and I know you'll make me proud." He gives a slight nod, still looking at me, then starts pacing again. I exhale the breath I'd been holding as long as he held the eye contact, and refuse to acknowledge the nervous lurch of my stomach. “The whole of the Corps of Cadets saw you march down just now. They know we’re on top and I demand that we stay there. You are a company now. A family unit. You will be punished and praised as a unit. Is that understood?”

“Drill Sergeant Stamm, yes, Drill Sergeant Stamm!”

“Good. Now, you have exactly seven minutes to get in, eat, and be back out here in formation. You are not squaring your meals like good little recruits, you’re chewing and screwing. Eat as fast as you can, then get the hell out. The cadets at the fine Denmark Military Academy want one evening where they don’t have to eat dinner with Worms. Understood?”

“Drill Sergeant Stamm, yes, Drill Sergeant Stamm!”

“Good. Company, dismissed!”

My recruit buddies are gone before I can even blink. I try to move but a hand grabs my arm, holding me back. Cadre aren’t supposed to touch us. I tense, but don’t dare turn around. Instead, I snap back to attention.

“Just a second, McKenna.” Matthews’s voice is syrupy sweet in my ear, his breath hot against my neck. It’s just the two of us, and the hairs on the back of my neck stand up.

“Corporal Matthews, yes, Corporal Matthews!” I yell it loud, hoping someone will hear and take notice, but everyone’s inside by now, even Drill. All the cadets on the PG have vanished, too.

I want to force my arm out of his grip, but I’m not allowed to move. I keep my eyes locked straight ahead so I don’t glare at him.

"I know you were at the infirmary today. And talking to Rev." He laughs. "You're slacking already, trying to find ways to skate through the year. It won't work, you know."

My heart pounds in my throat. Was he the one watching from the road? Was he following me? "Corporal Matthews, this recruit checked on this recruit's roommate, then went to a scheduled meeting with this recruit's mentor, Corporal Matthews!" I wish I sounded more sure of myself.

"You're just a stupid, weak girl." He hisses the words in my ear. "Play innocent all you want, McKenna, but we're watching your every step. There won't be a second of the day when I won't know where you are and what you're doing. The best thing you can do is save yourself a whole lot of grief and quit now."

I grit my teeth. His fingers dig into the flesh of my bicep. Tears sting my eyes and I try not to cry out.

"That's right. The sooner you figure out who's boss the better. Even your own brother can't save you here. It'll only get worse if you don't get the hell out of here. Understood?" He digs his fingers harder into my arm until I whimper.

It's all I can do to squeak out the proper response. "Corporal Matthews, yes, Corporal Matthews."

"Now, you've only got five minutes left for dinner. You'd better hurry that hot little ass up." He lets go of my arm, shoving me forward.

I let the momentum take me away from him and into the mess hall, as far away from Matthews as I can get. Alpha Company is already sitting down. I grab what I can eat with my hands—two hamburgers, skip the drink. The moment I sit down

I start shoveling the food in even though the conversation with Matthews has left me feeling queasy.

Kelly furrows his brow across from me. *What's wrong?*

For the first time, I'm grateful we can't talk at mess. Only in the privacy of our rooms or in academic buildings are Worms allowed to speak freely. I shake my head the smallest amount. *Not now.*

I jump when my recruit buddies around me start running to dump their trays. I'm not half done with my first burger but I go, too, and line up outside with the others.

Drill's not out yet, though, and my recruit buddies grab their Knowledge Books from the back pockets of their uniforms. It's what we're supposed to do when we have any spare time between orders. I've got mine out, too, but I can't focus. I keep scanning around for any sign of Matthews. Finally, after what seems like forever, Drill comes out and gives the command. "Back to the barracks, Alpha Company!"

"Drill Sergeant Stamm, yes, Drill Sergeant Stamm!"

"Forward march!"

Another cadence keeps us in step on the way back. Matthews stays in my peripheral vision, a sneer making him look more evil than usual. It's hard to remember we're both sixteen when he looks at me with such hatred. When we halt in front of the barracks and the corporals start in on their evening berating of the company, he comes right to me.

"You look a little sick, McKenna." His lips curl up. "Need to go to sick call?"

"Corporal Matthews, no, Corporal Matthews!"

"Are you sure? God forbid I keep you from letting everyone know how weak you are. I can get someone to walk you down there, if you need help."

"Corporal Matthews, this recruit is fine, Corporal Matthews." Upperclassmen have gathered around to watch the showdown. I can't blink, flinch, or even shift my weight. I've got to prove I can handle this.

He takes a step back and begins yelling loud enough for everyone to hear. "All right, so there's nothing wrong. Prove it. Drop and give me twenty, McKenna. Alpha Company, count along with me!"

I'm on the ground the second the order is given and, when he finishes drawing attention to us, he drops to the ground right in front of me.

"Begin."

Down, up, down. "One!" I yell out.

He locks his gaze on me and doesn't blink as he matches me move for move.

Down, up, down. "Two!" I refuse to break his stare.

Down, up, down. "Three!" He looks like he's not even working hard, but under the gaze of the upperclassmen, my muscles weaken quicker than usual.

Down, up, down. "Four!" I refuse to let Matthews win. I continue, while the company counts out twenty of the hardest push-ups I've ever done in my life.

When I'm finished, I jump back up and stand at attention. My face hot, I try to catch my breath. Matthews doesn't look happy. He brushes his hands off and goes over to stand next to

Lyons, the second in command.

Drill moves into my line of sight and meets my eyes, the slightest smile he can manage crossing his face. I've made him proud. I bite the inside of my cheek to keep from returning it. "Alpha Company! Dismissed!"

We sprint down the stairs, entering the basement door and climbing back up to the top deck, waiting silent and still for the orders of the evening. I'm not sure how I'm going to last another four hours until lights-out. The last seven days is finally catching up to me and the realization that there's an entire school year left of this crap weighs down on my shoulders.

I may have made it through the first week, but I haven't survived anything yet.

NINE

I DON'T KNOW WHAT I WAS THINKING. HOW I COULD HAVE possibly imagined things would get better once school started is beyond me.

My first class is Military History, where, like every other class I'm taking, I'll be surrounded by upperclassmen I'm not allowed to talk to. I may technically be a sophomore, but until I'm recognized as a cadet, I have to follow all the Worm rules. As far as I know, I'm the only transfer student here this year.

Like being a female doesn't make me enough of a target.

My heart pounds harder than it did when we met the cadre. In the computer lab, I tuck myself into the back corner ten minutes before class actually starts. I only hope the cadets can't sniff out my fear.

I log in to my school email. A message from Dad is short and to the point—as usual. He'll be heading overseas in a week. He'll be in touch again when he can. No details about where he's going or what he's doing. I'd email back asking for answers, but I know I won't get any. This does nothing to calm my nerves.

I shoot a note to my mom, telling her I'm doing fine and not to worry about Dad. I doubt she'll bother to respond, but I hope she does anyway.

An email from the commandant of cadets, Colonel Lee, lets us know that there will be a movie for recruits at the end of the month. We'll get to be at ease for two hours with the rest of the recruits instead of just hanging within Alpha Company. Oh, joy of all joys. I can't wait to sit in the dark with a bunch of smelly, stinky guys, and watch some war movie. Sounds great.

The next one is from my mysterious pen pal.

To: smckenna@dma.edu

From: jaxhax@mail.com

Subject: Warning

Sam,

I know you got my last message and I'm sure you're wondering who the hell is writing you like this. I'm an ally, I promise. You've done amazing things, but there are guys there that really don't want you to stay. If I were you, I would have left yesterday.

I get it. You're determined and you don't want to quit. Will you at least do me a favor? When you go to movie night with your company, sneak into the science building. I'll stash civilian clothes in the ceiling tiles for you. There's a coffee shop on Main Street. Meet me at ten.

If I can't convince you you're safer away from there, the least I can do is help you survive.

I stare at the words on the screen. Who the hell does this guy think he is? Doing what he's asking would require me to break at least three school rules. Before I can respond to say just that, though, cadets start filling in the front rows, then the back on the left side. I log out quickly, trying to blend in with the back wall.

When Matthews walks in, I sink lower in my seat. So, being in a class with random upperclassmen isn't bad enough? Now I've got to spend a semester with Matthews? He glares, tosses his bag on the floor, and sits next to another cadet in the row in front of me. When he bends down and whispers something in the other cadet's ear, they crack up laughing. After that, none of them look my way. None of them say a word to me.

This is going to be one long school year.

After my second class—where, thankfully, I don't know anyone—I rush to lunch. Even with walking through the gutters and squaring corners I make it before half my company. I grab a premade salad and French fries, and make my way to our assigned tables. I nod at Cross and Katie. We're not allowed to talk but it's amazing how much can be communicated through glances.

You guys okay?

Yeah. You?

Sort of.

I slide my eyes toward the library and mime eating really fast.

Both girls nod and we are done with our food and within the hallowed walls of books in five minutes.

"You're better?" I ask Katie as soon as we're through the door of the library.

"I guess. I didn't want to miss the beginning of classes, you know?"

"It's good to see you," I say, and I mean it. I'm glad whatever Matthews said to her didn't do any more damage than two days in the infirmary. That'll be bad enough to recover from.

"At least you guys have each other. It would suck if Sam had to room one floor down with the other sophomores." Cross sets her bag down on a table and sinks into the chair.

"All recruits have to stay on the same deck. It doesn't matter what year in school we are. We've got to earn the same privileges as everyone else." Then I nudge Cross. "But I'm glad we're all together, too. It's nice to know we've got each other's backs."

Cross nods in agreement. "Yeah, I'm sorry about what I said in the river. I can tell they're riding you hard. I thought once you got through that you'd be fine, but Matthews making you push after mess . . . I guess he's not backing down."

"At least we're all here now. It'll make company training a lot easier tonight."

"About that," Cross says. "I have to start conditioning this week for track, which means I'm not going to be around much in the evenings. I wasn't looking forward to leaving you alone on deck, so it really is a good thing you're back, Quinn."

"Isn't it a little early for track?" Katie pulls her binder out of her backpack and starts jotting notes in her planner in different colored pens for each class she's had so far.

I raise my eyebrows, then turn to Cross. "Yeah. Isn't track a spring sport?"

She nods. "It is, but Coach doesn't want to wait until spring to introduce me to the guys. He thinks it's going to take a bit of team building to get us all on the same page and comfortable together. He might be right, but being pushed with all those guys already? I'm just learning the ropes."

"You should try being in classes with them," I grumble, dropping my bag to the floor and sitting down, hanging my legs over the arm of the chair.

"So your morning wasn't so hot?"

I shrug. "I guess it could have been worse, considering I was surrounded by sophomores. I mean, I could have gotten beaten up or something." The girls laugh, and I take a second to laugh, too. Then I think of first block. "Matthews is in Military History. That class is going to suck."

They both make sounds of sympathy, but they're freshmen and are assigned to classes with other Worms. They don't understand what being a sophomore Worm is like.

"So, there was a guy in first block who was totally checking Cross out," Katie says, a huge smile on her face.

"Really?" It's strange to be talking about boys like we're just normal teenage girls and not taking on this huge, impossible task which will leave us no time to *be* normal teenage girls.

"Hispanic, I think. That dark brown hair and tanned skin. Yum!"

Cross shrugs it off. "I didn't notice."

"Come on, how could you not notice?" Katie fans herself, looking at me. "I mean *hot*, Sam."

"We're not allowed to date. You know that." Cross and Katie trade looks and I feel my face heat up. "What?"

"You're going to follow all the rules, aren't you?" Katie grins. "You're going to be the good recruit."

"I just want to make sure I make it through the year the right way. What's wrong with that?"

"So we can't date cadets. Technically, hottie in first block is a Worm."

"Still off-limits," I remind her.

Katie gives up when she sees neither Cross or I are going to talk about him. "Fine. If we aren't going to talk about how hot he is, I still think we should make a pact, just in case. If one of us likes someone, he's off-limits, okay? We can't be fighting over guys. You guys said yourselves we have to stick together."

"It's not like it matters since we *can't* date, but I'll agree to it if it will make you happy."

"I will, too," Cross says. "Any guy another one of us likes, completely off-limits. And, if we're starting this, I'm calling dibs on Kelly."

"Kelly looks like he was made for the military, like a real life G.I. Joe or something. And his eyes. God, give me an hour alone with him, that's all I want," Katie squeals. It would be great if she could muster that excitement for Corps activities.

I glance around to make sure no one can hear us. This is

probably exactly what the people who made the rules were worried about. "I really don't think—"

"I think McKenna's got her claws in Kelly," Katie says, her eyes sparkling with mischief. "Or Drill, maybe?" she says when I don't confess to an undying love for my recruit brother.

I hold my hands up. "I have no claws in anyone." I ignore the sudden sinking feeling I get just talking about this. Then I turn to Cross. "If you're going to break the rules and want Kelly—"

"I don't think it's a matter of me wanting him. He wants you. He follows you around like a little puppy dog," she says.

"Well, I'm not encouraging him. He's our recruit brother, he's a *freshman*, and besides, I told you, I'm not dating anyone this year."

"So," Katie says, dragging the *O* out in that way people do when something is super-awkward. She picks her backpack up off the floor and slings it over one shoulder. "Cross has dibs on Kelly. I'm not jumping into anything just yet, and goody-goody Sam isn't claiming anyone. Sound about right?"

I get up slowly, an afternoon with upperclassmen not looking as bad after the last ten minutes. "We'd better get going. It wouldn't be good to be late to third block on the first day."

Cross puts her hand on my arm, holding me back when Katie leaves. "Are you serious?"

"About what?" I hoist my backpack onto my shoulder.

"About not being interested in Kelly."

"I'm not dating anyone. I told you."

"Not quite the same thing, though, is it?" She drops her hand and I give her a smile.

"He's all yours, I swear. I've got enough to worry about."

Her face lights up. "Thanks, McKenna." She brushes past me and out the door, getting immediately into the gutter in front of me, and walking back toward the PG, a peppy spring in her step.

TEN

THE DMA CHAPEL, WORKDAY HOME OF REVEREND COOK, is open to all cadets, 24/7. Even when Rev isn't here, there's always an adult around in case cadets need to enter. No one has rank inside the chapel, not even the cadet colonel. For recruits who haven't made it through their freshman year yet, this means two things.

Number one: We have a place we can go at all times where we do not have to salute and be at attention.

Number two: We have a place we can go at all times to sleep, eat, and veg out, even if it is just between classes.

Both are equally important.

For me, it has a third meaning. It's where Dad and Rev agreed to set up weekly meetings between me and Jonathan, where we can talk in private without anyone getting in the way or saying

I'm trying to skip out on my recruit duties or fraternizing with upperclassmen.

Between first and second block on the fourth day of school, I walk as quick as I can to the chapel. The bell on the steeple chimes the hour and I slip inside just as I'm supposed to be meeting my brother. Someone plays the piano. Another student snores in the back pew. Up at the altar, three recruits are trading food gotten, most likely, from the student store. Kelly sees me and jogs down the aisle.

"Hey," he says. "How are classes going?" He stands close, maybe a little too close, and I'm irked that Cross and Katie planted the seed in my head that's making me analyze this.

I take a small step back. "Classes are fine."

"So what was up with Matthews Sunday night?" With no downtime to just hang out and a lack of cell phones, it's hard to keep up-to-date with everyone. "What happened?"

I shrug it off. "Nothing. He's just an asshole. He wants me to quit."

"That must be some target on your back."

"Welcome to life as a McKenna female." It comes out as a grumble and I sigh.

The wind today has made some of my hair come down from my bun and Kelly tucks it behind my ear. He lets his hand rest at the base of my neck and we stand like that for a second, the heat of his skin making me nervous. He gives me that dimpled grin again and I know it doesn't matter how much I deny it or tell Cross that she can have him. Even if I try to keep away from him, this boy is not going to give up.

“Good morning, Miss McKenna.” I turn toward the sound of the voice, my heart pounding at the thought of someone seeing Kelly touch me, even though I know who it is.

“Catch you, later, Mac,” Kelly says, not phased at all that Rev is cramping his style, and walks back to the front, where two other recruits are chowing down on a bag of chips.

I relax immediately. “Hey, Rev.”

“It’s good to see you smile, Sam. I’ve been thinking about you. How’s your first week been so far?”

I know he’s talking about classes, not Matthews, but I hesitate for a second anyway. “A little nerve-racking, but I think I’ll get the hang of it eventually.”

He smiles. “I don’t doubt it for a second. Ready to see Jonathan?”

Next to where he’s standing there’s a door that leads to a dark stairwell. I hold on to the rail as I follow him down. It turns three times before delivering us to the basement, a big open space with three doors lining each side. A light comes from under only one of them across the room.

“It looks as though the cadet colonel is already here. Enjoy your time with your brother.”

“Thank you, Rev.” I’m not quite sure what to do with all the politeness. I’ve been nothing but yelled at for the past week and a half. A friendly conversation with someone who outranks me is definitely outside the realm of normal right now.

“It’s what I’m here for. Oh, and Sam, remember: the chapel is open to all students all the time. But while there is always an adult here, I cannot vouch the safety of this place when I am gone. The fact that you have made it this far is a testament to your character and your upbringing. Though it may not appear to be so, there are people here who truly want to see you succeed, even if they seem greatly outnumbered." The steps creak as he makes his way back upstairs.

The basement is full of shadows. I hustle across the floor, staying to the center of the room. I'm not one who is afraid of the dark or anything, but I think, going here, I could learn to jump at shadows all too quick.

"Jonathan?" I tap on the door and hear a shuffling on the other side.

"Come on in."

I open the door and squeeze inside. For a second I'm not sure what this reunion is going to be like. The boy in the closet with me is not just my brother anymore—he's my colonel.

He glances up from his cell phone when I close the door behind me, and looks at me for a second before giving me a half-smile. If I were meeting Amos, he would throw his arms around me and pull me in for an epic bear hug. Jonathan just looks back down at his phone. "How are you? Are you okay?"

All I can do is nod, even though I'm not sure he even sees me move.

"Hey," he says, finally sliding his phone into his pocket and patting me on the shoulder. "The first two weeks are almost over. You knew it was going to be hard, right? You knew this was going to suck."

My lips start quivering.

"You've outlasted a lot of guys who've tried this. You and that other recruit in your company are the only females to attempt Declaration Day, much less survive it. You should be proud of yourself. No one will think badly of you if you want to quit. . . ."

"I'm not quitting." I refuse to lose the last bet I ever made with Amos. I know damn well he egged me into coming here because he *wanted* me to accept the challenge, wanted me to succeed, and I won't fail him.

And worse than that, if I quit I'll play into everything Dad thinks all females are—carbon copies of Mom. Weak and dependent. Unable to take care of themselves. I will not be that person. Surviving the DMA will show him I'm more than that.

"I know. I just wish Amos hadn't dared you to do this. You could have gone to any high school anywhere and gone through ROTC. You could go to West Point and get to be an officer the same way."

"That wasn't the bet, though."

"I don't care about the damn bet, Sammy. I've worked so hard to get here and now . . ." His words rush out. "You being here takes away something that's really special to me."

"I'm not trying to steal your thunder. Right now I'm just trying to survive."

"Well, maybe the best way to do that is to go home." He doesn't put much power behind the words. He knows it won't make a difference.

"Did you hear Dad's leaving again?" Dad is a safer topic right now.

"Yeah." The word gets caught in his throat.

"Do you know where?"

He looks down at the floor. "No. But it can't be good. This wasn't planned."

"He'll be fine. He always is." Unbelievable. I came here for a little comfort from him and now I'm doling it out.

He scuffs a shoe on the floor. "I know. Listen, I've got to go." Finally he meets my eye. "Anything else?"

I want to hug him. I want to feel my big brother's arms around me, strong and supportive. Even though it's not Amos, at least it would be something. I wonder about mentioning Matthews and my concern about what he might have said to Katie, but he pulls the cell phone back out of his pocket and starts scrolling again.

"No, nothing."

"You be good, okay? Follow the rules, keep yourself clean. I heard about the push-ups on the PG Sunday night. Impressive. If you're going to stay here, you've at least got to show them you're a McKenna."

Then he's gone without even a good-bye.

After another long week of training and classes, we're summoned to the parking lot behind Stonewall Hall for evening company time. "Come on, Katie. Grab your rifle. Let's go."

"This can't go on forever, right? I mean, they've got to let us rest at some point, don't they?"

"This is *military* school and we're Worms. We'll get to rest next summer." Though I know what she means. I could handle a nap right now, too.

She pulls off her boot, taking her sweet time. "I've got another blister."

I grab my med kit from my foot locker and try to take a deep, cleansing breath. "Let me see." Holding the moleskin up to her foot, I cut it to size and put it on. It only takes a minute, but already the deck is silent and the company is gone.

It takes her another minute to put her boot back on and lace up.

"We're going to get reamed for this. You know that, right?"

"You should have gone on without me." At least she's moving now, grabbing her rifle.

"You know I can't do that. Matthews has already made it clear that we'll get a smoke show if we leave anyone behind again. We're family, remember? But you better hurry now."

Outside the sun hasn't let up at all even though it's almost the end of September. Our company is lined up out on the blacktop, standing at parade rest. The cadre are walking through the lines, adjusting the way they hold their rifles.

I pick up the pace to a jog and fall in at the end of second platoon's line next to Cross. She doesn't have a track meeting tonight, and this is the first time she's been to company time all week.

It's not even thirty seconds before Matthews is on me. "Where the hell have you been, McKenna? What about you, Quinn?"

Katie is just getting into position next to me. She doesn't do well with Matthews yelling at her, but I can't glance at her to see if she's okay.

"Corporal Matthews, this recruit's roommate had a blister. This recruit was trying to help her, Corporal Matthews."

"Well, that just gives me a warm and fuzzy feeling inside,

McKenna. Meanwhile, your recruit *brothers* are working their asses off out here in the heat."

"At ease, Matthews," Drill calls from the other side of the company. "We've got work to do."

Matthews takes a step back and stops the assault. He glances between me and Drill, his signature sneer sliding into place.

I move into a perfect parade rest, right arm extended and the tip of the rifle angled forty-five degrees out from my body, matching the rest of my platoon. Drill takes over the company time and it's easy to follow along with his instructions. He's teaching us the manual of arms, a rifle routine we'll perform at the Parents' Weekend parade.

Like with all other company time we do out in the open, we've drawn a small crowd. With each set of instructions, we try our hardest to move as one, to be perfect, but there's no way we can be. Not yet.

Matthews and Julius prowl the lines, just waiting to jump on us.

"You call that parade rest, Quinn? Try it again! Attention!" Matthews barks.

Katie inhales quickly next to me, a sharp noise that means she's close to crying. Her rifle clinks as she brings herself back to attention.

"Parade rest!"

Katie moves, but it's slow and sluggish. There's no way he'll let that pass.

"What the hell? Is your blister messing with your ability to hold a rifle correctly, Quinn?"

"Drill— Corporal Matthews, no, Corporal Matthews." Her voice shakes when she says it and I cringe.

"Did you hear that, Julius? I've been promoted to drill corporal. Did you even know that was a rank?"

Julius bounds over. "Are you freaking kidding, Quinn? You've been here four weeks and you still don't know our ranks? Must be all that time you spent in the infirmary."

It's hard to take him seriously with an acne-covered face and gold and blue rubber bands on his braces. It's just not that intimidating, but Katie stammers like she's actually scared. "Corporal Julius, yes, Corporal Julius."

"And would you like to go back now? Your blister bad enough that you need to leave company time?"

A cheer comes up from the cadets on the sidelines. "Sick call! Sick call!"

Matthews looks toward the crowd, a smile on his face. "Why don't you, Cross, and McKenna stand over at the side and practice moving from attention to parade rest? If one of you doesn't know it, the other two are probably having problems."

I work my jaw back and forth, eyes straight ahead, but I don't move.

"Well, what are you waiting for? Female Alphas! Fall out!" Julius adds, his voice echoing across the open space while the cadets cheer.

My face is on fire as I pick up my rifle and jog out of formation. I stand between Cross and Katie, wishing I could disappear.

Matthews stops next to one of the cadets who has moved and is now standing directly in front of us—Evers from the first day, the one I totally mouthed off to. They talk quietly for a second. Matthews shakes his head, but Evers is adamant about whatever he's saying. When he's done talking, Matthews glances once at our adult supervisor before turning to us. "Cross!"

"Corporal Matthews, yes, Corporal Matthews." Her time with upperclassmen during track bonding makes her much more comfortable. She doesn't sound nervous at all.

"I'm worried about Quinn's foot. I don't want her to do any more *damage* to herself. Walk her down to the infirmary."

"Corporal Matthews, yes, Corporal Matthews."

"The two of you fall out."

As she turns, Cross glances my way, rolling her eyes. I ignore it, though, too focused on what Matthews is going to do to me. He's singled me out like this for a reason. The memory of being rude to Evers on the first day won't leave me alone. I'm finally going to pay for it.

"McKenna."

"Corporal Matthews, yes, Corporal Matthews!"

"Since the rest of the females have deserted you, I want to make sure you understand the proper movement expected of you. While the rest of your company drills the manual of arms, I want you to go from attention to parade rest and back two hundred times."

Because I can't disagree with him, I answer. "Corporal Matthews, yes, Corporal Matthews."

"Begin."

I keep my eyes focused on the row of windows on the first floor of Stonewall and tune out the laughter from all around me.

While my company works on a rifle drill I've known how to do since I was ten, I'm stuck doing drills we learned during Hell Week.

I move, snapping to parade rest, holding the position for five seconds, then snapping back to attention. The cadets cheer like I've just taken my first baby steps. Humiliated, I make the move again. Two down.

ELEVEN

"IF YOU CALL ME CROSS AGAIN, I'M GOING TO SLAP YOU. My name is *Bekah*," Cross—no, *Bekah*—says as she strums one of Rev's guitars, playing some rock song I've never heard.

"All right, *Bekah*," I say, and then repeat my question. "What are we going to do about my roommate?" My concern about Katie being able to hack it in the Corps has ramped up since training last night.

"Get her to quit?"

When I glare at her, she does some crazy-insane strum to end the song.

"What? Don't tell me you weren't thinking the same thing."

"We've got to stick together," I say lamely.

"You and I, yes. I can understand the logic. But if last night's debacle is any indication, we need to distance ourselves. She's still in the infirmary and Matthews already wants us to go check on her during sick call. All over a freaking blister."

Picking at the carpet up by the altar, I weigh my options. In a twisted way I know she's right. We're only going to survive if the two of us ditch her. But I can't imagine doing that. "I won't turn on her. We've just got to work harder to make her understand what she's got to do."

"Look, some people are made for this. You're here because of your family. I'm here because I got a scholarship, and if I wasn't here, I'd probably be in some alternative school or juvie. I'm not taking the chance they're going to turn on me and I know you don't want them to turn on you, either."

"You mean, you were ordered here?" I never pictured Bekah as a juvie kind of girl.

"We're not talking about me right now," she snaps.

I look at her for a few more seconds, trying to see something that she won't show me. "Katie'll be fine. I'll talk to her and make her understand."

"Good luck with that," she says, but her eyes are on Kelly and his roommate at the back of the chapel, playing cards.

"You talked to Kelly yet?"

"Nah. It's obvious he's into you." She shrugs, though, not too upset. "There's someone on the track team who's pretty hot, though."

"Is there any point reminding you we're not supposed to date?"

"No. But I'll keep it secret if anything happens."

I wish I had her nonchalance about everything rule-wise

here. Sure it's a stupid rule, like a lot of the DMA rules, but I can't bring myself to break them. "I didn't mean that. You can tell me anything. It's just I really don't think—"

"Just drop it, okay?" She starts strumming another song. "So, are you going to do it?" She's talking about the meeting with my mystery emailer that I'm supposed to have tomorrow night during the movie.

With Katie in the infirmary, I needed someone to talk to. I knew Kelly would demand to go so I trusted that Bekah would give me the most impartial advice. She'd jumped right on the idea, of course, and I haven't been able to make her see reason since. "No. Of course not."

"You're not even the slightest bit curious as to who's sending you secret emails and stashing clothes for you in the science building? Maybe it's some upperclassman that has the hots for you!"

"Yes, I'm curious, but that doesn't mean I can act on it. It's probably a trap, anyway. They probably just said they would help to get me to come and then they'll get me in trouble for being in civilian clothes off campus." I tell myself that what I'm saying is the truth, ignore the curiosity that always got me in trouble with my brothers at home. If there weren't so much at stake, I'd be planning my attack on the coffee shop right now.

"Are you always like this? 'I'm not going to break rules'? It's kind of annoying." She stops strumming and stares at me.

"About inconsequential stuff? Yes. Meeting this random person isn't going to get me closer to finishing the year."

"It figures," she sighs, sounding more resigned than mean.

"I'll just go to the movie and hang out with you."

"About that," she says, *tsk*ing. "I don't think I'm going."

"Have something better to do?"

"The track team is getting together for a social. Coach wants me to come and Matthews has already given me permission."

"You've got to be careful, you know. I know you want to hang out with them and everything, but—"

"I can take care of myself, Mac." Bekah gives the guitar one last strum before taking the strap off and putting it in Rev's case. "I've got to get to class. See you at third mess."

"Sure." I glance at my watch. It's almost time for my meeting with Jonathan anyway.

"If we don't get to talk before tomorrow, have fun at the movie and skipping out on some mysterious hottie's email."

I roll my eyes. "Yeah, thanks. Have fun making out with some upperclassman."

"Oh, I plan to." She grabs her pack and walks back to Kelly and Ritchie. All three walk out of the chapel and I head down-stairs to meet Jonathan.

He's on the offensive before I even close the door. "You going to the movie tonight?"

"Hi to you, too. I'm great. Yes, I'm going to the movie."

"I don't know if you should."

I can't read his tone. "You're kidding, right? It's the first time I've gotten even a little break since I started."

"You get a break every Sunday afternoon. You can watch movies then."

"This is the first time I get to do something normal."

"Do you know how this will look? You packed in a movie theater with almost a hundred guys?"

"What do you think I'm going to do, Jonathan? Jump all of them one after another?"

His face flushes red and he hesitates before continuing. "I just think you need to distance yourself from them. It's not going to be easy to keep your name clear if you're with them all the time."

I laugh at the absurdity of what he's saying. "You're being ridiculous. I'll be with my recruit buddies. None of them will let anything happen to me. None of them will *try* anything with me."

"There's already talk about the three of you."

"What do you mean?"

"Lyons says your roommate is in the infirmary all the time and the other girl is with the track team more than she's not—it won't be long before people start talking about *you* like that."

I ignore the implication that he thinks I'll give them a reason to gossip about the McKenna female. "I'm following the rules, Jonathan. I promise."

He changes the topic after that and we try to guess where they might have sent Dad, how many pills Mom's popping a day while he's gone. All too soon it's time to go. Even though he pisses me off, he's my brother, and I feel safe with him. I promise to keep my distance from the Worms, but I don't change my mind about going to the movie, even when he asks again. The higher-ups are giving me a chance to have a night off and I'm going to take it.

Katie's still at the infirmary so I'm the only girl when the recruits of Alpha Company pack ourselves in to the auditorium. I'm looking forward to the darkness that will surround me for the next two hours. Someone gave us all popcorn and soda—I guess it's the least they can do to make us feel a bit better about all the abuse. How sweet.

The lights go down in the auditorium and the movie starts promptly at nine, the exact time I'm supposed to be wearing civilian clothes and meeting my emailer. I'm ducked down in my seat, though, preparing for a two-hour nap before going to bed. When Kelly shuffles around, trying to get comfortable, his leg comes to rest against mine. I scoot to my right.

"You okay?" Kelly whispers. He keeps his eyes on the screen but he's got a grin on his face.

"Yeah. Just tired."

He shifts again, and before I know it, we're back where we started, legs pressed against each other and uneasiness hanging between us. I rest my left hand awkwardly in my lap, not wanting to get so near him that he thinks I'm doing a weird first date hand-holding maneuver.

Someone slips into the seat next to me and I wonder for a second if Bekah changed her mind. But when I look, even though the girl is blonde, she's not at all like Bekah. She's in camo while the rest of us are in PT gear and she doesn't have a recruit name tag.

I glance around, checking to see if anyone's noticed, but it's too dark in here for them to see that it's not Bekah. Shifting in my seat, I move a little closer to Kelly, despite what he might read into the movement.

"You're late," she whispers.

I look again. "Excuse me?" I try to keep my voice quiet, but I've got to talk over the war playing out on the screen in front of us.

"You were supposed to meet me at the coffee shop in town."

It takes me a second to process what she's said and what it means. She's the emailer. It was never an upperclassman after all. I almost laugh out loud. Bekah's going to be so disappointed.

In the light from the movie screen, I can see purple highlights in her hair. The makeup on her eyebrows is thick and anything but subtle. I lean on the armrest between me and mystery girl. "I couldn't risk it," I whisper, hoping that Kelly is either asleep by now or wrapped up in the shooting on screen.

"Girls' bathroom? I'm just asking for five minutes. It's important."

When she leaves, I sit there, my hands clenched into fists on my lap. Whoever-she-is has no idea how much trouble I can get in for civilian clothes and sneaking off campus. We aren't even allowed to bring them until after we're recognized as cadets. But she's emailed twice and is here now—the least I can do is hear her out.

Kelly turns toward me when I stand, but I stop him before he talks.

"Bathroom," I say, and head up the aisle and out into the hallway. It's empty, the upperclassmen in their rooms or off campus for the evening.

When I slip into the bathroom, I close the door and stand in front of it so no one can get in. "Hello?"

"I'm here," she says from inside the only stall. The lock

squeaks as she turns it and comes out.

I look at her uniform again and still don't understand. "I was worried you were an upperclassman. I guess I was wrong."

She stands next to a urinal they didn't bother removing when they made this a female bathroom this year. "Obviously." She picks at her black fingernail polish.

"If you're not going to tell me why you wanted to meet me, I need to get back to the movie. They'll miss me."

"Who will?"

"My recruit buddies."

"All the guys in there are glued to the screen. Your roommate's in the infirmary. The other female recruit is headed across campus as we speak to hang out with the track team."

"What? How do you know—"

Her gray eyes stare into mine. "You've got a lot of people who don't want you here. You know that, right?"

"I had no idea," I say, putting a southern belle hand against my chest. "Why ever would anyone hate little ol' me?" I clear my throat and talk like normal again. "What do you want from me?"

"Honestly? I want you to listen to me. To take me seriously. Lieutenant Colonel McKenna's daughter is probably made of stronger stuff than many other females, right? But even you can't do this on your own." She sighs. "Would you settle for letting me help you survive this year without getting yourself killed?"

I laugh. "They may not like me but they're not going to hurt me. Say some shit to scare me, make me feel like crap, sure, but you're overreacting."

"Am I?" She pulls a piece of paper out of her pocket and

hands it to me. "Do you know that right now there's an email circulating through the Corps offering money to the cadet who can get you out the quickest? They're also taking bets on when they think you three will quit. The winner gets over a thousand bucks at this point and more money comes in every day."

"You're lying."

"Here. Take it." She shoves the paper in my hand. "Take a look at your odds. See who thinks they can get you to quit the fastest."

Before I can say anything else, someone pushes against the door, then knocks. "McKenna?"

It's Kelly.

"Yeah," I say, my voice all breathy. "I'll be out in a second."

"You okay?"

"I'm fine, Kelly. Just give me a second."

The girl glares at the door, but the smile on her face tells me she's not all that mad.

"I'm coming in," he says, and pushes against the door with enough force that I stumble inward. My mystery emailer reaches out and catches me. I slip the paper in the front pocket of my hoodie just as the door swings open.

Kelly steps into the bathroom, closing the door behind him. His eyes get wide when he notices the girl in the bathroom with me. "Jax?" he says. "What are you doing here?" He's looking at her like he's seen a ghost. Or maybe an ex-girlfriend.

I'm perched on my windowsill, watching the stillness of the campus below. The movie was over hours ago, but I can't sleep. The piece of paper Jax gave me sits on my desk, the names of those betting against me burned into my brain. Matthews is at the top of the list.

Evers is right up there, too, but I already knew they wanted me out. They don't do anything to hide it or to help me along. Still, the fact that they're betting against me shows me how seriously they're taking the challenge. The rest of the names are unfamiliar.

If Kelly hadn't barged in and had a freaking middle school reunion right there in the bathroom I could have asked Jax more—how she'd found this information out, what else she knew. But I'd understood the look in Jax's eyes—the one warning me not to tell Kelly what was going on. She played it off like she was trying to find him and I slipped out and back into the movie.

Trying to sleep is useless. My mind won't quiet down long enough to even try and Bekah hasn't come back to her room yet—she would have stopped by to tell me all about her night if she'd returned. Our after-hours gossip session has become a nightly thing when she misses company time. I lace up my running shoes and sign out on my board, though I'm hoping no one will be awake to see it. I keep the door unlocked behind me so I don't have to fumble with a key when I get back.

The computers are humming away when I enter the lab, but the room is empty. In the dark, I head to the back corner, out of sight of the door, just in case. I know campus is patrolled, but I don't know how often or by whom. Better safe than sorry.

Two emails wait for me. I click on Mom's first.

From: mrsmckenna@mail.com
To: smckenna@dma.edu

Subject: Hi . . .

Hey Sam, just a quick note to see how you are. I miss you. Are you okay? Before he left, your father told me to stop worrying, but you know me. I know what Amos went through during boot camp and what Jonathan has gone through at the DMA. I just want to make sure you're good.

Mom

My fingers shake as I punch the keys, the words on the screen blurring as I fight off tears. It's more than she's said to me in a month and my first instinct is to spill everything. Instead, I shoot off a quick reply, telling her the big fat lie that everything's fine here. She doesn't need anything else to worry about.

I click to the next email so I can get out of here before someone sees me after lights-out and reports it to the cadet colonel himself.

From: jaxhax@mail.com

To: smckenna@dma.edu

Subject: ???

Well, as usual, Liam found a way to ruin things. LOL.

If you need anything, email me, but don't do details. Email isn't *that* safe, as you saw tonight.

I'm here to help, okay? More soon.

Jax

I send her a quick thanks, knowing this will most likely be the end of it. They want me out. The sheet she gave me is nothing new. And, getting involved with civilians in my Worm year, even if they're claiming to want to help me, is playing with fire. There will be time for friends and complicated relationships next year.

TWELVE

THE ROOM IS SO QUIET WITHOUT KATIE HERE THAT I CAN'T sleep. She'd recovered from the blister and participated in company time the last few weeks, but after training tonight, her ankle hurt so bad that Bekah and I had to take her back to the infirmary. She's talking about quitting now, and I'm trying to figure out if I should encourage that or try to get her to stay. That's the only reason I'm awake at 0015, stretching out my aching legs. And, that's the only reason I hear the knock on my door. It's mouse-light and at first I think I must be dreaming. But then it comes again and I wonder if Bekah is just getting in.

I crawl out of my bunk, muscles protesting every movement.

"McKenna." The whisper is hushed and I shuffle over to the door.

I open it just a crack—if the cadre know anyone's up, there'll be hell to pay. I squint into the brightness of the light I've let into my room. "What?"

Kelly grins beneath face paint. A black knit cap covers his hair. He pushes into the room and closes the door behind him. "Get dressed. Let's go."

"Go where?"

"Motivational march."

"You're insane. I'm exhausted. Not to mention I've got to get my room squared away." Our rooms are all the same, two beds in a bunk, two wall lockers, foot lockers up on top of them to save space. Desks are bare, books on a bookshelf, but no computer, no phone, no television. We have the same blankets and everything is uniform. Katie left her stuff scattered all around the room after the PT session and I'm going to have to clean everything or we'll do extra push-ups thanks to me.

"Come on, you don't want to miss this. Besides, we need your help with the TP. We'll get it from the rest of the barracks. Just grab the rolls from this one, okay?"

Jonathan warned me about MMs. Fun as hell, but equally likely to get you in a world of shit. I can't turn down the first one of the year, though. Part of the "fun" of military school is being part of a group, a family, and doing risky things with them. How can I turn down a group bonding opportunity like this?

"Give me five minutes."

"Meet us out back. Hurry." He slips out the door and closes it as quietly as he can.

I grab the camouflage uniform out of my closet. We get to

wear PT sweats tomorrow so I've got some time to clean them if we get dirty tonight.

The BDUs slide on easily, like they were made for me, and I slip my KB into my back pocket, not wanting to be caught without it, even on an MM. Boots laced up, I pull the wool hat down over my hair and slide out into the hallway.

It doesn't take long to grab all the toilet paper. In the dark the rolls in my arms are a bright beacon—anyone could see me. I head down the opposite stairs from where the cadre bunk and step as quietly as I can.

Out back, most of the company is waiting. Bekah stands next to Kelly and Ritchie and I huddle up with them. "Where's Wilson?" He's the only one in the company who can't seem to get on board with us being here.

Bekah shrugs. "He didn't come. And don't start feeling bad. He's an ass. He doesn't want to come; you don't get to feel guilty."

"Yes, *Mom*." I smile at her. "Glad to see you. We've missed you at training."

"I'm sure you have. But track duties called. Then these guys made me sneak into the other dorms with them to steal toilet paper. That's gross, right? I think that's probably gross."

I can't help but grin. "It'll be awesome. You'll see!"

"Come on, guys. Let's go," Ritchie says, grabbing Bekah's arm. She glances once at Kelly to urge him with her, but he's waiting for me.

"Way to go, Mac," Kelly whispers, grabbing some of the rolls of TP and putting them in his backpack.

Nix grabs the rest. "Here, put this on." He hands me a round container that looks like shoe polish. Leftover face paint from Declaration Day.

I feel a surge of pride as I realize they're accepting me as one of them, that they planned on me being a part of this. "Where are we going?"

"Back to House Mountain." Nix looks like a laughing jack-o'-lantern with his crazy grin. "Gotta leave a sign for the cadre, let them know Alpha really does lead the way! Maybe this'll give us a solid lead for Company of the Year."

"Good thinking." I follow Nix, Kelly, and the rest down the stairs. We move easily into a pace that will keep us moving for the next thirteen miles.

Everything looks sinister at night. Across the street, the trees reach out for us, pulling us into the darkness of the forest. Shadows play with my depth perception and night noises echo around me. I can't tell where anything is coming from.

The company slows to a crawl near the top of the mountain. Nix whispers something to Kelly, and Kelly nods and turns to me. "Campfire up ahead," he says. "We've got to go off trail. Stay to the left and we should miss whoever is up here."

At first, my eyes play tricks on me, the shadows dancing, but then I see a distinctive orange glow. I follow Kelly off the path. He pushes past a branch, and it whips back in my face, stinging my cheek and bringing tears to my eyes.

"Shit!" I hiss, clamping my teeth together to keep the word as quiet as I can.

Kelly is at my side in an instant, stopping me. "You okay?"

"Yeah. Just stings."

"Sorry." His voice is low, hushed so whoever is at the campfire won't hear us. His hand on my arm sends comforting warmth through me.

It's that, and only that, that makes me break. For the first time in six weeks—six weeks of feeling like scum as guys older than me, bigger than me, screamed in my face—I feel like I can trust someone. Kelly won't judge me. "It's okay. I'm just tired is all. Everything is worse right now, you know?"

The others keep hiking, their footsteps sounding out in the darkness. He doesn't move, though, just looks at me, his face shaded black from the war paint. In the moonlight and shadows, it's just us with the woods and the starlight for company. His hand comes to my face, cupping my cheek, his thumb tracing little circles as tendrils of warmth shoot down my neck. "You never give up. You don't let the cadre get to you. I know you're tired, but I think you're amazing."

I take a step away from him and laugh it off, trying to ignore the intensity of his gaze, but it's impossible. "Come on. Everyone's worked really hard. You beat me at tons of stuff during Hell Week and you're always at the top when we train."

"But you didn't stop." There's an accusation to his voice, like I should have begged for mercy, or at least his help, at some point. An expectation he wouldn't have had if I was male.

"Please," I say, suddenly annoyed, not sure if I want him to treat me like a girl or like one of the guys. Somehow I want both, even though it's impossible here. "If I start crying every time something happens to me, I'm going to be the laughingstock of the DMA." And who's to say he doesn't think of me the same way. Really, other than the fact that he's stuck by my side since the beginning, I don't know anything about him, and maybe he really does see me as some weak little girl, someone who needs to be watched over. Maybe he isn't being a recruit brother at all. Maybe he's assuming I can't hack it, and is coddling me until I quit. I wipe at my eyes again, pissed that my emotions are betraying me. "I'm fine. Please don't tell anyone I freaked out, okay?"

He steps toward me again, and this time I don't move, just look up at him. He reaches for me, his hands on my waist before I even know what's going on. "You can trust me, you know."

I close my eyes and just stand there for a minute. "I know." What we've gone through, what we're still going through—I feel closer to him than I have to any guy before. But in this place, thinking like that is dangerous, and what we're doing right now is dangerously close to being against the rules.

"It's not that," I say, taking a step back. And it's not. At least, it's not *all* of it. I can't let him touch me. If I let that happen now, let myself depend on someone else to get through this, I'll never truly be part of the DMA. I'm glad it's dark so he can't see me blush.

He tries to laugh it off, but I can tell I've hurt him. Rejected him. I wish I could explain the whirlwind of emotions spinning in my gut right now, but I can't even identify them enough to say what they mean.

"Tell me if you need anything," he says, stepping away, and it's like he's sucked the air from my lungs as he turns back toward the trail.

For a minute I can't move and then he's already a dozen yards away. I hurry to follow the glow of his flashlight. He's not waiting anymore but I don't have enough energy to devote to figuring out if I really just screwed up. I follow, keeping the glow of the fire to my right, plenty far away.

House Mountain has a clearing on top—the one we'd been on during Declaration Day doing buddy carries. It's maybe the size of a football field and can be seen from every angle on campus. Despite the worry over Kelly, I can't help but smile. Ten Alpha Company recruits have already started, lining up rolls and rolls of toilet paper. They must have gotten them from every bathroom on campus; there are hundreds of them.

"McKenna, grab a few rolls. Second Platoon's down on the lower end of the field. We're making the biggest *A* we possibly can. Wide, tall, just huge." The voice comes out of the darkness and I've got no idea who says it, but I grab a couple rolls and head down anyway. The sooner we get this over with, the sooner I can get back to my room and be alone with my sudden confusion.

Kelly, Nix, and Dove are already working on the right-hand side of the A so I get to work on the left along with Bekah and Ritchie. As long as we're not caught out here we won't get in trouble—one of the unwritten rules of the DMA. MMs, like sneaking around campus stealing uniforms or marching up the hill to show the entire town who rules the school, is definitely an approved activity by the cadre. Do something stupid and get caught red-handed, though, and we'll be pushing until graduation.

"Hey, McKenna. I'm here to help." Another recruit buddy,

Clark, grabs a roll of toilet paper from the pile and throws it in a big arc up the hill. He's built like a steamroller and must weigh about two hundred pounds. "I'm not gonna lie. You and Cross are pretty damn impressive. I had bets you'd all be out the first day and *definitely* thought you'd never make it this long. The corporals are riding your asses more than the rest of us combined—you especially—but you just keep on keepin' on."

"Thanks," I say, glad it's dark out here so he can't see how red I'm sure my face is. He holds his hand out to me, something shiny and round in it. I grab the can, looking at the name of the beer in the light of the moon. "Oh, I don't really drink." It sounds lame and I know it, but if I get caught drinking, I'm out of here.

"We're recruit buddies," Ritchie says, walking toward us with a beer in his hand. He's the tallest guy in our company by about three inches, but all skin and bones. His military-issued glasses make him seem a bit like Harry Potter. "No one's going to rat you out, Mac."

I grin at the nickname Kelly gave me that seems to be catching on, happy for the moment just to belong. I think of Kelly's hand on my face, of the hurt look in his eyes when I pulled away. I think of the words spit at us in the river on Declaration Day, of the pressure of being the only recruit, the only female, in classes with upperclassmen. And suddenly a beer doesn't sound so bad. What the hell. I pop the top and take a swig.

"Atta girl." Clark laughs. "Now, let's TP the hell out of this mountain." He pops his own can and drinks the whole thing down in a few gulps.

It takes me a couple tries to get the hang of throwing toilet paper rolls. It's not something I've ever done before, but after a few minutes, I can toss a roll across the field without ripping the paper.

Running up and down the mountain makes me thirsty and Ritchie hands me another beer when the first one is empty.

"Thanks." I take a few swigs from the second one, already feeling a little lightness in my head, and for the first time since I've been here I feel a little less scared, a little more free.

"Kind of a lightweight, huh?" Ritchie laughs as I stumble up the hill to get the roll I've just thrown.

"Not a lightweight." I don't even know what that means. "I've just never done this before."

"TPed a mountain?"

I laugh. "No, gotten drunk."

"Gotta learn sometime, Mac. And who better to learn with than your recruit buddies. We're going to be together for four years—might as well start trusting each other now."

"All right, Alpha!" someone yells from the top of the mountain. "Five more minutes and then we need to head back. Be sure to pack out your trash," he says, shaking the empty beer can in his hand. "We'll chuck it in the Dumpster on the edge of campus."

I quickly toss the last roll I've got, helping make the left line of the *A* a little thicker than before. Our finished product must be five stories tall and twenty feet wide. There's no way anyone will miss it. When I turn around to look down the mountain, the campus sways in front of me and stars zigzag across the sky.

"Doin'okaySam?" Bekah's words are smooshed together like she's trying to say one huge word instead of three individual ones, and I don't know if that's her fault or mine. She puts an arm around me and pulls me up against her.

"I think the world is spinning a little bit fast tonight."

She laughs. "Isn't it great? This is way better than getting yelled at." Then she pushes her mouth against my ear. "You and Kelly took a long time getting up here. Did you guys kiss in the woods?"

Thinking of Kelly stings a bit. "You know we're not supposed to—"

"Break the rules," she finishes. "Lighten up, Mac. What's the worst that could happen? They make us do some extra push-ups? Besides, you can't tell me nothing's up between you and Kelly. He can't keep his eyes off you."

"It's not like that." I want to say more but Kelly stumbles up and steps between us. He's messed up, too.

"What are you guys talking about?" He puts an arm around my shoulder and steers me in the direction of our recruit buddies. This time I don't pull away, even though I'm worried about what they'll think of us strolling around like this. So far, they seem to like me. If I get too chummy with one, though, they might turn on me. But . . . he feels solid, and warm, and just for a second while my head floats a little higher than usual, I let it happen.

When we get to the huddle of them, Kelly stage-whispers, "Guys! Mac and Cross are drunk!"

A cheer—much too loud for my liking—goes up, hanging in the air above us like it's a beacon for anyone looking.

"*Shhh,*" I say, jamming my finger against my lips and leaning in close. "You guys need to keep it quiet. My brother says they'll be looking for any reason to get us out of here."

"You don't have to worry about us, Mac," a voice says from behind me. "You and Cross have earned a place in the company."

The words wrap their way around me, slipping through my ears and not landing at all in any place that makes sense. I just let them talk and enjoy the warmth of my recruit buddies. The guys I'm going to survive this year with. My friends.

"Let's get down the mountain. Hopefully the hike will clear her head," one of them says. Kelly keeps his arm around me and helps me balance as we start heading down. I can't stop wondering if it's because he's trying to be helpful or if it's because he likes being close to me. When he tightens his grip to keep me upright, my insides go all warm and everything seems a little better. Thank God for beer.

A familiar orange light in the distance grabs my attention. It floats in the darkness, a little firefly maybe, bouncing back and forth, up and down. "It's so pretty. That little thing." I point toward the dot but my arm doesn't stay still.

"I don't think that's a thing," Kelly says, kind of laughing and it's then I realize he might be almost as drunk as I am. "I think it's that fire."

Campfires mean s'mores. All I want is s'mores. "Let's go. Maybe they've got food." My stomach growls then, as loud as a grizzly. I think for an instant that hunger is supposed to go with pot, but I can't focus on that for long.

"That would be awesome." Kelly jumps on the hungry train, too.

"My favorite part of s'mores," I say, "is the part when the

chocolate and the marshmallow mix together. You know, when they're both kind of liquid and you can lick it out of the inside." I think my voice is too loud. It sounds really loud to me, at least.

"I like to burn the marshmallows. Crispy black on the outside, still solid on the inside. Or, as solid as a marshmallow is, you know."

I nod. He is the wisest person I know. "That's good, too."

When we get closer to the fire, though, Kelly puts a finger to his lips. He creeps forward slowly, ninja-style, then motions me closer.

I lift my foot high off the ground and take a very exaggerated step, putting it down lightly and trying not to make any sound. I do it again before he shakes his head and points.

I follow the line of his arm, my gaze stopping on one of the people at the fire. It's enough to make me want to puke up my beer.

Matthews.

"What the hell? Why the hell is he up here?" It's not the stage whisper I used before. I yell it.

Matthews's head snaps up, his eyes on me in the darkness. Thank God we don't have a flashlight on.

Kelly's hand clamps down over my mouth. "Don't say a word." I try to pull away but he keeps me pinned against him. "Step back slowly, quietly. Maybe he won't see us."

Since his hand over my mouth is impeding me actually verbalizing anything, I just follow the movement of his body as he takes a step back, then another. Matthews keeps his eyes on the woods, on where he must think I am.

I stumble over something—a root, maybe—and fall to the ground. “Ouch. Crap!”

“Shh,” Kelly says. “Get up, Mac. We’ve got to get out of here.”

I trip once more but Kelly wraps strong arms around me and yanks me back to my feet.

Then we turn and run like hell.

THIRTEEN

KELLY TRIED TO CALM ME DOWN ON THE WAY BACK TO campus. He told me there's no way Matthews could have known it was me. But Kelly just did it so I won't flip out. I haven't been able to sleep since we got back, though, and now that the beer is out of my system and my head is starting to pound, I know nothing good will come of this.

There's no chance I'm falling asleep and so when the banging comes at 0530, I'm already in PT gear minus one major part of my uniform. My KB is nowhere to be seen.

"Out on the wall now, Worms!" It's Julius yelling this time, walking up and down the deck and pounding on each door he passes.

Since I don't have to wait on Katie this morning, I run right out, squinting in the bright hallway. It takes the rest of my recruit buddies longer to get out on the wall. Apparently none of them is worried about what happened last night. I stand as straight as I can, just hoping he doesn't ask us to pull out our KBs and start to read.

When we're all accounted for, Julius lets us in on the reason he's grinning. "Looks like some of you Worms tried to do something motivational last night. That's great. I'm sure Alpha will like it. But guess what? I don't. It means you broke curfew. It means you snuck off campus. So now you're going to pay." He drops the bag I didn't notice he was holding until now and I wince when it clangs against the ground. "Before marching down to first mess, you're going to make this deck shine. There's cleaner and rags in here. Every piece of brass—doorknobs, kickplates, *everything*—better be shining or we're going to smoke the hell out of you later. Got it?"

"Corporal Julius, yes, Corporal Julius." We try to sound off, but it's a little less than motivational. My head pounds in response.

"You can talk, but it better be a damn whisper." He sounds disgusted as he walks back off the deck, his flip-flops slapping against the floor as he goes.

"What does he mean about smoking us?" Kelly asks as he sits next to me at my door, rag and Brasso in hand.

I grab the can and put some cream on the rag, starting at the left side of the kickplate. "He's talking about a smoke show. Extra-hard PT—unsanctioned. Illegal. But it's not unheard of." I rub the rag in small circles, the cream smearing at first, until it works its magic and makes the brass start to shine.

"Extra-hard PT," Ritchie chimes in. "Hasn't the PT they've been having us do been extra-hard to begin with?"

I laugh out loud, then wince at the pain in my head and quickly cover my mouth. "I'm sorry. You're serious, aren't you?"

Ritchie's face goes red. "Hey, we can't all be born naturally fit. I am trying, you know."

"It's been hard for me, too." I don't think letting them know I'm tired will hurt their opinion of me at this point. "But smoke shows are worse. Way worse, I think."

"Well, then, let's make sure the hall looks amazing. I can't take 'way worse.'"

Kelly grins at me, rolling his eyes. They can't make PT hard enough to tire Kelly out. And no matter how hard it is for me, I'd never quit.

Ritchie moves away to help Nix at the next door and Kelly keeps his voice quiet. "You okay?"

"Head's pounding." Oh, yeah, and I've lost my freaking KB and am going to be the reason we end up getting smoked if I can't find it.

He laughs. "It'll go away. Just drink some water, take some aspirin. You going to see Quinn today?" It doesn't matter that she's injured anymore; she's not pulling her weight and they're already pushing her out. It's not going to be long before they turn on her and even though I want her around, I'm not sure I want to be beside her when she goes down. Besides, I've got to find my KB.

"Later, if I can get away."

"If you can't, let me know. I'll get over there and check on her."

"Thanks." I put more cream on my rag and continue working. I try not to glance at him, but I can't help it. He smiles when he catches my eye—apparently my rejection last night didn't hurt him too bad.

Matthews appears when we're in formation outside waiting for Drill to march us down to first mess. My stomach is growling, my head is pounding, but it's my heart that won't slow down. If he finds out about my KB, I'm dead. It's all I can do to keep my composure when he comes over to me. My aching head makes me feel out of my element and I don't even have time to get my game face on. I'm in front of the squad this morning, beating out Kelly for once, but it's not a great position. It means Matthews has easier access to me.

"Feeling good this morning, McKenna? Not too tired. No headache?"

My heart slams inside my chest. "Corporal Matthews, this recruit feels fine, Corporal Matthews."

"Not missing anything?" The sneer on his face says I am, and I know he knows.

"Corporal Matthews . . . this recruit doesn't think so, Corporal Matthews." It comes out stuttered and so obviously a lie that he can't keep the grin off his face.

He leans in a fraction further. "You've lost something important. Soon you're going to have to ask for my help." When he talks his teeth graze my ear. I can almost feel Kelly tense behind me and I pray he doesn't do anything and make this worse. "And I'm going to refuse. You'll have to explain this one away."

"Company," Drill says, his voice loud and dangerous. "Attention!"

Matthews snaps his teeth together next to my ear. I wince as he laughs and steps back, his eyes not leaving mine until Drill gives the order to march and I'm forced to move. All I want to do is curl up into a ball.

As eventful as waiting to march was, the actual process of getting to first mess is anything but. We're in and out within ten minutes, lined up and waiting to march back up for Saturday training.

"Get those KBs out, recruits," Matthews says, standing in front of me, his eyes staring threats into mine. "You're not going to waste time doing nothing. Every second of every day you should be breathing the DMA. Get them out!" He yells again when we move slowly.

I freeze. I can't move. Can't figure out how to get myself out of this without the whole company knowing I fucked up majorly.

I try to keep my eyes straight ahead, but they flick toward Drill. He's watching Matthews, worry lines on his forehead. I'm sure I must look like a startled deer or something because just as Matthews is about to speak again, Drill gives the order to march. I breathe a sigh of relief and force myself to focus on putting one foot in front of the other.

Matthews is right, though. I'm going to need help. Only an upperclassman can get me another KB. But he's crazy if he thinks I'm going to ask *him* for help. I just need to wait for my Thursday meeting with Jonathan and then everything will be fine. He'll find me one. He has to.

Finally, after second mess, we're released to the library, chapel, or to our rooms for the rest of the day. Without waiting to see what everyone's planning to do, I sign out to the chapel.

"Sam," Rev says with a smile when I knock on his door. The smile fades, though, when he takes in my face. "Come in," he says, standing to close the door behind me.

"I know you're probably getting ready for the service tomorrow. . . ." I let my voice trail off because I really don't want him to tell me to leave. He's the closest thing to Dad I have right now.

"How can I help?"

Pinching the bridge of my nose, I squint, trying to figure out the best way to say it. Like a Band-Aid, I guess. Just rip it off as fast as I can. "I lost my KB."

"Oh." He understands the magnitude of what's happened. I could be marching tours—hours of walking with a rifle as punishment—until Christmas for a violation this big. "Have you asked your corporal for one?"

"Matthews? No way. Besides, he knows." And Drill probably knows by now, too.

His eyebrows shoot up, shock all over his face. "He *knows*? What is he doing about it?"

"Nothing yet." I can still feel his breath on my neck, hear the snap of his teeth in my ears. "He's going to make me pay for it, though."

"Maybe Jonathan could help?"

"I've got a meeting scheduled with him for Thursday."

"I don't think this can wait that long, Sam. If Matthews tells—if more cadets find out you're without a KB . . ."

"I know." I can't stop clenching my jaw, a throbbing in my temples building. "I just don't want to let Jonathan down."

Rev smiles sadly, like he's heard this all before. "Which would be worse? Confessing up front or waiting until you're caught?"

I sigh and stand. "I know."

"I would help if I could. . . ."

"Thanks anyway, Rev."

"Good luck."

When I leave Rev's office, I hear a guitar in the sanctuary. It's not Bekah, though, like I expect. Kelly's sitting up front, strumming quietly and singing along. "I didn't know you play."

He smiles as I make my way to the front, singing the final words to a haunting, sad song that has my heart aching.

I can't stop myself from sitting next to him, leaning in to hear the quiet words he sings. "That was beautiful," I say when he finishes the song.

He sets the guitar down beside him and scoots closer, leaning against me, his hand just next to my leg. "My brother likes it when I play."

"Do you write?"

He shrugs. "Not really. I don't have time, you know?"

"We don't have time for anything anymore." I'm not sure what made me say that—like I'm implying if we went to a normal high school that maybe we'd have time to see where this goes.

He links his fingers with mine and I tense. It's been pounded into our heads for almost two months that we are brothers and sisters and I can't get the thought to go away. But his hand is warm and strong and I wonder if things will change if I let this happen.

"My brother takes a lot of work. I try to do things with him all the time. I think that's one of the reasons I like being here. People get to see me separate from him. Here, I get to do something for myself. For once, I'm not the kid whose brother has Down's." He shakes his head and laughs. "This is why you don't know I play. I get all introspective and weepy."

I squeeze his hand. It's all I can give him right now. More than I *should* give him. "My dad's a Ranger. Jonathan is the cadet colonel—I know a little bit about expectations. But while you're running from them, it looks like I ran right smack into them, and I'm letting everyone down in the meantime."

"What are you talking about?"

I turn toward him and lean in. "Promise you won't tell?"

"Of course not." He's holding both my hands now, gently, like he's scared I'll break. It's not how I want to be held, like I need to be protected, but I can't make myself pull away.

"I lost my KB up on the mountain last night."

"What?"

"It must have been when I fell. When we saw Matthews at the campfire and you helped me up. I didn't notice. . . ."

He lets go of one of my hands and reaches into his back pocket. "Take mine."

"No way," I say, trying to push the book back at him. "I can't take yours. You'll get yelled at."

"I can take getting yelled at. They'll eat you alive."

He's right and I know it. But owing him . . . God, it just pisses me off. I'm supposed to be doing this all on my own. "Thanks," I say, taking the book and putting it in my back pocket. "I'll get it back to you Thursday, as soon as I get a new one from Jonathan, okay?"

"It'll be fine," Kelly says, smiling at me despite how shitty I'm being. "I'll get another one." When he reaches for me, lifting my chin so I have to meet his eyes, I know he's going to try to kiss me.

I touch the top of his head, rubbing his buzz cut playfully and trying to break the tension. "You need a haircut."

He nods and closes his eyes, grabbing my hand and linking our fingers together again. When he leans closer, I try to scoot away. "Kelly, we're in the chapel. . . ." The words come out all breathy. I don't know what I want anymore.

"Then I'd better do this fast, huh?" His lips brush mine as he says the words and then I close my eyes because there's nothing else I can do.

The kiss isn't electric, but it's warm and gentle. An escape. Even though there are so many things wrong with this moment, so many reasons I should be saying no, I close my eyes and let him kiss me.

Too soon, or not soon enough, he pulls away. "I could do that all day," he says. He's smiling like he won a state championship and I wish I felt the same.

"Wouldn't sound like a bad plan if I didn't need to study."

He cups my face, planting a kiss on my nose. “Ouch.” His dimples make me smile. “But, considering I’m failing algebra, studying is probably better for me, too.” Standing, he reaches out a hand and pulls me to my feet, wrapping his arms around me. “But I’m not waiting two months to do that again, Mac. And next time, you won’t be thinking about studying.” Then he’s gone.

For a few minutes I had let myself pretend I was just a regular girl at a regular high school. So it wasn’t fireworks and tingling fingers. But it was nice. What’s so wrong with that?

With a missing KB, classes with Matthews, and Corps training, I’ll be slammed back to reality soon enough.

FOURTEEN

MONDAY NIGHT WE ARE SUMMONED TO THE HALLWAY IN our PT gear. We've got an hour until our nightly mandatory study hall and for once we've got no training planned. But being called on the wall by the corporals is never good. Kelly inches closer to me and I try not to notice. It doesn't work.

"In four days your parents will be crawling all over the DMA. They'll be holding your hands, kissing your cheeks, crying at how their little baby has grown up so much," Matthews barks out in his military voice.

Even though Parents' Weekend is all we talked about yesterday, none of us are stupid enough to celebrate our upcoming cadre-free time out in the open like this.

"Now, we want to make sure good Alpha Company Worms know how to behave. We don't want you to lose your minds on your first weekend off campus with your families."

"So," Corporal Julius picks up. "There are a few rules we need to make sure you understand. Number one: You are to be in your dress uniform at all times this weekend, even in your hotel rooms. Is that understood?"

"Corporal Julius, yes, Corporal Julius!"

"Number two: When you are off campus, you will still salute the upperclass officers and speak with respect to any upperclassman you come in contact with."

"Corporal Julius, yes, Corporal Julius!"

"And number three: You must keep an eye on your recruit sisters this weekend. All three of them. When they are out walking around, one of you will be with them at every moment."

What the hell?

"Corporal Julius, yes, Corporal Julius!" My voice is just a second later than the rest of my recruit buddies. Katie's back in the infirmary and Cross is with the track team again, so I'm the one bearing the brunt of the attention.

"Your recruit sisters are your real sisters now. Would you want the scumbags who are in the other companies pawing all over them, trying to get them to give up the goods?"

It's like I just stepped into the 1950s or something, and it's all I can do not to show my reaction. "Corporal Julius, no, Corporal Julius!"

"Would you want your recruit sisters to willingly give up their goods to anyone who asked?"

My face warms under the inspection of my cadre. Do they know about me and Kelly? I shouldn't have let it happen at all, but if they know and are going to make us pay for it, then whatever happens now is our fault. Kelly stiffens next to me. My eyes flick toward Drill but he's not looking this way. I just hope he hasn't heard anything; I don't want to let him down. I've got to end whatever is going on between Kelly and me.

"So, just to make sure you all understand the bond of brotherhood, we're going to treat you to one of the most sacred activities of this institution. Are you ready?"

"Corporal Julius, yes, Corporal Julius!"

"He asked if you were ready!" Matthews yells. "I can't hear you! Jumping jacks, go!"

There's not a clock on the wall, but I count to seventy-two before we're allowed to stop.

"Now, are you ready?" Julius asks again.

"Corporal Julius, yes, Corporal Julius!"

"Not good enough! Drop and give me twenty!" Matthews barks.

We fall to the floor as one, pushing and counting in unison. When the set of push-ups is over, we jump to attention.

Drill stands silently in the middle of the hallway, arms crossed over his chest, the black drill sergeant hat he hasn't worn since our first day now pulled low on his head.

"That was the saddest excuse for team unity I've ever seen." Matthews's voice is full of disgust. He walks to the end of the hall, pulling shut the fire doors that are always open, that we've been told can't be closed under any circumstances. The double doors at the other end of the hall clank shut, too. We're trapped. No adult on deck. No one to keep an eye on us. We're getting smoked.

"Alpha recruits." Drill barks the words out, his eyes skimming over me so fast it's like he's *trying* not to look at me. He knows about Kelly or my KB. Maybe both. He's got to. And it makes me feel like crap—like I've disappointed him or let him down or something. "It's time to show us what you're really made of. That you can handle the rigors of the Corps and honor your recruit sisters at the same time. This next hour is just a *taste* of what will happen if you screw up this weekend. Is that understood?"

"Drill Sergeant Stamm, yes, Drill Sergeant Stamm!" Our voices echo around the hall. I hear laughing and shouting at the stairwells—upperclassmen, I'm guessing, though I don't dare take a look. They must be coming to watch.

Matthews walks back to the center of the hall and pushes play on a CD player. The song that played when the cadre introduced themselves on the PG that first day starts with its eerie bell, moving instantly into the hard rock song, the stereo so loud the words are too distorted to hear.

But it doesn't matter. We're past hearing in an instant anyway.

The commands come in rapid-fire succession. Jumping jacks. Sit-ups. Running in place. Push-ups. Flutter kicks. High knees. Planks. Hello Dollys.

The songs come one after another. Songs about Hell. Jungles. Torture. Hate. Apocalypse.

Slick with sweat, I slip on the floor the next time I have to move to a standing position. A hand reaches out to catch me.

"Easy, Mac." Kelly sounds exhausted, but he helps me stand back up.

"Thanks," I huff back. My legs tremble with fatigue, my arms can barely go above my shoulders anymore, but I do the jumping jacks anyway.

Wilson pukes at the other end of the hallway, the stink of it filling the air and hanging over our heads. We continue to push, flutter, and jump our way through the commands.

"High knees! Make it count!"

I don't even know who says it but my muscles respond on their own, which is good, because I'd rather die right here on the floor than move another inch. Running in place, my knees come up, touching my hands which I hold out in front of me.

"Higher," Matthews snarls, grabbing me by the wrists and forcing my arms out at a ninety-degree angle.

I cry out, but raise my knees as high as I can after an hour of intense physical training, every muscle in my body shaking and straining for release. I'm determined not to fail tonight.

"Feel the pain, Alpha! Because if anything stupid happens this weekend—if something happens to your precious sisters, or if they allow something to happen to themselves—this is what you will feel every day until the end of the year."

I finally get what Matthews is doing right now. With the weird rants. He's trying to get our fellow recruits to turn on us. Trying to make them see us as baggage, another responsibility they shouldn't have to worry about.

"Understand this hate in your muscles. Hate us all you want, but you will be a unit. You will work together as a whole. Enjoy rewards as a whole. Suffer consequences as a whole. This is the family you have been given by the almighty commandant. This is the family you will live with, eat with, sleep with, play with, and be punished with!"

"Drop your arms, McKenna," Matthews says.

I do, and almost cry out with relief. But it's short-lived. He holds his arms out in front of him, a good three inches above where mine were. "Higher, McKenna. Do it right or don't bother doing it at all."

I grit my teeth and continue running, forcing my knees higher. Sweat stings my eyes so I close them.

"You are only as strong as your weakest link, Alpha. You will fail if this is how weak you are. Higher, McKenna!"

Groaning, I demand more from my tired muscles. Finally, I hit his hands with my knees. I can't keep the smile off my face. But I don't even get a second's grace.

"Push-up positions again. Go!"

We are not as whole as we were at the beginning. Some move slow, some slip when they are down, though they do not receive the same treatment that I do. They are left to fend for themselves.

"Down."

Nix, beside me, instantly goes to the floor. I'm close to collapse myself when Matthews crouches in front of me, his voice so quiet I have to strain to hear it above the scream of death metal on the stereo.

"Did you find your KB yet, McKenna?"

He wants to make me suffer.

"Corporal Matthews, no, Corporal Matthews." I don't even have the strength to yell. I've still got Kelly's but he's not worried about the particulars.

"Good. You know what kind of shit I hold over you?"

"Corporal Matthews, yes, Corporal Matthews."

"So, here's what's going to happen. The next time you need it, you're not going to have it. And the company will enjoy yet another smoke show on account of you. Not nearly so positive as this team building exercise you're enjoying right now."

I keep my eyes straight ahead, focusing on a cinder block in front of me, counting the pock marks in the wall to keep from looking at him. He's going to turn them all against me, one by one, until even my recruit brothers will want me out. I'm shaking violently, my arms on the verge of giving out.

"I'm glad we had this chance to talk, McKenna. I look forward to many more talks like this before you quit the Corps and go running back home to Daddy. Then again, you could leave now and save us a world of trouble and you a world of hurt. Why don't you give up, McKenna? Just think, you could wake up tomorrow in your nice warm bed, safe and sound at home. All this could be a bad dream."

"Jumping jacks! Go," Julius yells.

My recruit brothers jump up and begin counting, but Matthews has a hand on my shoulder, pushing me down farther, the weight of him threatening to make my arms collapse. Why isn't anyone doing anything? Why isn't Drill stopping this?

"You could get out now, go home. No one expects you to make it. No one *wants* you to make it. You don't belong here, McKenna. Females don't belong here. Sooner or later you're going to figure it out. Let's just hope it's sooner, before something bad happens. God forbid you get *injured* during a training incident or that the

Society decides to do something to encourage your departure."

I grit my teeth, summoning the last bit of strength I have as his fingers dig into my shoulders. It'll do no good to respond; it would probably make things worse.

"That's enough, Matthews." Drill's voice breaks through my thoughts. I hold my breath, waiting to see if he has enough control over Matthews to make him obey.

Matthews lets out a growl at being called off by Drill. "Leave, McKenna. Now." He pushes down on me as he stands up, and I sink to the floor, collapsing under the weight of being one of the first females at the DMA.

Breathing hard, I struggle, trying to get my hands under me. Kelly reaches out a hand and I grab it, standing up and breathing out a sigh of relief.

As soon as I'm steady, Matthews is there again, his hot breath sluggish on my neck as he whispers, "Remember, McKenna. The DMA is a dangerous place for females. Watch out."

Drill speaks next, so close by that Matthews winces and takes a quick step back. "Showers, everyone. Study hall in five minutes! Matthews," he says, more quietly as the rest of my recruit buddies turn and run. Matthews is still too close for me to move without running into him. "At my door. Now."

"Yes, Drill Sergeant," Matthews spits out. He glares at me for a minute before taking a step back, giving me just enough room to slide by. Drill waits until I'm at my door before he moves away from me, his eyes on Matthews the whole time.

I slip into my room and close the door behind me, collapsing on the bed in a heap of sweat and exhaustion. The only thing I want to do right now is crawl into a hole. Drill had to call Matthews off because he thought I couldn't take it. He thinks I'm weak.

But that's not the worst of it.

God forbid you get injured during a training incident or that the Society decides to do something . . .

Matthews threatened me outright. Not just that he was going to make my life miserable, but that there's some kind of Society that might go so far as to hurt me. I've never heard of them, but that doesn't mean they're not real.

And if they're something Matthews knows about, it's not likely that they're anything good.

I slam my Military History textbook shut during Wednesday night's study hall. There's no point in staring at the pages when the dates swirl together, making rivers and contrails on the page.

"Not going well?"

Kelly sits across from me in the library, struggling over his algebra textbook. His foot has been touching mine for seven minutes and right now I don't have the strength to even try putting up a fight. It's been two days since the smoke show but I'm still so sore it hurts to move at all. "I'm just confused," I say.

"By dates and battles? That doesn't seem like you."

I toss my pencil down, giving up the study hall as a loss. "Okay, how about exhausted? That seems like my excuse for everything lately."

He's looking at his homework, though, not really listening. "Your roommate back from the infirmary yet?"

"Who knows. She might as well move in there. It's been two weeks this time. Sounds like a nice break."

"You don't mean that," he says, raising his head to look at me. "You're not one to slide through."

"Then maybe I should join a sport; Cross hasn't been to company training since the beginning of September. She's got an excuse every night." I'm trying not to let the fact that Cross missed Monday night's smoke show bother me, but it's hard to ignore that I seem to be the only female in the company right now.

"Okay." He puts his pencil down and steeples his fingers in front of his face, leaning on his elbows. "Therapy time. Why are you here? I mean, I know your brother is cadet colonel and your dad went here. But, what made you come?"

I stare at him for a long second. *Liam.* Jax called him Liam. It suits him. And somehow when I think of him as just plain Liam, it's like he's just a regular guy, someone I can talk to.

"Honestly?"

He looks up from his book, scooting his chair closer. Now it's not just his foot touching mine, but his leg. His lips twitch when he sees me swallow hard. "Of course."

I pull my foot away from his—the closest thing to rejection that I can dish out right now. "It was a dare."

He drops his hands and leans in so he's partway over the table, his voice quiet and conspiratorial. "You're kidding, right?"

I can't keep the grin off my face. "No. I'm not. My oldest brother, Amos, gave me the dare two years ago when girls at the DMA was just an idea." I tuck a stray piece of hair behind my ear and study the table. "I kind of have a problem with saying no to dares."

He smiles so big I see a second dimple that I've never seen before and I feel my resolve to stay away from him wavering. The *shhh* from the librarian when he laughs makes me start, too. I haven't laughed like this for weeks. It feels good.

"That's a pretty major dare, Mac."

I shrug it off. "We've done worse," I say, though I'm not sure that's true now that I'm here.

Kelly looks like he wants to say something, and then squints instead.

"What? Go ahead. Say what you want to say."

"Well, the point of going to a military high school, other than being put here by a judge, is to stand out, you know? To thrive, rise through the ranks, and get into a military university. I mean, you're good, but I just can't imagine them letting you be a drill sergeant, much less the cadet colonel. You're a *girl*."

I look around, acting shocked and checking to see if anyone overheard. "A girl? Are you serious? Who told you? How did you find out?"

He grins and blushes. "I'm sorry. I didn't mean it like that. I just meant . . ."

"I know. I'm not the most popular person around here. I figure if I toe the line and keep my name clean, though, I can finish strong, even if I don't get the chance to prove I have leadership potential."

"So your oldest brother, the one who gave you the dare—where is he now?"

Gritting my teeth, I pick up my pencil and press it hard into the paper, tracing over words I can't even read through the tears that are suddenly there.

"Mac?" He leans across the table, his fingers brushing mine. He doesn't hold my hand, but he keeps it where it is, lined up with mine, pinkie to pinkie. I think about pulling away.

Blinking quickly to keep the tears back, I shake my head. I promised Dad and Jonathan. I *swore* I'd keep it a secret. But I can't. I need someone to talk to about it—that's something neither of them will ever be able to understand. Maybe I have more in common with Mom than I thought. "He killed himself on R & R last Christmas."

"Oh, shit. I'm sorry, Mac. I didn't mean—"

"We've kept it real quiet. Dad doesn't want anyone to know, you know? A McKenna weakness like that wouldn't be too great to broadcast." I spit the words out, still pissed that Dad could think Amos was weak at all.

He pauses, like he has more questions about Amos. I look away when he meets my eyes, his face full of pity. It makes me want to get up and leave, and I think he knows it. "So . . . what's it like being in classes with cadets instead of recruits?" He's eyeing my pages of notes. "Awkward conversation change, I know. But I don't have any idea how to respond to that."

"It's okay. No one knows how to respond to it. I'll take topic changes any day." When my hand shakes, he moves his just a bit, so his pinkie and mine are crossed. I swallow and pull my hand away, putting both of them in my lap to keep from chewing my nails. It takes me a minute to even remember what he asked and I have to clear my throat to make my voice work. “Classes. They’re weird. I don’t say a word in Military History—I think Matthews would eat me alive. In all the other classes I keep quiet as much as I can and let the upperclassmen do all the talking.”

“And they let you in as a Worm? Knowing you were a sophomore?” To his credit, it doesn’t look like the lack of hand-holding bothers him too much.

“As long as I complete recruit training and Worm rites of passage, they don’t care.”

“Well, I’m glad you’re here,” he says, giving me that dimpled smile that might make me melt if we were anywhere but here. Then he clears his throat and picks up a pencil. “Now, about this math homework. Damn multistep equations. I hate them. Ever wonder why there are letters in math? It doesn’t seem right, does it?”

“Need help?” I’m not an ace at math, but algebra I can handle.

“Nah, I’ve got to figure this out on my own.”

“Suit yourself. I’ve got to get another book. But when I get back, it’s my turn to ask you a question.”

His eyes get really big and he feigns nervousness. “I don’t know if I’ll survive until you get back. If it looks like the numbers have killed me, you may have to use mouth-to-mouth to resuscitate.”

Laughing again, I push the chair away from the table and stand up. “You wish.” I grab the book off the table and head back to the stacks. I know what I want to ask him—we never have gotten a chance to talk about Jax. I’m dying to know how they connect and why she’d reach out to try and help me.

I run my fingers over the spines of the books, looking for another one that might help me make sense of the Military History homework. There are two that look promising and I grab them, about to turn the corner. The sound of voices stops me in my tracks. They're hushed but the closer they get, the clearer they are.

"What I'm doing isn't working. Her roommate basically lives at the infirmary now. I nearly killed her the other night. Shit, I've seen *guys* crumble with a smoke show *half* as bad." It's Matthews. I'd recognize his voice anywhere. I slip away from the voices and around the end of the bookshelf so they won't see me when they walk by.

"The Society meets next week. We can't change our course of action until then. The other female?" This voice could belong to any one of the faceless cadets I don't know.

"We're going to get to her another way," Matthews says to the invisible voice and follows it up with a laugh. I stay where I am until their voices fade away, then take a step backward, sliding as quietly as I can down the aisle and into the main part of the library. If they see me here, there's no telling what they'll do. Breathing hard back at the table, I pack my stuff as quickly as I can.

Kelly looks up from his textbook. "What are you doing? Everything okay?"

I glance around, hoping Matthews isn't still in the vicinity, and shake my head at Kelly. "I need to head back to the barracks." That's twice I've heard about the Society this week. Could this have something to do with the bets to get us out of here?

He stands up and starts packing his stuff. "Did you get the book you need?"

It takes me a minute to figure out what he's talking about. "Nah, I'll find something online."

He shrugs. "Time for a study break anyway. I'll head back with you. I'm about as sick of algebra as I can get and you know the cadre. They don't want you girls walking around alone."

I don't bother telling him Matthews would probably love to get me alone—that the Society would be proud of him, too. "Thanks," I say, glancing around once again before heading out the door and taking a left toward the barracks.

"You sure you're okay?" Kelly is taking the steps two at a time to keep up with me and I force myself to slow down. We're not supposed to be talking, but there's no one around.

I whisper, "Yeah, everything just kind of catches up to me sometimes."

"I know you're worried, but change doesn't happen overnight, Mac. Give them time. Once they see how amazing you are, they'll want you here just as much as I do."

His words drift over me and they're nice to hear, but I can't let anything risk my position here, or his. "Kelly, we can't do this."

He drops his gaze to the ground, breaking military bearing for a second by putting his hands in his pockets. "I know. It's just . . ."

"Nice. It's nice for me too, but—"

"We've both got goals here and dating's just going to get in the way of them." He shrugs. "Another time, maybe."

"Maybe," I say, though I know nothing other than a stray

kiss in the chapel will ever happen between us now. "Thanks for understanding."

He laughs. "Thanks for having the guts to say something about it. I know you're right, but I didn't want to stop."

I nudge his shoulder. "You're a good friend, Kelly." We walk in silence for a bit longer, but something about Matthews's conversation won't stop repeating itself in my mind and now that we've gotten over the non-relationship stuff, I need his opinion. The bell tower hasn't chimed the hour yet so we still have a few minutes. "You ever heard of anything called the Society?"

"No. What are you talking about?"

"I don't know. Nothing." I kick a rock, frustrated and disappointed that he can't help. "Just something I heard."

"Where'd you hear it?"

"Matthews. I've heard it from him twice now. He's got to be talking about some group, but I've never heard of it."

"Maybe we'll learn about it after we're recognized?"

"Yeah. Maybe." But it doesn't sound right. The way Matthews said it, it sounded like the whole Corps wasn't involved. He made it sound evil.

FIFTEEN

"SIRS! GOOD MORNING, SIRS! THIS IS THE OUTSTANDING Alpha Company, sirs! Today is the twenty-third day of the tenth month in the year of our Lord twenty-fourteen. Uniform of the day is low quarters, Winter Class Bs, garrison cover. Upperclassmen, you have twenty minutes to fall out. Freshmen, you have fifteen minutes to fall in."

I stop yelling and take a breath. Morning calls are another one of those weird duties recruits have to do, like we're fricking human alarm clocks. Upperclassmen in royal blue robes start exiting their bunks and heading for showers. Some still have their eyes closed. The one who opens the door next to where I'm standing rubs the sleep out of his eyes.

I keep my gaze straight ahead. Holding my arms straight

down at my sides, I walk at attention to the other end of the hallway.

"Looking good, recruit," a cadet wearing only boxers calls out as I walk by. They're supposed to wear robes, but after my first time doing morning calls, I've already realized they don't all follow the rules. The one who just addressed me heads to the bathroom, giving me a glimpse of a sculpted back decorated with a tattoo—thick lines that could form a circle except for the skulls that break their circuit. The letters *P* and *S* run vertically down the middle, and a square sits dead center in the design.

"I don't know, Evers. She could stand to shake her ass a little bit more."

It's then that I realize that the boxers-only guy is the cadet from the first day and the one who got Matthews to single me out during rifle drills. I move my eyes away from the tattoo and force myself to look straight ahead. Shit.

Evers turns, stopping in front of me and blocking my way. "Please. This one's a tease. She's going to show it off but I'm sure she won't let us touch."

My face reddens and I break out of my straight line to move around him. At the other end of the hall, I stop, sweep my right foot behind me, and do an about-face, turning around to look down the hall again. Thankfully, Evers goes into the bathroom and lets the door close without saying anything else. I've dropped Jonathan with two punches before. Evers might require a few more hits, but if I'm fast, I think I could take him.

Once I yell the same information again, I head back to

where I started. As more upperclassmen come out, I slightly cross my eyes, not wanting to focus on the half-naked bodies all around me.

"McKenna, what kind of music do you like?" The voice is quiet, coming just from my left. The one who wasn't happy I woke him up.

I ignore him and keep looking straight ahead. We were warned never to talk to the upperclassmen. This could just be a trick to get me in trouble.

"It's me, Huffman. Stamm's friend, Alpha Company flag bearer and self-proclaimed shitbag," he says under his breath.

My cheek twitches. No one would call themselves a shitbag unless they were serious. Cadets who fit the name around here really own the title, though. They don't iron their uniforms, come to formation late, and skip PT.

"I'm not one of those lame-ass tools who's going to rat you out. If you tell me what kind of music you like, I'll play something for you. Besides, the parade's tomorrow. You need to relax before you go on display."

God, I'd kill to listen to some music right now, but there's no way I'm getting caught in this trap.

"Fine, let's do this: I'll say some bands and you just blink really hard if you hear one you like, okay?"

Blinking isn't against the rules, though, so what can it hurt? I close my eyes, and keep them shut for longer than normal, then open them again to show him I understand. I just hope no one sees him leaning out his door to talk to me.

He starts with country and after two or three names, switches to rock. When I don't blink at any of those he makes a clicking sound with his tongue. "Boy, you're a tough one."

When he finally mentions one I like, I blink and then open my eyes really big. Amos used to blast his music in the car when we'd go for long drives together.

"Well, well, well. What a surprise. I wouldn't have pegged you for a rap girl, but okay. Here goes."

I hear his door close behind him and soon the loud bass of my favorite song is blasting through the basement. I allow my face to relax just slightly, but have to make a conscious effort to keep myself from nodding along with the beat. For a moment, I'm somewhere else—riding shotgun with Amos on the autobahn, not stuck here, in a world where no one wants me.

When I'm done with my next round of morning wake-up calls, I park myself back in front of Huffman's door. He's just coming back from the shower and gives me a wink as he passes by. "I may be one of the few, but I'm glad you're here, McKenna. I think you and the rest of the females will make life around here more interesting. Let me know if you need anything."

I blink really hard and continue listening to the music for the few minutes I have left.

Jonathan tried to beg off from today's meeting. Apparently he's got a lot to do before Parents' Weekend. I wouldn't let him, though, and run to the chapel after first block is finished.

He slides his phone into his pocket. "I only have a minute. You've got to be kidding me about the KB."

I lower my gaze to the floor. "We were on an MM—"

"Don't tell me. The less I know, the less they can say I'm helping you out. And as far as the KB . . . I can't get you one." He at least has the decency to sound a little remorseful.

"What do you mean you can't get me one? Only upperclassmen—"

"If I help you with this, they'll think you can't do anything on your own—that I'm going to bail you out every time you get in trouble. You'll have to find another way."

"It's not like I can ask Matthews for mine back."

"Well, you're going to have to think of something. And you'd better not ask any of the cadets in your classes for one."

"What? Why not?" But I can tell by the disgusted glare he aims my way that he's heard something about me.

"You could ruin a lot more than your year here if you're screwing an upperclassman."

"If I'm *what*?" For a second I forget that he's the cadet colonel and wind up to hit him. He grabs my fist in his hand, though, twisting my arm behind my back. I cry out. "I'm not! I'm not! Jonathan, let me go."

"All I'm saying is that it better stay that way. The things Lyons is hearing about you guys is getting worse. If any of them are true and you're hooking up with cadets—" He drops my hand and I shake my arm out, backing away from him.

"You know what? Don't worry about the KB. I don't know what made me think that you'd actually want to help me. No, if it makes you look the slightest bit weak, you're not going to do it, are you? Never mind that I'm your sister, that I'm doing the hardest thing I've ever done in my life. No, Colonel McKenna has to be a hard-ass, just like Dad." I push the door open and walk out, ignoring the command of my cadet colonel as he demands I stop.

When I get to the computer lab I log in to my email, ready to give my mom an earful—well, eyeful—of Jonathan's latest asshole move. She's beaten me to the punch, though.

From: mrsmckenna@mail.com

To: smckenna@dma.edu

Subject: About Parents' Weekend

Sammy,

I can't come this weekend. Sorry.

Mom

I stare at the computer screen for way longer than I need to, reading the lines over and over again. She knows how important this first Parents' Weekend was for Jonathan. She's got to know how much I'm counting on her. But once I headed down the military track, I was never her top priority.

I log off without even bothering to respond. Whether she's here or not, I've got a long night ahead of me preparing for tomorrow's parade. I might as well get started.

"Are you going to tell me what's wrong or are you just going to shine your boots all night?" Katie's in the barracks tonight, for once. She's starching both our uniforms so that we can iron them.

"What do you mean?"

"I mean you look like someone killed your freaking cat or something."

I spit on the tip of my boot, rubbing it into the polish to bring out a shine that even Matthews won't be able to critique. "It's nothing."

"You're lying."

"So what if I am?"

"Look, I know I haven't been around much. I don't mean to keep getting injured—"

"There's a difference in being hurt and sliding through freshman year." I want to take my words back as soon as I see the hurt on her face. "I didn't mean that. I'm sorry. . . ."

"Of course you did. You don't think I know I'm not doing as much as the rest of you?" She grabs the iron out of her footlocker and plugs it into the wall. "I know I'm missing training. You and Bekah have more friends than I'll ever have. I'm going to recharge this weekend. I'll be at a hotel, eat real food, watch some television, and then I'll come back and be ready to be part of the company."

I don't even bother responding. The fact that she gets to see her parents . . . I can't even.

"What? You don't think I can?"

"It's not that. I'm just having a shitty day." I rub my boot much harder than I should. The shine transforms to a dull polish. I've ruined it. "Shit!" I throw my boot across the room and it thuds against the wall locker before hitting the ground near Katie's feet.

"What's going on, Sam?"

"My mom's not coming." I scrunch up my face, barricading the tears before they can fall.

"What?"

"She's not coming to the parade, to Parents' Weekend, to any of it." My mom's chosen her hatred of this place over me. I can't win, no matter what I do.

"God, Sam. I'm sorry." She presses down on the iron, the smell of hot starch filling the room, reminding me of mornings at home when Dad would get his uniform ready.

Standing, I reach for my boot and put it away in my wall locker. I'll deal with it in the morning. "It's not worth getting upset over," I say, though the shaking in my voice probably makes it hard to believe. "I'm going to go take a shower."

I grab my bath caddy, sign out, and walk quickly to the bathroom. At least in the shower I can let the tears fall.

Katie's sleeping like the dead two hours later when I sneak out of the barracks and head to check my email, hoping maybe Mom will have sent another one to explain her earlier message.

Sam, I can't come this weekend. Sorry. Mom.

No reason why. No *Love* at the end.

The lab is dark and I slink to the back to my normal computer. But when I log in, there's no new email from Mom. Just Jax.

To: smckenna@dma.edu

From: jaxhax@mail.com

Subject: RE: RE: PW

Saturday morning. 2am. Bell tower by chapel. Come alone. (God, that sounds dramatic, doesn't it?)

I know your mom's not coming for the weekend. Sorry about

that. I do have some info to share, so come, okay?

BTW, you've got them all stirred up about your KB. What the hell happened?

J

I shoot back an email agreeing to meet. Maybe when I'm with her I'll be able to pretend to be human for just a few hours.

SIXTEEN

I CHECK MY BELT BUCKLE ONE MORE TIME BEFORE heading out. Today is my second time being inspected by Jonathan and the commandant. And it's the Friday of Parents' Weekend. I can't afford to screw up like I did last time. But who knew the command sergeant major was going to make me drop and do push-ups on my way to inspection? I've wrapped rubber bands around my shirt stays—little pieces of black elastic that connect our shirts to our socks beneath our pants to keep the hem from coming untucked—just to be sure.

I slip out onto the wall right as Matthews is making his way on deck.

"Good to see you decided to join us, McKenna." It's all I can do to keep from rolling my eyes. "You remember the drill. You'll miss formation and head straight up to the admin building to get inspected. If you don't win, the smoke show when everyone returns Sunday night will be in your honor." He takes a step to the left and inspects Bekah for what I think is definitely too long a time, his eyes roaming down, then up, then lower again.

So. Gross. She needs to say something to Drill about that. That could give a whole new meaning to jumping the chain of command.

But I'll keep those thoughts to myself. He hasn't actually done anything that I've *seen* and the red blush on Bekah's cheeks hopefully means she's embarrassed, rather than enjoying the personal inspection a bit more than she should be.

"So, go!" Matthews's voice makes me jump and it takes me a second to realize he's actually talking to me. His eyes are focused somewhere near Bekah's name tag.

"Corporal Matthews, yes, Corporal Matthews!" I turn and run before I get yelled at again.

The recruits from the other companies are already lined up and I'm breathing heavy when I make it to my place in line for inspection. I hate this part of Corps life—where what I do can negatively impact my company.

"Good morning, Recruit McKenna."

"Sir, good morning, sir!" I yell into my brother's face.

He winces and his eyes are red. Late night for the colonel, it looks like. I wonder if his responsibilities are getting to be too much for him. "Recite the honor code, recruit."

"Sir, a cadet of Denmark Military Academy will not lie, cheat, steal, or tolerate those who do, sir!"

He nods, a sharp, crisp movement, but his heart is not in it.

He used to love torturing me at home. What's going on? "Very good. Now, let me see your KB."

I pull Kelly's KB out of my back pocket and hand it to him. He flips it open and studies the inside front cover for a long moment and the recruit next to me shifts uncomfortably. I try not to freak out.

"Recruit McKenna." He sighs my name, like he's our father, disappointed in me for some trouble I've caused.

"Sir, yes, sir!"

"This isn't your Knowledge Book, correct?" He knows it's not.

I try to give him a look that says I want to kill him, but his eyes are still on the inside front cover. Why won't he look at me? I swallow around the sudden lump in my throat. "Sir, no, sir."

"You do understand that a recruit is required to carry their KB with them at all times?"

What the hell are you doing, Jonathan? "Sir, yes, sir." My voice comes out shaky and I force myself not to react. I can't show him he's freaking me out. The recruit next to me snickers.

"Then it appears you've broken a cardinal rule of recruitdom."

I blink several times, my heart thundering. I don't know how to respond to this.

"You'll have to do tours to make up for it. Ten should suffice. Tomorrow and Sunday. Understood? And," he says, pulling another KB from his pocket, one I recognize. How the hell did he get it? "Keep a better hand on your original Knowledge Book, understood?"

This weekend, even if Mom can't come, is supposed to be the first weekend I'll be able to really relax since the beginning of the year. Thanks to Jonathan, though, that's gone. Marching all weekend with a rifle is going to be anything but the time away from this place that I need.

I reach out and take my old KB, sliding it into my back pocket with the other one. "Sir, yes, sir," I say through clenched teeth, forcing myself to look straight ahead and not at him.

"Good. Now," he says, stepping to my right and looking at the recruit next to me. "Bravo Company. Recruit Mills. Very squared away," he says, actually sounding impressed.

As soon as we're released, I bolt from the building. I don't even care about the smoke show I've just caused my company. Matthews gave him my KB right now for a reason. Maybe he doesn't know Mom isn't coming? Or is there another reason? Something the Society is planning?

By the mess hall, Alpha Company is lined up and waiting for me to head in to breakfast. I double-time it and fall in next to Kelly, whose eyes are straight ahead, scanning lines in a Knowledge Book he magicked from some upperclassman.

"About time, McKenna!" Matthews yells. I'm sure even the squirrels behind the barracks jump to attention. "So? Did you win?" The sneer on his face tells me very well that he knows the answer to that, but he's not going to let it go.

I meet his eyes. "Corporal Matthews, no, Corporal Matthews."

"What was wrong with you this time?"

"Corporal Matthews, there was a problem with this recruit's KB, Corporal Matthews."

"Got that squared away, have you? Then get it out!"

I feel the weight of the extra book in my back pocket. When

I get my original book out, I flip to the first page. But where I should be getting a brief history of the DMA, a giant X is drawn in black Sharpie, thick and bold, covering all but a few words and making the page unreadable.

"In order to read, your eyes have to be moving, McKenna."

"Corporal Matthews, yes, Corporal Matthews."

"Then get reading!"

I flip the page, but the same thing is on the next page, and the next one after that. On every page of the KB I'm forced to carry around, an X blocks the words underneath. It's useless. *What the hell?* Jonathan had to have known it was like that when he gave it to me.

My breaths come in shallow gasps and the world tilts at an angle around me. Kelly glances my way, breaking his attention stance, and it's almost enough to undo me.

Matthews glares at me for a second longer before shaking his head. "You disgust me, McKenna."

"Corporal Matthews," Drill says, stepping into my line of sight.

Just great, Sam. Let Drill see how weak you are—how you can't even stand up for yourself against Matthews.

"Yes, Drill Sergeant?"

"Send the company in for breakfast."

I want to close my eyes and melt into the ground. As if being chewed out by Matthews and disappointing Jonathan weren't enough shitty things to happen before eight o'clock in the morning. Now Drill thinks he needs to swoop in and rescue me. My cheeks burn with embarrassment.

"Yes, Drill Sergeant. Alpha Company, dismissed!"

I don't even hesitate, but break into a sprint to get out of the line of sight of anyone who has permission to yell at me.

Kelly's waiting for me after second block, his wool uniform jacket zipped up against the cold. He nods toward the chapel and I follow, waiting until we're inside before talking. The last thing I need is another reason to get the company in trouble today. "What's up?"

"I just wanted to see how you are." He steps toward me, then catches himself and moves back. "Sorry. I forgot."

"It's okay." I reach into my pocket. "Guess we're in for another smoke show Sunday night. Here's your KB."

He tucks it away. "They would have found a reason to give us one anyway. Don't sweat it."

"Easy for you to say," I grumble. Sitting down in a pew, I pat the cushion beside me. "I haven't had a chance to ask you my question since we left the library so fast the other night."

"Okay," he says, leaning back against the pew. "Shoot."

"Tell me about that girl who came to the movie looking for you." If I'm going to meet up with her and let her help me, I need to know who I'm dealing with.

"Who, Jax?"

I nod. "Yeah. She seemed to know you pretty well."

"We're best friends. Have been for years. We tried dating last year but it didn't really work. Guess I have a thing for girls who don't like me." He nudges me. "She's not really military-geared and she doesn't understand why I'm here."

"Isn't that the story of our lives?"

"I guess so," he says, then smiles. "Maybe I'll invite her to one of the dances. When she sees me in my dress blues, there's no way she'll be able to turn me down. Not like I'm going to take you or anything. You're my recruit sister. It's kinda gross if you think about it." He laughs, the sound filling the chapel and making me smile for once today.

"You calling me gross? That's rude!" I punch him lightly in the arm.

He glances at his watch. "Thinking of you as gross is helping to heal my broken heart."

"See? Rude! Get out of here. I'm fine and you've got an algebra test to study for. See you later, okay?"

He laughs. "I'm going, I'm going. See you."

I watch him leave, then shut the chapel door, leaning back against the solid wood.

"Recruit McKenna, it's nice to see you." Rev steps out of his office and comes toward me. "Are you excited to see your mother this afternoon?"

I shake my head. "I don't get to see her."

"She's not coming?"

I barely have the energy to shake my head. "It doesn't matter." I brush at tears suddenly hovering, threatening to fall. "Even if she did come, I wouldn't be able to do it. Jonathan gave me tours this weekend."

His eyes go wide.

"Over the KB. Remember I told you Matthews would use it when it would hurt me the most? Well, Jonathan called me out during Commandant's Inspection and gave me tours."

His walrus mustache is working overtime as he gazes at the wall.

"Not only that, but *someone* completely ruined it."

"Ruined it? What do you mean?"

I pull it out of my back pocket and hold it out for him. "See for yourself."

He flips through, and I get a whiff of Sharpie even now. My jaw tenses and I have to force myself to relax. "Jonathan did this?"

"I don't think so." I brush at my eyes, annoyed that the tears are still falling. "I think it was Matthews."

He doesn't disagree with me and I'm not sure if that makes me happy or worried. "After the parade today, when everyone leaves campus, will you bring this to me?"

"Why?"

"I'd just like to take the time to look at it a little further. If you think Matthews had a hand in this, it could be . . . interesting."

"Please don't say anything, Rev. The last thing I need is for him to think I'm ratting him out."

He opens the book again, looking at the last page and nodding, like he knew what he expected to see. "I won't tell anyone your suspicions, but I'm going to need to see this again."

"Please . . ."

"It's not even about the DMA right now. Your father would have my head if I didn't look out for you like I promised. You know how hard it is to fail your father, don't you?"

"Fine," I say, after waiting a second to make sure my voice is steady. "This afternoon."

SEVENTEEN

AFTER THE LONGEST DAY OF CLASSES I'VE HAD HERE, freedom is just a parade away. Bagpipes whine and scream before they kick into gear, playing the song that we'll march onto the PG to for the Parents' Weekend parade. The sun beats down and in my dress uniform—our blues—I'm already sweating despite the late October breeze. I glance nervously at Kelly next to me.

"You okay?"

I nod slightly, but I'm not and his look tells me he knows it. Katie's parents took her home last night to go to the doctor and I don't know if she's even coming back. And Bekah got approved for some extra leave—Matthews came and told her at lunch. She's already gone.

So, it's left to me to be the one on display, the only girl marching in the Parents' Weekend parade. All those parents out there, the alumni of the DMA, and the commandant will be focused on me. I'm nervous as hell.

"Remember, Alpha Company. No one locks their knees. This is our first major parade and inspection. Recruits will be passing out left and right. None of them will be you. Do you understand?"

"Drill Sergeant Stamm, yes, Drill Sergeant Stamm!"

"Then, let's go!"

"Alpha leads the way!"

When he gives the cue to march, we each step off with our left foot. We've been practicing for this since we started training, going so far as to have a Corps parade every Friday, but it still doesn't prepare us for the crowd surrounding the PG. The cheers go up as soon as we step onto the grass and even with my eyes straight ahead I can see flashes from cameras on all sides.

I grit my teeth and bite the inside of my lip, a slight scowl rounding out my military bearing. We're like a well-oiled machine and I know we look the best we ever have. The energy helps us to sharpen our motions. Up on the PG, we make our slow march around. The whole Corps is on display today. It's the only parade all year that the recruits are in the front. Normally, we're in the back—out of sight, out of mind.

"There she is!" someone yells from a crowd of civilians to my right.

"Get her out of here! Old Corps! Old Corps!" Another person shouts support for the single-gendered Corps of last year.

We turn left at the far end of the PG and march back toward our barracks, the hisses coming from this side as well. A man up ahead takes a step forward, close to the parade route. "Get out of here, McKenna. The Society will make you sorry if you don't go!"

The words pull at my focus and I stumble on the grass. "Ignore it," Kelly hisses, but my confidence is shaken.

I try to find the man who yelled, but he's gone, blending in with the crowd here to watch the Corps strut its stuff. The Society, though. It's what Matthews keeps saying.

"Alpha Company—halt!" Drill says when we are marching in place. "Parade rest!"

I take a step to the side, spreading my legs a bit and snapping one arm behind my back while the other holds my rifle out in front of me just a bit, the butt of it resting against my foot.

"Buck up, McKenna," Matthews says, appearing to my right. "If you don't want to be the laughingstock of the DMA, you'd better not trip again. Everything they said is what we're all feeling, but you're the one intent on being here, so show us why you think you belong."

I nod just slightly, keeping my eyes straight ahead. I refuse to screw up again today.

Once the pomp and circumstance is through with, we come to a halt behind our barracks. Standing at attention, we wait for the order to go be with our families. I kind of wish everyone would have to stay until lights-out tonight.

"Alpha Company, you made yourselves proud today despite a few screw-ups," Drill says, his eyes falling on me.

The heat comes to my face before I have a chance to gather my wits. His words hurt but I won't let him see how much it kills me to let the company down like that.

"The cadet colonel has announced that you will be released from recruit protocol at 1700 this evening until you must report back at 1700 Sunday evening, except for those of you marching tours this weekend." His eyes stay on me. "Even when on campus, you may walk at ease with your families. If you leave campus, however, you must be in your dress blues at all times and carry yourselves as a proud recruit of this fine academy. Understood?"

"Drill Sergeant Stamm, yes, Drill Sergeant Stamm!"

"Very well. Enjoy your weekend. Remember: if we hear of anyone going against the rules, you will all pay the price Sunday evening. Now, everyone but McKenna, get lost!"

A cheer goes up and my recruit buddies scatter in every direction, running to catch up to their families. Even Kelly vanishes, too excited to see his family to wait for me. I stand, unmoving, until the area empties.

"At ease, McKenna."

I take a deep breath. I'm not sure I can take getting yelled at again, especially by him. "Drill Sergeant Stamm, this recruit is sorry—"

"I said 'at ease.' Take a break." He takes a few steps toward me, his eyes scanning the area.

I do the same. We're alone. "Yes, Drill Sergeant."

"You've done a really good job here."

I have to force myself to sound happy. "Thank you, Drill Sergeant."

"What?" he asks. "You don't think you have?"

"I tripped during the parade. Earlier today you had to call Matthews off me. At the smoke show the other night . . ." I clear my throat and stop talking. I've got to be strong for five more minutes.

"McKenna, I'm not calling him off because I think you're weak."

"Then why?"

He opens his mouth to answer, then lets out a sigh instead. "Just be careful this weekend, okay?"

His words don't sound like they're coming from someone ranked above me. It sounds like he actually cares. "Of course, Drill Sergeant."

He bends down a little so we're eye to eye. "Your recruit buddies aren't going to be on campus to keep an eye on you. I'm not going to be here either . . ." For a second, his eyes drop from mine and he's looking at my lips, but it happens so fast I think I must have imagined it. Even still, my heart thunders in my chest until Drill clears his throat like he's getting back into character.

The clock tower chimes 1700, 5:00 p.m. Freedom.

"Dismissed, Mac." A little red creeping into his cheeks at the slip—he'd called me what my recruit buddies call me. "Recruit McKenna."

I walk away slowly, glancing back once to see him standing there, his eyes following me. He looks kind of sad but that doesn't make any sense. He's getting ready to go home for the weekend. If anyone should be looking sad, it's me—stuck here by myself, with ten hours of marching and remembering the few seconds Drill and I spent alone the only things I get to look forward to.

I make my way up onto the PG, taking deep breaths and steeling myself for the walk to the chapel. Almost everyone is gone, whisked away by their families to spend a weekend being pampered. The only people left are a group of older men circled around Matthews. I hang back at the edge of the PG, standing near a tree.

They don't notice me and their voices carry easily.

"You've done a fine job so far this year, Corporal. Even with all the ruckus and the threats against our fine academy you are holding your own. Removing the problem will secure your position in the Society."

I promised Rev I'd be at the chapel right after the parade, but he's just going to have to wait.

"I understand, sir," Matthews replies.

"Do you?"

I move behind the tree so they won't see me if they look this way.

One of the guys turns and puts his arm around Matthews, but it's not a friendly hug. The man holding him in place, baring his teeth as he talks, has two stars on his shoulder and a Purple Heart on his uniform. "Of course he understands. He's done as ordered and has already laid the groundwork."

"But he's got a hard task ahead of him, General Matthews."

My corporal's father has pulled out all the stops for today.

"I don't think it will be so hard after this weekend. Her mom's not coming; she's marching tours. The recruits that went home will be strengthened in their resolve to survive. She'll be all alone come Sunday evening," General Matthews reports.

Corporal Matthews can't keep the grin off his face.

"Then I think we can go," the older man says. The general's

assurance is enough for him.

The men stand straighter and each man puts a fisted hand over his heart before turning toward the mess hall. Matthews is the last to make the motion, but he does it just the same, and then leads the way, laughing with one of the older men. I'm left alone on the PG.

Once I'm sure I won't be seen, I hurry to the chapel, the whole reason I was up on the PG in the first place. "Okay." I start talking the second I open the door. "I know I'm late, but I told you I'd come. Here I am."

"Sam— Oh, of course," Rev says, looking shocked when I come into his office without knocking.

Sitting in the chair where I usually sit is a guy in jeans and a polo shirt. When he turns to look at me, I realize I know him, though I never thought I'd see him again. "Tim?"

Amos's Army roommate stands up, a sad smile on his face. The last time we were together was at Amos's funeral. "It's good to see you, Sam." He reaches out, his arms pulling me in for a hug I'm not expecting and am not ready for. I don't squeeze back and, when his arms slacken, I take a quick step away from him. Being close to him . . . well, it's bad.

"What . . . what are you doing here?" I glance at Rev for an answer.

"Tim's been keeping up with your progress here—he lives in town. He's heard about your KB trouble."

"You said you wouldn't tell anyone," I whisper, retreating toward the door. "You promised."

Rev walks out from behind his desk and reaches for me. "Tim

is a friend, Sam. We can trust him."

Dad had promised me Rev was one of the good guys, and less than a day after I tell him something private, he's shared it with someone I barely even know. Sure, Amos trusted him, but Amos is dead.

"I promise I'm on your side, Sam. I'd do anything for Amos, and he'd want me to look out for you."

I look between the two men—Rev, who I've grown to trust, and Tim, the guy Amos used to talk about all the time, his best friend. After a long, tense moment, I reach into my back pocket.

Rev and Tim exchange a look. "Sit back down, Tim." It's not an order, but it's close enough. Tim sits and I scoot by him to hand Rev the book.

"I need it back by Sunday evening, seventeen hundred hours."

"I'll make sure you get it."

I glance once more at the KB that's caused me so much trouble, knowing I shouldn't be letting it out of my hands again.

"I'll take care of it, Sam. I promise." Rev slides the book into the pocket of his uniform.

"Sam, I meant what I said," Tim says. With my hand on the door, I turn to look at him. He hands a piece of paper to me. His address is written on it. "I'm here for you, okay? I live about two miles from campus. You're welcome anytime. I cared a lot about Amos. I want to help."

After a minute, I nod. "Thank you." I pull the door closed on my way out and slide Tim's address into my pocket.

Once back in the barracks, I change into sweats, tying my

tennis shoes and getting ready to go for a run. I've got to find something to keep me busy for the next few hours or all I'm going to see is the blue tint of Amos's face when I opened the door and saw him hanging.

EIGHTEEN

WHEN THE CLOCK FINALLY HITS 0130, I PULL THE HOOD OF MY sweatshirt up and walk out of the barracks. The night air is cool and I tuck a stray bit of hair behind my ear. I'm watching the shadows, the trees that move in the breeze, for any sign of life. There's nothing. The campus is dead silent.

By the bell tower, a weeping willow's branches sway, brushing the ground with long fingers. I slip beneath them and secure a hiding place in the dark, where no one can see, and wait. Boots thud on the pavement and I try to calm my racing heart. She's in camouflage again, a cover pulled down low over her face, and smaller than I remember. When she gets close I step out.

Jax doesn't jump or anything, just jerks her head up in acknowledgment and keeps on walking, leading me out the western gate of the school and across the road to the football field.

Beneath the bleachers she finally stops and turns toward me.

"I'm surprised you came." She puts a cigarette in her mouth and lights it.

"I'm not sure I'm staying." After Rev's betrayal and the mysterious Society I keep hearing about, I've got to be sure Jax is on my side. "I need to know I can trust you. Who are you?"

"I'm Jax."

That doesn't tell me anything. "Does Kelly know you're talking to me?"

"No, he doesn't. And I'd like to keep it that way, if you're okay with that."

I'm not sure how I feel about keeping this from him, but I agree. "So why the emails? The weird meeting on movie night?"

"It's a long story."

"I've got all night," I say, crossing my arms and going toe-to-toe with her. "But this is our last meeting if you're not going to be honest with me."

She sighs, taking a long drag before talking. "You know there were supposed to be five females, right?"

"Yeah . . ." I'd forgotten all about the girl who never showed up.

"I was number five. I was supposed to be here with you."

"Why didn't you come?"

She takes another drag, exhaling a big cloud of smoke. "Look at me. I'm five-foot-nothing and am way better with computers than I am with getting yelled at. I probably would have punched one of those assholes in the face the first time they yelled at me."

I can't help but laugh. "It's crossed my mind a time or two."

"But the difference is, you wouldn't do it."

She's right. Asshole or not, Matthews still outranks me. One thing you grow up with in a military family is a healthy respect for the chain of command.

"So why enroll in the first place?"

She looks at the ground before taking a deep breath and squaring her shoulders. "I don't really fit in around here. Kelly was the only one who ever saw me as anything but a freak. The rednecks don't really like goths. When he decided to come here, I couldn't imagine doing anything but following him. It turns out I'd much rather be at my computer hacking into the DMA than actually attending."

"What do you mean?"

She tosses the cigarette on the ground and crushes it with her combat boot. "I knew there was going to be crap because of the whole female thing, so I thought, since I wasn't going, I'd at least try to keep an eye out for you. I started watching emails, flagging things that stood out."

"Bekah and Katie haven't said anything about emails from you."

"Your roommate's days are numbered. Everyone knew that during Hell Week. And Bekah, it's weird. It's like she's got a free pass for being in track."

We're going after her another way. It's what Matthews had said in the library. Not a free pass at all. "How do you know all this?"

"They say lots of things in emails."

"They?"

"I can't nail down all the players but some of them were on that list I gave you. They're bad news, Sam."

I scrub a hand across my face. "It's just a bunch of guys blowing off steam. We're threatening their good old boy system and they don't like it."

"I don't think so," she says. "They think you marching tours this weekend will be enough to break you. If you aren't out by Christmas, it's going to get bad. You've got their panties in a twist, I'll tell you that. They didn't think any of you would last this long."

The sound of boots on the cobblestones makes us both jump. She grabs my hand and pulls me farther into the shadows. The footsteps get closer.

We're under the bleachers, but we weren't being quiet at all. I close my eyes and wait to be discovered. Me out of bed in the middle of the night, free weekend or not . . . no way is this going to end well.

As soon as the footsteps recede, we both let out our breath. "You'd better get back. But listen. Matthews, one of your corporals, is definitely in the inner circle of whatever is happening." Her voice is quieter now.

"That's not a surprise. He's definitely got it out for me." I want to tell her about my KB and the Society, but I'm not ready to give that to someone outside the DMA yet.

"Is there *anyone* on campus you trust?"

"Kelly and my drill sergeant," I say without hesitation.

"Good old Liam," she says fondly, and I feel a weird, possessive twinge. I want to ask more, but she looks at her watch. "Liam's okay. I'll check out Stamm to be sure he's safe."

"Thanks. For meeting me, for trying to help."

"It's nothing. I chickened out. But someone's got to be the first female cadet, right? If I can help you get there, maybe me being too scared to come will pay off somehow." She glances at her watch again. "I'll email you soon, okay?"

"Okay." I take a step away. I don't want to leave her. The feeling that I've got someone on the outside I can talk to, someone who may not understand but who's in my corner, helps me breathe just a little bit easier.

"Lunchtime. Be back in thirty minutes," the cadet in charge of marching tours barks when we near the cafeteria again.

Thank God. Three hours of marching down, two hours to go today. Same schedule tomorrow.

The three other guys marching with me—Evers, Huff, and another cadet who got caught with tobacco—scatter. Sauder, our drill sergeant for the day, waits to take my rifle and lock it in the guard shack. I hand it over. "Sir, thank you, sir."

He grunts but doesn't respond, so I turn and head toward the mail room. I'd kill for my cell phone but it's against regs so Mom has it at home. I pull my phone card from my pocket and punch in the numbers. Her voice mail picks up right away. "Hey, Mom. It's me. Just calling to see how you are. . . . I wish you were here." I hang up quickly so she can't hear the shaking in my voice. Then I dial Jonathan's cell phone number before I lose my nerve.

"Colonel McKenna." There are voices in the background, and the clink of dishes or something.

"Hey, I need to talk to you. You want to have dinner tonight after I'm done marching tours? Maybe get a pizza?" My voice is a bit more demanding than it should be, talking to the cadet colonel and all, but he's my brother first, and he set me up with the KB. I deserve an explanation.

"Why are you calling me? Where are you?" His voice is a low growl. "I'll be right back, guys." The phone is muffled and then I hear the sound of cars passing by as he steps outside. "You're supposed to be marching tours. Now's not really a good time, Sam."

"Oh, really? Then when would be a good time to talk about how you totally rigged that inspection?"

"I didn't rig anything." His words are like knives. One thing he definitely got from Dad is the military man temper. "But you want to talk? Fine. Tell me what happened with you and Matthews."

My throat swells up. "What?" I can barely manage to get the word out.

"With you and Matthews. What happened? He came to me today to file a complaint."

"A complaint? I don't understand." I put my hand against the wall. This does not sound good.

"He says you're hitting on him, looking for a way to get ahead. That you won't leave him alone."

I'm flabbergasted. "No way. You can't believe him."

"These are serious charges, Sam. First of all, it's against the rules of the academy for cadets to date."

I ignore pointing out that the whole stinking military has fraternization rules and that I've heard about them since I was old enough to understand. Not to mention, if I *were* going to be stupid enough to do something here, it certainly wouldn't be with Matthews. "I'm not dating Matthews. I have no interest in him whatsoever."

"So you didn't follow him the other night when your company was on an MM? I've got five upperclassmen that saw you."

"Of course not!" My face burns. I didn't follow him exactly. . . .

"He's saying you've been throwing yourself at him since Hell Week. That your roommate is on the verge of leaving because she can't stand constantly getting in trouble for you trying to date cadre. He says she'll corroborate his story."

Katie would never turn on me. Would she? I try to remember any time where we haven't gotten along. Sure I yelled at her the other night, and told her she needs to pull her weight . . . but without someone forcing her to turn on me, I can't believe she actually would. "Jonathan, she's been in the infirmary since day one. She doesn't know anything. I swear he's lying. I would never—"

"Stop right there, Sam. You can't go around accusing people of lying. That's serious shit here. And besides, you don't have any proof."

"Does he?"

Jonathan is silent.

"So you'd believe him over me? Even though *he* doesn't have any proof either? Listen, something's going on, okay?" I lower my voice. "I heard Matthews and his dad on the PG after the parade yesterday. He's setting me up. He's trying to get me kicked out."

I can tell by his hesitation that he knows. "This is ridiculous. If you have something concrete, I might be able to help you. Until then, my hands are tied. I'm hanging up."

"Wait!" I yell into the phone.

"God, Sam. Not *everything* is about you, okay? Go march your freaking tours and get over yourself." His voice is shaking. "I know it's hard here. If you can't cut it, just give everyone a break and quit."

The line goes dead. My hands shake as I stare at the phone in my hand.

Outside, Sauder is yelling, calling us back together to continue our tours, but my legs refuse to follow the orders. I know I need to move. I need to go march the afternoon away, but I can't believe it's come to this. Even my own brother is choosing the Corps over me. How the hell am I going to survive now?

NINETEEN

SUNDAY EVENING, AFTER I'VE COMPLAINED TO REV ABOUT the call with Jonathan and picked up my KB, and before we're back to acting like Worms, Bekah shows up in my room. Katie hasn't come back yet and I haven't heard anything from her, but Bekah's too involved with my story to care about our missing recruit sister.

"She called him Liam. Like he's got a first name."

"Liam is a sexy name. He looks like a Liam, you know? God, I want to . . . I don't know . . . *eat* him or something."

I throw my pillow at her. "He's our recruit brother and you are definitely not a zombie. Stop talking like that."

She's grinning like the Cheshire cat, though, and I know she's hiding something.

"So, spill," I say. "I told you about the meeting with the

mysterious Jax. Now tell me about Matthews getting you early leave and you disappearing all weekend. What happened?"

But before she can spill, we're interrupted. "On the wall now, Worms!" Matthews barks.

I roll my eyes at Bekah and stand up to put my shoes on.

"What's this about?"

I've forgotten she's never had the privilege of being part of a moment like this. "Smoke show. This is about the time they all start." We jog out of my room and onto the wall.

Before we're even standing at attention, Matthews is on us. "Too slow. Do it again. Now!" Matthews's voice makes us all jump to action.

I rush back into my room and Bekah follows. "This should be a fun evening."

"Yeah, well, this is what we do every night while you're away team building with track." I stand by the door, hand on the knob, and wait. It doesn't take long.

"Get out here now! On the wall! Let's go."

Both of the corporals are yelling now and I rush to my position again.

"McKenna, it's come to my attention that you had the balls to call the cadet colonel on his personal cell phone over the weekend."

How the hell did he find out about me calling Jonathan? I swallow hard before I speak. It doesn't matter right now that Jonathan is my brother, apparently. "Corporal Matthews, yes, Corporal Matthews," I yell.

The smile on his face makes him look like a piranha about to pick his teeth with my bones. "And you, let me get this straight, invited him to *hang* with you and eat pizza?"

Closing my eyes, I take a deep breath. No matter what I say here, I'm dead. "Corporal Matthews, this recruit called this recruit's brother in hopes of spending some time together, Corporal Matthews."

"Are you freaking kidding me?" He's so close to me, I can smell the burger he had for dinner. "He's not your brother anymore. He's your *colonel*! And please tell me that the rumors of you off campus in the middle of the night without signing out aren't true."

I lose focus on the hallway, blinking hard. Everything's moving too fast. And then I remember the sound of footsteps on the walk. Someone overheard us. Someone connected to Matthews.

Matthews is having me followed.

He shakes his head, taking a step back and turning away from me, facing my recruit brothers. "If it had been any of you other Worms, you'd have been doing push-ups until graduation! But no, just because McKenna's brother is in charge of the Corps, she thinks she'll get away with it." When he turns back to me, his eyes flashing, I know he's about to deal me a deathblow. "Let me see your KB, McKenna!"

"Corporal Matthews, excuse this recruit, Corporal Matthews?"

"Did I freaking stutter, McKenna? Your KB. Now!"

When I give it to him with a shaking hand, he holds it up, the small book of DMA history that is causing so much freaking trouble right now. "Take an eye!"

"Snap!" In unison, all my recruit buddies snap their heads to Corporal Matthews, the word a signal to the cadre that we're all listening and moving as one. But I can't.

"I'm dead," I whisper to Kelly.

"In my hand, I have your recruit sister's KB. A book she cared so little about that she left it on the side of House Mountain the night of your MM. A book she *defaced* with permanent marker!" He flips through the pages, making sure each of my recruit buddies get a good look at the black Xs. "Get it back!"

"Pop!" Again, in unison, my recruit buddies turn their heads, this time facing the wall in front of them.

"You filthy, disgusting Worms. I have never heard of anyone losing their KB before. Never in my two years at the DMA has anyone lost such a precious piece of our legacy. Never in my two years at the DMA has anyone had the balls to mark through *every single page*. But for that same person to treat the chain of command with such disrespect shows her lack of willingness to be part of the DMA, to be fully invested in what we are trying to do here." He takes a breath before continuing. "You make me sick, McKenna, and now your recruit buddies are all going to see what happens when one of their own screws up."

"Push-up position," Corporal Julius demands.

We drop to our hands and knees, quickly getting into position.

"Hold there." Matthews continues the order. "Alpha Company. You are only as strong as your weakest link, and right now your weakest link has long hair and tits. Down!"

I lower myself, nose almost on the floor, back straight, heart pounding.

"Hold there," Corporal Julius barks. "Is she worth all this? The pain you know you're going to endure tonight? Is it worth it to have her here? Up!"

I lengthen my arms, wondering how long this barrage is going to continue. If someone in charge walked in, Matthews would get in a world of trouble. Where the hell is Drill? The adults?

"Right now, you're in second place for Company of the Year. Can you not join together as recruits of the finest company at the DMA and get rid of your weak link? Animals kill those among them who are weakest. If you can get her the hell out of here you've got a chance of being top dog again. Down!"

Near the ground again, I risk looking to my left. Kelly's eyes are wide, but he stares straight at the ground, not looking at me.

"By now you should know all your uniforms inside and out. What goes with each, how each one looks when it's up to military standards. You have two minutes. I want you in summer blues. Go!"

I push myself up and run to my room, throwing my wall locker doors open. Short-sleeved shirt, wool pants, shirt stays, black socks, black shoes, belt, name tag. My fingers slip on the buttons and I have to attach my shirt stays three times before they'll actually stay. My belt buckle is smudged with a fingerprint, but I make it out on the wall before any of my recruit buddies. The muscles at the corners of my mouth want to turn upward but I don't allow myself a victory—even one as small as this.

It takes another minute before the rest of the company is out and by the time the last one is against the wall, the corporals are yelling orders again.

"Battle dress! You have three minutes! Go!"

I run back in, ripping my shirt off so fast two of the buttons pop off. I'll deal with that later. Brown undershirt. Camo pants. Camo blouse. Combat boots. Cover. It's the easiest uniform we've got.

Kelly beats me out to the wall but I'm just seconds behind him. I stand at attention again, not able to catch my breath but still holding my own. Weakest link, my ass.

"Alpha Company! You've got two recruits who think it's fun to get out on the wall before the rest of the company. They're leaving you behind. Does that make you happy?"

"Corporal Matthews, no, Corporal Matthews!" The answer is muffled coming from each of the rooms.

"So stop where you are now and switch it up. Dress blues. Go!"

Kelly and I run back into our rooms. I tug the camo blouse up over my head and drop my pants to the floor. Back to wool pants, but this time I've got a long-sleeved woolen tunic to put on—something that takes someone else to zip and button closed.

I'm screwed.

I hear doors slamming as my recruit buddies make their way out to the wall. Straining, I try to do up the buttons, but there's no way—and Matthews knows it.

"Come on, McKenna! Everyone's waiting on you!"

I'm sure they are, Matthews, since you rigged the freaking deck on me. Never mind that I'm not the only female having this problem.

Bekah's obviously the focus of Matthews' little game.

He kicks the door like they did during Hell Week and this time it bends, a crack in the wood appearing and slithering halfway up.

Tunic unbuttoned, I open the door and stand out on the wall.

"What the hell do you think you're doing?" Julius is in my face, yelling so hard he showers me with spit. "You're practically naked, McKenna!"

I'm not, but he obviously doesn't see it that way.

"And what the hell are you wearing? A BDU shirt with dress blues?"

"What?" Matthews runs to stand in front of me.

Eyes straight ahead, Sam. Don't look. Don't flinch. Just tune them out.

I'm reciting my fives times tables in my head to drown out their voices when doors slam up and down the hallway. Shit, I've missed the order.

"She loves her camo so much, why don't you all get back in it. And don't think we're going to let some scuffed boots slide. You'll be doing push-ups till the sun comes up if you look like crap!"

BDUs, right. I run into my room and dig through the pile of clothes on the floor until I have everything I need.

I hear one of my recruit buddies cry out as I'm coming out of my room and I look for the source of the noise.

"Don't be looking around, McKenna! Eyes locked straight ahead!"

"Corporal Matthews, yes, Corporal Matthews!"

Another cry from down the hall. "Be a man, Wilson. You were pretty damn impressive tonight. Just rewarding your hard work." Matthews's attempt at a whisper makes me want to laugh. Until he stops in front of Kelly. "And, you. If you got rid of your dead weight," he says, tilting his head in my direction, "you'd probably be the top-ranked recruit in our company—maybe on the whole of the DMA campus. Figure out where your allegiance lies, Kelly, and you'll make one damn fine cadet."

Matthews drives his fists into Kelly's chest not once, not twice, but three times. Even our camouflage uniform requires us to wear name tags and he's punching Kelly right on top of the tag, digging the pins into his chest.

But Kelly doesn't cry out. As far as I can tell, he doesn't even flinch.

"Impressive," Matthews says, and takes a step back. "Now for room inspections! Let's see if Alpha Company's weakest link can at least do something right and have her room up to standard."

I stand in the door at attention, holding the orange baseball cap in my hand and out at a ninety-degree angle from my side. It's a pointless exercise. My clothes are scattered all over the floor. They're going to rip me a new one.

They slide into my room like two snakes, just hissing around for something to call me on.

"Bed doesn't have military corners!" They rip the sheets off my bed, throwing them onto the pile of clothes left from the fashion show we just put on.

"Underwear drawer not up to standard." Matthews pulls the drawer out and upends everything in it, my bras and underwear showering onto the floor.

"Undershirts and BDU shirts not the standard folded and

rolled length. Gonna need to redo those." Julius dumps that drawer onto the pile.

"Trash can is in the wrong place." Matthews kicks it across the room, crumpled up paper scattering like snowballs.

"Window blinds not at the correct length. Shit, McKenna, can't you do anything right?" Julius jerks both window blinds off the wall and tosses them on the heap as well.

"Get busy, McKenna. Lights out in fifteen and room inspection at 0500." Matthews grins before he slams my door, leaving me alone with debris from tonight's battle scattered across the room like shrapnel.

A quiet knock on my fractured door around 0100 doesn't wake me—I'm still trying to put my room back in order. I've been at it for two hours, but it takes a long time to make everything perfect. Kelly and Bekah slide in and let the door close behind them. I'm too tired to start the conversation so I just grab another shirt.

"We wanted to make sure the corporals were in bed for the night before we came." Kelly moves straight to my curtains and starts to untangle them. "So, the smoke show was . . . interesting."

"Feeling bad for not standing up for me?" My argument is unreasonable, I know, and I feel childish even saying it. Messing up the fold of the shirt, I throw it down on the ground, grabbing another one instead.

He won't meet my gaze. "I couldn't—"

Bekah walks over to Katie's bunk and starts working on the military folds we have to put in the corners of the sheets. She keeps her eyes moving between me and Kelly.

"Ruin your reputation. I get it." I can't forget the way Matthews drove his fist into Kelly's chest. "Your little bonding moment with Matthews was clear enough."

"It's not like that, Mac."

"Please. I've been around military guys my entire life. You may not have a family in the military, but if this is how you treat your female *friends*, you're well on your way to climbing the ranks."

"Look, we didn't come to fight, Mac. Matthews treats you like shit. Everyone sees it, but you know we can't say anything. We came to help," Bekah says, folding and placing the blanket on top of the bed. "And to see what Matthews was pissed about."

Gritting past the annoyance at being thrown to the wolves, I try to get the conversation back on track. We can't be up much longer. I give them a rundown of what happened over Parents' Weekend with the tours and Jonathan, including what Jonathan said about Matthews's charges.

"There's no way your brother could believe that." Bekah grabs the socks off the floor and begins rolling them to put in the drawer.

"Clearly you don't know my brother. He'll believe whatever he wants to believe and nothing I say is going to convince him otherwise."

"Your brother's a dick," Kelly says unapologetically.

I hold my hands up in surrender. "No arguments from me."

An uneasy peace fills the room and the three of us work in silence to get everything back in order. When Kelly leaves, I'm ready to tell Bekah good night, too.

"Can I tell you something?" She's almost vibrating with electricity.

I sit down on my bed. "Sure."

"I'm dating someone."

"What? Who? When did this happen?"

"This weekend at track's big get-together. There was alcohol, dancing. It was amazing. It felt so good to be *human* again."

"Please tell me this is some townie and not a cadet."

She at least has the decency to look a little ashamed. "He lives three floors below us. Shawn Evers."

If I were drinking something, I would spit it out all over the table. "You've got to be kidding. He's a freaking junior." Not to mention a complete asshole.

"I know, I know. But he's gorgeous." She can't keep the smile off her face.

"You know what he said about me during morning calls, right? I did tell you that story?"

"Yeah, but he's just—"

"You've got to end it. You saw what they did to me out there tonight. Matthews is trying to prove that I have the hots for him to get me kicked out. They're going to eat us alive, Bekah. Please . . ."

"Shawn's not going to tell anyone. He knows how it'll look. He's going to keep it a secret. Besides, he and Matthews are friends. Matthews was at the party—"

We're going to get to her another way. It's what Matthews had said about her. If they'd gotten Evers involved, Bekah might not even see it coming. "Matthews can't be okay with you dating.

He's the one who won't even let me blink wrong and he's going to let you break a major rule? Not to mention, I have no idea how you'll even pull this off. You're going to . . . what? Email each other?"

"We'll be together whenever we have practice. And, somehow we'll find time. Near Christmas we'll be recognized, right? That gives us a little more freedom."

"Not enough to date upperclassmen." My mind flashes to when Drill's eyes glanced at my lips for just a second. "It's late." And I'm frustrated. "We can talk this through tomorrow."

"There's nothing to talk through, Mac. I like him and he likes me. I hope you're okay with it, but even if you're not, please don't say anything."

"Of course I won't," I sigh.

TWENTY

KATIE SHOWED UP TWO DAYS AFTER PARENTS' WEEKEND leave was over and got sent to the infirmary three days after that. It's two weeks into November before she moves back into our room. Her doctor's note says she's still not allowed to do company training or PT, either. I resist the urge to point out how unbelievable her injury and the doctor's note are when she seems just fine walking to and from classes.

I've gotten used to having the room to myself and am still trying to adjust to life with a roommate again. "Sorry," I say as I bump into her shoe polish.

"It's okay. I think I'm doing this all wrong anyway. At the infirmary, someone did it for me."

Of course they did. Everyone knows the staff at the infirmary does everything from polishing to starching. Even sick and injured cadets have to adhere to military standards, whether they can do it themselves or not. "Here, let me help." I shouldn't have to do this by now, but I ignore the grumbling I want to voice and pick up her boot instead. Besides, if she's going to go along with whatever Matthews wants to say about me, I need to be as nice to her as I can.

"Are you okay?"

"Why wouldn't I be?" I don't meet her eyes—I've always been a bad liar.

"You just seem . . . distracted. I know I haven't been around, but if you want to talk . . ." Her words drop off.

"It's just my mom."

She gives me this look of sympathy. "I'm sorry you didn't get to see her on Parents' Weekend. Thanksgiving is only a week away, though."

"I'm staying here over Thanksgiving." The email came earlier today. It shouldn't surprise me, not after the past eleven months of coming in last place with Mom, far behind mourning Amos and her daily pills. "Jonathan and I have plans." Or, we should.

"So you guys are talking again? I'm surprised you want anything to do with him after the KB incident. That was a jerk move on his part."

I hadn't even bothered to tell her about what Jonathan had said about her over Parents' Weekend. "I know, but we're still family, right? And it's a holiday." I'm ready for a break, but if Jonathan won't speak to me, it's only going to cement the fact that Platoon McKenna is dysfunctional.

She nods encouragingly. "I'm sure you guys will get to do something fun together."

I drop her boot to the floor when I'm done polishing and pick up the other one. "Here you go."

"Thanks."

"Attention on deck!" Matthews yells. "The cadet colonel is in the hallway."

"Speak of the devil," I mumble, meeting Katie's wide-eyed gaze.

The door to our room slams open. Katie bumps into her wall locker.

"Room! Attention!" I yell at the top of my lungs, even though Katie and I have already snapped into position.

"At ease," Jonathan says, glancing at Katie as she slides into a parade rest stance that's still not correct. "Glad to see you're back in the barracks, Recruit Quinn."

"Colonel McKenna, this recruit is glad to be back, Colonel McKenna." Her voice shakes when she talks. If she'd been with the company more than in the infirmary, she'd be over the nerves by now.

Matthews hovers in the doorway, a grin on his face, which means whatever is coming will likely not be good. I brace myself as best as I can.

"Recruit McKenna."

"Colonel McKenna, yes, Colonel McKenna?"

He swallows hard, then continues, his eyes on my face but not meeting my gaze. "I'm going away for Thanksgiving." He glances at Matthews and then back at me.

I don't know how to respond without getting chewed out by

Matthews, so I remain still and silent.

"So, anyway, that's what I came to say. Have a good Thanksgiving. . . ."

When he turns to leave, I snap to attention. "Room! Attention!" My voice doesn't waver, but the room blurs when Jonathan disappears around the corner.

Matthews is still standing by the door, the grin changed to a full-fledged smile now. "Aw, sorry to hear that, McKenna. Guess you'll be about the only one on campus next week." His laugh hangs in the room even after he leaves.

"So that does it," Katie says, turning to me when we're alone again.

Blood rushes in my ears and I sit down at my desk, not sure my legs will hold me up anymore. "What?"

"You're coming home with me for Thanksgiving."

But that's the last thing I want. "No. I mean, thanks for the invitation, but no."

"Sam, you can't stay here alone. That's ridiculous. It's a *holiday.*"

"I *know* it's a holiday. And I'm going to spend it alone." I can't go to a house where I don't know anyone—not this time. Not when it's the first Thanksgiving without Amos here. . . . I thought at least Jonathan would understand. "Just go home and have fun. We'll hang out when you get back, okay?"

I turn back to my desk, trying, once again, to focus on the paper that's due this afternoon that I don't even care about anymore. But to make sure Katie knows I'll be okay, I blink away the tears, pick up my pencil, and begin writing again.

TWENTY-ONE

I PULL ANOTHER HANDFUL OF CEREAL OUT OF THE BOX I'D bought at the school store before everything shut down for break. Only about sixty-eight hours until everyone starts showing back up on campus. Not that I'm counting or anything.

It's my own damn fault, really, feeling this alone. I'd sworn Katie to secrecy—she wasn't allowed to tell Kelly that I'd be here by myself. I didn't even email Jax. If no one in my family cares enough about me to want to spend time with me, I'm not going to force my crappy mood on anyone else.

I close up the cereal box—it's the second one I've gone through since everyone disappeared—and stretch. I promised myself I would go for a run after my afternoon pity party and the light is fading fast.

A big crash outside my door makes me jump. I wish there

was a peephole, but there's not. I grab my rifle from the rack. It's not loaded, but I could still leave a mark if someone's sneaking around.

When I open the door, though, Drill is standing outside my door. "Sorry," he says.

I've got to keep my smile at bay and my heart calm. "Drill Sergeant Stamm, this recruit—"

"We're on break, Mac. Quit with the third person." He smiles and I feel my face go red. "And don't you dare sandwich my name."

"Thanks, Drill. But . . . how did you know I was here?" I let out a relieved breath and slip the rifle back into its place against my wall. He notices, though, and laughs.

"Rev might have mentioned you'd be here all alone over the break." He gestures at the broken glass on the floor. "This was a plate of dinner for you."

My heart almost stops. He thought about me and brought me Thanksgiving dinner? That's not something a drill sergeant would normally do . . . is it? "Oh."

"But it's obviously not anymore. At least the pie didn't get ruined. I'll run out to my car and get it." He shoves his hands in his pockets and starts to walk away.

"Wait. You brought me pie?"

He stops and turns back. The grin on his face is the most amazing thing I've ever seen. "I come from a military family, too. I know what it's like to not have family around at the holidays."

I let him think that everyone is just away—not that they don't want to spend time with me. It's nicer than the truth. "Thanks."

"I'll go get the pie."

"I'll clean this up."

By the time Drill is back, I've swept the remains of the broken plate into the trash and mopped up around the spill. He stands in the doorway, looking strikingly different in civilian clothes. It's just jeans and a green T-shirt with an old-school video game character on it, but tonight he looks like he's just a guy coming to visit, not someone I'm not allowed to be friends with.

"I can just leave the pie here," he says, though he's holding two plates, and the words come out slowly. Had he brought dinner for both of us, too?

"Stay. I can't promise to be good company, but you're more than welcome to hang around."

He comes in and hands me a plate with whipped-cream-covered pumpkin pie wrapped in Saran Wrap, the smile back. I'm glad I invited him in. My mouth waters and I sit down at my desk, ready to dive in. "Did you make this?"

"If you count taking it out of the box and slicing it, then yeah. I did." He pulls Katie's desk chair out and slides it over in front of mine.

I pull the wrapping off and hold it up to my mouth, licking off the whipped cream. "God, just this little bit is better than anything I've had since I got here."

He laughs again. "That's pretty sad. . . ."

I like the way he laughs, solid and strong, like he's not worried about anything, least of all the fact that my knee is touching his or that my hair is piled in a ridiculously unsexy bun on top of my head. "Yeah, well, you know what the mess hall food is like."

He hands me a fork, his eyes on the wrapper that I'm still cleaning off. "For when you're done licking the plastic." He meets my gaze, his cheeks blushing a beautiful shade of red. "I mean, the pie itself is probably pretty good, too."

"So, pie," I say, stabbing a forkful, reminding myself that Drill is totally off-limits, even in his civvies.

"Yeah," he says, clearing his throat. "Pie."

We eat in silence for a few minutes. It's the most comfortable I've been on campus since Dad dropped me off months ago. I don't want it to end, but it does, too quickly. "Why didn't you tell me about your KB?" He sounds hurt, like I've betrayed him somehow.

I'm guessing Matthews told him. "Gee, let me see," I say around a mouthful of pumpkin pie. "You're my drill sergeant. I screwed up and didn't want you to know how bad."

His fingernails are white where they press against his fork. "I told you to come to me with problems."

"It's fixed now. It's fine."

"So you can totally read through all the words marked in black?"

"I don't want to cause waves, okay? You've already done too much to keep Matthews away. I just want to get through this year and—"

"You shouldn't have to stay quiet to survive the year. This shouldn't be happening."

I stop the fork halfway to my mouth, my eyes snapping to his face. "It's nothing worse than what I expected. I knew things weren't going to be easy." He's obviously angry and I'm scared that it's directed at me. "I'm sorry I'm not better—"

"And now you're apologizing. You haven't done anything wrong, Mac. You're . . . you . . ." His eyes rake over my face, searching for something. He closes his eyes, taking a deep breath, and when he opens them again, he seems calmer, the Drill I trust completely. "You have some whipped cream . . ." His eyes are on my lip again and my heart speeds up, galloping along at a dangerous pace.

Reaching up, I wipe the edge of my mouth.

"No. You missed." He leans in, his face a breath away from mine. His thumb grazes the corner of my mouth, the rest of his fingers reaching out and brushing the hair at the nape of my neck.

I'm frozen in place, unable to breathe because his hand feels so strong, so right. My jaw fits perfectly in his palm. If he asked, I'd stay like this forever. Forget family drama, forget the Corps and their rules about fraternization, and just stay right here, hovering over pie, linked by whipped cream and losing myself in his crystal blue eyes.

He clears his throat. "Sorry," he whispers, dropping his hand like I've burned him. "I shouldn't have touched you."

It's hard to speak with my heart pounding so fast, but I try anyway. "I didn't mind. . . ." My face gets warm.

He laughs, but it's a disgusted humorless sound. "I'm in charge of you. I can't put you in that position." He scoots back. "Also, I'm kinda scared your dad would kill me."

A smile tugs at my lips. He's thought about me—about what kissing me would mean, about how Dad would react. I slide forward on my chair, closing the space between us that doesn't feel like it should be there in the first place.

Slowly, like I'm a hummingbird that would flit away with the smallest movement, he reaches out, his fingers brushing mine, just slightly. Doing this is wrong. So incredibly wrong. But I don't stop him and I don't pull away.

Then his phone rings.

I jump, and he jerks his hand away from mine. "Saved by the bell," he laughs nervously. He stands up and clears his throat, pulling the phone from his jeans pocket. "Yeah?" His voice is rough, scratchy, and he won't look at me. He rubs a hand over his head.

I can't take my eyes off him. The way his T-shirt stretches across his shoulders and wraps tightly around his biceps. When he turns back around, I drop my eyes, but then look away completely because staring at my drill sergeant's crotch is definitely not a way to ease the tension in the room. My face is on fire. I close my eyes and take three deep breaths.

"I can get her a message. What is it?"

His eyes meet mine, turning from sultry to sorry in zero point two seconds. The room is suddenly cold. Who would be calling him about me? I try to read something, anything, in his face, but I can't.

"I'll get the message to her tonight. Yes, sir. Happy Thanksgiving to you, too, sir." He ends the call and stands still, not turning to look at me.

"What is it? What's wrong?"

He moves toward me awkwardly, like he's not sure where he

should be. He keeps meeting my gaze and looking away, almost like he's nervous, though that's ridiculous. Drill doesn't seem like he could be nervous about anything.

I move to my desk, organized to military regulations, notes written in small regimented handwriting. I focus on that so I don't have to meet his eyes.

"Sam." He looks frustrated, his forehead crinkled like what he's got to tell me is too much.

I try to swallow but can't make myself. I don't know if he's ever called me Sam before, but the way he says it now makes me scared. "What . . . ?" I have to clear my throat and start again. I'd give anything to be five minutes in the past, where we were about to cross a completely forbidden line.

He hands me his cell phone. "Call your mom. She needs to talk to you."

A call like this could only mean one thing: something's wrong with Dad. I try to push the phone back into his hand. Clenching my teeth, I shake my head just slightly—it's all I can do without falling apart. "It's Thanksgiving. You should get back to your family. . . . I've got some studying to do. I'll call my mom over the weekend. . . ."

"You need to call home, Sam."

My hands vibrate with energy I can't contain. I take a deep breath, not wanting to know what she's got to say. "Can't you just tell me?"

"I don't know what it is for sure. Your brother just said you need to call."

"Wait. That was Jonathan?" Tears sting my eyes knowing I

was that close to talking to him on Thanksgiving and one slides down my cheek as I realize he didn't care enough to tell me this news himself.

Drill pushes the cell phone back at me and reaches out to hold my free hand in his. There's no fire this time, only warm strength. "Come sit down and call. I'm right here." He sits down on Katie's chair and I sit on mine. Drill rests our linked hands on my leg.

I hit the green button and hold the phone up to my ear, though I can barely hear the ringing over the pounding in my head. "Please don't let her answer. Please don't let her answer." I whisper the words over and over. As long as she doesn't answer, nothing's really happened. If she doesn't tell me, I can pretend that everything's normal.

It's something we're always waiting for as military brats: the knock at the door or a call that tells us our parents are dead. That we're going to be orphans. And there's no one who would understand that better than another brat. I squeeze Drill's hand when Mom picks up.

"Hello?" Her voice is shaky and I can tell she's been crying.

"Mom?"

"Oh, God, Sammy." She breaks down, sobbing on the phone. The sound cuts through me, ripping holes in the fragile existence I'm living here. I pull my hand from Drill's and punch my leg, digging my fingernails into my palm.

"Mom? What is it?"

"It's going to be okay, baby. It's going to be okay."

I'm not sure if she's comforting herself or trying to convince me, but either way she's doing a piss-poor job. I stand and start pacing, waiting for her to get herself together. My stomach heaves and I know I'm going to lose it if she doesn't say something soon. "Mom . . . What the hell is going on?"

"It's your father. He's MIA, Sammy."

I double over, leaning against my desk. Drill is next to me in a second, one hand on my back, another on my shoulder. His touch is just enough to calm my breathing.

"Tell me what you know." I try to sound unconcerned, like Dad goes missing in action all the time.

"They're not saying much . . . not even where he was to begin with. But he's been out of contact for three days." She chokes off another sob and I hear her take a drag on a cigarette. She only lets herself smoke when Dad's gone and I can't imagine how many she's gone through since she heard the news. "They're looking for him and two other soldiers in his company."

I don't know what to say. I don't have anything but questions. When I move to start pacing again, Drill pulls me against him and wraps his arms around me. If I'd had any strength before this, it's gone now. I close my eyes and tuck my head against his neck. His heart races in his chest but his arms are still, a wall of strength holding me together. "So what happens now? Do you want me to come home? Stay with you 'til they find Dad?" I hold my breath, not knowing what answer I want her to give. Drill freezes against me.

"No, baby, of course not. You need to stay. There's nothing you can do here and I'm climbing the walls—no reason for you to see this."

"Call me if you need me." I lean away from Drill and wipe

my hands across my eyes to bring him into focus. *This number?* I mouth to him, and he nods. "Use this number, okay? Drill can probably get to me faster than Jonathan." I try not to let her hear the anger I'm feeling toward Jonathan right now.

"Okay," she says, taking another drag on her cigarette. At this point, I kind of wish I had one. "I love you, Sammy."

"I love you, too, Mom." I choke the words out, refusing to break down again until I get off the phone. The phone beeps when she hangs up but I hold it in my hand, unwilling to break even the small connection I still have with her.

"Are you okay?" Drill's voice is quiet, hesitant. He takes a step back, putting distance between us. He's an arm's length away and looks like he's in pain, standing on the verge of reaching out to me.

But we've crossed a line neither of us meant to cross. I still feel him against me, the safety I felt even when there's no chance of any comfort at all right now. It felt right. And that's the last thing I have the strength to deal with right now.

I nod. "I'm sorry, I shouldn't have—" I gesture toward the tear stains up by his shoulder.

He shrugs it off. "Don't be ridiculous, Sam."

"No. You're my drill sergeant." I'm suffocating in here, so close to him and this whirlwind of thoughts and fears and revelations that I can't deal with.

"You need someone right now."

"Well, it can't be you."

He looks hurt. "Kelly's in town, right? I'll call him, let him know. Maybe you can spend the rest of break with him."

"No," I choke out. I don't want to spend the rest of break with anyone.

"He's your recruit buddy. He'll take care of you."

It's not Kelly that I want to take care of me. But what other choice do I have? It's not like I can ask Drill to take me home to *his* house.

Finally, I agree. "Call him. And thank you." It's only a whisper, but it's the best I can do.

When I move to go past him, he steps into my way. He reaches down, his thumb brushing away a tear on my cheek and I close my eyes, holding as still as I can. His hand stays there, resting against my jaw just like before. Before my world came crumbling down and the thought of breaking the rules seemed huge and amazing. Now I'm scared that if I breathe I'll fall apart right here. "If there's something I can do . . ." He lets the words drift off, dropping his hand and wincing like it hurts to stop touching me.

"I'll be okay," I whisper, not trusting my voice to do more than that.

TWENTY-TWO

KELLY HAD BEEN A SOMEWHAT WILLING PARTICIPANT IN keeping my mind occupied, running with me twice during the last couple days of break and taking me to the local theater to watch some action movie. I'd kept the secret of Dad's disappearance from him, though. Ever since the smoke show when Matthews hit him, he's been . . . off.

When the pounding starts at 0530 on the first Saturday in December, I jump to the ground from my top bunk. Going through the routine is much easier than waiting. Waiting for a phone call from Mom, for a fleeting glance from Drill, for the next attack from Matthews and the Society.

Katie mumbles but I bust my butt, tying my running shoes.

"Hurry up, Katie. I'm not waiting."

She mumbles again and I glare at her for a second. She turns over, covering her face with the blanket, when I finally open the door and head out to the wall without her.

Kelly rubs his eyes next to me, his shoes not even tied. "What the hell is going on?"

"Recognition?" I whisper back. According to Jonathan—before he stopped talking to me—recruits are recognized as cadets sometime around Christmas. After that, things change a little bit—we get phones in our rooms and we're allowed to have computers. We get to stop walking in the gutters. It's going to be heaven. And it's the only thing I've got to look forward to right now.

He shrugs, still trying to wake up.

"Where is everyone?" Drill reappears on deck and counts the meager number of us who have shown up. He walks slowly down to the other end of the hall and back, stopping in front of me.

"McKenna? Where's your roommate?" He hasn't talked to me alone since Thanksgiving. He keeps his eyes locked on mine and I have to force the shadow of a smile from showing. He's kept the secret of my dad's disappearance for a week and in moments like this I can almost pretend it's not happening at all.

"Drill Sergeant Stamm, this recruit's roommate is still in this recruit's room, Drill Sergeant Stamm."

"Will you go get her?" It's not an order, more of a request. Kelly's head turns a little as Drill takes a step back, addressing all of us on the wall now. I'm scared if I look at him, he'll be able to figure out that I've got a crush on our drill sergeant. "Everyone whose roommate is not on the wall in sixty seconds will be marching tours this weekend instead of going to the football game. Is that understood?"

"Drill Sergeant Stamm, yes, Drill Sergeant Stamm!"

It takes five minutes, but finally we are all out on the wall. Bekah is grumbling and Matthews stands possessively close to her, protecting his best friend's property, I guess. She's gotten out of the two smoke shows we've had since Thanksgiving, even when she's not at a team event. I guess dating an upperclasshole has its perks.

"I know what you're all thinking. It's what everyone is wondering about right now. Recognition." Drill sounds tired, like he's been up all night, and his hands are curled into fists.

My heart speeds up. Could this be it? Could we finally be getting some freedom? But if it is, why does Drill look so pissed?

"But it's not going to happen. At least not right now." Drill's eyes fall on me and he shrugs. "Some of the upperclassmen feel that all of the weakest cadets have not been weeded out yet. That there are still some here who should not hold the title of cadet. You won't get recognized until after Christmas."

For the first time since Hell Week, my recruit buddies and I break military bearing and groan.

"What?" Kelly says. "That's bull, Drill."

I glance at Matthews. He's loving every minute of this.

"I didn't say it wasn't. What I said was that this is the consensus of the Corps as a whole." Drill looks down at his hand, rubbing a spot on his ring finger. In just a few short months he'll wear one of the DMA class rings. It should be the happiest moment in his time here besides graduation, but he doesn't look happy about it right now. "That doesn't mean you won't be recognized into

Alpha Company, but that's something else entirely."

"Is there anything we can do? Any way we can change the Corps' mind?" Kelly pleads.

"Motivational marches are always an option, but they won't help. Not this time." Drill's eyes fall on me again and the next sentence he says is just for me. "This was a directive from the cadet colonel. You would have to move mountains to get it changed."

"So, it's *her* fault," Wilson snarls. He's wanted me gone since day one.

I shrink into the wall, wishing I was invisible or that Dad had instilled in me a spine that could stand up to this. Sounds like the corporals might finally get their wish. If Wilson turns on me, others might follow. If I don't have anyone in my corner . . .

"I never said that." Drill's voice is harsh, leaving no room for doubt about where he stands. The Corps as a whole might not want me here, but he does. I shake my hands out at my sides to get some feeling back into them even though I'm supposed to be holding still.

"You didn't have to." Wilson's New York accent comes out when he's angry. "Can't we just ditch her? Get her the hell out of here?"

It's the first time any of my recruit buddies is brave enough to say it to my face. I expect Kelly to speak up but he remains silent. His jaw works overtime, clenching and unclenching.

I glance to my left but he won't meet my eye and suddenly I'm glad I didn't tell him about Dad. The silence goes on so long I can't stand it anymore. "I'm not leaving. I don't care what you guys say or what you try to do. I deserve to be here just as much as any of you. I've worked just as hard." I don't mention that they're not riding Bekah as hard as me, or that she's missed out on most of our training, not to mention all the smoke shows I've endured without either her *or* Katie. Maybe that's the problem, though—I'm making it on my own and the boys can't handle it.

"I didn't sign up to be here when the Corps gets watered-down," Wilson says. "The others are sliding through. It's only a matter of time before you start slacking off, too. If you three make it, they're going to have to let other girls in," Wilson argues. "Then we're going to be jogging and doing modified push-ups just to make things easier for you."

"Cut the crap, Wilson. You know the cadre are riding Mac harder than the other two," Nix says, standing on the other side of Kelly. I want to give him a hug.

I can't believe Drill is letting us do this, but I'm not backing down now. "Let's forget for a second that I've done every damn thing we've been asked to do. Girls have just as much right to be here as you, Wilson. Besides, I pushed more than you during the last smoke show and I'm pretty sure I've never puked on deck before." Drill's standing against the opposite wall, watching me, his head cocked to the side as he listens. He smiles a little as I finish. Well, I'm glad someone's enjoying this.

"Pack your bags and leave, McKenna. Let the Corps stay true like it used to be."

I don't respond to Wilson this time. Blood pounds in my ears and I don't care anymore that I'm supposed to be standing at attention. I turn and look at Kelly, wanting, no *needing* him to stick up for me. But he doesn't.

Kelly continues to stare straight ahead, the muscles in his jaw tense.

"All right, all right. Get it back under control," Drill says when it's obvious Kelly isn't going to say anything. "I just needed to inform you of the change. Don't expect Recognition before Christmas. You probably shouldn't even expect it after Christmas. It's easier to not get disappointed that way. Just continue on. Show the upperclassmen that you deserve to be recognized. Now square yourselves away and get ready for PT."

Our five-mile run finishes at the obstacle course again. My lungs burn, the December air creeping inside and not letting go. My body feels like it's freezing from the inside out. I pull my hands over my mouth and nose, struggling to slow my breathing and get a few lungfuls of warm air.

"We're working on the obstacle course again today," Drill says once the stragglers have caught up. "We've got two weeks until Christmas break and after that it'll be snow-covered until March most likely. Each recruit will go through the course three times. We'll be timing each run. Your cadet colonel is here to make sure you're each putting your best effort forward."

I bend over, putting my hands on my knees, still breathing hard, and not looking at Jonathan. I certainly didn't expect a hug from him, but *some* recognition that he sees me or an acknowledgment that he's worried about Dad, too, would have been nice. Winter air stings my lungs and huge clouds of mist float up every time I exhale. Pulling my hood up, I straighten, trying to focus on the task ahead. There's no way I'm going to win, but I've got to prove to them that I belong here.

"You okay?" Kelly says, jogging over to me.

I take a step aside, putting some distance between us, still pissed about before. "I'm fine."

Bekah stretches an arm up in the air. "What the hell are you doing over here, Kelly?"

He looks stunned at her anger. "I'm just checking on Mac."

"I'll check on her. She doesn't need your help." For once I'm grateful for Bekah's no-bullshit take on life.

"What's that supposed to mean?"

"It means you messed up, dude."

He looks at me, the teal eyes that I liked so much at the beginning of the year full of concern. "Mac?"

I shake my head. "If you don't know what you did, don't worry about it."

"I'll tell you, dick. You left her for broke back there on the wall. Her recruit buddies were rioting against her and you just left her there to take it on her own."

"Wait a second," he says, looking from Bekah to me and back again. "No, that's not what happened. She always says she can do this on her own . . . that she doesn't need to be protected . . ."

"That doesn't mean you don't stand up for your *friend*," Bekah fires back.

I expected to be abandoned by some recruit buddies. I expected upperclassmen to be against me from the start. But for Kelly to turn on me . . . I didn't see that coming at all.

"Just leave it, Bek. It's not worth it." I glance at him once more, just to make sure he understands I'm talking to him. "*He's* not worth it."

"Cross, McKenna, you're with me. Kelly, hurry up and go with the company," Matthews yells from where he stands with Jonathan and our adult supervisor.

I keep my grumbling to myself and run over to where he points, jumping up and down to keep myself warm. At least over here I don't have to deal with Kelly anymore. Bekah gives me a shrug and I just roll my eyes. A whistle starts the first recruit on the course and I watch as Wilson stumbles on the first obstacle.

"Listen up, Worms," Matthews sneers.

I immediately slide into parade rest, but Bekah stands at ease, having more guts than I ever would.

"Colonel McKenna and I have been discussing your physical fitness levels this morning. He watched you both throughout your run and he raised some concerns about your ability. So, when you come back from Christmas break, PT is changing. Instead of being with the company, you'll be going to remedial PT. Until you're physically fit, we don't want you hurting your precious little selves in company PT. Is that understood?"

I can't believe it. I'm in better shape than half my recruit buddies. So is Bekah. Now we're being put in remedial PT? I look from Jonathan to Matthews, then back to my brother.

"You have a problem with that, McKenna?"

Bekah elbows me in the side.

"Corporal Matthews," I say, loud enough for Jonathan to hear. "This recruit is wondering if there are any other recruits in the company being put in remedial physical training, Corporal Matthews."

"Of course not. Everyone else is where they need to be. Everyone else has proven themselves. You haven't."

I clench my hands into fists at my side. We have and they both damn well know it.

"Do you understand, McKenna?" His eyes dart to Jonathan and back at me, but at this point I don't care that I'm breaking all protocol.

Telling me I'm not prepared when that's all I've done for the last year—putting me in a PT class for losers? How the hell can I understand? Bekah should feel the same, but she's nudging me with her elbow again and I know I've got to say something.

"Corporal Matthews, yes, Corporal Matthews." The words come out quiet and dangerous.

"Good. Now sit back and watch. Don't want you injuring yourselves, do we?"

I don't even wait until he's out of earshot to start in on Bekah. "Did you know about this? This is bullshit." I kick the ground, wanting more than anything to pick up a rock and throw it at Jonathan.

"It's whatever, Sam. Don't worry about it."

"You're kidding, right?" But her face is relaxed, like she's not even pissed off. "They're putting us there to separate us even more. If we don't go through PT with our recruit buddies, we lose company bonding time. They think we're weak and they're trying to get us to quit. You should be angry."

"Well, I'm not, okay?" She sits on the ground, crossing her legs and leaning back against a tree to watch the guys on the obstacle course, enjoying her morning off. "They're just boys playing at being in control. So we run a little less, do fewer push-ups. It's not that big of a deal."

It may not be a big deal to her, since she's suddenly got some kind of special pass with Matthews, but it is to me.

I'm too pissed off to sit. Just so Jonathan can see it, I put myself through a round of push-ups, sit-ups, and jumping jacks off to the side, obviously alone, while the rest of my company does the obstacle course together.

TWENTY-THREE

WHEN CHRISTMAS BREAK FINALLY COMES, I'M ON MY OWN again, like freaking Harry Potter. Other than getting a cup of coffee with Jax, this vacation promises to be full of suck.

Jonathan didn't even bother coming to me this time to let me know we weren't hanging out. Mom's too busy staring at her phone to have me come home. She called once to let me know they found the soldiers who had been with him, but there's still been no word about Dad. I've found not thinking about it much less stressful than picturing the million horrible places he might be.

Three hours after the last cadets have disappeared from campus, I put on my dress blues and take my second trip off campus since coming in August.

The town is small, just four main streets and a few more

stoplights. Uneven cobblestone sidewalks line narrow roads and even though it's only 1700, many of the shops are closing for the night. The sidewalks are busy, people bundled up, heads down against the wind, bags in hands. I shiver against the cold as I walk past stores where Christmas lights twinkle in the windows. The week before Christmas used to be my favorite time of year. This year, though, all alone with the anniversary of Amos's suicide looming overhead, I can understand why people decide to kill themselves during the holidays. They're downright depressing.

The coffee shop Jax wants to meet at sits on a corner of Main Street with window seats that are perfect for people-watching. It must be the only place not closing. A bell next to the door chimes as I walk in, and then again when I shut it tight against the wind.

"Do you want anything, dear?" The waitress rubs a wet rag over the counter next to me.

"No, thanks." I'm the only customer, but I don't want to order on my own. I find a seat at the window. "I'm waiting for a frien—" But just then I see Jax outside. She tosses a cigarette on the ground and smashes it underfoot.

The door chimes, but she doesn't need any help announcing her presence. "Two coffees, black." As the waitress walks past, Jax hands her a five-dollar bill. Her makeup is just as thick as it's always been, but her hair is down this time, almost white-blonde with streaks of green. She's wearing black skinny jeans with chains that clunk against the seat and not worried at all about the condescending look the server gives her as she surveys Jax's outfit.

"Hey, Jax. What's so important?"

She looks at me, her eyes scanning my face. "Shit. You look just as bad as Liam."

"He's changed. He skips company training as much as Bekah now, but he won't tell me where he goes." Not that I've talked to him since the remedial PT conversation. I'm still pissed about him not standing up for me.

"Hmm . . ." is all she says.

The waitress puts a cup of coffee in front of Jax and slides another cup in front of me. I pick it up to drink so I don't have to talk. The coffee burns the whole way down.

"Whatever the problem is, you're both feeling just as sorry for yourselves. Only he's doing it at home, in sweats." She shakes her head and laughs. "But, believe me, drama follows Liam around like a sad little puppy dog. He wouldn't be himself if he weren't pissing someone off."

I clear my throat. "So, your email . . . ?" I don't want to talk about Kelly right now. I need to talk about something I might have a chance to solve, as remote as that possibility might be.

She moves right on. "Matthews and Evers email all the time, but they only talk about your roommate and Bekah. They're eerily silent about you. Like they don't talk about you. *Ever.*"

"Is that weird?"

She shrugs. "It is if it means you're being talked about somewhere else."

"Well, that's not comforting."

She pulls out a piece of paper. "Different subject. Do you know what blood wings are?"

"Of course I do. Everyone does."

"Remember I don't go there and am not wrapped up in all the ridiculous rites of passage. Enlighten me."

I think of Matthews drilling his fist into Kelly's chest, how much it must have hurt. Does she know about it? Did he tell her? "It's kind of a trial by fire, a way to test how strong you are," I say when I'm done explaining the basic idea. Kelly hadn't even winced. Wilson had gotten them, too. "Why?"

She sighs. "I don't have it all figured out yet, but from what I understand there's a group of cadets that uses them as a way to mark the freshmen they want to recruit for some disciplinary committee."

"What?" I wrap my hands around the coffee mug, willing my fingers to warm.

"Look," she says, tapping the paper in her hands. It's a photocopy of a handwritten letter. "Blood wings are only to be used by the committee."

I scan the paper, but it still doesn't make sense. Is this the Society? Is that why Kelly's distancing himself? He and Wilson are joining them? "I can't believe it. There's got to be other people who use blood wings on campus. They do it all through the military. . . ."

She shakes her head, handing me a second letter, dated 1897. "No, see? Whatever this committee is—"

"The Society." I force the words out. Suddenly it's not just a name anymore. Talking about them with Jax makes them all too real. "They call themselves the Society."

"Okay," she says, though she doesn't press me for how I know this. "The Society has been around a while. Sometimes secret, sometimes not. You know, they'd make themselves known back when it was more acceptable to exclude people based on race or class or whatever. This letter gives the Society sole permission to use blood wings at the DMA. Blood wings are specifically banned for hazing cadets other than by Society members. Any cadets found using that form of hazing on freshmen without authorization from the Society will be drummed out of the Corps." She points at a specific sentence.

It takes me a minute to read it. The old-timey writing is full of curlicues that don't need to be there. "You're talking about a secret society." I want to tell her it's ridiculous—that the DMA wouldn't have secret societies—but they're rife throughout military schools and the military itself. The thought that one would make itself known the year that females start participating in the Corps isn't too shocking, I guess. "Where are you getting your information?"

"I'm good, right? It's amazing what you can find when you know your way around the internet."

There's no way Jonathan would let a secret society have control over the Corps. They'd be higher than he is and he wouldn't want that to happen at all.

She must read my doubt. "Look, this paper is proof they were working a hundred years ago. There's nothing I've found that shows beyond a shadow of a doubt that they are active now. But everything you've told me points to it."

I think about my KB, about how worried Rev and Tim seemed.

"You want proof? I'll find it." She takes another sip of coffee.

But I don't want proof. I don't want it to be true. The thought of having to go back for another semester of what I've just gone through is almost too much to take right now. Jonathan said we'd lose some recruits after the holidays and I can see why. Secret society chasing them or not, why would a normal kid want to go back and go through it for another semester?

"If we're going to go down this path, let's start with Matthews. Maybe I can figure out who he spends all his time with. That might clue us in," I say, though the thought of spending any more time around Matthews does not sound pleasant at all.

"It's a start. I'll keep digging, too."

I drain the last of my coffee. "Thanks, Jax. I don't know what I've done to deserve you. . . . "

"It's not a problem. I told you I owed it to you guys when I bailed on you at the beginning of the year. You're sticking it out. The least I can do is help."

"Thanks, anyway. I mean it."

"Forget it. Oh, I was going to invite you over for New Year's, but Liam says you guys have a weird recruit meeting at midnight. What's going on?"

"What? We don't have a meeting. . . ."

"Liam said it was really important. He isn't allowed to miss it."

My mind works overtime. There's no Corps-wide or even recruit-wide meeting, but if what Jax said about the Society using blood wings is true, and Kelly is being initiated, maybe *they* have a meeting. "Look, I know you and Kelly have history, but . . . does Matthews ever email Evers about *him*?"

"Liam? No. Why? What are you thinking?"

"It's just a theory, okay? I don't have anything solid, but Matthews gave Kelly and Wilson blood wings at a smoke show before Thanksgiving. He's been acting really weird since then . . . pulling away from me, you know?"

She shakes her head. "God, could he be any stupider? I'll look into it."

I let out a breath. "I'm glad you're not mad at me for telling you."

"Liam's sweet, but he's stupid. I'll kick his ass six ways to Sunday if he gets involved with them. I reached out to help *you*, Sam. If Liam's gotten himself wrapped up in something like this, then he'll just have to unwrap himself from it."

After we take our empty mugs up to the counter, we walk back to campus. Jax tells me stories of the civilian high school here. Their Drive-Your-Tractor-to-School Day and the bonfires they have on the weekends when the weather is nice. She's known Kelly since they were in kindergarten together and I'm jealous—not just of their friendship, but of being grounded somewhere. She may not belong at the DMA, but she belongs here.

In sixteen years, the only place I ever belonged was with Amos.

Two days later, when I haven't seen anyone on campus, and Jonathan doesn't answer his door no matter how long I pound on it, Rev demands I go see Tim. The ghost of Amos won't let me rest and since it's nearly been a year since he died, Rev takes it upon himself to force my hand. He thinks I'm spending too much time alone. Tim had offered his house as a place to go when I first saw him this year, and Rev thinks it'll be no problem to show up on his doorstep. So, with the piece of paper he'd written his address on, I head into town to find Amos's old roommate.

Past Stonewall Jackson Memorial Cemetery and the old houses that have been around town since the DMA was founded, I find Tim's house. It's near the hospital and in the newer, poorer part of town, but he's got a fenced-in front yard and a nice porch. Music blares from inside, the wood beneath my feet bouncing with the bass. At least I won't be waking anyone up.

A simple knock won't be heard, so I ball my hand into a fist and pound on the door. When no one answers after a minute, I bang on it again. Inside the music stops and my heart starts thudding. I haven't seen Tim since the day in Rev's office, and before that at Amos's funeral. Neither of us was in any shape to talk to each other that day. He should be stationed somewhere, but Mom said after Amos died, he came back here to work for a landscaping company. Quite a drop down for someone who had such military promise.

Tim opens the door and squints at me like he can't see me even though I'm standing right in front of him. Dark circles hang under his eyes; he looks like he hasn't slept in days, hasn't shaved for weeks. He's wearing gray sweatpants and an old DMA T-shirt.

"Sam?" He sounds unsure as he blows a cloud of cigarette smoke out the front door. His eyes are glazed over. Who the hell gets drunk in the middle of the day?

"Hey, Tim. You . . . you said I could come over if I ever needed to. . . ." Suddenly I think this is a bad idea. Retreating would be the best option but I can't make myself move.

He stands in the doorway, just looking at me like I'm some sort of alien with ten eyes or something. More footsteps thunk on the floor inside and someone behind Tim clears his throat.

"Get out of the way, Tim," Drill says. "Let her in."

TWENTY-FOUR

HIS IS THE LAST VOICE I EXPECT TO HEAR AND I MOVE backward, stumbling down a step before catching myself. "Ouch. Shit!" Wincing, I keep all my weight on the ankle that didn't just betray me and try to ignore the heat in my face. "Drill Sergeant, this recruit didn't know that the drill sergeant would be here. This recruit will leave, Drill Sergeant." The third person thing sounds lame out here, but I can't make my brain work.

He's wearing a soccer jacket with three white stripes down the arm, zipped up high to keep the cold off his neck. His jeans fit exactly right where they rest, low on his hips, and he wears soccer shoes, too. He leans against the door frame, looking so relaxed and gorgeous in his civvies that I want to scream about the unfairness of it all. "Don't be ridiculous. Stay, it's fine. Right, Tim?"

God, if this guy standing in the door wasn't my *drill sergeant . . .*

"Right. Come on in, Sam. We're having a party." Tim looks relieved that someone told him what to do. He stumbles backward a few steps and disappears into the house. A few seconds later the music starts again.

I should definitely leave, go back to the DMA. After Thanksgiving, the last thing I need is to be alone with him. But I can't go without knowing. "Drill Sergeant, how does the drill sergeant know Tim, Drill Sergeant?"

"At ease, Mac." He waves the words away. "Tim's my brother." Now that he's said it and I've seen them this close together, I don't know how I could have missed it. The eyes, the wrinkles both their foreheads get when they're concerned. It's so obvious now. "This is my house, too."

"Wow. I should go. Really." When I turn, he reaches out and takes my arm. Just that small touch sends jolts of electricity through me.

His eyes lock on my arm where his hand is touching me. I don't understand the little tug at the corner of his mouth. "Tim said it's fine. Come on in. It's freezing out here." He steps back, his hand on the door opening it wide for me to enter. He doesn't move aside, though, and I brush against him as I step into the house.

Boxes are stacked almost floor to ceiling in the small, cramped hallway. "Here, follow me," Drill says. He shuffles sideways to move past, pausing for a second when we're face-to-face and making my heart stutter before sliding by. I follow him past the boxes and into the kitchen. "Want something to drink?" Moving quickly, he shuffles papers together that are spread out on the kitchen table. He adds them to a pile on a chair and then moves the entire stack. "You can sit here."

Drill opens the fridge, then grabs a Coke and pops it open. Beer bottles clink as he lets the door fall shut. When he hands the can to me, our fingers touch. I wonder if it affects him the same way it does me.

"Thanks."

"Mom and Dad are off visiting Megan, our sister. She's stationed in Colorado."

Drill's sister is military and his brother was Amos's best friend? Now it makes sense why he was watching over me. Having a logical reason for why he cares about me doesn't make me feel so great, though.

He sits there, looking anywhere but at me, fidgeting with his fingers.

"Is he always like this? Tim?"

Drill shakes his head. "Normally he's pretty great."

"He's drunk. How great can he be?" I wish I could pull the words back, but it's too late.

"He's not always drunk. This Christmas has been rough for him."

It's bad for everyone, I want to say, but the words stick in my throat and I find something really interesting on my Coke can to study. It sounds like an excuse I used to give for Mom. *She's not always drugged up.*

"Why are you here, Mac?"

I fiddle with the tab on the can, breaking it off and pushing it inside before I talk. *I think there's a secret society after me and I'm scared. I miss my brother.* "I just needed to get off campus. And I thought maybe Tim might have heard from my mom. They talk sometimes. About Amos or whatever." It sounds so pathetic. *I miss my mommy.* I've survived a semester of Matthews. I should be able to survive two weeks alone.

"If she'd called I would have come right over."

"I know." I push the chair back. "I'm gonna go." As I walk past him, he reaches out and wraps his hand around my arm. The heat from his hand makes me shiver and I stop as suddenly as I started.

He stands and turns me gently so I'm facing him. "Mac . . ." His voice is quiet, hesitant, like he's scared he might break me if he talks any louder. "Stay awhile. For the whole break if you want. We've got movies, video games . . . your mom will call if there's news. Just stay."

The beginning of a "no" lodges in my throat because I'm sure staying here with my drill sergeant is so against the rules it's not even funny. I fight the urge to lean into him. More than anything, I wish the look on his face wasn't just one military brat caring about another military brat, but something *more.* Being a normal teen sounds so good right now. Spending Christmas break wasting time, not worrying about Dad being MIA or the possibility of secret societies . . .

"Okay. For a little while." I don't promise how long. "I'm going to need some food, though."

He laughs. "We've got Domino's on speed dial. Follow me."

The living room isn't much cleaner than the kitchen. Beer bottles and soda cans cover every empty space there isn't a pizza box. Sitting on a futon, Tim holds a video game remote, staring at a screen on pause—presumably from when I knocked on the door earlier.

"Ready, Tim? I've got some serious ass to kick." Drill sits down on the futon and grabs the other remote, unpausing the game and beginning to shoot a machine gun almost immediately. Tim doesn't say anything but he starts playing, too.

"There are some sweats upstairs in my bedroom if you want them," Tim says. "That is, if you want to break DMA rules in front of your drill sergeant." He laughs like it's the funniest thing in the world, his eyes never leaving the screen.

Drill grins when I look his way. "I won't rat you out if you don't rat me out later when I drink a beer."

"Deal."

He pauses the game again, stands up, and walks over to a duffel bag against the wall. When he turns to me, he's got PT sweats in his hand. "Here, wear these. They're clean, at least. Take a left at the top of the stairs, second door on the right," Drill says. "We'll get your PT gear from campus tomorrow."

I take them and try to ignore the fact that I'm about to be wearing Drill's clothes. They smell like fabric softener and some spicy body wash that is totally him. My face heats up and I take the stairs two at a time.

The bedroom is an extension of the downstairs. Boxes everywhere. Running my finger over his dresser, covered in a thin layer of dust, I stop and stare at what's in front of me: a framed photo of Tim and Amos—one I've never seen—in-country. They're wearing their desert BDU pants but no shirts. I can't help notice their smiles. Amos looks happy in the photo. This is not the same Amos who came home last Christmas. That Amos was . . . broken.

"It was the October before we came home on leave. Hot as hell, even then." Tim stands in the doorway, leaning, just like Drill does.

I reach out to the frame to touch Amos's face. I'd forgotten the way the left side of his mouth crept up higher than the right when he had a secret. Brushing away a tear, I sit on the edge of the bed and hold the frame in my hand.

"It's my favorite picture of us." Tim steps into the room, stumbles, and plops down onto the bed next to me. "Sorry I'm like this tonight. Tomorrow it'll be a year."

I close my eyes and have to force the words out. "I know." It's hard to imagine that a year ago today my brother was planning his suicide. "I found him, you know?"

"No. I didn't. I'm sorry." And somehow from him, it's not pity. He *gets* it.

The sun is setting outside and he hasn't turned on any lights yet. But somehow it's easier in the coming darkness to tell my secret. "We were supposed to go shopping for Christmas presents. We had just moved to Fayetteville and he had just come home on leave. I walked up the stairs to his room. His door was closed and when I opened it there he was, dangling from the fan in the middle of the room. He'd pushed his bed up against the wall, knocked the chair over. I don't know how long he'd been there, but I tried to lift him up. I tried to help."

Tears fall down Tim's cheek. I reach over to hold his hand but he scoots away.

I don't know if I should go on, but I can't stop. Even Dad doesn't know the details about how I found him. My teeth are chattering now and the room is suddenly way too cold. "I never got to ask him why. He didn't leave a note."

Tim reaches out and takes the photo from my hands. "He loved you, you know that? He loved you more than anything. You and the colonel." He spits Dad's rank out like it's poison. "He didn't want to let you guys down."

"How could he ever let us down?"

He sighs, pain in his eyes. "I think it was my fault."

"What? Him killing himself?"

"I told him he should tell. I *told* him that you guys would understand that he was gay. You're *family,* for Christ's sake." His eyes are red and full of pain when he meets my gaze. "God, your old man flipped out."

Some puzzle piece I'd had all along clicks into place and sadness overwhelms me. I should have known. It's obvious, now that Tim's said it out loud. The girlfriends who were never serious, the need to please Dad in the military. We'd been so close, but he'd held his secret even closer. "He could have trusted me. I would never hate him for that."

"Your dad did," Tim says. Someone in Platoon McKenna not following Dad's battle plan for our lives. Yes, Dad would have been furious. "Amos called me and put his phone in his pocket so I could hear the conversation. When he told your dad . . . I could hear your old man screaming over the phone. After that, he didn't want to even try to tell you."

I remember the fight last Christmas. I heard them yelling in Dad's office and I just turned my iPod up. Maybe if I had gone down . . .

"All right, Tim. You've spent enough time strolling down memory lane for one night. Time to get you to bed," Drill says, walking into the room and breaking the moment. I wonder how much he heard—what he must think of my screwed-up family that values appearance so much Amos couldn't even trust us with a huge part of himself—a part of him that was so obvious now that the truth is out in the open.

"Sleep sounds good." Tim's lying down, tugging at the blanket even while I sit on the bed.

Before Drill can say anything to me, I walk to the bathroom, close the door, and lock it behind me.

Thirty minutes later, after the tears have finally stopped, I walk out of the bathroom, Drill's sweatpants rolled three times at the waist so they don't drag on the ground. Wrapping a rubber band around the end of my braid, I follow the sound of gunfire into the living room.

Drill doesn't look up when I walk in, but he scoots over and pats the futon next to him. I sit down, picking at my fingernails and trying to keep my eyes off the screen. Instead of stupid video game characters fighting a battle, I wonder if that's what Dad's going through, wherever he is. Maybe he's hurt, maybe someone's holding him captive. Maybe he's scared. Alone. Maybe he's somewhere thinking about what tomorrow is. Maybe he feels the same huge guilt about Amos that weighs my shoulders down right now.

Drill pauses the game when I sniffle. "Shit. I'm sorry. I wasn't thinking." Without waiting, he gets up and turns the game off. I shiver and he grabs the blanket behind my head, shaking it out for me.

He wraps it so gently around my shoulders that I have to laugh. "I'm not going to break." I wrap my arms around my stomach, wishing he couldn't see how easy it would be for me to crumble. "At least I don't *think* I'm going to break."

He reaches for the remote and turns on the satellite. "What do you want to watch? Comedy? Action? Romance?" He starts flipping channels when he sits down next to me again.

"It doesn't matter."

He settles on a channel that shows reruns. There's a comedy on about nerds and he turns the volume low.

I feel his leg against mine, his arm a heavy weight on the blanket. He's watching me, probably to see if I'm going to lose it and be all *feminine* on him. I force myself to keep my eyes on the screen and laugh through the nerd show, then one about a group of friends at a coffee shop. Much later, when the screen turns to infomercials, I turn to him.

"Did you know about him?"

He sighs and turns to face me, leaning back on the armrest and pressing his leg against mine. "Tim told me last Christmas after it happened. I just figured you knew and didn't want to talk about it."

I take a deep breath and close my eyes. This conversation is too emotional. It just makes me want to be closer to Drill, and getting any closer to him now . . .

Despite the warning sirens going off in my brain telling me to walk away, though, I settle farther into the futon. Right now, I need him more than I need the DMA. "I think I always knew, somehow, but he never told me. And I thought we told each other everything. . . ." I miss Amos so much right now it feels like I'm crumbling to pieces. The hole in my heart is so big tonight I don't know how it's ever going to get better. I put my hand on Drill's.

"I guess he just thought you had an image of him and he didn't want to disappoint you, or something. I don't know. I'm no good at this." He rubs his free hand over his face, the frustration obvious when he looks down at me. "Mac . . ."

But I can't stop now. I need to know if this strange thing between us is more than a drill sergeant looking out for his recruit or a military brat looking out for one of his own. If he feels what I do right now. To hell with the rules. I need to be *close* to him.

I lean in toward him, my eyes on his lips now.

His arm muscles tense under my hand. "I can't . . . shit, do you know how hard it is to be your drill sergeant?"

That's not what I expect at all and I'm starting to pull my hand away. "I'm sorry," I say, the humiliation of being demoted to remedial PT still a fresh wound in my mind. "I'm trying as hard as I can—"

He grabs my hand, though, and slides his fingers between mine, locking us together. "No. I don't mean like that. You're an amazing recruit. You're going to make a damn good cadet. But seeing you every day, being in charge of you, knowing that I can't touch you. Knowing what Matthews says to you and not being able to beat the shit out of him. Knowing that I can't kiss you whenever I want to . . ."

My heart is pounding. If I move a fraction of an inch my lips would be on his. "Like right now?" The electricity in the room crackles. I lick my lips, suddenly not sure what I'm doing anymore. I feel out of control, like I could do anything I want tonight and no one would hold it against me, least of all Drill.

"Yes," he breathes out, holding as still as he can as I inch closer. "Like right now."

His blue eyes are wide, staring right at me. My lips are just a whisper from his now. We're balanced on the edge of a cliff. One breath closer and we'd be in a free fall.

TWENTY-FIVE

HE LETS OUT A FRUSTRATED GROWL, LEANING BACK BUT NOT moving off the futon. "God, if you were *anyone* else but my recruit, we would not be talking right now."

I lean back, trying to regain my senses. "Well."

"You don't say." He laughs now, still tense but a little more relaxed. "It's late. You staying?"

I raise my eyebrows and stand up. "I probably shouldn't." But the thought of going back to the dorm, where one brother won't talk to me and my other brother's memory will haunt me in the dark sends a shiver down my spine.

"You can stay." His voice is quiet, understanding, and he won't break my gaze.

"If you don't mind . . ."

He throws a pillow at me, breaking the spell. It thumps me in the leg. "Of course I don't mind."

"Hey!" I grab the pillow and throw it back at him, the charge of the last few minutes dissipating.

He catches it easily. "Grab the other end and pull up."

I watch what he's doing, then mimic the move. The futon that we sat on moments ago is now a bed on a wooden frame. My eyes get big. "I can sleep on the floor. . . ."

"Just go with it. I promise I won't take advantage of you no matter how much you try to throw yourself at me. Besides, we're on Christmas break. In my twisted mind, I can make this okay somehow." He tosses two pillows on the futon and lies down on one half, leaving me enough room to crawl under the blanket on the other half. He turns on his side, looking up at me. "Do you trust me?"

The mattress suddenly looks small, like a life raft in the middle of the ocean. I swallow hard and then lie down beside him. My voice is weak, breathy, but I answer him anyway. "I've trusted you from day one."

The smile that lights up his face is all I need to forget the crap I'm going to have to deal with in the morning. He inches closer, laying his arm over my stomach and pulling me tight against him. "Then I'd better not do anything to screw it up, huh?"

The smell of bacon makes me think of home before everything turned to shit. When Dad was stationed stateside and Amos, Jonathan, and I used to play forts outside, even during the hot summers in Louisiana. After Mom lost her battle to make me a girly-girl and when all of us were equal. Before Dad and Amos started bonding over the military.

When life was good.

I roll over, completely disoriented after my first full night's sleep in five months. I stretch, enjoying the lazy feeling of sleeping in. Then last night slams into me like a wrecking ball. The truth about Amos, the boundary blurring with Drill.

His side of the futon is cold. Quickly, I unbraid my hair and run a hand through it, trying to tame the bed head before pulling it back into a ponytail. Hushed whispers in the kitchen give me pause, and I stop just outside the door.

"I don't know what it means. I've told you that. Rev and I are looking into it."

"So meanwhile, I'm just supposed to pretend like nothing's happening?"

"Pretty much, Dean. If you draw attention to it, they'll go into hiding. We need *proof*."

A loud thump makes me jerk and I bang into the wall. The boys go silent and my face burns.

"Come on in, Sam," Tim says from the kitchen.

Drill's face is pink when I walk into the kitchen. His eyes scan my face and I shiver under his gaze, thinking about the feel of his body against mine last night. I'd stayed awake a long time, just being next to him, listening to him breathe.

"Were you talking about me?"

Tim turns slowly, spatula in hand and a Kiss the Chef apron on. "When did you wake up?" He wants to know how much I heard.

"Just a second ago. Is there coffee? I need coffee."

Drill walks over and sets a mug he's holding in front of me. "I just poured it." He tugs my ponytail as he goes by and can't help smiling.

I hope Drill woke up before Tim. Tim seeing me and Drill like that, curled together on the futon, would be bad. "Thanks," I say, focusing on Tim.

He glances between me and Drill then turns back to the bacon he's cooking on the stove. Drill grabs the coffeepot and pours coffee into another mug. "We were just talking about your KB. Who might have drawn in it?"

"Matthews." Or Jonathan, I think. At this point, I'm not sure what he'd do. But I don't say that out loud. "He's the one who found it up on the mountain that night."

"Do you know who he was with?" Drill sounds hopeful.

"I don't. I didn't know anyone well enough back then to recognize them."

The smile falls from his face and he bangs his hand down on the table, the same thump that had made me jump earlier. A tremor goes through me. With what we might be up against, I kind of like knowing that Drill could be dangerous if he wanted to be.

"So tell us what you do know." Tim blots the bacon off and sets it on the table. When he pulls the eggs out of the oven, he plops them down, too, and both he and Drill sit.

I chomp down on a piece of bacon to give myself time to think.

"Tim was one of your brother's best friends. And you said last night you trust me," Drill says. It sounds like an accusation.

Again, Tim looks at Drill, then me. "Let us help." The way he says it is genuine, like Amos would say it if he were here.

I rub my eyes and then sigh. "I think there's a group after me, maybe a secret society. I know it sounds crazy—"

"It doesn't," Drill insists, trading a look with Tim that I don't understand. "You're a military brat . . . you know they exist."

"I've heard scary stories, that's all. Look, I'm taking care of it. I don't want you to risk everything you've worked for at the DMA. I can handle this."

"We want to help, okay?" Tim says. "Have you heard any names? Of people or what group might be after you?"

"The Society. That's all I've heard. Real original, right? And as far as members go, besides Matthews, I think an upperclassman named Evers might be in on it. I don't have any proof, though. . . ."

Drill looks up at this, his eyes wide. "Why Evers?"

"He just . . . I can't explain it. He and Matthews are really close. . . ." I can't bring Bekah into this. Not yet. If Drill knows she's dating Evers, he'll have to report it and she'll get kicked out.

Tim grabs a piece of paper, scribbling something. "Have you seen this anywhere?"

He's drawn a picture of Evers's tattoo. "Why?"

"Whoever screwed up your KB drew that on the last page." He's right, but I'd forgotten all about it. "So, recognize it?"

"Evers has a tattoo like that on his shoulder." I flush when Drill looks at me, clearing my throat before continuing. "He likes to walk around shirtless during morning calls."

Drill stands, pacing the floor. "Why didn't you tell someone about this?"

"It's a tattoo, that's all. I never even thought about it and the drawing together. As for why didn't I tell someone? Because I don't know who I can trust. Because anyone could be involved. Because my own brother told me to either keep my mouth shut or go home."

"Jonathan knew?" Tim looks like he could beat the shit out of Jonathan. "He knew and didn't do anything about it?"

"He said he needed solid proof. All I've got are guesses. And, nothing's *happened*. Not really . . ."

"Amos never would have dared you to do this if he had known something like this would happen," Tim says.

"Something like what?"

But Tim's lost in his own mind. I don't think he hears me. "And if it *did* happen on his watch, you know damn well he would've protected you."

Unlike Jonathan. The unspoken words hang heavy in the room.

Tim scrubs his hands across his face and lets out a frustrated sigh. "What are you guys doing today? I need to make some calls."

"I guess I should go back to campus. . . ."

Drill looks at me, studying my face. "No. We'll go get you some clothes, but you're staying here until break is over."

I don't want to say no. "Okay. Thanks." I try to smile at him but it sucks. The whole situation sucks. "I'll wash your clothes and get them back to you once I get mine from campus." I don't want to. What I really want to do is keep his shirt since I can't have him.

He grins, finally, taking a step toward me. "Keep 'em. They look better on you anyway." Then he takes another step and heads into the hallway. "I'll take a shower then we can go."

Drill thumps up the stairs and Tim just laughs. "They look better on you?"

"Shut up," I say, and walk back in to lie on the futon, my head spinning a million different directions. Secret societies. The anniversary of Amos's suicide. The feel of Drill's arm across my waist last night.

I pull the blanket up over my head, sheltering myself in the dark, hoping Drill will take a long time in the shower and leave me to my angst for just a little bit.

TWENTY-SIX

I STAY OFF CAMPUS THE REST OF BREAK, SPENDING IT FREE of anything DMA-filled, except for Drill. There's plenty of Drill. We run every day, he lets me beat him at a video game every once in a while, and we get to know each other. Drill tells me about his family and where his parents have been stationed over the years. It's almost normal, except for Tim's daily report on what he's found out about the Society, which pretty much equals nothing every day.

Christmas Day itself didn't suck like I thought it would without Mom and Dad around. We made homemade pizza instead of roasting a chicken, and we ate ice cream out of the container instead of pie. We didn't swap presents but we spent a lot of time talking about family, about happy memories. And for just a minute, things didn't seem so bad.

Despite wanting to know what Kelly is up to, I stay off campus on New Year's Eve. His involvement I've kept to myself. Without proof, I don't want to betray him. Besides, with school starting back soon, I want to be focused on Drill for as long as I can.

Before the first class of the new semester, I log in to my email. There are only two I care about. Suddenly Worm outings in January don't matter much when the Society is deciding my fate.

I click on Mom's first—it'll be quicker. No way would she put serious news about Dad in an email. The subject says as much.

From: mrsmckenna@mail.com

To: smckenna@dma.edu

Subject: No news—just checking in

Sammy,

It was good to talk to you over Christmas. I wish I could have come, but I needed to stay here. Thanks for understanding. There's no news on Dad yet.

Focus on school, on getting through the rest of the year. I love you, baby. Talk soon, okay?

Love,

Mom

I send her a quick reply, trying to ignore the feeling in the pit of my stomach. Dad's strong, though, and fighting fit. Even if he is in trouble, he's probably never been happier. He lives for this. And the last thing he'd want any of us to do is distract ourselves by worrying about him. He'd want me to press on, to complete the objective. And that's what I'm going to do. For him. For me.

I save Mom's email to process later, and click on Jax's.

From: jaxhax@mail.com

To: smckenna@dma.edu

Subject: Tunnels

THERE ARE TUNNELS UNDER THE DMA. THEY MEET THERE. MORE WHEN I GET IT.

I look around, but no one is sitting close enough to read it, and thankfully Matthews doesn't appear to be in this new class. Still, I minimize the window while the last of the cadets come in and I think of a reply. I've never heard about tunnels under the DMA, but that doesn't mean they aren't there. If we know where they're meeting, maybe we can sneak in there and listen in on their plans.

Drill enters and scans the nearly full room, then sits in the chair next to me. He jerks his head up in a greeting. "McKenna." No "Mac." No "Sam." We'll never be just a pair of normal teens at an ordinary high school.

I try to ignore the small grin he gets when he sees me here and how much I want to touch him when he's this close. I clear my throat. "Drill Sergeant Stamm, good morning, Drill Sergeant Stamm." He smells like aftershave and there's a small nick on his chin. I want to ask him why he's in a sophomore English class as a junior, but I don't know how to walk this line. How can I ignore what happened over Christmas?

Thankfully, Professor Williams, my Military History professor from first semester, starts to speak. "Good morning, gentlemen." He has a leather bag slung over his shoulder and is wearing an Army sweater with leather patches on the elbows. "Oh, and, uh, ladies. Lady. Please forgive me, Miss McKenna. It's nice to see you again."

I smile but can't make myself answer him.

"Now, this is sophomore English," the professor says, sounding unsure as he reads the title on a piece of paper. "And I am . . ." He reaches for the glasses stuck on top of his head and slides them down on his face as if that will help him remember. "Professor Williams."

Some of the cadets laugh, but he's grandfatherly, just like he was last semester, and I instantly want to come to his defense.

"Coming around now," he says as he hands a stack of papers to the nearest cadet, "is the course syllabus. You'll notice a large part of your grade comes from outside reading and group work."

When I get my syllabus I scribble a note on the edge to talk to the professor about making an exception to his group work rule. I'm hoping he'll give me permission to work by myself again.

Professor Williams continues. "You would do well to choose your groups wisely. Many cadets have failed this class due to their, um, unwise group selection." He clears his throat, his eyes falling on Drill. A wide smile crosses his face. "A prime example sitting in the back row. Good to see you again, Mr. Stamm."

"And you, Professor," Drill says with a grin. "Listen to him, guys. He's not wrong about the failing part."

I glance sideways at Drill and the grin slides into a full-fledged smile, which throws me completely off-kilter. He shrugs before turning back to the front.

"I'm sure you're eager to know what we'll be doing in here. Our focus will be on researching the DMA, looking for famous military heroes from within our ranks. We'll write reports to publish in our very own DMA newspaper."

The guys are mumbling to each other under their breath, none of them sounding happy about research, reading, or publishing. The perks of being in a class you're forced to take. They should be happy it's only a semester long.

"Now, our first assignment will be to research different branches of the military DMA grads have gone into to get an idea of the breadth of people available for us to study as the semester goes on. After some presentations, we'll pick a direction in which we want to start off. Sound good?"

My classmates nod and grin at each other. They get to decide what they want to study? Suddenly they think they've got it made.

"The partners you choose for the first assignment will be the ones you'll work with the entire semester. There will be no switching partners after today. I think most of you all know each other, and while I'm sure there will be some uneasiness regarding Miss McKenna among us, I'm sure one of you will make her feel welcome. Partner up and start brainstorming some topics."

I hear names yelled across the room; some cadets get up and move around.

Drill speaks up after a few seconds. "McKenna's my recruit. I'll partner with her, Professor."

Spending hours researching and writing a paper with him? Late nights where we're actually allowed to be together? I bite the inside of my lip to keep myself from smiling.

"How chivalrous of you, Mr. Stamm." Professor Williams sounds like he means it, and I like him even more. He's been here for years—he must know how hard it would be for Drill to stand up to them and work with me.

A cadet in front of us snorts, nudging the guy next to him. He holds his hands in front of his face, moving them like he's groping an imaginary girl. "Chivalrous, my ass!" They both erupt in laughter.

Drill grins, though it looks like he's plastering it on his face for show. He lifts his head in acknowledgment. Even though I know he's playing it up for them, it still hurts.

Campus seems different at night, with no one out here to scream at me for not keeping my eyes straight ahead. Pulling the hood of my PT sweatshirt up to block the bite of January, I glance around, sticking to the gutters just in case anyone notices me. Only a few cadets walk around campus at this time of night, but most are heading back to the barracks, not toward the armory.

I shouldn't be out past curfew, but Katie promised not to tell anyone where I'm headed. Remedial PT is useless and I've got to do something to stay fit or this year is just going to get worse. I've got to show them I'm tough—that I can do whatever the DMA throws at me. It might require a lack of sleep, but at this point, I've got to focus on something other than Dad and the Society or I'm going to go crazy.

I'm almost to the safety of the armory when I hear a voice behind me.

"McKenna?" Drill's voice comes from only a few steps back, but I hadn't heard him at all.

I stop, coming to attention. "Drill Sergeant Stamm, yes, Drill Sergeant Stamm." I don't want to wake anyone up, so I speak quietly. We still haven't figured out a balance between what we had over Christmas and how we're supposed to be here. The air between us is thick with longing, with *something* we aren't allowed to be.

"What are you doing?" He sounds more concerned than upset. "Are you okay?"

"Drill Sergeant Stamm, this recruit is heading for the armory, Drill Sergeant Stamm." My eyes scan the darkness behind him. I don't see anything, but that doesn't mean there aren't people watching.

He raises his eyes. "What? Now?"

"Drill Sergeant Stamm, this recruit couldn't sleep. This recruit wanted to get some weights in, Drill Sergeant Stamm." I feel stupid, talking this way, especially to him. Heat burns my face. I should have just stayed in my room and done sit-ups.

"I was on my way to the weight room, anyway. Come on." He starts walking and I hurry to keep up. "You shouldn't be walking out here alone, though. Next time, just ask." When we reach the armory, he opens the door and shoos me in before him. "After you."

"Thanks." I bite my lip as I pass, keeping my eyes on the armory floor. Only the emergency lights are on and the polished floor shimmers with the reflection.

Huff stands by a basketball hoop, lobbing a ball up and

missing spectacularly. "There you are, Stamm," he yells, grabbing the ball and passing it to Drill. "Hey, McKenna," he adds, a huge smile on his face.

I grin but don't say anything, glancing at Drill and waiting for him to tell me I need to go back to the barracks. But he just lobs the ball back through the air to Huff. "Don't worry. You can be at ease if it's just the three of us. This shitbag's not going to rat you out." Huff tosses the ball back and Drill catches it easily. "Mac's going to lift with us." It's not a question. He rolls the basketball against the wall and heads across the court to the weight room. "Huff made a New Year's resolution." He punches Huff on the shoulder. "Ready to lose some of your shitbag status?"

"I didn't make it of my own free will," he grumbles, but gives me a grin. They head straight to the bench press—typical males—and I go across the room, starting with some lat pull-downs. I watch Drill, stern but patient as he coaches Huff on proper bench press technique. He's calm, relaxed, the version of Drill I saw at Christmas. The one who almost kissed me.

I shake my head to clear it, to keep my thoughts away from his lips and the electricity that flows through me, charging me with energy and confidence whenever he touches me. I'm on my second set before Huff has even done five reps on the bench.

"Come on, Huff," Drill yells, using his drill sergeant voice. "You can do better than that. Stop slacking."

"God, chill out, man. I'm not one of your recruits." He's laughing, though, so he's not too pissed. "Why do you think I'm making you do this with me in the middle of the night? If anyone knew I was actually *trying* to get a little better, they'd laugh me out of here. Besides, I like my remedial PT."

Drill helps him put the bar back in the holder. "You've got fifteen seconds. Then we're doing it again."

"Yes, Drill Sergeant." Huff sits up and turns, searching the room for me. "Mac, how the hell do you put up with this shit? He's like a freaking drill sergeant or something."

I laugh, the weights clanking down as I finish my set.

"Time's up," Drill growls, trying to sound tough. He's standing up by Huff's head, arms out in a spotting stance, ready to catch the weight if it's too much for Huff. "Lie down and give me eight more."

Huff leans back, grumbling about his taskmaster, but picks up the weight and begins. Drill talks to him about what he needs to start eating as I make my way around the room, working two more machines before Huff's done with his third set.

"It's been nice having you guys in PT with me, Mac. I enjoy looking good for the ladies," Huff chimes in between labored inhalations.

My smile's gone in a second and I lower the weights I've been using to work my quads, pumping through a fury-filled extra set. "Yeah, well, it's not by choice."

Even though he's still holding Huff's weight bar, Drill looks over at me. "I'm sorry, Mac. My hands are tied. Corporals are in charge of their recruits' fitness."

"Isn't there an SOP for changing back? Say I want to get back into Corps PT. How would I do that?" I push with all my might, attacking the weights since I can't hurt Matthews.

"The recruit would go to their corporal and request a change.

You'd have to take a PT test and score within a certain range to be able to move."

I stand, legs shaky after too much work, and walk over to them. Huff's raising his arms above his head to stretch them. He's breathing hard and I almost feel bad for him. "And if the corporal won't listen or won't let a recruit test?" Matthews had demoted me to remedial PT. I'm guessing he won't want me moving out anytime soon.

Drill huffs out a burst of air. He knows I'm right. "Then I guess you'd come to me."

I nod toward the bench press. "Can I work in?"

Drill raises his eyebrows and takes a step back. "Sure."

It's hard to keep the grin from my face, knowing I've impressed him with my weight room terminology. Amos and I used to work out all the time before he was deployed so I know my way around. I grab two tens and two fives, adding them to Huff's one hundred-five pounds. I also know when I'm overdoing it. I've never benched this much but I was gearing up for it at the end of the summer. Being in here with Drill and Huff is *almost* like being at home with Jonathan and Amos. I was always doing stupid things to push myself and impress them. And here I go again.

Huff whistles. "You're way past me, Mac." He raises his hand and heads to the treadmill.

I ignore Huff's comment. I'm too focused on the weight I'm determined to push. Lying down on the bench, I slide up so my head is directly under the bar.

"I'll spot you." Drill stands above me, looking down, his

hands under the bar but not touching it.

I blow air into my hands and rub them together, drying them off so my grip is sure. Gritting my teeth, I hold the bar, lifting it just a fraction and letting my muscles settle into the familiar pain. When I grunt with the unaccustomed weight, Drill moves to grab the bar. "No." I grimace.

Eight grueling reps later, I put the bar back in the rack, my arms completely spent. I swipe the back of my wrist across my forehead and sit up, trying to catch my breath. Drill sits down on the bench next to me.

"Want to tell me what that was about?"

"What?" I'm looking around for water, but the fountain is across the room and I'm not ready to move yet.

"Whatever you were just trying to prove to me by lifting that much."

"I'm just working out."

"Bull."

"Fine. Consider this me coming to you about getting out of remedial. I want to join Ranger PT." It comes out of the blue and I know it's crazy, but I can't take it back now.

He raises his eyebrows, really studying me, and I can't hold his gaze for long. "Ranger PT is serious shit."

"I know. But I'm not going to let Matthews push me around. I can out-PT half the guys in the company—"

"That doesn't mean you're ready for Ranger PT."

"Then get me there." I turn toward him. "You're working with Huff. Add me into the mix. I won't make the move until you say I'm ready, but at least give me a shot." I don't want to beg, but I will if I have to.

He looks at me for a second longer, then runs both his hands over his face, scrubbing it like he thinks he can clear away the thought of me in Ranger PT.

I stand up, putting distance between us. "Never mind. I'll figure out my own way to get into Ranger PT. I'm sorry I asked." I thought after getting closer to him at Christmas that he'd understand how much I have to prove myself, that he might even help me get there. Maybe I was wrong.

"Mac, wait," he says as I'm moving across the room toward the door. "It's nothing like that. It's just— You've got enough that you're fighting right now. Why make it even harder? You can work out with us at night. I'll help. But test for Ranger PT next year."

I don't want to admit he's right. It's not in my nature to back down, but he's offered a solution that might work. With everything going on this semester, delaying Ranger PT is probably not such a bad idea anyway. "Deal."

"If we're going to do this, we're starting now. It's going to be hard."

I don't think he's talking about us, but I allow myself a second to pretend. Then I turn my thoughts back to PT. "I know." I swallow, proud because I know he wouldn't do this if he didn't think I could manage it. "I won't let you down."

"You couldn't, even if you tried." He points toward the bench press. "Now let's get back to work."

TWENTY-SEVEN

JONATHAN TOLD ME ABOUT THE RANDOM SNOWSTORMS IN Virginia, but I didn't believe him until today. It's the end of January and when I wake up at 0500 to get my uniform ready for the day and change into PT gear, the PG is covered with white. Not just an inch, though. There's almost a foot of snow on the ground, where last night there was only dead grass.

I can't even begin to comprehend. No one is out walking to the gym, or the armory, or anywhere, for that matter. Normally there are at least a few cadets ready to lead PT heading out and about. But today—nothing.

It's a rare, quiet moment—one I'm going to soak up. Not like I have anyone to share it with anyway. Bekah spends all of her time with Evers and the track team. Wilson and Kelly are starting to miss company time regularly, too, though Kelly gives no explanation that I've heard and Matthews obviously doesn't mind.

It hurts. Despite knowing that he might somehow be involved with the Society, I miss my friend.

Once I'm dressed in DMA-issued sweats and a hoodie, I sit by the window. A snowplow pushes its blade along the PG, scratching and screeching as it moves snow to the sides of the path. One light pops on in another barracks, then a second, and a third. Even with the snow, the campus comes alive early.

No point in delaying any longer. I turn on the light, ignoring Katie's groans, and iron my uniform of the day. Better be prepared just in case. Thirty minutes later, my uniform so starched it could stand on its own, Matthews yells for us to get out on the wall. "Good morning, Alpha Company!"

"Corporal Matthews, good morning, Corporal Matthews!"

"I'm assuming you all saw the beautiful white stuff that fell last night. In celebration of the first snowfall of the year, there will be no classes today and PT is canceled."

Cheers go up from my recruit buddies. I'm reserving celebration until I find out what kind of hell he's going to put us through today. While Kelly's been ignoring me, Matthews's onslaught is harsher than ever. Earlier wake-up calls, harder smoke shows. And I just have to take it, knowing that he's pulling Kelly away from me—offering him something I obviously can't.

"Today, you will participate in one of the finest traditions the DMA has to offer. Today you will compete against the rest of the freshman companies in a snow sculpture competition. You will plan and execute this snow sculpture. You will let your cadre know what you are building so that we can supply spray paint to make it the most beautiful sculpture the DMA has ever seen."

Another cheer goes up.

We're making snowmen? Seriously?

"Meanwhile, you will also be planning and preparing for the PG Battle, another first snowfall tradition. You will be making bunkers, tunnels, and ammunition out of snow in order to defeat all the other companies in a snow battle. As always, you are expected to win. You have ten minutes to get dressed in BDUs and begin morning wake-up calls. After reveille and breakfast, you will begin work. Judging will be at 1400, the war will commence at 1500. Points will be awarded toward Company of the Year for each activity today. You all are in the lead right now, but not by much. Any questions?"

"Corporal Matthews, no, Corporal Matthews!"

After much arguing and annoyance out in the cold in front of the barracks, we decide on Phineas and Ferb for our sculpture. Why? Because we're eight, apparently, and my recruit buddies think it's cool. Kelly runs off to tell Matthews what colors spray paint we need and we begin designing it.

"So, they need to be at their rocket ship. Think we can make it really tall? Like, eight feet or something?" Ritchie asks.

I glance around at the snow. It doesn't look like it's melting anytime soon. "Probably," I say. "We've also got to worry about the snow war."

"Okay, here's what we do," Wilson says. He loves being in charge. He's a shitty leader, but no one says anything against him because Matthews loves him, so if he's in charge, we're bound to get everything approved. "Nix, Ritchie, McKenna, Quinn, and Cross will work on the bunkers and ammo for the snow war. The rest of us will work on the sculpture. When the spray paint comes, you guys can jump in and help with that part. Sound good?"

"We're on it," I say, leading my small group around to the side of the barracks, glad to be away from him. "Making snowballs will be a hell of a lot easier than building a rocket ship. Besides, if the sculpture sucks, we can totally blame them."

Kelly exits the basement of the dorm next to ours and I wave him over. "Why were you in there?"

"Talking to the cadre." He glances down at the ground, then back at me. He's about as good at lying as Jonathan is, but I can't deal with it today. The PG is covered in white, we don't have PT, and there are no classes. There are more important things to do today, like have fun.

"Wilson's taken charge and wants you with him."

He takes off jogging without even saying good-bye and I stand there until he's gone around the side of the barracks.

"Hey, don't worry about it," Katie says. "Let's just make snow-balls."

I push my suspicions about Kelly to the back of my mind and focus on the third Alpha Company female. "Where did Bekah go?" She'd been right behind me when we walked over but some-time in the last few minutes has disappeared.

"Who knows—track practice?" Katie shrugs.

"I guess." She hadn't said anything about it before we came outside, though. "You doing okay? I've been so busy with new classes we haven't really had a chance to talk."

"Not to mention the midnight PT. How are you surviving on three hours of sleep?"

"Not too well, but I've got to do it." I haven't told her I'm working out with Drill, but the extra time with him in the evenings is worth any lack of sleep I'm getting right now.

"I guess . . ." She sighs, letting her words drop off.

"How about you?"

"I miss my parents. I miss sleeping. I miss normal school."

"Don't talk like that, Katie. We're almost done."

"Five more months? That's not almost done. That's dragging hell out a little longer."

"Don't quit on me now." I didn't inadvertently keep the secret society stuff from her, but I'm glad now that I haven't said anything.

"I don't want to, but . . ."

I grab another pile of snow and pack it down tight, changing the subject so she doesn't have to dwell on her misery right now. "I've never made snowballs before."

"What?" She laughs at this, her worry about the DMA sliding away with something as simple as snowballs to focus on.

"Nope. According to Mom, snowball fights might ruin my manicure or something. She tried to keep me girly. Dresses, jewelry, heels."

"And yet here you are." Katie laughs.

"And here I am." I look around, the PG alive and buzzing with activity—cadets and recruits moving around, laughing, and tossing snowballs, white explosions erupting everywhere before the fight is even starting. "And here *you* are, almost done with freshman year."

She adds three more snowballs to our pile. We've got about fifty by now, but I know we're going to need a ton more. "Yeah," she sighs. "For now."

Drill steps out of the barracks wearing camo, the uniform tight across his arms. He scans the ground in front of the barracks until he finds me, a smile lighting his face.

My face heats up. "I don't know, this place is kind of growing on me."

"Yeah, like a tumor," she mutters, though she can't keep a smile off her face, glancing between me and Drill.

After a quick chew-and-screw lunch—where we eat and get the hell out—we run back to our statue to spray-paint. Those of us who were in charge of preparing for the snow war are now the artistic directors. Those who did the heavy lifting before are now working on fortifying our bunkers and finishing out our tunnels.

It's scary how much my recruit buddies know about Phineas and Ferb. The statue actually looks really good, and they even have the annoying sister yelling at them from a few feet away. The spray-painting takes longer than we thought, though, and we are just putting the finishing touches on it when the judges—all the drill sergeants and Jonathan—come up to our barracks.

They stand there, marking things on their scorecards, mumbling under their breath. Jonathan doesn't even look at me, though I stare at him. Kelly elbows me and I jump, turning to look at him. "What?"

"I know he's your brother, but you can't stare at the cadet colonel like that," he hisses under his breath.

"I'm just trying to get his attention." He hasn't met with me since before Christmas.

"Yeah, but right now he's not your brother—he's your colonel." He's taken the words right out of Matthews's mouth.

I nod and take a step back, glaring at Kelly now, rather than at Jonathan. "Better?"

"Oh, just wonderful. Very grown-up of you."

"I am a year older than you, you know." I give him a smug smile and he just rolls his eyes.

Jonathan's voice makes me jump. "Good job, recruits. Alpha Company has won the statue contest every year for the past seven. Good to see we can count on you this year as well. Now, finish getting ready for the snow war. Don't forget, when you hit someone, you can take them prisoner. When you get rid of a company, grab their flag. The company standing at the end with the most flags wins! Now, get out there and kick some ass!"

"Colonel McKenna, yes, Colonel McKenna!"

As soon as he walks away, we're high-fiving each other. If we can win this, we might be able to solidify our lead in the points. Originally I'd just wanted to make it through the year—but to win Company of the Year, too, would just be the icing on the cake.

We talk through our strategy for the snow war, which basically involves just beaning the hell out of people and hiding behind bunkers. Wilson puts himself in charge of guarding the flag.

The PG is crawling with cadets, upperclassmen and freshmen

alike. Evers has positioned himself at a bunker within throwing distance of mine. "Wait a second, upperclassmen are playing in the snow war?"

"Of course they are," Kelly says. "They should get to have fun, too. You'll be fine." He pounds me on the back and I stagger forward a step before standing still again. This is not the same Kelly who wanted to protect me earlier in the year. This Kelly is different, more *indifferent* than I'm used to. And it scares me to think that the Society has gotten its claws in him.

Just then the cannon goes off, announcing the start of the war. I dive behind the bunker with Kelly and lie flat against the snow. My fingers are frozen as I try to grip a snowball. I inch my head up above the lip of the bunker and scan—snowballs fly from every direction. Cadets and recruits run around, diving, dodging, and rolling out of the way. My recruit buddies are in the middle of the fray. Bekah's still nowhere in sight. Katie is behind the bunker next to us, just a few feet away.

From the side of the barracks Kelly came from earlier, three cadets carry a plastic bin filled with snowballs. They glance around and point in my direction. I duck back down behind the bunker.

"They've spotted me." I know we're going to be prime targets in the war but I want a fair chance to help the company before I'm taken prisoner.

"You're kind of hard to miss, McKenna." He still won't meet my eyes, brushing off my concern like he would a fly. "It's just a snowball fight. Have some fun!"

Kelly grabs some ammunition and crouches, running from

the bunker we're behind to another one a few feet away, chucking a snowball out into the middle of the PG as he goes. When it explodes, Evers whips around and looks our way. He glares and points a finger in my direction.

I don't have enough ammo to waste one on Kelly for his idiotic move. Evers is filling his arms full of snowballs from the plastic bucket, keeping his eyes on me. Katie is okay a few feet away. I inch my head up and look around, but still can't spot Bekah anywhere.

"Katie? You see Bekah?" I grab a snowball and wind my arm back, prepared to attack, and scan the field in front of me for a target. Evers is closest, but I don't want to push him.

"No sign of her."

I turn the other direction, determined to take down some of Bravo Company.

The first snowball hits me from the side, my shoulder stinging with pain. It's not a nice soft one that explodes on impact, like the ones we made. When I reach for it on the ground, it's a solid lump. I squeeze it in my hand but I can't break it.

The fucking snowballs are frozen.

The second one comes from somewhere near Kelly. He's looking out at the PG, but he glances nervously in my direction.

At the next bunker Katie's not doing much better. She's lying on the ground in a fetal position, her arms up over her head, protecting herself. Three upperclassmen charge toward us, Evers included, pounding Katie with iceballs from all sides.

They run away, laughing, but Katie's arms are slack and she's not protecting her head anymore. She's not moving.

"Jesus. Kelly, help her!" I turn to him, but his eyes are wide and he's frozen in place. "Kelly! She's not moving! Someone help her!" Where is everyone else? Where the hell is Bekah?

I get on my feet, running over to her, dropping to my knees next to her. "Katie. Come on, Katie." I shake her and she groans. "Thank God." She keeps her eyes closed, though, tears dropping into the snow.

"Mac!"

Just as I lift my head to see who yelled for me, a third iceball hits my forehead and everything goes black.

TWENTY-EIGHT

KATIE'S GONE. NOT *DEAD* GONE, BUT DONE WITH THE DMA.

The infirmary nurse called our parents after the snowball fight, and she vanished in a whirlwind of hugs and tears. She finally found her way out.

Mom offered to come get me, but she's got Dad to worry about and after all this time, even my "He's doing what he loves. He's going to make it through" speech isn't helping. The only thing keeping me from running home is the knowledge that Dad's too stubborn to die.

I push the blanket back on the bed and am careful to avoid the squeaky floorboards as I sneak out of my room and make my way downstairs. The nurse has a room behind her office where she sleeps when cadets are here so I don't turn the lights on. Her television is blaring, though, so I doubt she'd notice me anyway unless I banged on her door. From the infirmary, it's only a two-minute walk to the armory. The weights are clanging already. I guess they didn't think I was coming after all.

Huff is busy benching his weights, so Drill sees me first. He can't move from his spotting position, though, and taps his foot in frustration. "Mac."

Huff finishes his set and puts the bar back in the cradle. When he sits up he grins. "Hey! How's the noggin?"

I feel the lump on my forehead and wince. "Sore."

He stands, glancing at Drill, who hasn't taken his eyes off me or moved. "I think I'm going to call it quits tonight, Stamm. I'll see you in the morning, okay?"

"See ya," Drill says, his eyes still locked on mine.

Drill is across the room and he's hugging me as soon as Huff is out the door. "Are you okay? Jesus, Mac, they were *frozen*."

"I'm fine," I say. I repeat it when his arms squeeze me even tighter. "I promise." I say a silent thanks to Huff for giving us a few minutes alone, broken rules or not, and lean my head against Drill's chest. He's warm and solid, just like I remember, and I don't want to let go.

"I saw you trying to help Katie. Saw you fall. Everything happened so fast." His jaws are clenched.

"I know who threw the snowball that knocked me out." It's what I've been dreading telling him. I keep thinking he'll take off, beat the crap out of the cadet who did it, and then get in a world of trouble. But I can't keep something like this from him and I certainly can't tell Jonathan.

He leads me to the bench and we sit down. "Who?" He's

talking in his dangerous voice again, his eyes turning from concerned to pissed so fast I can barely keep up.

I choke on the name at first and have to clear my throat to try again. "Lyons."

"Second-in-command Lyons? Your brother's best friend?"

I nod. "Jonathan must have known this was going to happen. He's been in on it since the beginning."

"That's a huge leap, Sam. I could see Lyons in some secret society. But your brother letting people hurt you?" He shakes his head. "I don't buy that."

"You don't know Jonathan like I do," I insist. I want to explain how it all makes sense now. Jonathan pulling away from me this year, trying to use the phone call over Parents' Weekend to get me to quit. He's been with the Society all along. But before I can, Drill pulls me to him, wrapping his arms around me. Without hesitation, mine come up around his shoulders. In a flash of movement, he's lifted me onto his lap and I straddle him, every inch of my body tingling and craving to be just a little bit closer.

We hover on the brink of what's next, just like we did over Christmas. My fingers ache to pull his face toward mine, to feel his lips against mine, to see what would happen if we finally decide to take the plunge.

He breathes first, pulling me closer. But instead of kissing me, he rests his head on my shoulder. His heart thunders beneath the skin and I put a hand on his chest to feel it. I let my lips press lightly once, then twice, against the smooth skin of his neck.

"I'm worried about you." His words come in a rush of wind and I'm not sure he's actually said anything until he continues. "I don't want anything else to happen to you."

"I'll be okay," I breathe into his skin, urging him to believe it. I couldn't leave now, even if I wanted to. It's gone too far to turn back.

"You'd better get back to the infirmary." The hand that's not keeping me pressed to him slides up and down the length of my spine.

"They're releasing me back to the barracks tomorrow."

"I know. I'll send someone to meet you. I don't want you alone."

I tense, pushing against his chest to sit up and meet his eyes. "I can take care of myself."

"Matthews and Evers are just pricks, but I thought Lyons was a stand-up guy. If he's involved with this, there's no telling who else might be." Jonathan's name hangs between us, unspoken. "I need to talk to Rev and Tim." He moves me gently, waiting until I'm steady on my feet before standing himself. "I'll walk you back."

"Okay," I say, though it's not okay at all. I don't want a babysitter, but the Society's taken their game to the next level, and I'm not sure I have a choice anymore.

"What do you mean you're not going to be there?" While I was in the infirmary and after Katie left, Matthews moved Bekah into my room. At first I was happy, but now every day seems to begin not only with Matthews yelling but with a fight of some sort between Bekah and me.

"I have track—"

"Team building, right? Well, it's getting ridiculous." The pounding in my head hasn't stopped in the week since the ice-ball, though the nurse assures me every day when I'm forced to report for sick call that I don't have a concussion. It's fine with me as long as I'm still able to do what I need to do during company time. Which is what Bekah isn't doing.

"Kelly and Wilson aren't going to be there either."

"Oh, they've joined the track team, too?" Their absences scare me more than Bekah's, but I can't explain that to her—I don't know how much she knows about Evers, the Society, and their new initiates.

"Of course not. They have a study group." She's halfheartedly ironing her camo pants to the point where I want to jerk the iron out of her hand and do it myself.

"For someone who studies so much, Kelly sure does have shitty grades."

"I thought you guys weren't talking anymore. Isn't that why you're in such a bitchy mood all the time?" She's digging, searching for information, but I'm not going to give it to her. Not if she's just going to report back to her boyfriend and he's going to use that information against me.

Leaning back against my wall locker, I close my eyes. The truth is, I'm pissed because for the past week with her here, I haven't been able to sneak away to the armory. Drill and I have had no free time to talk about what he's found out about Lyons. There are cadets after me and yet I'm the one left in the dark. "Yeah, I guess."

"Well, you need to get over it. You're the one who said you

didn't want to date him. You can't be upset if he starts finding other friends, Sam." She picks her pants up and shakes them out, totally undoing the creases she just attempted to put in them.

I hold out my hand. "Here, I'll fix them."

"Thanks." She smiles gratefully. "And don't worry about tonight. Matthews won't be there either, so it should be pretty easy."

I have to grip her pants to keep from dropping them. "What? Where's he going to be?"

She shrugs. "Evers just said it would be an easy night on deck so it didn't matter if I didn't show up."

I wish I had time today to email Jax and see what's going on. It's not going to happen, though. Not today. I grab the can of starch, my hand only shaking a little bit.

Seven hours later, head throbbing and arms trembling, I hold myself in the lower half of the push-up position waiting for Drill to call an end to the smoke show.

"Feel the pain, Alpha. Feel it," Drill says. He walks to the end of the deck and hits the light switch, plummeting us all into darkness.

Ritchie groans next to me. Even without Matthews and Julius here to make it horrible, this smoke show is by far the worst we've had all year. But with Drill it's different. He's not trying to tear us down, he's building us up for something.

"You got this, Ritchie," I grit through clenched jaws. My heart flutters, not even enough strength left to fight.

Instead of the typical hard-core I-want-to-kill-you music

we've had so far, the next song starts out with a helicopter. The piano and a single singer come in next. I raise my head, looking through rivers of sweat but there's nothing but darkness.

"Close your eyes." Drill's voice is quiet now, the worst type of voice he can have.

I do as he says.

"Listen to the words," Drill says directly behind me. I adjust my back to make sure it's as straight as possible even though he can't see my push-up form in the darkness.

"Lift your left hand in front of you."

Shifting my weight to do as he says, I let out a cry. There's no way my one arm will hold me after the last hour. The song has moved from Parris Island training to the fields of 'Nam, singing of dead friends and darkness.

"Scoot over, Mac."

I do as Drill says, shuffling to my right, then raising my hand again. He's beside me now, in push-up position just like the rest of us.

"Alpha, lower your left hand onto the hand of the recruit buddy to your left. Lean your shoulder into him. Let him support you."

And just like that, Drill is there, a rock to lean against. I lean into his shoulder, easing some of the pain. I support Nix to my right, his body heavy on my shoulder. We all shake, we all sweat, including Drill, who did every exercise with us tonight.

"Now listen to the words of the song. You are Alpha. You eat together, breathe together. You live together and you die together. Never forget that. Feel the weight of your recruit buddy. Know

that you are holding him up. Feel the weakness in your own muscles. Know that you would not still be up if your recruit buddy wasn't helping you. This year is all about you becoming a unit." His last words about unity echo the chorus of the song.

My eyes sting, and Nix, who never cries, no matter how bad the smoke shows get, sniffles to my right. I'm not alone in this moment and Drill is fully responsible.

"Thank you," I whisper as the music fades.

He leans closer to me. "You belong here. Don't let anyone tell you different."

When the song ends, Drill shifts, giving me a chance to get my balance back before standing up. A few seconds later, the light comes back on and I shut my eyes against the intrusion.

"On your feet, Alpha," Drill barks, but he reaches down to help Nix up.

Then he reaches down and offers me a hand. "Help your brothers up."

Soon we're all up, standing in a semicircle around Drill. We pant, arms around each other while waiting for our next instructions.

He begins speaking, so quietly that we have to lean in even closer to hear him. "I'm original Alpha—was in Alpha Company as a Worm, just like you. I was corporal cadre for Alpha last year. Alpha is in my blood, just like it will be in yours if you make it through the rest of this year. So listen up. You've got study hall in ten minutes. I've got to be quick." As he talks, he looks each of my recruit brothers in the eye. "You've been judged this whole year—by your cadre, by the cadet colonel, by the commandant himself. And even though no one has recognized you as cadets yet, you've made me proud.

"Now I've got a mission for you. If you succeed, you will be legendary among all members of Alpha Company, past and present."

There's excitement in the group and we all lean in closer. Are we breaking into barracks? Stealing the local university's mascot? What crazy thing is he proposing we do? Because looking at the faces of my recruit buddies—we're going to do it, whatever it is.

"It's February. Now is when things are going to get easier on most of you—the upperclassmen will let up a bit, there will be less hazing on the PG, less . . . everything. It's meant to get easier as the year goes on, not harder."

"You said most of us, Drill. What do you mean?" Nix doesn't get it. If I could see the good in everyone like he does . . . well, I'd probably be on my way out the door by now.

"Mac's year is only going to get harder from here on out. She's got a chance, boys, a real chance of being a model recruit and cadet at this academy. She's squared-away, works hard, doesn't complain. But there are people here who don't want her to succeed. You've got to take it upon yourselves, as fine, upstanding members of Alpha Company, to make sure those people don't get in her way."

Before I can protest, he continues. "I'm not saying she needs babysitting, or saving, or taking care of. But you do need to watch her back." Drill leaves no room for argument. "So, fellas, this is your mission. Assign roles, make guard schedules. Let me know if you need anything. You've got to keep Mac under your watchful eyes twenty-four/seven. Help her survive the school year. Is that understood?"

"Drill Sergeant Stamm, yes, Drill Sergeant Stamm!"

I grit my teeth when the others respond, glaring at Drill to make sure he knows I'm pissed.

"Nix, Ritchie—you seem closest to Mac. I'm putting you two in charge."

"What about Kelly, Drill? He should be involved in this."

Drill shakes his head. "I'm putting you two in charge. Kelly, Wilson, and Cross are to have no knowledge of this mission. Is that understood?"

I feel the curiosity flow around the circle, but they won't ask. They'll follow orders because Drill has earned our respect. I try to catch his attention, but Drill just gives me the smallest of nods. He's found something out.

"Drill Sergeant Stamm, yes, Drill Sergeant Stamm." They both respond and squeeze my shoulders. I try to shrug them off but they don't budge.

"Obviously, Mac is not going to help," Drill says, a smirk on his face, though he's not upset and he doesn't mean for his words to hurt. "You're going to have to take it upon yourselves to figure out her class schedule and make sure she's not alone on any walks across campus. If you do this—if you see her through and make sure she finishes this year—you guys will have earned your place in Alpha Company." He clears his throat. "Now, helicopter showers—in and out as fast as you can. We've been at this long enough. Mac, a minute. Everyone else, dismissed."

Nix and Ritchie hang back while everyone else runs to their

room to get their shower kits. We've got five minutes to shower and be at our desks studying.

"You guys are dismissed. I'll make sure she's okay right now."

"Drill Sergeant Stamm, yes, Drill Sergeant Stamm!"

He raises his head, looking at a spot across the hall. I move there with him, but he doesn't say anything yet. Recruit buddies pop out of doors, head to the bathroom, and leave the hall free once again.

"What is it?" I can't read the expression on his face and it makes me nervous.

His hand reaches out, but he pulls it back when he hears a door open. "I know you don't want this, but don't fight me."

"It's ridiculous—"

"What's ridiculous is—" He sighs. "Do you know where Kelly is tonight?"

"Cross said he had a study group," I stammer, the words sounding as false as they are.

He lets out a burst of air. "But you don't think it's true, do you?"

I shake my head.

"You knew Kelly was somehow involved in this and you didn't think it was important to tell me?" Hurt, then anger, cross his face.

I look down. "I didn't know for sure. . . ."

"What made you think it?"

"The blood wings. Matthews gave him and Wilson blood wings during a smoke show."

"You should have told me," he says, and this time he's not angry, he's hurt.

"I can take care of myself against Kelly. I'm not helpless."

"Accepting help doesn't mean anyone will think any less of you. It means your recruit buddies care about you. It means *I* care about you." He closes his eyes and takes a deep breath. "This isn't what I needed to tell you. I just got a text from Huff. He's been keeping an eye on Matthews, but he's lost him. No clue where he's gone."

"Lyons?"

"No sign of him or Evers, either."

I close my eyes, leaning back against the wall. His words confirming what I want to deny. "Jonathan?"

He shakes his head. "I don't know."

"Do you think they're together?"

"That's the million-dollar question, isn't it?"

I can't listen anymore, because if I listen, then I'll get scared. And if I get scared, I'm going to want to run. "I need to go. . . . I've got to go to the library. I need to check my email."

"I'll bring my laptop up here for you." He grips my biceps, forcing me to look at him. "Sam, you're not leaving the barracks tonight. We don't know where they are. What they're doing. They hurt you once already. I won't let them do it again."

I turn and walk into my room without being dismissed. I close the door behind me and sink to the floor, leaning my head back against the door until I hear him walk away. Only then do I let myself breathe again.

TWENTY-NINE

THE CHAPEL IS ALMOST EMPTY WHEN I COME IN AFTER second block. Ritchie's on Guard Sam duty and goes to sit in the pew at the back, leaning his head back and closing his eyes. "God, I'm tired."

"I told you, you don't have to follow me around."

He opens one eye and rolls his head lazily toward me. "I'm not disobeying Drill."

And it's true. Their homemade schedule and constant tagging along for the last few days have proven that. "Fine. I'll be done soon, I hope."

"I'll be here," he says, and closes the one eye he's been looking at me with.

I knock on Rev's door and hear a shuffle inside. Drill opens the door and ushers me in, glancing in the hallway before shutting it behind him.

"Don't worry. Ritchie's out there," I mutter.

"It's not him I'm worried about," Drill says. "Take the chair. I'll stand."

I want to tell him I'll stand but there's no point. The sooner we can get this over with, the sooner I can get back to classes. I smile halfheartedly at Tim, sitting in the chair next to mine.

Rev clears his throat. "Any news on your father, Sam?"

"No, sir. I talked to Mom briefly while I was in the infirmary, and I've had a few emails, but there's nothing to report. He's still missing." Out there somewhere, hunted or caught, in pain or dead.

"Well, no news is good news most often in these cases. Your father is a strong man. He'll get through this."

I like the way he talks about Dad in present tense. Someone should have faith that he's still alive and will get home, not being tortured somewhere or eaten by worms. . . .

"This will be the only time we meet like this," Drill says. "It's too dangerous."

"Agreed. Though I thought it important to make sure we're all on the same page. Sam has a right to know what we're thinking," Rev says, leaning back in his chair and steepling his fingers. "Sam, I trust you are recovering well."

"I am. Thank you." My face burns under the attention. "So what's the news?"

Drill grits his teeth, and his arm muscles tense and relax, tense and relax. "Cross is dating Evers."

I turn around in my chair. "She's been dating him since . . . Parents' Weekend."

Drill closes his eyes, letting out a sigh.

"Sam, we need to know who is helping you figure this stuff out. The one who thought it might be a secret society, who drew the link with the blood wings." When Tim speaks, I can see exactly where Drill got his commander's voice.

It's hard for me to question him, but I don't want to bring Jax into this now. "What? Why?"

"I might have a lead. I need to find some information, though."

"Tell me. I'll get whatever you need."

"I'm not sending this information over email. I need to meet with whoever is helping you." He leans in toward me.

"I'll be fine. It's okay. Nothing's happened other than scribbling in my KB."

"You're forgetting the near-concussion you're getting over," Drill says, walking around the chair and bending down in front of me. He takes my hands in his, squeezing them. "Not to mention that we're about to start the Weekend Warrior competitions. Look at me, Sam."

Finally, I move my eyes to him, scanning his face before locking on to his eyes. It's Drill. I trust Drill. The last thing I want to do is pull Jax into this any more than she already is, but I don't think I have a choice anymore.

When I've given them a history of Jax and her email address, the meeting is over. Tim will get anything new to me through Drill. Operation Guard Sam will continue as planned, and Rev will work his confessional magic to try to talk to Jonathan and get our meetings back on track.

Drill walks me out of the office. Ritchie's snores greet us in the chapel. "My fearless guard for the day." I nudge Ritchie and he jerks awake.

"Hey, Mac." He clears his throat, rubbing his eyes, then jumping to his feet when he sees Drill. "Drill Sergeant, good morning, Drill Sergeant."

"I'll walk Mac to her next class. Go on and grab lunch. You can pick her up after class."

"Drill Sergeant, yes, Drill Sergeant." Ritchie pats my shoulder and jogs out the door.

"You don't have to walk me yourself."

His eyes scan the chapel. "If it were up to me, I'd be next to you twenty-four/seven." He moves closer and I take a step back, pressing against the wall. Resting an arm up by my head, he leans in.

I can't tear my eyes away from his face. If I can just kiss him once, I know everything will be okay. That we'll make it through. I'll be able to wait until the end of the year if I can just take one second for myself right now.

A cough makes us both jump. I take a step away from Drill before I even look to see who it is.

"Dude, I could have been anyone. How stupid are you?" Tim smacks him on the back of the head.

"That's my cue to leave," I say, unable to meet Tim's eyes as I skirt around both of them and head to the door.

"It won't happen again," Drill says.

"It better not, dill weed. If you lose your position as her drill sergeant, there's no telling who they'll put in your place."

Drill holds his hands up in surrender. "I said it won't happen again. Let's get to class, recruit." He holds the door open for me, giving me a conspiratorial wink.

THIRTY

"THE WEEKEND WARRIOR COMPETITION. THAT'S WHAT WE'RE all out here for on this cold-ass March Saturday." Matthews rubs his hands together as he paces back and forth in front of our company. "You'll have a total of four of these challenges between now and the end of April."

"That's right," Julius picks up.

While Julius is talking, Matthews moves to stand in front of Kelly, who's been looking worse lately, like he's not getting much sleep. Dark circles outline his eyes and he's lost weight. I've told Bekah I think he's getting sick, but she gets defensive and says it's nothing. I don't like how close they've gotten lately.

Drill stands in front of us now and I try to focus on the instructions. "Each of you will have a chance to go through the obstacles laid out for you. Your speed and success will determine the company score. This will, of course, go toward our Company of the Year score. We're slightly behind Charlie since the snow battle." Drill glances at me, then continues. "We'll definitely be able to make it up, though. So, first platoon, choose your order and get ready. When the gun goes off, your time starts."

Our little mission is simple, really. We've got to move through a mock town to get to a rendezvous point. Once we're all there, we low-crawl through a mud pit covered in barbed wire to get to the safe zone.

I try to ignore how this could be what my dad is going through right this very second. How scared he might be. It'll do no good to lose my focus and bring the company down. If I can just get through this without screwing up, I'll be thrilled. The gun goes off and first platoon is gone, Wilson leading the charge. They yell and scream support to each other as they work their way through the challenge.

It seems like the entire Corps is out here watching. Ropes are set up to keep them separate from us. Evers stands over to the side, whispering to Matthews. Kelly and Bekah stand together, though they're not talking. Their eyes are focused on first platoon. Almost too focused, like they're specifically trying *not* to look anywhere else.

"Second platoon, get ready," Matthews says, stepping away from Evers and handing a clipboard to Rev, our supervisor for today. "Kelly, you'll lead the charge. Cross, you're second." He assigns Ritchie, Nix, and Dove their places. "And you can be last, McKenna. See if you can lead from the rear."

"Corporal Matthews, yes, Corporal Matthews."

I wait until Dove reaches the wall we've got to get over, and the second he jumps, I take off.

Imaginary foes and traps wait around every turn. I press my back against the wall, glancing around the corner, and wait until the "explosion" goes off, sending green smoke up into the air. Running and diving to the ground, I let my momentum carry me, flipping over once then returning to my feet at a run. Thank God I've recovered from the snow battle.

The next obstacle is jumping across the roofs of two "buildings" they've built. They're only a foot off the ground, but the leap requires a running start and I barely clear it, the heel of my combat boot not even on the second roof. Luckily the forward momentum helps pull me to safety and I don't lose any points. I jump down on the other side, where my platoon waits for me.

"Good job, Mac," Ritchie says, patting me on the back. Nix and I trade fist bumps.

"We'll celebrate later, guys. We need to move now." Kelly doesn't look at me; his eyes are fixed on the mud pit. "Same order. Let's go."

One by one, my platoon aims themselves for the mud pit and dives in, pulling themselves frantically under the barbed wire. Blanks fire overhead and when I hit the mud, I keep myself as low as I can. They're simulating live fire and, just like Declaration Day, I'm not going to be one to "die" in my company. I keep myself as close as I can to Dove's boot, pausing only long enough to be sure he's not going to kick me in the face. Globs of grit get in my mouth before I remember to keep it closed; the exhaustion of the run makes breathing hard.

But then something slams into my side. It feels like a rocket has split me right open and I scream before I can stop myself, the pain in my ribs so excruciating it sucks all the air from my lungs. I look down, clutching my side. The mud doesn't turn red, though. The gaping wound is all in my mind. But I can't breathe. No amount of forcing will make my lungs work.

Dove crawls on, oblivious to what's happened, so I know whatever it was only happened to me. The crowd is cheering as I try to suck air into my lungs to yell for help. Black spots dance in front of my face. Am I going to die, right here in the mud pit while the rest of the Corps watches and cheers?

I finally take a breath. Then another. Pain stabs at my side and tears blur my vision. But the thought of Matthews celebrating—of all those boys out there celebrating right along with him is enough to spur me on. I can't give in to the pain and let him win.

I force myself to move, put one arm in front of the other and pull myself inch by inch through the mud. It hurts like hell every time I inhale.

A black circle surrounds my vision. Dove looks miles away. He turns back. His mouth opens. He stretches his arm out to me.

It all happens in slow motion, like we're stuck in some movie and have to keep going until the director yells cut. So that's what I do. Using my left arm only, I pull myself on in a slow, stuttered movement that gets me barely anywhere. Then I reach out and do it again. And again.

I keep doing it until Dove and Ritchie grab hold and pull me out from under the barbed wire. "You okay, Mac?" Ritchie's voice is quiet, the ground spinning as I try to figure out where I'm supposed to be headed.

"Fine," I manage. "Just go."

Then I see the end, my company standing in a semicircle ten steps in front of me, waiting. I'm going to be last one in the company to cross the line. Ritchie stays with me but at least he knows enough to let me finish on my own.

"What the hell happened, Mac?" Ritchie bends down, whispering in my ear despite the cheering going on all around us.

I put a hand protectively over my side and that's when I feel it—a lump the size of an egg near my ribs. "Get Drill and Rev, but don't tell anyone else," I say through clenched teeth. "Rubber bullet. I've been shot."

THIRTY-ONE

"HAVE YOU HAD ENOUGH, SAM? YOU NEED TO LEAVE." Jonathan's been at this for fifteen minutes in my hospital room but he won't give up. My ribs, though not broken, are pounding, and my throbbing head can't take much more. I glare at him from the hospital bed but don't bother to respond.

"You've got bruised ribs from a training accident. Your grades are slipping—"

My head whips around to look at him.

"Don't look at me like that. Of course I know your grades. I'm in charge of everyone. Not to mention you're my sister."

"Oh, you'll claim that now, will you? If you could control your cadets maybe this wouldn't have happened," I spit out, then instantly regret the outburst. My side throbs and getting frustrated has set off firecrackers in my eyes.

"That's enough, Recruit McKenna. He may be your brother, but he's still your colonel and you'll treat him with respect." Drill moves slightly, coming into my peripheral vision. He hasn't left my side since it happened.

"The colonel might get respect, but my brother doesn't." I continue to glare at Jonathan, daring him to do or say anything right now to piss me off.

Drill meets Jonathan's eyes and continues, his words cautious, guarded. "Right now, they're one and the same."

I realize I've messed up. We've got to walk a fine line with Jonathan. If he's involved with the Society, I could be in more trouble than I thought. "Colonel McKenna. I apologize on behalf of my recruit. She's hurt and needs to rest. Can we continue this conversation later?"

Jonathan doesn't say anything, but he's looking at Drill, sizing him up and trying to figure out what's going on. All Jonathan knows is that I got hurt. I hinted that I had been kicked in the mud pit by a recruit brother. It could have easily happened and Jonathan doesn't care enough to ask too many questions.

"Did you call Mom? Let her know I'm in the hospital?"

"I did, but she can't come. She's got other things to deal with right now, Sam. She's headed to Landstuhl."

I clench my hands beneath the blanket so I don't reach for Drill. Landstuhl is the military base in Germany where injured soldiers are taken before being sent back to the States. That means they found him. "Dad?" My heart pounds, tears sting my eyes. "When did you hear? Why didn't you tell me?"

"I heard right before the challenge. I didn't want to distract you. I was going to tell you after."

"How is he? Is he okay?" I know the question is stupid. If he were okay, they'd just patch him up and send him back out in the field. Sending him to Landstuhl means he's hurt. Bad.

"We'll know more once Mom gets there."

"You're kidding, right? Tell me what's wrong with him." But now that I've said it, I'm not sure I want to hear. The look on his face—it's the same look people gave me at Amos's funeral.

"He was missing awhile. He's sick. He'll be out of the Army when he gets home." He chokes on the words, looking for the first time in a long time like something's affecting him. "Can't be a Ranger with just one arm."

Searing pain shoots up my side when I jerk back. My stomach heaves. I slap my hand down over my mouth and Jonathan pushes the trash can closer, sliding his arms under me to help me turn onto my side. I don't know if it's because of the pain or because of what he just told me, but I can't stop myself.

When I'm done puking, I glare again. "Get out."

Jonathan nods. Guess he's happy for a reason to get away from me and back to his Society. "I'll leave. But you've got to, too. You've made your point. You can do it. But think about Mom. She's lost Amos, Dad's . . . What would she do if something worse happened to you? Go home."

Leave? After everything I've been through? I can't. The weight of this moment presses down on me, making it hard to breathe. If I leave, Mom will be happy. I'll be able to help with Dad. But next year, when a new class of girls comes in, they'll be forced out, too. I won't let another girl go through this. If they fail to run me off, they'll have to stop.

It *has* to stop.

My head is swimming. Jonathan's face wavers in front of me and I'm not sure where to focus my eyes.

"I can't," I manage, then close my eyes, moving slowly to roll onto my other side, facing the window, with my back toward Jonathan.

I don't bother looking at him again even though he stays a few moments longer. He bangs the trash can against the side of the bed when he picks it up but soon the door closes behind him and the smell of vomit recedes. The room is silent, and so is the hallway.

"Say something." My voice is weak and shaking. It doesn't even sound like mine.

Drill pulls the little vinyl chair over next to my bed. When he sits down, he finally meets my gaze, his eyes full of pain. "What am I supposed to say?"

"I don't know." I breathe the words out and hope inspiration will strike. When it doesn't I move my hand slowly, reaching for him.

He sighs, leaning into my touch and resting his head on the mattress near my side. Slowly and gently he moves his arm so it's hugging me around the waist. "When Ritchie told me . . ."

"I told the doctor he couldn't tell anyone what really happened. Not even my mom, though I don't know if that will work if she can find the time to call."

Lifting his head, he nods. "Good. We'll keep it quiet. Let them know that you're not the kind of person who is going to run off and tell."

I don't want to think about the Society. If they did it, and Jonathan's part of it, that means he let it happen. "It could have been an accident. . . ." I let my words trail off because I know how stupid they are. "Matthews and Evers were talking before we started. Kelly and Bekah wouldn't even look at me. You don't think they knew—"

"I don't know."

I don't press it because the thought that any of them—Kelly, Bekah, or Jonathan—knew about this but didn't stop it is too much to take in. "What happens now?"

He tightens his arm, squeezing me in a small hug. He looks so tired. "Tim's on his way here. He called Jax—she's watching their emails. They'll take shifts staying with you. I'm heading back to campus. Huff and I need to put some feelers out, see what's going on."

I don't want him to go. I don't care that his brother will stay here with me. I want it to be Drill.

"I know," he says, even though I haven't voiced any of this to him. "I'll stay until Tim comes, okay?"

But Tim is here too soon. Within a matter of minutes, Drill stands, scooting the chair back where it was. Before he leaves, he moves in close, his words just a whisper of breath against my ear. "If you need me, call. I'll be here in a heartbeat."

I nod, tears burning my eyes. I don't know if they're for me or Dad right now, but it doesn't matter. He kisses my forehead and I close my eyes, determined to remember the feel of his lips on my skin, the strength he's pouring into me.

"Stay safe," he whispers. When he pulls away his eyes look watery, too. But Drill is Drill. He won't let them fall. "I'll be back soon."

I try to give him a smile, something to let him know I'm okay. But all I can do is sit there and watch him leave.

Sometime in the middle of the night while Tim is here, trying to sleep on the stupid little chair they say turns into a bed, they come in and take my vitals and give me more pain medication. I can't get back to sleep, so I'm awake when Jax comes in after five to take her shift. Around six, after she's fallen asleep, they bring breakfast.

Jax is curled up in the chair and I let her sleep, even though her phone pings every few minutes with new notifications. I don't want to know anything yet.

Sunlight streams in the window above her head, haloing her in a soft gold morning ray, but she's got to be uncomfortable and sore as hell. "I can feel you staring at me." She doesn't open her eyes but stretches out one leg, then the other.

"Sorry. I didn't mean to wake you."

"'S okay. What time is it?" She reaches her arms up above her head and stretches like a cat.

"Eight. You missed a delicious breakfast of cold oatmeal and Jell-O."

"I don't eat breakfast." Her stomach growls and she grins. She reaches for her phone, her finger sliding over the screen, her eyes darting back and forth as she reads. "So. What's the word with you?"

"They're releasing me in an hour. I'm heading back to school."

Her eyes lock onto me. "You're not serious."

"I am."

"You can't go anywhere near that school right now. They *shot* you."

"With a rubber bullet. I'm fine." I push the blanket back and swing my legs over the edge of the bed. Lying still all night coupled with the painkillers helped me forget how much moving hurts. The shooting pain that lances down my side makes me glad I'm still sitting. I close my eyes to keep from getting sick, but that only makes it worse. "What's going on with your phone?"

"I get a copy of each email one of them sends." She glances down again as a new message comes in. "Look, I know you're trying to show them you can take whatever they give you, but give yourself a break, Sam. What good is it going to do to go back injured and in pain? They'll just be on you even harder to get you to quit."

She's right, I know, but dammit, I need to be there. "I've got to show them I'm not scared."

"No one thinks you're scared."

"They will if I don't come back." When she doesn't look like she's going to budge I've got to think quick. "What are the emails saying?"

"Nothing. Absolutely nothing."

"Then why do you keep checking? What's going on that you're not telling me?"

"Dean and Tim are just keeping me updated." Hearing Drill's first name disorients me for a second. She flicks through the screens on her phone again. "Your brother is on his way here. There's no sign of Evers or Lyons on campus. Matthews is prowling the deck."

"You've got to get out of here. Jonathan can't see you. If he's part of it I don't want him to see you."

She stands and stretches, reaching her arms above her head. "I still think you need to go home."

"I'll make you a deal."

"I'm listening," she says hesitantly.

"I'll be extra-super careful at school, I promise, but you've got to do some recon. I need proof. If I don't stop them, who will? How long is this going to last, Jax? Five years, ten? Girl after girl after girl? I only have to survive three more months and then it's done. The ones who come after me will have it easier."

She nods, her lips a thin line. "I don't like it, but I'll do it. These bastards deserve to pay." She stands up and gives me one last look. "I'll see what I can find behind mystery door number one." Then she's gone.

If we don't figure out who's involved, I've got no hope of staying. And my new goal, the one I've only just figured out, will be pointless if I can't stick it out long enough to see it through.

I've got to stay. Because it's not just about me making it through the year or surviving a dare anymore.

I'm bringing down the whole damn Society.

Jonathan signs my discharge papers, shakes the doctor's hand, and glares at me. "Do you need help?"

"I'm fine," I say, holding my hand out to the wall as a guide until I get to the wheelchair they're forcing me to ride out in.

"We'll go back, pack up your stuff, and I'll take you to Tim Stamm's house until we can figure out what to do about transferring you to the public high school."

"I'm not leaving." I sit down in the wheelchair trying to keep the wince from showing.

"It's not safe for you here."

"It was just an accident."

He looks down at me for a second and I wonder what he's thinking. Does he know that I'm lying to him—my cadet colonel—an act that could get me kicked out of the DMA? "Dammit, Sam, this isn't a joke anymore. Forget the stupid dare and *go home.*"

"I know it's not a joke. But it would be nice if you'd believe in me. Support me."

He bends down, his voice just a hiss of air in my ear. "I can't do anything without *proof.* Proof you don't have. Proof you'll never be able to get." Then he stands up, speaking normally again. "Besides, you're just a girl trying to survive at the DMA. What you want to do is *impossible.*"

My heart thunders in my chest, shooting pain up and down my side with each pump. Did he just admit to knowing what's going on? "It's not impossible. Hard, sure, with people standing in my way. But I can do it."

"This isn't like jumping into the river or doing a night hike or any of the other hundred dares we did over the years." He pushes the brake down on the wheelchair and jerks roughly on my arm.

"I wish you'd just drop it. Drop everything. This is too much."

"I'm not trying to add to your stress, Jonathan. I'm not trying to ruin things for you, you know."

"Trying or not, you are."

I glance at my watch, the only jewelry I'm permitted as a recruit, so he won't see the tears in my eyes. "All I wanted was to be with you. To make Dad proud."

"That doesn't mean you have to be here. Be a cheerleader, a track star. Succeed at something else. You don't have to take this from me, too."

"All I've ever been is military. You, Amos, and Dad made sure of that."

"Be yourself, okay? Be military in college. Just don't do it *here*."

I want to ask him if he's being himself. If the guy he is here, the hard-ass, squared-away soldier tangling with a secret society, is who he really is, but I don't. By the time I get situated in the car, I'm breathing hard and everything around me is spinning.

"All right, you want to stay? Stay. It's third mess. I'll drop you off at the mess hall. You can march back with your company since you think you're invincible." He spits the words out, disgusted.

To him, it's always a competition. But if he's part of the Society, it's gone way beyond good old-fashioned sibling rivalry now.

During study hall, Nix walks me to the library. He's scanning the PG as we move around it, looking at faces and name tags of each cadet we walk by. Drill hasn't clued them into the Society, but he's told them to keep tabs, to notice who is around. Some look at me curiously—the girl who ended up in the hospital after a Weekend Warrior challenge, though they don't know why. Others glare at me—the girl who won't give up.

My legs are still jelly and the painkiller they gave me at the hospital is wearing off, making every step a trial. When we get to the door of the library, I let out the breath I was holding. "Thanks." In just a few seconds I'll get to sit down with Drill and, once again, try to be a normal teen working on a normal paper, not one whose life is crumbling down around her.

"Get out of my way, recruit."

The words make me jump.

Evers pushes me aside, knocking me into the door and the door handle into my ribs. Pain explodes in my side and I can't help but cry out. When I catch my breath enough to look up, Evers is smiling. And even when he's smiling, Evers looks evil. I'll never understand what Bekah sees in him.

Nix lunges forward and I put a hand on his arm, holding him back even though it feels like my ribs are slicing into my lungs. "Don't," I grit out between clenched teeth.

"Oh, forgive me. Did I bump into you, Recruit McKenna?"

"You messin' with my recruits, Evers?" Drill takes up the entire doorway of the library.

"Wasn't looking where I was going. Didn't mean to. I apologized." Evers doesn't move, challenging Drill.

For a second the air is frozen around us, each of us holding our breath, trying to outlast the others. Drill moves first, stepping toward Evers. "Inside, you two. And don't let me catch you getting in the way of upperclassmen again."

"Drill Sergeant Stamm, yes, Drill Sergeant Stamm!" we yell, scuttling inside.

"Jesus," Nix mutters under his breath. "I'd pay good money to see those two square off."

If I close my eyes I'll see Evers's face again, the threat written plainly for anyone to see. He's untouchable, or at least he thinks so. "I wouldn't," I say. "Listen, I've got to work on a project. . . ."

"I'll be here until you're ready to go." Nix sits down next to me.

"At least go get on the internet or something. You don't need to be bored out of your mind and I know you wouldn't lower yourself to actually study." I grin so he knows I'm playing, but I've got to get him away. Drill and I need to talk and I don't want Nix overhearing anything. He disappears into the movie room, though he sits by the door so he can see me.

When Drill finally reappears, my foot is tap dancing on the floor. "You okay?" he asks, sitting across from me. "How do you feel?"

"I'm fine." I ignore the steady throb coming from my side. "What's going on?"

"Not here." He changes the subject before I can ask him more questions. "So, I pulled General Denmark's old journals from the archives for the article we have to write." He reaches into his backpack and pulls out four old leather-bound books, setting them on the table between us. Beneath the table he stretches his legs out, resting one against my calf.

"Right. Normal high school stuff. A paper on the man who

founded this wonderful institute of learning." I pull the top one off the stack and open it. The handwriting is small, but uses all the curlicues they liked in the old days, making it look very impressive and important, though it's probably just about what he ate for breakfast. "It doesn't look like anyone has read these in the last million years. This is going to take forever to get through."

"I don't think so. We'll keep it easy. Focus on the founding of the DMA. Why he really opened it and what happened in that first year."

I bite my lip to keep from grinning. His foot presses against mine. I scoot my chair in closer and now we're knee to knee. He drops a hand below the table, leaning forward like he's trying to read the journal I have open upside down. A second later, his fingers open and close on my knee, sending tendrils of electricity shooting in every direction.

Heat sears my face. I shift a little, sinking down in my seat, his hand moving an inch or two higher on my leg. To keep from looking at him, I start skimming the journal. The words aren't familiar but something about it . . . "Wait a second." I slide up in my chair, bending down over the pages, ignoring the sting of pain in my ribs at the sudden movement. "I recognize this handwriting."

"You make a habit of reading a dead military general's journals?" But Drill sits up, too, paying attention.

"Not usually, but I've seen this writing before. It was in the letter about blood wings Jax showed me over Christmas." I'm whispering now, scared that someone will overhear. "But why would Denmark write that letter?"

I see something click in Drill's eyes, and he grabs the journals, tucking them back into his backpack. "Where's Nix?"

"He's on the computer. Why?" I search his face but he's not giving anything away.

"You need to go back to the barracks." His eyes scan the room, taking in every cadet here.

"Why? Tell me what you've figured out."

"I've got to be sure first. It can't be. I mean . . ." He shakes his head and doesn't even continue. "Get Nix. Get back to the barracks. I'll come talk to you soon, okay?" He's zipping his backpack and pauses before he walks away. "Be careful."

"Why don't I just meet you in the armory tonight?"

"No," he says. "You're hurt." He leans in close, despite all the people around. "Promise me you'll stay in the barracks tonight, Sam." There's an urgency in his voice I've never heard before.

I nod in agreement because I don't know what to say. He stays until I go get Nix and we all leave the library at the same time.

But a week later, Drill still hasn't explained his little freak-out. He acts like it didn't happen at all. Other than class stuff and how to write our paper, Drill says nothing more of the handwriting. Matthews refuses to let me participate in company training or the Weekend Warrior challenges so I continue reading Denmark's journals, but they just leave more questions than answers.

After English, I hang back, waiting for all the other cadets to leave before approaching Professor Williams. Drill notices and waits with me. "What are you doing, Mac?"

"Miss McKenna, Mr. Stamm. How may I help you?" Professor

Williams smiles and leans back against his desk.

"Sir, we think we've found something interesting to report about General Denmark."

"That's wonderful, Miss McKenna."

"We've run into a problem, though." I keep my gaze on the professor. Drill stiffens at my side. "See, I've been reading through the journals and this one"—I pull the journal in question out of my backpack—"just stops."

"Sam," Drill says through clenched teeth. "I told you I'd look into it. I'm sorry, Professor . . ."

"You haven't talked to me in a week," I snap, tired of being left in the dark and not caring that Professor Williams is hearing this. "I'm not just going to sit back and wait."

"I'm on it. Can't you just—"

"If this has something to do—"

"Is there something you wanted from *me*, Miss McKenna?" Professor Williams's head pivots back and forth between us like he's at a tennis match.

"In this journal Denmark's talking about a select group of cadets he wants to put in charge of disciplinary hearings, but then just stops. There's nothing more. I've looked through the next journal, but it doesn't mention anything else about this group."

"Professor," Drill says, "this isn't the focus of our project, it's just something on the side that Sam got interested in. It's not important."

"Generally I encourage this type of associative research. If one thing leads to another, then the researcher has an obligation to put the pieces together, to give us a whole view of the subject for the report."

I shoot Drill a look, happy to be right.

"However," he continues, his voice laced with warning, "I have to agree with Mr. Stamm. I think you should stick to the Denmark we all know about. Sometimes when a person stops talking about something . . . it's for a reason."

There's a knock at the classroom door and Evers walks in. Drill grabs the journal out of my hand and slides it into his backpack, nudging me to take a step back.

"Professor Williams, I need to talk to you about a project."

"Cadet Evers, we were just finishing up here." He turns to us, clearing his throat. "Thank you all for your update. Again, staying broad, focusing on just a general character sketch—that's the assignment."

"Thank you, Professor," Drill says. "Recruit McKenna, you've wasted enough of the professor's time. Let's go."

"Thank you, sir." I follow Drill out of the room, glancing back once at Evers but he's already shutting the door.

"Keep walking. Go to your next class. We'll talk later." I start to argue but he won't let me. "Just listen for once, okay? Please, Sam," he begs.

"Okay, but we're not done talking about this." I push open the door to the building and step outside.

THIRTY-TWO

CADETS MOVE LIKE ANTS AROUND THE PG AND I KEEP TO THE gutters, eyes straight ahead, though I'm committing the name of each cadet I pass to memory. Some of the names are becoming familiar and I'll add them to the list when I get back to the barracks. Possible members of the Society. Evers has kept a low profile since his meeting with Williams, but even though Jax is looking, we haven't found a connection between that visit and the professor's mysterious absence from classes for the past week.

I pull open the door to the lab. A few cadets are scattered around. Drill is in the back row at the computer I usually use.

"You can sit back here, recruit. I'm just finishing up work on our PowerPoint." He sounds genuine enough, but his eyes don't meet mine—they're scanning the other cadets in the computer lab.

"Hi," I say quietly when I sit next to him. Ritchie, my sidekick for the evening, sits a few computers down. "Any word on Professor Williams?"

"No. Still the same story—his wife is sick and he's taking emergency leave."

"You don't really believe that, do you?" With Bekah as my roommate it's been impossible to sneak out for PT with him and Huff. We haven't even had a chance to talk it through, but it's got to be the Society. Evers must have known what we were talking about and now Williams is gone. "Drill?"

"Stop," he whispers. He's not looking at me, but he's serious. His jaw is tensed and his hands curl into fists on his lap.

Jonathan moves to the first row of computers and Lyons enters seconds later. Drill sucks in a breath and I almost stand and salute, doing my stupid recruit duties and yelling, "Officer on deck!"

Drill puts his hand on my arm to keep me seated. "He hasn't noticed you yet. Just sit." His eyes don't leave Jonathan and the senior beside him; he looks upset.

They're deep in conversation, sitting at the computers but not logging on. Even though they're hunched close together, Jonathan's hands are moving, a sure sign he's worked up about something.

To my left, Drill sits alert, muscles tense, like he's waiting to spring. "Do what you need to do, but be quick about it. I'm walking you back to the barracks."

When I've logged in to my email, Jax's is the only unread mail I have. Finally. It's been three weeks since the shooting. Three weeks since I've heard from her.

I try to ignore Drill next to me. He's like a coil of balled up energy, ready to strike. My eyes skim the email.

> To: smckenna@dma.edu
>
> From: jaxhax@email.com
>
> Subject: News
>
> We need to meet. I know who shot you. But more than that. I have a NAME.

Drill's quick intake of breath makes me jump. His eyes are on my computer screen and I log off the computer without responding.

"I'm ready," I whisper, my voice shaking. I glance at him again but his eyes are back on Jonathan.

"I'm going to stop and talk to him. You go by like you don't even notice. I'll meet you outside."

It's just Jonathan. I shouldn't have to sneak by him. But he's with Lyons, and with our suspicions, we've got to be cautious. Ritchie sees us getting ready and packs his stuff up. As Drill passes Ritchie, he whispers something and goes on ahead.

"Colonel McKenna, glad to see you here," Drill hoists his backpack on his shoulder and walks over to the aisle of computers Jonathan is at. He stands blocking Jonathan's view of the aisle, of us.

Ritchie nudges me and we walk by as quickly as we can.

"My recruits have some questions about Junior Ring. . . ." His voice fades away as Ritchie and I make our way out of the science building and onto the PG.

"What was that about?" Ritchie asks.

"I wish I knew."

"What's going on, Mac? Everyone knows there's something up."

The night's gotten colder and I shiver, standing there waiting. My side is almost pain-free, the remnants of the bruise all but gone. It's not fair that my recruit brothers are doing all this work and don't know what's going on. I'm about to tell him when Drill appears.

"Ritchie, head back to the barracks," Drill says as soon as he's next to me.

"Drill Sergeant Stamm, yes, Drill Sergeant Stamm."

I shrug, promising myself I'll tell him later. "Drill . . . ," I say. As soon as Ritchie is out of hearing range, we start walking. My teeth chatter. I feel like if I could just get warm, things would be better.

"We need to meet with Jax. All of us need to be on the same page. Let's meet tomorrow night in the armory. I'll text Jax."

It's about time that he tells me what he's been keeping to himself.

"And, Sam?" He takes a step toward me. His breath is white, hanging in the air for just a second before disappearing. "I'm sorry. About all this."

The lump in my throat makes it impossible to talk.

After the trumpeter sounds retreat on the PG the next night, I lie in bed, counting the seconds until Bekah's even breathing comes from the bottom bunk. I want to know if she was in on the shooting, if she knows who Evers is involved with—but we're past confiding in each other.

When she's finally asleep, I move quietly around the room, pulling on my hoodie and tying my shoes. I leave the door unlocked when I leave but don't sign out.

"Where are we going?" Nix whispers once we're outside.

"The armory."

"Any chance you're going to tell me why?"

"You'll find out soon." I lead him the back way around campus, behind the barracks on the service road to keep out of the lights around the PG.

Drill's waiting impatiently by the door when we get there. "I thought something had happened," he says, and I immediately feel guilty.

"I had to wait for Bekah to fall asleep. If she found out, she would have told Evers."

"Get in here. Hey, Nix."

Nix looks confused at the sudden "at ease" of everything but enters the armory anyway. "Drill Sergeant . . ."

"Man," Jax says before I even make it halfway across the basketball court. "You have got them in a tizzy. They thought you were gone after the bullet."

I wrap my arms around her, squeezing tight before stepping back. "Thanks for coming."

"I wouldn't miss this for the world. It's bad, though."

"What do you mean?"

"I still don't know who we're dealing with on campus. I've hacked a lot of emails lately. Some of them are DMA addresses. That's what Evers and Matthews use. Lyons, too. That's how I knew who took the shot."

"You're sure about Evers?" Drill asks.

"Yeah. I've got the email that confirms it."

"Good. We're going to need every little scrap of proof we can get."

"So, besides the obvious, why's it bad?"

"I think the Society could be bigger. It could be *huge*." She's talking fast. "Once in a while, they get emails from an unknown address. The message is just a bunch of weird code, and I can't figure out what it's saying. I don't know all the receivers, but it goes to *hundreds* of people. The only thing I know for sure is a name. The Pandora Society."

There it is, as simple as that. Three words for a group that wants me out so bad they might kill me. A group my brother might be in charge of.

Drill shakes his head. "We don't know that for sure. The people threatening Sam could be any number of groups. . . ."

"Wait," I say. "You've heard of them?"

He nods.

"The discipline committee Denmark created." I don't ask because it's all falling into place. Why he didn't want me asking Williams, why he freaked when Evers walked into the classroom.

He nods again. "But they haven't been active for decades."

"You're right. They've been pretty quiet for a while," Jax says. "I can't find anything certain. But I *think* that's who it is. And if I'm right, these are some pretty bad dudes."

"Am I missing something? Who are these guys?" I wish my voice sounded a bit stronger.

"Denmark's discipline committee was a group of cadets whose only job was to remove from the DMA any cadet who didn't measure up to their standards. From what I can tell, they were first trying to deal with African-Americans, maybe gays. Trying to keep the DMA, and the military as a whole, pure."

"Right. Like Hitler, or Voldemort." I try to laugh it off. "It worked out so well for both of them."

"The Pandora Society is no joke, Sam," Drill says.

I stop laughing. "I don't think it is."

Drill pushes the issue. "The reason there are only rumors is because anyone they've set their sights on won't talk—or *can't* talk. Once they mark someone to remove from the DMA, the person is gone. The Pandora Society doesn't fail. They're good at what they do."

"I guess I should be honored that they came out of hiding just for me."

"So, I've been trying to decode the emails, and then I realized it doesn't matter. It's not what they're saying right now; it's *who* they're saying it to. Once in the Society, always in the Society." Jax pauses, waiting for her words to sink in.

There are other secret groups like that—Skull and Bones, which is rumored to be a favorite society among presidential hopefuls, the Illuminati, the group that supposedly plants members in the government to try to control the world. But this is just the DMA . . . if it's bigger than this campus, it could stretch all the way up the military ranks.

"I think they might have some kind of secure server. Something I can only hack from the inside. If I can get into it, I can see who these emails are going to. And if I know who they're emailing . . ."

"You'll know who's in the Society," I say. "What's your plan?"

"After the Junior Ring Dance, the Society is going to decide positions for next year and which initiates will become full-fledged members. Remember the tunnels I emailed about?"

Drill shoots me a look. "What tunnels?"

"Jax found some old plans for the school. There are tunnels underground and she thinks that's where they meet." I wasn't trying to keep it from him, but he looks hurt just the same.

"I'm going to go down there and get what I need," Jax says.

"It's not like you can just go to the dance with Matthews and tag along to the meeting. How are you going to get in?"

"Easy. I'll follow Kelly. Once I know where they are, I'll wait until the meeting is over. Then I'll sneak in to find the server."

"What? No. That's not an option."

"We need the names, Sam. Besides, the only way we're going to get Kelly back is if we prove to him how bad they are."

Why the hell isn't Drill saying no? This idea is crazy. Drill agrees with Jax, though. "It's all we've got, Sam. We've got to figure out who we're dealing with. I can't keep staying up twenty-four/seven trying to watch everyone. Even with Huff's help we can't do it all. If we can get a list of members, we can go to the commandant. Secret societies are banned. They'll be kicked out of school."

"It's too dangerous. I don't want anyone getting hurt because of me."

"You can't do this on your own." Nix puts his arm around my shoulder. "They've trained us all year to be a unit, to go into battle. You—*this*—it's worth fighting for, Mac."

"*She's* not part of the family, though," I insist, nodding at Jax. "What if they hurt her?"

"They *won't*." Jax sounds so sure of herself. "Kelly won't let anything happen to me. I know you think he's switched to the dark side, but if it's me or Matthews, he'll choose me."

"Nothing's more important than this right now," Drill says. "After Junior Ring, we'll know exactly who we're dealing with."

I don't think everything's going to be okay at all, but Jax looks determined. She doesn't understand that if something happens to her, or any of them, it's going to be my fault. I couldn't save Katie and that thought weighs like a heavy brick in my stomach as Nix and I make our way back to the barracks.

"Sirs! Good morning, sirs! This is the outstanding Alpha Company, sirs! It is the tenth day in the fourth month in the year of our Lord two-thousand-fifteen," I yell through the uniform of the day. No one cares, anyway. What they care about comes next. "Juniors, attention, juniors. Today is Junior Ring Ceremony!"

The roar on deck is deafening. Even knowing what Jax is going to try to do tonight, it's hard not to get caught up in their excitement. I bite the inside of my cheek to keep from smiling.

Until Evers walks out of his room. "You should have gone home after you got shot, McKenna. It would all have ended then. Now you've ruined everything."

I keep my eyes locked straight ahead, trying not to let any reaction show on my face. My heart speeds up, though, and I want to take a step back. He's got a shirt on this morning, as opposed to the other days when he walks to the bathroom in just his boxers. He's moving a little slower than normal, left arm cradled around his stomach. There's a bruise on his arm, partly covered by his sleeve. His eyes are hard, furious.

Before he disappears into the bathroom, though, I notice the blood. Up on his shoulder, where his Society tattoo is. Blood oozes out and through the fabric of his shirt. Something happened to him.

I finish morning calls and head straight to inspection, eager to see Jonathan for the first time since the hospital. He's losing weight. There are shadows under his eyes, dark circles that only make him look worse. Maybe the pressure of the Society is getting to be too much for him.

Jonathan refuses to choose me as the most polished recruit during inspection, even though the guy he does choose has scuffed low quarters and a smeared belt buckle. Just another chance for me to screw up our Company of the Year points. I skip first mess and head directly to the chapel.

"How can I help you, Sam?"

I shut the door to Rev's office behind me and sit, though I can't stay still. My leg shakes, bouncing up and down while I drum my fingers on my legs. "Professor Williams is gone. Jax is going to try to get into the Society's secret cave, or whatever she thinks is in the tunnel. Jonathan and Kelly both look sick. It's all because of me and it's too much." Dad would hate to see me so shaken. He'd tell me to stand up, to take it like a man.

"You've got them scared. I would assume that they never thought a female, even one of your caliber, would bring into question their core beliefs. Everyone makes choices about how they live their lives, the way they're going to move toward success. You have chosen an honorable route. Honorable people, people of character and moral uprightness, can be intimidating. With your family name behind you, I'd say you have a chance of being a shining star at the DMA. It doesn't sound like this Society is ready for that much change."

I think of what Evers said this morning, how I'd ruined everything. "Well, it's not fair."

Rev chuckles. "My dear, my job is to teach about the unfair parts of life and how to shine even in the midst of strife. Many of these boys could not do what you are doing. I know you feel alone, but you've got a strong corps of students and faculty behind you. Supporting you."

A banging on the door makes me jump and I stand quickly, glancing at Rev.

"Just a moment," Rev calls out. He points to the corner and I step over three stacks of papers to get there. When I'm in place, he opens the door and hides me at the same time. "Can I—"

"Have you seen Mac?" Drill sounds frantic.

"I'm here." I step away from the corner and Drill takes two steps, wrapping me in his arms and squeezing for all he's worth. I breathe in, relaxing instantly at his touch, at the smell of his aftershave, spicy and crisp.

"You scared the hell out of me. Are you okay?" He scans my face.

I nod. "Why wouldn't I be?"

"Ritchie couldn't find you. He's supposed to be walking

everywhere with you. You're supposed to have someone with you." He sounds angry, but his hands are gentle and he rests his forehead against mine and closes his eyes.

"I'm sorry. After inspection I just came here."

"It's not safe—"

"I know. I understand. . . ."

Rev clears his throat. "I think I'm going to go get some coffee from the mess hall. I'll be back in fifteen minutes or so."

"Thanks, Rev," Drill says without taking his eyes off me. When the door closes, he takes his hands from my face only to link his fingers with mine. "What the hell were you thinking?"

"Something is wrong with Evers. He's got bruises on his arms."

"What?"

"And his tattoo—it's bleeding, like it's been cut. During morning calls he said I'd ruined everything. I just . . . I have a bad feeling." I can't shake the thought that something is pressing down on this campus, just waiting for the perfect moment to implode around us all.

"Maybe you messed up his mission when he shot you and you didn't quit. If they've done something to his tattoo, removed it or burned it or something, it might mean they're booting him from the Society."

"Great. Just another reason for him to be gung ho about getting me out. Now I definitely don't want Jax getting involved."

"I know you're scared, but it's all we've got right now. If we don't figure out who's in the Society, we'll never take them down. I'll follow her tonight, okay? She'll be safe. As long as you stay at the dance, no one will suspect anything. We've got to act like it's business as usual, like we don't know anything's going on." He sighs, sitting down in the chair I was in just a few minutes ago. He looks so tired.

I walk over to him and he pulls me down onto his lap. I fit perfectly, his arms wrapped around me to keep me close. "Kelly and Bekah are sneaking out and going to Wintergreen."

"I heard. Lyons rented a condo at the ski resort. You're sure they're going?"

"Bekah told me earlier." Though time has dragged most of the year, now I don't have enough of it. I thought I'd at least get a chance to tell Kelly I know and beg him not to sign on to what the Pandora Society wants him to do. "I need to talk to Kelly."

"I don't think that's a good idea. The less they know you know, the better right now."

I resist the urge to argue. I know he's right. "I guess. Do you think Jonathan's really involved?"

"I hope not. I really, really hope not." He pauses. "If I'm following Jax, I won't be able to protect you. Your recruit buddies are going to be watching, but they don't stand a chance against the Society. The only people I trust are *my* recruit buddies, but there are only so many of them." For the first time since everything started, he looks scared. "How am I supposed to make sure you're okay?" His hands grip my shoulders, thumbs trailing along my neck.

"They'll all be at the meeting, right? I'm going to be the safe one tonight." And as much as I want to call it off, we can't back down now. We have to figure out who is involved if we're going to take them down.

Rev whistles as he enters the chapel and I stand up. The ghosts of Drill's hands are still on my shoulders, giving me strength I wouldn't have otherwise.

"I'll be okay. I'm more worried about Jax tonight than anything."

"I'll take care of Jax. Huff will watch over you."

"I don't want to keep him away from—"

"Give him some credit. It may be our junior year, but some things are more important than getting drunk, even when it's the only time the entire faculty looks the other way and lets us do it out in the open."

"Thank you. For helping me. Even when I act like I don't want it."

One corner of his mouth turns up. "You're Alpha, Mac. You're one of my recruits. And you're . . ." He takes my hand but doesn't step closer. It seems safer this way, less intimate, although I still feel the need to be close to him, even though I know I shouldn't. "If you were anyone else . . ."

I smile sadly. "If I were anyone, you wouldn't give me a second thought."

Drill squeezes my hand, a last hurrah before we go to battle. "I think we'd better go out at different times. Stay and talk to Rev. Call D.C. Your mom and dad should be back by now, right?"

Talking to Mom might be just the thing to keep me on track. Besides, knowing Dad fought and survived gives me the strength I need to do the same.

"Wait until Ritchie gets here before you leave. I don't care if you miss class or not." Drill looks at me for a moment before he opens the door to Rev's office. "Be safe tonight."

THIRTY-THREE

JAX KNOCKS ON MY DOOR TEN HOURS LATER, A DRESS BAG in her hand. "I know you said you'd go in your dress blues, but that's ridiculous. You've got the chance to wear civilian clothes, and if you're going to prom, you might as well dress up for it, right?"

"You really didn't have to." I haven't worn a dress since Dad finally got Mom to back off on making me a girly-girl like her, but when she unzips the bag, I can't help but smile. The dress is the color of arctic ice, a blue that matches Drill's eyes to a tee. The fabric is shimmery and silky and will reach the floor when I put it on. I don't even ask how she knows my shoe size, but the two-inch heels she hands me are incredible. "It's perfect. Thanks."

"Hey, what are friends for?"

I want to tell her I don't know, that I've never really had a friend like her before, but I can't get the words out and it doesn't seem like she's waiting for an answer anyway.

"Where's the infamous roommate?"

I lock the door behind us, just so we get some warning when Bekah reappears. "She got a pass to go into town to get her hair done. I declined her invitation to come along."

"She still distancing herself?"

"Ever since the shooting it's gotten worse. With Kelly, too."

She shakes her head but doesn't respond. Instead, she shakes the dress out and holds it up to me.

I can't stop the eye roll. "Are you sure you have to do this?" Maybe she's got a bad feeling, too, and just needs a push to cancel the whole plan.

"Please. It's a high school dance. What could go wrong?"

I don't even bother bringing up the drunk driving, pregnancies, and fights that tend to happen at normal high school proms, because this isn't a normal high school. This is the DMA.

"Get dressed, McKenna. I need time to do your hair."

"My hair? Really?"

She laughs. "Relax. For one night, just relax."

I try to do what she says, and relax. Business as usual. Everyone goes to prom.

The armory, where we first swore our oaths to the DMA, is all decked out for the party. Streamers hang from the ceiling; strings of lights line the walls. A giant replica DMA class ring stands in the corner. One by one, the juniors, looking sharp in their dress blues, and their dates stand under its arch and smile for the photographer.

Music thumps through the speakers and bodies press together on the floor. Most of the guys in Alpha Company have dates from their hometowns or local high school girls they've met at games throughout the year.

I spend the first hour of the dance leaning against the wall, watching Drill and Huff scanning the group and moving around, talking to their friends and celebrating. But after a while, Nix gets impatient babysitting a wallflower and pulls me out on the dance floor.

"We're at a dance, Mac. At least attempt to play the part, okay?" But his eyes are on Kelly, and even dancing, I constantly scan the room.

Matthews and his date are practically having sex on the dance floor, though he looks at Bekah frequently. None of the faculty uses their chaperone status for anything other than catching a show. Bekah dances with Wilson, though Evers dances close, keeping an eye on her. She looks stunning in a floor-length green dress with a slit almost up to her hip. Her hair falls in perfect curls around her face, the rest in a trio of braids that weave like a snake down her back. Even though we're not talking anymore, I hate to think how the Society is going to try to get rid of her once I'm out of the picture.

"You doing okay?" Ritchie says, trying to be quiet but yelling over the music. He and Nix have been alternating babysitting duty for the last hour.

"Huh?" I pull my thoughts away from Bekah. "Oh, yeah, I'm fine," I get out, but I pull away, fanning myself. "I need a drink."

"I'll come with you."

"Stay. I'll be right back." We've been dancing for two hours and no one's disappeared yet. Maybe Jax got the date of the meeting mixed up.

Away from the press of the crowd I can breathe a little easier. It's hot as hell inside and I grab a napkin off the table to wipe the back of my neck. When I feel a hand on my side, snaking around to my stomach, I jump.

"It's just me," Drill whispers in my ear, dropping his hand to his side. He turns to grab a cup and fills it with punch. "You look amazing." His gaze keeps moving down to my dress, though each time his eyes come back to my face. He runs a hand from my shoulder to my fingers, making me shiver.

My heart races as I take in the sight of his uniform. He looks good too. It's hard to swallow and I glance back at the people dancing. "Someone's going to see." The words come out breathy and for a second I'm not sure I even said them.

He leans into me, grabbing a grape and popping it in his mouth. The heat of his body sends me into a tailspin. "Let them."

"Stamm," a voice says.

Drill freezes. I wish I could disappear.

"Stamm," Huff says again.

His eyes half closed, Drill sighs and pulls away just enough that I can slide to the side and breathe some cooler, less Drill-filled air.

"They're on the move. You need to go." Huff looks nervous, glancing from Drill to the packed dance floor just a few steps away.

"Make sure she gets back. Make sure Ritchie and Nix are

outside her room. If anything happens to her—"

"It won't. I won't let it. I care about her, too. Now, go, before you lose them completely."

"Get back to your room. Stay safe." Then he's gone, off to fight my battle for me.

Back at the dorm, I try to swallow away my fear. Ritchie heads to his room to change into PT gear, grab a blanket, and park outside my room for first watch. I change into camo and sit at my window, trying to keep my leg from bouncing completely off.

Out on the PG, just a few people are around. No one is walking in straight lines, though. How the commandant willingly lets this happen is beyond me. It's amazing what private schools can get away with.

Where the hell are you, Jax? The clock has ticked slowly past midnight, then one. She should be back by now. I need to be doing something—searching barracks, looking for a way in to Jax's mysterious tunnels to rescue her—but the watchdogs outside my room won't even let me go to the bathroom without an escort.

I cross my arms on the sill and lay my head down, looking at the PG sideways and imagining everything at the DMA tilting over over over until it collapses into a pile of chaos. Then I close my eyes.

A noise from somewhere behind me makes me jump, my heart in my throat. I grab the closest thing to me, my KB, and hold the history of the DMA out in front of me like a sword. "Who's there?"

"It's me, Sam."

"Shit, Jax. You scared the hell out of me. What time is it? Did I fall asleep?"

"It's just after four. Where's your computer?"

"I don't have one. It's against regs."

"Fine, let's go."

I can barely make sense of what she's talking about. "Go? Go where?"

"Tim's house, I guess."

"Why?"

She holds something up in her hand—a small flash drive the size of her thumb. "I got it."

The list of Pandora Society members.

I grab my hoodie and pause only long enough to lock the door before we run outside, Ritchie and Nix following close behind, thankful that it's still the middle of the night and we'll be able to get to Tim's house without anyone seeing us.

Soon, at least, we'll know who we're dealing with.

Jax looks worried, but she's smiling, eager to take the next steps in our battle. "Boy, have you decided to bite the toe off a big fucking lion."

THIRTY-FOUR

THREE DAYS AFTER JUNIOR RING, THUNDER CRACKLES across the sky, exploding over Stonewall Hall. The rain that's plagued us for forty-eight hours has left the campus a muddy, soggy mess. Drill's been off deck every evening this week, busy with Tim as they sort through the list of names we got. Over three hundred in all, but no DMA students. It's way worse than that.

The list reads like a who's who of military brass. Matthews's dad is front and center at the top of the list, not that it surprised any of us. We don't have anything on the students here other than our "possible Society members" list. And there's no way we can tackle the big list—not yet. There are too many heavy hitters for us to go throwing accusations, even with the proof we've got. We need to start small.

Another clap of thunder makes me jump. "Crap. Weekend Warrior is going to suck."

"About that . . . ," Bekah begins.

I haven't had the courage to ask her about Evers yet, but I'm going to tonight. "Let me guess. You'll be at a track meet."

"All weekend long. It's an invitational."

"Why not just tell your coach you can't go?"

"I got a scholarship to come here because of track."

"It's a military school. Your coach will understand. You just want to hook up with Evers all weekend." She doesn't have a quick comeback like I expect and I turn to her. It's my opening. "Uh-oh. Trouble in paradise?"

"It might not be . . . paradise . . . anymore."

I keep my "I told you so" to myself and pick my pen back up, acting like I don't care. It's a surefire way to get her to open up.

"Fine. He got in a fight with Matthews and Lyons after the dance." After the Society meeting. "They're not hanging out anymore. He's getting really moody."

I'm sure he is. Drill's assumption that he's getting kicked out of the Society must be right. And if he's out, that puts Bekah in a dangerous place. She's turned her back on me but I can't stop worrying about her. I reach for my shoes to keep myself busy.

"What are you doing?"

"It's almost company time. Just preparing for the inevitable."

She glances at her watch, then bites her lip. "Crap. I've got to go to a study group." She throws a book into her backpack and hoists it on her shoulder.

"You're kidding, right? I mean—"

The knock on the door is so conveniently timed it's not funny. Kelly pokes his head in, looking at Bekah. "You ready? Wilson's waiting."

"Yeah." She doesn't sound happy, though, and for the first time she drags her feet as she leaves. "See you later, Mac."

At least Kelly has the decency to look a little embarrassed as he and Bekah sneak off, again missing company time. But if they're gone, maybe Matthews won't be here for the smoke show. Maybe that means Drill is finally back.

"On the wall, Worms!" Matthews and Julius yell five minutes later, running up and down the hall, kicking the trash cans into our rooms and letting the doors slam shut. Guess I can't be that lucky.

I don't know how long it's been, but we're all at our breaking point. Matthews orders us onto our backs, heads off the floor, legs hovering six inches above the ground. "Still haven't gotten rid of your dead weight, Alpha. I know you think she's one of you but she's going to do nothing but hold you back! The rest of this year, and even in the coming years." Matthews screams over the music; he's been yelling so much tonight he's almost as hoarse as he was at the end of Hell Week. "She's going to hurt you every step of the way. Look at what she's cost you already. You are the only class in the history of the DMA to not be recognized as cadets before Christmas! And now it's almost the end of the fucking year! It's pathetic. That's *her* fault!"

I grit my teeth as he gets closer, determined to keep my legs up as long as he's talking. My abs shake, sweat drips down my face, but I won't break. And that's more than some of my recruit buddies can say. Nix is already sitting up on my left when Julius gives the command to change to jumping jacks.

Before I can get up, though, Matthews crouches in front of me, his face contorted in anger. "You think you can get to us? Like we don't know what you set up on Junior Ring?"

"Corporal Matthews, this recruit—" My racing pulse has nothing to do with the PT now.

"Save it. You can come at us with guns blazing. It's not going to make a difference. We have always ruled this school. We will continue to rule this school. You're just a blip on our radar. One that will be gone before the year is over."

"Corporal Matthews," I say, my lips turning up, mimicking his signature sneer, "the corporal said that at the beginning of the year. But this recruit is still here, and will be here long after the corporal is gone, Corporal Matthews."

He pushes down on my shoulder and my abs can't support the weight. My head slams against the floor and I immediately roll onto my stomach, trying to find grip on the slick floor. I start pushing up but a sharp pain in my side sends me back to the ground. It happens a second time. Then a third.

Matthews's boot. Kicking me in the side—right where the rubber bullet hit. I feel something crack. Spots cloud my vision. Tears stream down my face, mixing with the sweat. I cry out but no one hears over the music and they're all too focused on their own pain to see what's happening to me on the ground at the end of the hall anyway.

"Keep it up, McKenna. Things have changed in the Society.

You'll pay for that one."

When he steps back I struggle to get up, bent over and keeping an arm protectively at my side.

"Five minutes 'til lights-out, Worms. Hurry the hell up!" Matthews storms off the deck and I suck in a ragged breath.

"You okay, Mac?" Ritchie and Nix are standing next to me now, but they're both going to get reamed if Matthews sees us talking.

I nod, taking one shaky step, then another. I just make it to the bathroom before I throw up.

THIRTY-FIVE

THE NEXT DAY, CAMPUS IS SOGGY BUT AT LEAST IT'S DRYING out. It takes everything in me to march to the mess hall. I've got to focus hard just to stay upright. I think Matthews cracked a rib last night.

"Company! Halt!"

I force my body to stop its forward momentum, wincing as I do. At least we're corporal-free for second mess. I don't think I could handle looking at Matthews without either throwing up or punching him.

"McKenna, stay back a moment," Drill says after he dismisses the company to lunch. The thundering feet of my recruit buddies fade away. "Are you okay? You didn't look well this morning and you look worse now."

I want to tell him what happened last night, but not here,

where anyone can see. *I'll tell you tonight.* I mouth the words, then speak loudly in case the upperclassmen milling around are paying attention. "Drill Sergeant Stamm, this recruit is fine, Drill Sergeant."

"Very well. Fall out," he says, but he's not happy.

Jogging, even though every step sends shooting pain spider-webbing across my side, I head into the mess hall. I trudge over to the soup and salad bar, my stomach rolling from the pain in my ribs.

"Tomato soup, please. And, can I have it in a cup?" I say to the cafeteria lady. It's all I can manage. I'm not sure I'm going to be able to keep anything down.

"Right away, dear." She moves around behind the counter and, a few seconds later, hands me a cup of soup. "We're proud of you, sweetie. Keep it up."

Her kindness is almost too much. I try to smile and walk away, heading to my table. I sit, but the smell of food just makes me feel worse.

"You okay, McKenna?" Kelly whispers. It's the first time he's spoken directly to me in months.

I shake my head before I remember he's the enemy. Nix is at the other end of the table—too far away to notice, and I can't take the time to alert him. I've got to get away. Pushing my chair back, I abandon my food and wind my way through tables full of cadets talking and laughing. I shouldn't have come.

Outside, the PG comes in and out of focus as I head to the barracks. My head spins and more than once I almost fall. Once inside the safety of the stairwell of Stonewall Hall, I lean against the wall to catch my breath.

The door opens but I can't even force myself to stand at attention. Kelly is in my face. "Okay. Enough. What the hell is going on?"

"What are you talking about? I'm fine." I force myself to start walking up the stairs. We're still not supposed to be talking and the last thing I need is another reason for Matthews to smoke us again tonight.

"I'm your recruit brother, Mac," he says. He takes the stairs two at a time until he beats me to the landing. "I know I haven't acted like it, but I am."

His face is so close to mine I can smell the mint ice cream he had for dessert. "You *are* my recruit buddy, but you're something else, too." I put my hand on his chest over his name tag, where Matthews drilled the pins into his skin. "I know, Kelly. I don't understand why, but I know you're involved with the Pandora Society."

His eyes go wide but he doesn't deny it.

"I don't know what they're giving you that your company can't—"

"My whole life people have depended on me. My brother, my parents. Everything I do revolves around them somehow. Help Mom to help my brother. Help my brother to help Mom. It never ends." He releases my hand and then punches the wall. "Matthews doesn't expect anything from me other than for me to be the best soldier I can be. He pushes me to be the strongest version of myself. It's not about me helping anyone else. For once, it's just about *me*."

I don't laugh only because it would hurt too much. "Sure. You, turning against your company. Against me."

He looks hurt. "It didn't start out that way."

"Of course it didn't." I push my anger at Kelly aside. If he's opening up, I've got to keep him talking. "Something's changed in the Society hasn't it?"

Kelly shakes his head. "Yes—no. How do you know about this?"

"Your *friends* have been trying to get me to quit all year," I say, my ribs pounding the more agitated I get. "They've just gotten a little more aggressive lately. That means something's changed."

"What do you mean 'more aggressive'? What's wrong, Mac?"

"Screw it. You really want to know?" I pull up my camo blouse and the brown shirt underneath, my ribs purple and black for him to see.

"What the hell?" He bends down, putting his hand on my side and inspecting the bruise. "What happened?"

I hiss in a breath. "Your precious Society. Matthews. The changes a little more than you expected?"

"He didn't—"

"Like hell he didn't. His boot did this last night when you were conveniently away. Still think he's a good guy?"

"I didn't know. I swear I didn't know, Sam. We had an initiate meeting." He pleads, gripping my hands in his. "You can't think I would have let them do this if I had known. I knew they were *saying* things. But I didn't know he'd kick you."

"That's not all they've done. They hit me with frozen snowballs. They *shot* me."

"Why didn't you tell me?"

"Because you're *with* them, Kelly. You're one of them! You and Wilson both!"

"You've been going through this all alone?" His face is scrunched up and he won't meet my eyes.

"Of course not. Jax has been helping me. And other people." There's no way I'm letting him know about Drill, Nix, Ritchie, and the rest of them. Not if he's going to take their names back to Matthews.

He drops my hands, holding his out in between us. "I'm done. I swear. I never knew they would go this far. It's over." He just keeps shaking his head.

"I wish I could believe you. But I don't." I turn before he can answer and start climbing the stairs again, using the handrail to steady myself. When we get on deck I dig my room key out of my pocket.

There are voices behind the door, hushed.

"Is Cross in here?"

"She shouldn't be." I'd been too focused on my side to even notice she didn't march down to lunch with us. "Maybe she and Evers made up." But I hope it's not true.

"No chance of that," he says. "Evers is completely out."

I push the door open and step into the room. "Bekah?"

We stare at each other for a second, her in her bra and me about to throw up because the person holding her against the wall has his shirt off, and a circular tattoo on his shoulder, just like the one on Evers. He turns to look at me, his eyes glazed over and lips swollen red. No, it's definitely not Evers.

THIRTY-SIX

"WHO'S IN—" KELLY STEPS TOWARD ME.

I turn and push him out the door, closing it behind me and trying to get the picture of Matthews out of my head. "Forget it. Let's go."

"Mac, what the hell is going on?"

"Just go back to the mess hall. I'll be okay."

"Who was in the room?" He puts his hand on my arm when we get outside, stopping me.

I jerk away from him. My hands are shaking and the dizziness is getting worse. Bekah is with Matthews now. "You want to make up for this?"

"Yes. What can I do?" Kelly pleads.

"Give me something I can use. Anything to help me fight them."

And then he does. He gives me the name of every single Pandora Society member at the DMA—Lyons, Matthews, Evers, Harper, Watkins, and more. Twelve in all.

And Jonathan's not one.

I breathe a sigh of relief, committing the names to memory to tell Drill later. "Thank you."

"It's the least I can do. I feel like shit, Mac."

I chuckle, even though it hurts like hell. "You think you feel like shit, try being my ribs for a few minutes. Now help me get to the chapel before I pass out."

Later, after Rev listened to Kelly's confessions, I call Mom. Dad's doing better and he's started physical therapy. It's a huge step. Just five minutes talking to her helped more than I could ever have thought possible. She sounds stronger and that helps me find the strength I need to show Drill the evidence of Matthews's latest attempt to get me to quit.

I slip out of my room after lights-out, not having to worry about sneaking past Bekah because she hasn't come back to the room yet. Kelly's joined Nix with tonight's watch, his guilt driving him to join the Guard Sam platoon. He doesn't ask questions, but follows us down the stairs and out into the night.

Drill and Huff are hard at work in the weight room. I stand at the open door, watching Drill finish counting a set for him. "Good, Huff. You're doing really good. You'll be ready to test for Corps PT at the end of April when we do fitness tests."

"I don't know about all that. . . ."

"Don't talk yourself down. You've worked really hard. Now,

why don't you get on the treadmill and run a 5k."

"Dude, you're killing me."

Drill laughs and stretches his arms above his head.

"Hey," I say when Huff is on the treadmill, earbuds in, and Drill heads toward the water fountain.

"Feeling better?" Then he notices Kelly and Nix standing near me.

"No, not really." I sit down on one of the weight machine seats and lean back, wincing as I stretch out my ribs a bit too much.

He keeps his eyes on Kelly. "What's he doing here?"

"If you'd be quiet, maybe I could explain."

For a second, his mouth curls up on one side. "I'll shut up."

"About time." I smile, trying to let him know that it's going to be okay. "Evers is out of the Society. Lyons is, too. Matthews has been promoted."

"What? How?"

"I'll explain everything, I promise. But you need to listen." I look toward Kelly. He's hanging his head and won't meet Drill's eyes. "Kelly's done with it all, too. When I showed him my side he realized what was going on."

"Your side?" He takes a step toward me, concerned.

My fingers shake as I reach for the hem of my PT shirt. I lift the edge of the fabric, pulling it up just enough so he can see the bruise.

"What the hell happened?" He looks like he's ready to murder someone. He uncurls one hand enough to rub the sweat off his forehead.

I swallow. "Matthews. During the smoke show last night."

"Son of a bitch!" His right hand explodes outward, punching into the metal bar of the weight machine. It must hurt like hell, but he does it again.

"Drill . . ."

"I'm going to kill him."

I stand up, wincing at the movement, and step toward him, putting a hand on his chest. "I need you here right now." I take a shaky breath, wondering how to proceed. "I think I've come up with a plan. Kelly says Jonathan had nothing to do with the Society—that Lyons was pressuring him to get me to quit all year. Jonathan said he needed proof. Well, here it is. Kelly's named the twelve Corps members; we've got my medical charts. He can't ignore the proof if we take pictures to show him my side."

After looking at me for a few seconds he takes a step back, reaching into his pocket for his cell phone. I struggle out of my shirt, thanking God that I'd been able to manage changing into a sports bra earlier without needing Bekah's help.

After he takes three photos, from the front, the side, and the back, he helps me back into my shirt. "Ouch." I wince.

"Sorry." His face is pale and he looks sick.

"It's okay," I say quietly. I glance at Kelly and Nix, but they'd turned away when I took my shirt off and haven't looked back yet. "I don't want to complain about you touching me."

"Just wait until I'm not your drill sergeant anymore. You won't be able to keep my hands off you," he whispers.

"I think I could be okay with that."

He tries to smile but he just ends up sighing. "Sam, if this doesn't work . . ."

"If it doesn't work, then Jonathan's lost control of the Corps and we're in way more trouble than we thought." I want to lean against him for just a second, borrow some of his strength. But I can't, not yet. If I touch him now, I might forget how to stand on my own.

Bekah is in bed but sits up when I get back from the armory. "Where have you been?" she asks, her voice wary.

"Around," I say.

"You look like hell."

"Well, I feel like hell."

"Look, I don't know what you think you saw today—"

I flip on the light. "Are we really going to do this?"

"You don't know what's going on."

"I have more of an idea than you think." She's working her way up the ranks of the Society to keep herself safe.

"Me and Matthews . . ."

"Are together now. I get it. Do you have any idea what they've done to me? Do you even care?"

"Of course I care!"

"And you've just let it happen?"

"I thought they might give up after the snowball fight. Then Evers screwed everything up—"

"Wait. You knew about that? You knew about that and didn't do anything to stop it?"

"They told me to disappear. I didn't know about the iceballs until after it happened."

"You're not their *slave*, Bekah. They expect us to do whatever they tell us to, and you're just sliding right into that role. What happens when they turn on you?"

She pales but doesn't say anything.

"Don't look upset now. You've made your choice. You have to know it's only a matter of time 'til they get rid of you, too."

She blinks her eyes quickly. "It was my choice to be with Evers. But," she says, wiping at her eyes, "Matthews—"

"Stop right there. No one's making you date him."

"You've got it all worked out, don't you? Making me out to be the bad one here? I may have started out enjoying it . . . but now . . . they've got too much on me. If I turn my back on them now, they'll tell everyone what I've done. You know the rules. They'll drum me out and then . . ."

"Then what, Bekah? What do they have against you that's so bad you'd let them hurt me like this?"

She wipes her eyes. "If I get kicked out of here, I'm done. I go to jail."

"What are you talking about?"

"I may have gotten a track scholarship to come here, but only after the ultimatum." She sighs and starts at the beginning. "I was at a party that got out of hand. When my friends and I left, we were drunk. While I was driving, I hit someone. He didn't die, but he'll never walk again. The judge gave me two options. Juvie or military school. If I don't make it here, I'm done. By the time I figured out what Evers was into, it was too late. They had too much on me. Now I've got to stay with Matthews. If I break up with him, he'll force me out of the school. I don't have a choice."

"You've always got a choice. Wilson's going down with the

Society. Kelly's done with them." Right now, Drill should be showing Jonathan pictures of my injuries and I'm praying Jonathan makes the right choice. Bekah's got to do the same.

"You don't understand. . . ."

"I want you out of this room."

"What?"

"You may not think you have a choice, but I know I've got one. I want you out. Gone. I don't care where the hell you go. Move in with Matthews for all I care."

She's standing now, taking a step toward me. "Mac . . ."

"I'm sorry, Bekah. I really am. But if you're not going to walk away from them, we're done." She may not be directly involved, but she's connected enough that I won't ever trust her. "Stay away from me. Stay away from Kelly. And tell your precious Society boyfriends that they're done threatening me. Now"—I grab her by the arm and open the door—"get out."

THIRTY-SEVEN

THEY'RE WATCHING ME. THE PEOPLE KELLY WARNED ME about: Matthews, Evers, Lyons, Watkins, Harper, Wilson, and the others. One of them is never far from me, scooting in behind me in the mess hall line, waiting outside my classroom buildings, standing on the PG at night, just staring up at my window.

Kelly's not getting off easy, either. His room is destroyed every day while he's in class, and we're awakened every night with pounding on his door. His eyes are bloodshot but still he refuses to take a day off Guard Sam duty.

Matthews has been absent from deck the past few days, but he's still on campus. Jonathan still won't talk to me. The tension is thick, rising with the heat of April. It feels like everyone is just waiting for something to happen.

"Did you hear me, Mac? We should head back to the barracks." Nix is packing up his books.

I can't sleep. I can't eat.

"What's the hurry?" I glance down at my paper, covered only in doodles. Great. Another study hall wasted.

"Drill wanted us back on deck early. Remember?"

I don't, but that doesn't mean much. Minutes, hours, and days blend together in a haze of exhaustion and pain, though the pain is a little less each day. Outside, Nix has to grab my arm to catch me as I stumble up the stairs. "You need to sleep, Mac. You can't keep staying up all night."

"They stand outside my window twenty-four/seven and they bang on Kelly's door all hours of the night. I can't sleep knowing they're there."

"I've got watch tonight," he says. "Give me your key and I'll come in. I'll sit by the window if it would make things better."

We're at my door now, and I erase my destination on the whiteboard.

"Good, you're here," Drill says, walking on deck.

Nix snaps to attention and I sort of slide into it, though my hands aren't lined up with the seams of my pants and I know he's going to notice.

"Is she okay?" Drill confronts Nix, as if he had something to do with the state I'm in.

"She hasn't slept in days. The Society isn't *doing* anything, but they're *everywhere*."

"Hey." Drill is looking at me now, his blue eyes so strong I just want to sink into them. "It's going to be okay. Your brother is coming up on deck to make the announcement. It worked. Your plan worked."

I blink, the words not registering.

Nix talks for me. "Matthews is gone?"

"He must be. I was about to call the company out on the wall. Just stay here."

I nod because it sounds too good to be true. For once, Jonathan is going to do something right. I breathe a little easier, imagining the full night's sleep I'll get to have tonight.

"On the wall, Worms," Drill says, his voice echoing down the hall. My recruit buddies pop out on the hall, one by one, standing at attention. Kelly comes to stand on the other side of me. Bekah slides in next to him but keeps her eyes focused on the ground.

Jonathan appears at the end of the hall and I try to catch his eye. He's in full cadet colonel mode, though, and won't break his stance, or his stare, to look at me. I'll thank him later, though. I'll get Rev to set up another meeting so that I can make sure he understands how much this means to me.

"Attention on deck!" Drill's voice booms from the end of the hallway and I stand a little straighter.

Jonathan marches on deck, his steps slow and even, looking every inch the person in command that he was the first day of Hell Week. "Good evening, Alpha."

"Colonel McKenna, good evening, Colonel McKenna!" We sound strong, sure of ourselves.

"Take an eye," he says.

We continue standing at attention, but each of us turns to look at Jonathan.

"I'm sure you've all heard the rumors around campus about one of your corporals. Before you all arrived on campus, I trained each and every member of the cadre. I explained what was expected of them, how they were chosen leaders of this institution and that everything they did from that day forward would be an example of the DMA as a whole." He takes a breath, scanning my company but skipping over me without meeting my gaze.

"Unfortunately, every so often one or two cadets decide to take training into their own hands. This is against the rules of the DMA and when it happens those cadets are taken before the disciplinary committee."

I stop breathing. The disciplinary committee? No, he was supposed to take it to the commandant. He was supposed to take it to the board of directors. I look frantically up and down the hall for Drill. He's standing in the stairwell, flanked by Lyons and another Society member, his face wiped clean of emotion. The floor tilts beneath me and I have to lean on the wall to keep from falling.

"Matthews, front and center."

"Yes, Colonel," Matthews says, jogging to stand next to Jonathan, directly in front of me, not an ounce of worry on his face. My mouth goes dry and I have to force myself to keep my fists tight at my sides.

"I cannot discuss the specifics of this case with you, but Corporal Matthews has crossed a line. He knows it. The Corps knows it. Kneel, Matthews," Jonathan says.

Without looking away from me, Matthews lowers himself onto his knees. He's not embarrassed, like he should be, to be degraded like this in front of Worms. He's happy.

Jonathan reaches out, unpinning Matthews's epaulettes, pieces of fabric denoting rank that all cadets wear on their shoulders. When he takes them off, Jonathan continues his speech. "From this day forward until the end of the year, you will be a private at the DMA. You will get no honors or privileges above your station. Your room will be stripped to award you only that which a private can possess. You will earn privileges as you climb the ranks again next year. Do you understand?"

"Yes, Colonel."

But he's not leaving? He gets to stay after everything he's done?

"You are to have no contact with the recruits of Alpha Company. Do you understand?"

"Yes, Colonel."

"Recruits of Alpha Company," Jonathan says. "From now until the end of the year, you are not to have any further contact with Private Matthews. He is no longer in your cadre and you will not perform any duties he demands of you. But," he says, his eyes locked on mine for the first time tonight, "he is still a member of the DMA Corps of Cadets and ranked above you. You will treat him with the proper respect of anyone above your rank. Do you understand?"

No!

"Colonel McKenna, yes, Colonel McKenna!"

"Very well. Good night, Alpha Company."

"Colonel McKenna, good night, Colonel McKenna!"

Jonathan reaches a hand out and helps Matthews to his feet. Then both of them leave the wall. My jaws throb from clenching so hard and Nix puts a hand on my arm when I try to step forward. It's over. The Pandora Society has complete control.

"What the hell just happened?" Someone speaks and it takes me a second to realize it's me.

"It'll be okay, Mac. He lost his rank. He can't touch you anymore. *They* can't do anything anymore." Kelly's words don't help, though, because they're not true.

"He lost his rank *because* of me. If anything, Jonathan just made it worse, not better." My hand is shaking too hard to get the key in my door. Nix takes it from me and pushes the door open for me.

"Holy shit, Mac."

I nudge him inside, then step in with him so I can see what's wrong.

The room's trashed.

My sheets are shredded to ribbons, my blanket torn. My wall locker is upended and every drawer is upside down on the floor.

"Did you leave your room unlocked?"

I shake my head because the words won't come. Blood thunders through my ears and I reach for my chair.

"Yeah. I think I'm going to be sleeping in here tonight," Nix says.

"I'll go let Drill know." Kelly turns and runs down the hall.

They can get into my room. Whenever they want. Oh God. They're not going to stop. Not ever.

Not until I'm gone.

THIRTY-EIGHT

THE DAYS MOVE LIKE MOLASSES, THE WARMTH OF SPRING spreading into our bones and making us a little slower, a little more stir-crazy. Tension rolls across campus, boiling just beneath the surface. I watch my back every step I take, jump at every noise. Every second of every day spent just waiting.

"Rev," I say, as he comes out of the chapel. "I wanted to call D.C. and check on Dad."

He glances left and right, fingers twitching at his sides. "I was just on my way to find you. Come here." He takes me by the arm, not leaving me any room to argue, and pulls me into the chapel. "Are you okay?"

Nix walks in behind me to stand guard.

"What do you think?" I'm jittery, like I've had too much coffee with a few sides of energy drinks. I lower my eyes and fiddle with nails I've almost completely chewed off from nerves. It's been a week since they broke into my room. Everywhere I look, I see a member of the Society. Staring, whispering threats, just *being* near me. Will they be in my room the next time I go back on deck? Waiting for me?

"Have you seen your brother today?" His words are hurried and he looks around again, like someone's going to jump out of the shadows.

"No. Why?" Ever since last week when he stripped Matthews of his rank, Jonathan has been strangely absent from Corps functions. Lyons has been picking up a lot of Jonathan's duties.

"I'm not sure. I hear things, you know? Sometimes when people come into the chapel, they don't even realize I'm here."

"Lucky you," I mutter, wishing he would get to the point.

"There have been whispers all day."

"Come on, Rev. Please."

"Your brother's being drummed out." The words come in a burst of air.

"What?" I can feel the color drain from my cheeks and I shiver. Nix comes to stand next to me. I lean into him.

"You're a smart girl. Your brother took the rank of a major player—if not the *leader*—of the Pandora Society here at school. They want your brother out and they have the power to do it. The official ruling will be fraternization with a female recruit."

I can't breathe. Jonathan's being kicked out of the DMA because of me. It's all my fault. "Bekah wouldn't touch Jonathan." But she has hooked up with other upperclassmen. It wouldn't be a stretch to say she'd been with Jonathan, too.

"You and I know the truth doesn't really matter right now."

"What about her?" His look tells me all I need to know and I reach out to steady myself on the table. "She's out, too, isn't she?"

Rev sighs, the heart of the matter finally coming out. "After this evening, you're the only McKenna here. The only *female* here."

Nix is helping me up the stairs to deck when Drill opens his door.

"Nix, up on deck. McKenna, in here," he says. When Nix is gone, he closes the door. "You heard about Jonathan and Bekah?"

"Yes." I feel like I'm moving through a dream. Everything is happening in slow motion.

"I think it's time for you to leave," Drill says. "Your brother is out. You understand that, right? You might've thought he wasn't on your side, but whatever he was doing, he was walking a careful line with them. He was the *only* thing keeping you safe. Without him here, I . . ." He jerks his hands into the air, like he's out of options.

"Don't give up on me, please." My voice shakes and I hate it. I hate the whole damn situation.

He reaches for my hand and pulls me close. "It's not worth you getting hurt again."

I feel like I'm on the losing end of our argument, but I can't back down. "Your sister went through West Point and made it. You think that would have happened if there weren't girls before her to pave the way?" He looks more defeated than I've ever seen him. "I might not be able to win," I say, "but they'll know the end is coming. That it can't go on forever. They can't control everything."

He sighs, dropping his hands to his sides. "I knew you wouldn't quit—it's one of the things I love about you. But I had to try." He brushes past the word, like it's something people say every day. Drill moves toward the door, but keeps it closed while he continues. "We'll keep up the guard on you. No going anywhere alone, no more late night training sessions." He puts a finger on my lips when I start to protest. "No. We'll worry about PT next year. There's too much at stake now for you to worry about something that petty. You've got to watch your back. Every second. Every day."

I try to put on my face everything I'm feeling right now. The gratitude, the love, because I don't know when we'll get a chance to be alone again. If we'll get a chance. The Society has upped their game. Who knows how far they'll go now?

Four hundred people—cadets, professors, and other bigwigs at the DMA—in two lines wearing dress blues is an intimidating sight under normal circumstances. By the time Bekah got to me, her whole body was shaking. I wanted to tell her I wasn't mad at her anymore. That I was sorry for everything that had happened. I was so worried about what was coming next, though, that I just watched as she passed me and walked out the gates of the DMA for good.

Now, with a pain in my chest I can't quite get a hold on and knees that are threatening to give out as the sun goes down, I wait for the second cadet of the evening to get drummed out.

I'm assigned the last position by the gate, probably so I'm the last thing Jonathan sees. A way to rub his failure in his face. The drums have been beating for the last ten minutes as Jonathan makes his long walk to the gate of the DMA. Each time he passes a cadet, one of his brothers for the past four years, they turn their back to him, refusing to acknowledge him or even look in his direction.

I can't think about how I feel. I cannot let myself care about this right now. This summer there will be plenty of time—if I survive until then. The clouds above me have been moving in all day, a solid, menacing presence that rumbles low and deep. I stand at attention but I can't keep my hands from shaking.

When Jonathan steps into my line of sight, I put my hand on the stone pillar for support. He walks hunched over, the weight of a rucksack, Army-issued, hanging on his shoulders. He wears jeans with holes torn in them, and a white T-shirt. His eyes blaze with anger when he reaches me.

"Jonathan . . . ," I whisper. There's no way I can fix this.

"Go to hell, Sam."

"I never meant—"

"You and Amos always had to be better than me. He jumped right into the Army when he could. I can't help that I'm not the oldest, but I'm the one who wants to follow in Dad's footsteps. Amos *quit*." He spits the words like he's disgusted to even say them. "And, you. You can't be a Ranger like Dad. Why the hell did you have to come here? What's it going to prove if you survive?"

I shake my head. "I didn't mean for this to happen."

"I won't graduate from the DMA. West Point will never take me since I got drummed out of here. I busted my ass for *four years* to make a name for myself. And you come here and ruin everything in nine months." He leans in toward me. His teeth are clenched and his voice is a quiet hiss in my ear. "I hope they kill you."

He turns and walks through the gates without looking back and I can do nothing but watch. He's my only brother now.

And the Society has made me lose him, too.

THIRTY-NINE

"WHAT DO YOU MEAN THINGS HAVE CHANGED?" FIVE OF US cram into Rev's already overly full office the first weekend in May and it's stuffy, hard to breathe.

"They're not done with you yet." Jax sighs and Kelly nudges her in the side, encouraging her on. "They're not going to just let you finish the year. They're going to do one more push to get you out now that Bekah's gone. They're going to hijack the Worm Challenge."

The room is silent and Rev's old clock *tick-tick-ticks* until I want to scream. But I sit there for a full minute staring out the window before I speak. "How?"

"I don't know." Jax looks at the floor. "The normal channels have gone silent."

Drill runs his hands over his buzz cut. "Look, I know this must be hard—"

"You have no idea," I whisper. It's all I can say without breaking down. If I speak any louder, all the crap that's been building up is going to force its way out. I can't let them see me cry.

Rev clears his throat and stands. "Dean, why don't we give you two a few minutes? Jax, Kelly, can I get you guys a cup of coffee?"

"Sorry, Sam." Jax puts her hand on my shoulder and squeezes. "I know how hard you've worked for this."

When they're gone, I reach for Drill's hand and my fingers slide between his easily, like they're meant to be there. "Is it weird that I've never called you Dean?" I like how his name sounds on my lips.

He lifts my hand a little, resting it on his leg and tracing circles on my skin. "We need to figure out what we're going to do. I'll go get your stuff from Stonewall if you want . . . to go home. . . ."

It sounds so easy. Packing up and leaving. Getting the hell out of the DMA. "Is that what I should do?"

"I don't know. I really don't. I want you safe—that means gone. I want you to beat the bastards—that means staying." He leans forward, resting his head on my shoulder. "This year has been a nightmare," he says, then continues hastily. "But I didn't say that. I don't criticize. I'd hate to lead the Corps."

"I think you'd be a great leader." I mean it with all my heart. "And I'm not just saying that because you're you."

"Well, if it's up to me that will never happen. But thanks."

"Why aren't you a member of the Society? You seem like their ideal candidate. Good soldier, strong, squared-away. Way better than Evers and Matthews."

"Not true. Most secret societies, at least the ones who rule by intimidation like the Pandora Society, are for people who want things a certain way. They've been at every military school and through all branches of the military. You may be born into it because your dad or grandfather was in it, but you've still got to prove you belong. And for this one, you do that by hurting fellow cadets to make a core group stronger. Everyone else is cast aside. I don't work like that."

"I'm glad you don't."

"I didn't apply to be a drill sergeant, you know."

"No, I didn't know that. What happened?"

He shrugs. "Got called into Colonel Lee's office during cadre week. I think he knew what he was up against with females coming in. Maybe he even knew something about the Society—though he probably won't admit it. But he needed someone near you females who wasn't wrapped up in the Corps' image—only in giving everyone a fair chance to succeed."

"Well, I'm glad he chose you." From day one I've known I'd do whatever he asked of me and this . . . whatever we have . . . makes it hard to think for myself rather than think of Alpha first. But I can only put off my decision for so long. "If I leave after all of this, after everything they've done, I'm throwing it all away. Every step I've gained toward acceptance, toward being part of the DMA—it'll be gone." And I would fail.

"Yes."

"And if I go, what I've gone through, what Bekah went through, what *Jonathan* went through, will be pointless." He squeezes my hand and I lean against him, resting my head on his shoulder.

"You could still expose the Society. Still give the board of directors something to think about."

We'd spent weeks looking at the list: cops, bankers, military brass, members of the board of directors, and Matthews's dad.

"Tell me what to do. I'll do whatever you want."

He laughs, the skin around his eyes crinkling in amusement. "No you won't." Then he gets serious again. "It's your choice. I'll back you either way, but this is a decision you've got to make."

I stand, unable to sit still, but pacing doesn't help either.

"I'm going to step out. Give you some time to decide, okay?"

Nodding, I reach for his hand and squeeze. "Thank you."

"For what?"

"Believing in me."

"You make it really easy. If you choose to continue, we'll come up with a plan. We'll help you make it." He plants a kiss on my forehead before walking out, closing the door behind him, and leaving me alone to make a choice that could cost me my life.

I want his words to be true. That with their help, I'll survive the Worm Challenge. I *need* his words to be true.

I just don't know if they are.

FORTY

"ALL RIGHT, ALPHA," DRILL SAYS ON THE SECOND SATURDAY in May, the day of the Worm Challenge. "When you finish tomorrow morning, you will all have earned your place here at the DMA. You've gone through a lot this year, but you've stayed strong. Now, this is an eight-hour challenge." He's dressed all in black, his arm muscles tense and stretching his T-shirt. The black drill sergeant cap is pulled down low over his face, covering his eyes in shadows.

My legs shake as I stand on the wall next to Kelly and Ritchie. "Breathe, Mac," Kelly says. Our truce has turned into an uneasy friendship.

"You'll start in pairs, hiking the thirteen miles up House Mountain. At the top, you'll be given an orienteering map, compass, and flashlight. You'll have the remaining time to solo-navigate your way down the mountain, stopping in at three checkpoints. The final step will be completing the obstacle course." He crosses his arms, just putting on a show. We had our real meeting in secret last night. The one without Wilson where Alpha voted to forgo any chance of Company of the Year to protect me. "If you want your time to count toward the Company of the Year, you've got to cross the finish line before 0700. Are there questions?"

"Drill Sergeant Stamm, no, Drill Sergeant Stamm!" We're the only ones on deck, but as soon as we go outside, the Society will be watching.

"Good. Then pair up and meet me outside."

Kelly nudges me, though we'd worked this out last night, too. "Mac?"

"Yeah," I say. "Partners."

He hovers close, waiting for me.

"She'll be right out, Kelly."

"Drill Sergeant Stamm, yes, Drill Sergeant Stamm." Now that he's been ordered, he won't disobey. He runs to the edge of the stairs, his combat boots thumping against the ground. We count the thuds as he jumps to each landing until he's down in the basement and we're alone.

Drill strides toward me purposefully, grabbing my arms and pulling me close. His lips hover millimeters from mine, and his eyes look like they're begging for permission. "Here's the cell phone." He pulls it from his pocket and checks to make sure it's on. "I've turned the GPS on. Everyone knows their roles."

I nod and reach for the phone, but he moves his hand near my hip, letting the phone drop into my pocket. "I don't want anyone to get hurt. . . ." I let the words trail off.

"My friends and your recruit buddies will stay back unless there's a problem. Jax will watch your progress. She's hacked into the phone. If you stop moving, she'll start recording. If they try to make a move, we'll get everything they say and then we'll beat the shit out of them."

He moves his hands to my hair, and mine are pulling at his shirt, urging him closer. He nudges me back against the wall, pinning me in place. One hand leaves my hair and travels down my neck and my side, coming to rest on my hip. He leans in, my body igniting every place he presses against me. "I need to kiss you."

I need it too, but all I can do is nod. Then, for a moment, his lips are on mine, pressing hard. I want to melt into him, to let the world around me disappear. I stand on my tiptoes and lean against him, trying to get as close as I can.

But as fast as it starts, it ends, and too soon he pulls away, breaking every inch of contact. "I wish I could ask you to stay. To not do this. If I do, you'll hate me. If I don't, and something happens to you, I'll hate myself."

"I'll be fine." My voice is breathy and I close my eyes, trying to focus on the task at hand. "I'll be fine." I say it again so I'm forced to believe it.

"I've got guys at each of the stations. In eight hours, it'll all be over." He pulls me close once again, his arms squeezing me, threatening to crush my ribs.

"When this is over," I whisper, standing on my tiptoes so my lips are against his ear, "you'd better finish what you just started."

A shadow of a smile crosses his face, and I leave before the fear overwhelms me and I can't stop myself from staying safe within his arms.

Two hours later, around 0100, Kelly and I are huffing at the top of House Mountain. We've run almost the entire thirteen miles to the top and have a good lead on the other Worms.

"First recruits to check in," Lyons says, standing behind a table with water on it.

I grab a paper cup and swallow the water down, trying not to glance at Kelly. A member of the Society up here waiting for us, fallen though he may be, is definitely not a good sign.

"Here are your maps."

"Cadet Colonel, thank you, Cadet Colonel." I take mine, my hand barely steady. It makes me sick to call him a rank he hasn't earned.

"Good luck, recruits." The look on his face makes it clear just how much luck he wishes us.

Once Kelly has his map, we step away. I hand him my map to look at. I aim my headlamp on the paper for him to see, trying not to gasp. The map itself looks normal, but there's a small circle in the bottom right-hand corner, an exact copy of the mark in my KB and the tattoos both Matthews and Evers have: the Pandora Society insignia. Kelly raises his eyebrows and brushes a finger across the inked in mark, but he doesn't mention it. "According to the map Lyons gave you, it looks like you're going south from here for about four miles, then east toward the ridge. Once you wind your way down to the river, it's a straight three miles north back to campus." He says it not only for my benefit but for the cell phone, too. Back at Tim's house, Jax is probably staring at a map, trying to figure out my course. "You know to check your compass every fifteen minutes."

I nod, though I can barely breathe. "I know." I don't want him to leave me alone up here. This is how they're going to do it. They've changed my map. If I draw attention to it, I'll fail the challenge. If I don't go, they'll know I'm onto them. I've got no choice now.

"You're going to be okay, Mac." He coaxes a small smile out of me, even though he looks just as nervous as I feel.

"Then why does everyone look like this is a funeral?" I want to take the words back as soon as I say them. *I hope they kill you.* I try to push Jonathan's words away. "There are cadets crawling all over these woods. I'm going to be the most watched recruit during this whole mission." I say it loud, for Lyons's benefit. But he and I both know that it's a lie. They're watching trails the DMA uses every year for the Worm Challenge. Not a new one drawn up by the Society. If Jax can't figure it out from Kelly's description, if something happens to the GPS, I really will be on my own.

Kelly grabs me and pulls me into a hug. "I'm sorry, Mac. For everything. I was stupid."

"You were." I squeeze him back, trying to laugh a little. "But you've made it up." I pull away. Holding my compass up, I check my direction. "See you at the bottom, right? Alpha leads the way." It's hard to get the words out, but somehow I manage.

He hands me back my map, checks his headlamp and mine, then takes a step back. I slip into the woods before he can say anything else. I'm no good at good-byes.

They've started me out going downhill. My strides lengthen and it's easy to jog at first, even as I jump over logs and curve around boulders. As night slinks around me, though, the clouds move in, blocking the moon and any hope of extra light to help me through this. If I turn my head constantly, my headlamp gives me some idea of the near obstacles, but I can't see anything beyond fifteen feet.

The forest is alive with the sounds of crickets and tree frogs. Cicadas screech their way through the trees, but all the sound does is mask anyone else who might be out here. I don't see another cadet until I come upon my second checkpoint two hours later. It's almost 0300.

I smile at Huff when I get to the table. "Four miles down."

"Here's some Gatorade," he says.

I grab the bottle from his hand and he holds his walkie-talkie up to his mouth. "Cadet Huffman, Checkpoint Two-A. Recruit McKenna checking in."

I chug the drink down, little streams of it eking out the corners of my mouth, as Huff confirms my status and that I'm about to leave. When I'm done, I wipe an arm across my lips. "Thanks."

He shrugs. "The least I can do. I'll call Drill as soon as you leave and let him know, too. You doing okay?"

"Yeah. No sign of anything." They're smart, having me check in to make everything appear normal. I wonder when the map they gave me will take me where they want me.

Huff scans the darkness. "You know where you're going?"

I nod, trying to sound more confident than I feel. "Yep. No worries."

He tries to grin, but even he looks worried now. "Be safe, okay?"

There's a churning in my stomach that's not from the Gatorade, but I nod and check my compass before taking off again at a run. It would have been easy to tell him about the map, but anyone could be hiding in the dark, listening.

The woods are blacker this way, deeper somehow. My thighs burn from the uphill turn my path takes and it's not long before I have to slow to a walk.

Each step seems to take more energy now. I check my compass every fifteen minutes to make sure I'm on the Society's preferred trail.

Staying focused and alert for this long in the middle of the night is not easy. I scan the forest for a hint of anything that seems off, but it *all* seems wrong. A branch snaps in the woods and I jump, then stop in my tracks. I flick my light off, giving my eyes a chance to adjust to the dark.

The clouds have lifted a little bit, and somewhere to my left I can hear the waterfall where I think the checkpoint is supposed to be. Wind whispers through the trees. Or my imagination's playing tricks on me.

My heart gallops and I try to swallow down my nerves. "Dammit, Sam. Get a grip."

Dad did things like this all the time as a Ranger. Amos did it, too. Every cadet who's gone through the DMA has completed the Worm Challenge. There are hundreds of years of tradition that say I'll make it.

Then again, there's the Pandora Society. As old as the DMA itself. And they'll do anything to keep me from surviving.

The whisper comes again, this time closer and to my right. I take a step back and crouch down at the base of a boulder. Shadows move as a cloud streaks across the moon.

Then the atmosphere changes—it's thick with anticipation. When something clamps on to my ankle, I can't do anything but scream.

FORTY-ONE

"EVERS, SHUT HER UP," MATTHEWS GROWLS IN THE DARKNESS. I'm about to yell out again when the hand leaves my foot and clamps over my mouth. I bite down as hard as I can.

"Ouch! You stupid bitch." Evers grabs his hand away, balls it into a fist, and rams it into my stomach.

I double over in pain, gasping and trying to suck in air. He grabs my hair and jerks my head back. Then I see Matthews standing just inches from me. I refuse to let them see me scared. I imagine they're Jonathan and Amos, playing a trick on me, and answer how I'd answer one of them. "This is your master plan?" Evers's eyes shine in the darkness but I force my voice to sound strong and sure. "Lure me off into the woods? Kidnapping and ransom? Not the best ways to regain favor in the Society, I don't think."

"Just wait, McKenna. You'll see how I plan to get my position back." There's no joking, no sneering now as Evers talks. This is his last chance. *I'm* his last chance.

"So, what? The Pandora Society isn't going to let me finish the Worm Challenge? You couldn't get me to quit so you sabotage the one thing left that will prove I'm as good as you?"

"I said shut her up, Evers," Matthews growls.

Evers punches me in the stomach again, the wind blowing out of my lungs. Black spots form in front of my eyes before I can finally suck in air.

"The box was opened," Matthews says, his voice strange and hollow, sounding now like he's reciting lines in a play. He moves toward the waterfall.

Evers gives me a shove, pushing me after Matthews, and then speaks. "The box was opened. And within, all evil things were set loose upon the world." Water rages over the edge of the falls and thunders to the river below; no one will be able to hear us at all soon.

"But the most powerful item of all remained. Hope," Matthews says, the leader of this weird chorus.

"Hope that the future does not have to repeat the past."

"Hope that what is in the world can be made pure again," Matthews replies. "The box was opened. But hope will see it closed again."

"Hope will see it closed," Evers repeats.

I try to laugh through the fear. "Is that it? You're going to chant at me and leave me by a waterfall until morning?" A breeze rushes through the trees, their trunks bowing. I wonder if they will hold up to the pressure, or crack under the strain.

Where is Drill? Where are the cadets he said would be watching my every move?

"Not by the waterfall. Under it." Evers's voice is cold. Hard. He looks to Matthews for assurance.

Matthews just grins. "God, I'm going to love every second of this."

"You ruined my life, you little slut. I was going to rule the Society next year. All you had to do was quit." Evers shoves me once more until I can't help but run into Matthews.

"But you made a mockery of this school. Of our traditions. Our values." Matthews jerks on my arm, pulling me to the edge of the cliff. Water disappears, crashing on the rocks below. "Because you refused to play along, Evers lost his place in the Society. He wants it back now."

"And you're the one who can give it to him?" My voice shakes.

"Of course I am. I'm the leader of the Society now. I don't want you here any more than any other cadet, but you have elevated me through the ranks more quickly than I could have hoped. For the rest of this year, and the next two years, I'll rule the Society. Rule the school." Matthews's eyes shine with excitement. "Enough. Evers, you know what you have to do if you want back in."

"Get into the harness," Evers says, holding the contraption out in front of me.

"You're kidding, right?" I look into the darkness, but there's no one there. No one's coming.

"Don't you realize you're out of chances?" Matthews growls.

"This is it. Now get in." Evers puts the harness on the ground and Matthews tightens his grip, pushing me forward, my feet stepping into the leg holes.

Evers jerks the nylon fabric up around my legs, pulling much harder than he needs to, to get the fabric situated around my hips. He cinches the straps tight until they're digging into my thighs.

"I still don't get your master plan. Now you're going to, what? Cut off circulation to my legs?" Maybe if I can keep them talking, one of Drill's friends will find me. My eyes scan the darkness again. Still nothing.

"Looking for someone?" Matthews laughs. "Stamm, maybe?"

I shake my head. "No."

"That's good," Evers chimes in. "Because no one's coming. We took care of your map a few days ago."

"And on our way out here, we took care of three cadets, some of Stamm's closest friends, if I'm not mistaken, including Huffman—a friend of yours too, I think." Matthews laughs. "And just as he was about to make a call to your drill sergeant. Bad timing, I guess."

It's hard to breathe now, knowing they hurt people because of me. Knowing no one's coming.

Something glints in Evers's hand, shining in the moonlight, and he works it back and forth against a climbing rope.

My teeth start to chatter. "A knife? Come on, Evers. You may be a dick, but you're not evil. You can't kill me." I try to laugh it off, because the alternative is too terrifying.

"Oh, we're not going to kill you." Evers picks up a rappelling rope, the knife slicing easily through almost the entire rope. "If you fall, it's just a tragic accident."

"You've seen the list. You know who's in the Society." Matthews's mouth is close now, his lips brushing my ear like he's whispering something sweet. "A recruit dying in a training incident? It'll be easy to cover up. No one will look twice. They'll just say girls weren't cut out to be at the DMA anyway."

I try to shrink away from the truth but the hands are too tight, holding me still.

Evers jerks on the waistband of my camo pants, pulling me closer to him. He presses the knife against my thigh, between the harness and my leg, making a jerking motion. The nylon gives way, leaving only one leg strap fully functioning.

"Look at me," Evers snarls. His fingers are tight on my jaw. "This is it. This is where your choices have led you." His tongue snakes out and wets his lips.

Without thinking, I spit in his face, angry that he thinks he can make me beg. Angry that this is happening at all. Terrified of how far they'll go but knowing I'll never give into them.

Matthews spins me around to face him, grabbing the rope that Evers has already cut and securing it quickly. "Let's get this over with," he says. It's fraying where he cut it, just one little coil still in place. It won't take much weight to make it give and send me plummeting into the water.

"Hold her there. I'm going to get a rock, make sure she sinks."

"It has to look natural. Don't go off-book like you did with the rubber bullet, Evers." Matthews sounds annoyed.

"The waterfall is fifty feet. She's bound to hit a rock or two on the way down. Who's gonna know if we knock her out before she goes over?" Evers takes a few steps into the darkness.

"You can still make this right, Matthews," I plead. "Let me go. Right now. This can be the end of it."

He shakes his head. "You think you know so much. Like you're better than me. My father is the head of the Pandora Society. You can't touch me, bitch."

"But I did, right? I mean, I'm the one who got you stripped of your rank."

The back of his hand smacks into my cheek before I even know he's moved. My face is on fire, tears blurring my vision.

"Hurry the hell up, Evers!" he shouts into the night, pushing me back a step.

My boot slides when it leaves the dirt and lands on a rock. I plant the foot that's on land and refuse to move. He'll have to throw me over.

But he doesn't. His head snaps around at the sound of someone crying out. "What the fuck?" Matthews takes a step to the side, his grip on my arm loosening just slightly. "Evers!" But he's too far away to see in the darkness and it's hard to hear anything over the roar of the water. "What the hell happened now?" Matthews's voice is worried, no longer so sure of himself.

"We happened, Matthews." Drill flicks on a flashlight, his face shadowed in army paint.

My heart stops.

Matthews releases me and he turns, his hands balling into fists as he steps closer to Drill.

I stare at the light wavering through my tears, determined to focus despite the pain. I crouch where I am, ready to drive my

shoulder into someone's stomach, ready for a fight when it's time.

Drill keeps the light focused on him. "It's over. Let her go."

"You want to take me on, Stamm?"

"Let McKenna go, then you'll get your chance with me."

Laughing, Matthews takes a step toward Drill. "You're crazier than I thought."

"Come on. Man to man. Let's go."

Matthews hesitates and I know he's scanning the darkness, waiting to see if anyone else is going to come. "What the hell!" He steps forward into the clearing.

Drill drops the flashlight on the ground, highlighting a space he steps into, muscles tense and ready. Just waiting for Matthews to make a move. They circle slowly, sizing each other up.

"Evers is down, Stamm!" Jonathan's voice slides through the trees.

Jonathan! I want to cry out, but before I can another hand clamps over my mouth. "Don't yell, Mac, it's us. You're safe." Kelly releases his hand and I turn to see for sure. "We've got to move. Now."

I shake my head. "Not yet. Let's just wait—make sure Drill and Jonathan—"

"We've got orders, Mac. We have to get you out of here." Kelly's voice is full of urgency.

"You ready to rappel?" Nix whispers, his eyes on my gear.

I shake my head. "They cut it. It's ruined. They were going to make me . . ." But I let the words trail off. If I say it, then it's real, and I'll freak.

"Here. Use mine." Kelly's moving fast, taking his harness off as Nix helps me untangle from mine.

Drill lands a punch to Matthews's stomach, then charges when he's bent over, carrying them both to the ground in a whirlwind of limbs.

"Where's Jonathan?" I'm doing what Kelly says, trying to pull up his harness while my eyes scan the darkness for any sign of my brother.

"Hurry," Kelly whispers, pulling his harness up around my waist and tightening it. Nix secures the rope they used to climb up the falls. "You remember Hell Week, right?" Kelly says, checking the ropes once more. "Easy as pie. Ritchie's down below."

I want to say thank you, to hug him and tell him I'm sorry for everything that's happened.

"Go, Mac. You've got to get out of here. We're right behind you."

I close my eyes, take a deep breath, and step off the ledge. Pushing back, I let the rope slide through my fingers. It only takes two jumps to get down.

At the bottom, Ritchie unhooks me, my hands shaking too hard to be useful. "Let's go." He gives my arm a tug but I can't stop looking up.

"What about—"

"Kelly and Nix are coming. The colonel and Drill have it under control. Now, hurry," he says. "The guys we took out aren't going to stay down for long. Jax intercepted an email. The rest of the Society found out what Matthews and Evers were planning. They're on their way out here right now. We've got to get out of the woods."

We start running along the trail by the river, a much easier way to go.

"The phone worked great. We've got their whole conversation on tape. Matthews and Evers are going down. The *Society*'s going down."

"What about Jonathan? How—"

"Jax finally hacked into Matthews's dad's email tonight. Kelly was right. It was all there—how he'd ordered Matthews to pressure Jonathan all year to get you to quit. How they kept him from sleeping like they did Kelly, how they threatened to hurt you if he wouldn't get you to leave. Drill called him and Colonel McKenna demanded to be part of this. He hadn't even left town yet."

"You guys are amazing." The relief makes it easier to run. Jonathan never really turned his back on me at all.

Ritchie shrugs. "We'll be even more amazing if you pick it up and we finish the Worm Challenge."

Kelly and Nix catch up, giving each other celebratory high fives as they run. Kelly grabs my hand and doesn't let go, pulling me on even though my legs are dead and all I want to do is sink down on the ground and curl up into a ball.

The static of a walkie-talkie breaks the silence. "Mission complete," Drill says through the buzz. "I repeat, mission complete. Get back to campus, you four. All hell's going to break loose."

"Ready, Mac?" We're out of the trees now, the last two miles a road run to campus. The clouds are gone, and a hint of sun glows on the edge of the horizon. Kelly's green eyes sparkle and both dimples shadow his face.

"For what?"

"To finish the Worm Challenge!" He squeezes my hand. Ritchie grabs the other and we run onto campus together, Nix leading the way. When we round the turn for the last climb up to the obstacle course, the guys back off. I glance at my watch: 0645. It'll be close, if we make it at all.

"Where's the rest of Alpha?" I huff, muscles straining as we climb the hill.

"Look around."

From the trees that line the side of the trail, one by one, the rest of the company—minus Wilson, the only Alpha recruit the Society has left—comes out. They'd waited for me.

Kelly starts a cadence as we all fall into step, climbing the hill to the last obstacle course together.

Falling into formation, my recruit buddies let me go first, though none of them are far behind, over the walls, through the tunnels. I hesitate for only a second at the rope, the cheers from the guys behind me urging me on. The rope bites into my skin, but I use the memory of Amos to fuel me.

I'm going to win this battle for him.

Back at the bottom of the rope, I wait. The rest of the obstacles we can do as a team and I'm not going to go off on my own. I've blazed enough trails this year. Together, Alpha Company crosses the finish line with two minutes and three seconds to spare. We did it.

The cheer is enormous and even through the exhaustion, I give myself a second to smile. Arms grab me and pull me into a hug. I know this hug. "Jonathan," I get out, before he squeezes me again.

"God, Sammy." He shakes his head and pinches the bridge of his nose. "Are you okay?"

"I'm fine. You came. Nothing else matters."

He nods, fighting the tears that he won't let fall. McKenna men don't cry. "I'm sorry I was a dick. I didn't want them to know I was onto them. That you'd given me proof. Getting Matthews demoted was all I could do without doing more harm than good. I didn't mean any of it." He looks me in the eyes. "*None* of it, Sammy."

Drill runs through the recruits, giving congratulations, but his face is anything but happy. He leans his head between us, talking just loud enough for me to hear. "We need to go. Now."

FORTY-TWO

THE KITCHEN IS PACKED—DRILL, JONATHAN, AND TIM pace like caged animals. Jax sits on the counter and Kelly fidgets. "I can't stop shivering," I say, my words sounding loud in the silent kitchen. When I got here I changed into a pair of Drill's sweats, but even they can't warm me up.

Kelly goes to Tim's cabinets and starts opening them. When he finds what he wants, he pours the coffee grounds into the filter and sets the pot to brew. Then he sits next to me at the table, his eyes scanning me from head to toe to head again.

"Stop staring at me like that. I'm fine." I wish I wasn't shaking so he might believe me.

Drill walks to a basket on the kitchen counter. He grabs an apple and slices it, opens the pantry, and pulls out some peanut butter. He plops them on the table in front of me. "Eat."

I pick up a slice and chomp down. "Happy?" I ask around the fruit.

"Something needs to happen to those bastards," Kelly growls. Even though he isn't part of the Society anymore he hasn't stopped apologizing.

"They'll pay, believe me." Drill uses his dangerous voice again.

"So the million-dollar question is how? What do we do with the names? The information?" I chomp down on another bite of apple.

"We don't have to rush into this," Jax says.

Drill lets out a snarl. "No one expects you to do anything right now. Just rest."

"I can't, okay?" If I stop even for a second, everything will come flooding back: the waterfall, the knife, the cut rope. The fact that they were actually trying to kill me. I know I'm going to have to deal with it. I just can't right now. "I need to do something. Anything. If Jax thinks we can take them down, we do it." I turn to Jonathan. "So, Colonel? What's the plan of attack?"

"They're lying low. Going to the local cops is pointless—half of them are on the Society's payroll anyway. We've got to go to the board of directors and hope things haven't changed too quickly, that the Society hasn't had time to put more people in place."

Drill nods. "Forget about jumping the chain of command. If we make the list of cadet members public, the board of directors will have to make sure something is done."

"So we go to the board." My voice is breathy and my head is light, like I'm about to pass out. I look at Jax. "We'll do it." I swallow hard. “You’ve got the evidence?”

“Right here,” she says, pulling a flash drive out of her pocket. It had taken some doing, but Jax’s hacker skills paid off. She’d gotten photos of all the DMA cadets with their Pandora Society tattoos, the emails proving Evers shot me, the photos from Matthews’s kicking incident, and the recording from the Worm Challenge. We’ll hold General Matthews’s emails back. We need to make sure something gets done at the DMA before we take our chances releasing the bigger list. If this works next year the DMA will be Pandora-free.

“That’s it. It’s decided,” Tim says, his voice commanding.

“Okay,” I say. “But I need to make a call before we do anything.”

Tim stands up. “The phone’s right there. Your dad’s number is next to it. He’s expecting you.” How Tim knew what I was going to do, I don’t know. But then I think of Amos. Dad was the first person he always went to when he was in trouble. Of course he would know it’s what I want.

Once they’re in the living room, the television on, machine guns firing, I grab the phone and the number. My heart pounds so loud as I sit at the table, I’m scared I won’t hear if anyone picks up.

“Colonel McKenna.” His voice is brusque and serious on the phone. No extra syllables to spare. But I shatter all the same.

Tears spill down my face and my throat swells up. I’m not even sure I can talk. “Daddy?”

* * *

"It'll be okay," Rev says two days later, standing next to me on the steps of the admin building. "I'll be there with you."

The building is tall and imposing and I'm afraid I'll lose my nerve. I still can't stop shaking so I busy my hand tugging at the collar of my dress blues. Drill, Tim, Jonathan, and Kelly stand with us.

Tim's cell phone beeps and he pulls it out of his pocket. "Jax wishes you luck. Actually, she told you to kick some ass, but . . ."

I'm too terrified to laugh though. In the last two days, three helicopters had hovered above campus, chopping their way to the landing pad next to the football field. Helicopters that could only be bigwig military officers—the people who had summoned me here after Jonathan requested a meeting.

Tim's phone chirps again. "Jax again. The commandant's out," he whispers, like he's scared someone will overhear us. "The board of directors just sent a press release."

"The first casualty of the war," Jonathan says.

Drill shrugs, clearly not upset over the "loss of life." "He should have stood up to them. He got manipulated like all the rest." He keeps his eyes on me, avoiding a look at my brother that will just start another argument between them. It's been nonstop for two days.

"I guess there's nothing left to do but go in there and tell the truth."

"I'll be right here when you get out." Kelly doesn't hug me but he's there, a solid presence at my side.

"I know you will." I glance down at my blues, smoothing the

tunic even though there are no wrinkles.

"You look fine," Drill says. He tugs on a stray piece of hair and I can't help but smile. Then I turn and walk up the stairs to see what my future holds.

It takes a minute for my eyes to adjust inside.

Raised voices from behind heavy wooden doors make me want to reach out for Rev. I take a step back, feeling the edge of a chair dig into my legs, my heart beating too fast to be able to survive long.

Evers's voice is louder than the others. "It's what they wanted—what *you* wanted."

The noise makes its way out from somewhere deep inside.

The other voices are not as loud but are equally strong. "We should be pressing charges against you. Using the DMA to do something like this—"

"Say whatever you want. You knew it would end up like this. You knew this would happen. And that's why no one said anything when you found out we were still active."

"This is the end of the road for you, Cadet Evers. You're out of the DMA. Out of the collegiate military academies."

"You can't do that!"

"I can, and I will. You're dangerous, Cadet Evers."

The door jerks open so hard it slams against the wall inside the conference room. Rev steps in front of me.

Evers struggles to pull his DMA ring off. "Take this damn piece of trash. It's worth about as much as this fucking school." Winding up like a star pitcher, he rips the ring into the room where it clatters against the far wall. Then he turns.

"You," Evers hisses when he sees me. "I should have dropped you off the waterfall when I had the chance."

Blood thunders in my ears. I want to rip his eyes out, to kill him, to hurt him like he hurt me. "You're pathetic," I spit out, thankful for the adrenaline that keeps my voice from shaking.

"You're going to *ruin* this school. You already fucking have."

"Did you get what you wanted when you tried to kill me? Did you prove your point?" The words are out before I can stop them.

"Hell, yes. I'm better than you. Always will be. You needed to be put in your place."

"As opposed to the place you're in?" I look at him. Finally, really look. He's got stubble on his face and a split lip that should have had stitches. Both his eyes are swollen and bruised from the beating Jonathan gave him in the woods. "The place where they're kicking your sorry ass out the door, and I'm here for round two?"

He lunges for me, but Rev is there, his hands on Evers's chest. "Now, now, Mr. Evers. I doubt you want another incident on your record." Then he lowers his voice. "Get the hell out, now. Before I finish what her brother started. You're a disgrace to the DMA."

"No," I say, my voice shaking. I nudge my way between Rev and Evers, knowing this is the last time I'll have to stand this close to him. "Don't go yet." I pull my arm back and strike fast, my knuckles connecting with his cheekbone.

He stumbles back, shaking his head. Putting his hand against his cheek, he glares at me.

"What? Not used to a girl who puts up a fight?" I couldn't have surprised him more. "Now you can go, asshole."

Evers throws his arms up the air. When he's out the front door, leaving behind a trail of profanity, I can finally breathe again. "God, that hurt."

"You okay?" Rev turns to face me.

"Not yet." My hand throbs and I cradle my fist in the crook of my arm. "Let's finish this."

A gentle cough makes me jump. "Recruit McKenna, they're ready for you." The commandant's secretary holds the door to a large conference room open for me. There are uniforms all over the place; at least fifteen people of varying rank sit around the conference table. "Reverend, this is a closed meeting. You may wait outside."

"The *reverend* will be coming with me." I push past her and wait to be sure Rev follows without even giving her a second glance.

FORTY-THREE

EVERYONE STANDS WHEN I ENTER AND THE MAN AT THE HEAD of the table, someone I've never seen before, motions to a seat. When I sit down, Rev stands close behind me.

"Miss McKenna, thank you for coming to meet with us. My name is Colonel Keene. I'm the acting head for the DMA board of directors. As you can imagine, our board has been thrown into upheaval since the training *incident* and the evidence the cadet colonel released to us."

It certainly has—the most major change being Matthews's father, who is sitting at the end of the table. He wasn't on the board of directors last week. He must have pulled rank to be part of this today. My nerves go into overdrive.

Colonel Keene continues. "I'm sorry about the . . . unfortunate timing. Cadet—former Cadet—Evers's meeting wasn't supposed to take that long. The last thing we wanted was an altercation."

If I'm going to get through this, I have to push Evers as far to the back of my mind as I can. Rev puts his hand on the back of my chair.

"I would like to apologize to you on behalf of the Denmark Military Academy board of directors and family," Colonel Keene says across the table. "There were always going to be those cadets who did not want things to change, but we knew nothing of the Pandora Society."

"Thank you, sir. But your apology would mean a lot more if I believed it."

Rev lets out a loud breath behind me and I'm sure we're both thinking the same thing. Keene's name wasn't on the list, but including Matthews, there are four others at the table who are DMA grads and Pandora Society members.

"We are taking immediate action to ensure this does not happen again. All members of the Pandora Society on campus will be drummed out this evening. They will not be allowed to continue their education here. Furthermore, we will be doing some restructuring to ensure that the Corps is as strong and safe as it can be. Commandant Lee is released from his position and a new commandant will take his place."

I glance around the room at this and none of the Society members looks particularly happy. I fight to keep my military frown in place.

"Also," he says, leaning forward, "and I tell you this in the strictest confidence." He pauses, waiting for assurances from me.

"I won't reveal anything that happens in this meeting, sir.

What you do from here on out for the DMA is up to you."

"Thank you for your discretion in this matter. Next year, a new group of females will enter the Corps and we'd like *you* to be in command of their training. Since you will be a junior next year, we'd like to offer you a drill sergeant position."

"I'll stay." I hadn't given a lot of thought to what I was going to do next year, but like I told Drill, if I don't stay, all this is for nothing. If I'm not here next year, there will be another group of females who have to blaze the way. I can't let them be alone in this. "But there are conditions."

Colonel Keene is about to speak but someone at the end of the table interrupts him. "You're not in a position to be blackmailing the DMA, young lady."

I turn to look at the man who spoke. Matthews's father, the supreme leader of the Pandora Society. "Actually, after the 'training incident,' I am, General Matthews."

Rev hands me a piece of folded paper like we'd actually scripted this before. I unfold it and glance down. It's blank.

"If you don't want the names of the Pandora Society, and I mean *all* members—not just the ones at the DMA—released to the media, allowing for a full-scale investigation into the cover-ups that have happened here this year, I'm pretty sure I'm allowed a condition or three." I swallow, hoping he doesn't call my bluff. Blackmailing a leader of the United States Army isn't exactly easy.

Thankfully, he sits back down, scowling, arms crossed over his chest.

Colonel Keene clears his throat—he may not be in the Society, but he knows there's more at stake here than what's obvious. "What do you want, Miss McKenna?"

"My brother gets reinstated as cadet colonel. His drumming out is removed from his record and he gets the highest recommendation to West Point for going beyond the call of duty and saving a recruit's life."

Colonel Keene nods. "It will happen today."

Rev puts his hand on my shoulder and squeezes. I can't keep the smile off my face.

"Any more *conditions*?" General Matthews asks.

"Just two." I swallow around the lump in my throat but have no doubts as to my next request. "My roommate, Rebekah Cross, was a target of the Society as well. No matter what *stories* came out about her, they were a result of the interference of the Pandora Society. She gets reinstated as well."

"I'll see to it." Colonel Keene writes something down on his notepad. "The last item?"

"The Worms haven't been recognized yet. I'm sure it was just a paperwork snafu," I say, staring at General Matthews. "But we will be recognized. Tomorrow."

"I think those are very reasonable demands, Miss McKenna." Colonel Keene seems relieved.

"Now, if we could get on with the agenda?" General Matthews slides a paper across the table to me. "This is the list of Pandora Society members at the DMA that your brother so graciously provided, plus Recruit Wilson, who I understand is an initiate into the Society. If you will, please verify that the names on this list are correct."

I hold the paper gingerly and when I get to the last name, I look over them all again. "There are only eleven names here."

"Yes," General Matthews says. "Is there a problem?"

Matthews's name is missing. It's not on the list. If he's not on the list it means he'll be here next year. Yes, there's a problem.

I feel Rev tense behind me. *Easy, Sam.*

Scanning the table, my eyes stop on General Matthews. He sits there, the image of calm, but there's a dangerous glint to his eye and I have to look away. "Miss McKenna, is there something wrong? Have we missed someone?" General Matthews's voice is as oily as his son's.

I shake my head, pushing the paper away from me as fast as I can. I grip my hands together in my lap to keep myself from jumping across the table at the general. My foot bounces up and down. I need to get out of here.

The Society is letting me down and the Board thinks I won. But it doesn't matter what I do. The Society will always be in control. General Matthews's presence here—his ability to keep his son at the DMA despite everything he's done and all the proof we've turned over—is evidence of that.

"Just one more thing," Colonel Keene says, and I want to scream. I can't stay under the heavy gaze of General Matthews when he knows I know what he's doing. "We'd like you to meet the new commandant. You and he will be working very closely together, assimilating the new class of females to the Academy."

"Yes, sir," I say, glancing around the table, wondering who will be the next commandant. *If he says General Matthews, I will throw up all over their polished conference table.*

"He'd like to meet you in his office."

I nod and stand, grateful for any excuse to get out from under the general's gaze. "Thank you, sir."

"You did great in there," Rev says when we're back in the hallway. "General Matthews is a powerful man and you stood up to him. Eleven gone is better than none."

I want to believe what he says. "Matthews'll be alone next year. I'm not scared of him anymore," I say, hoping the words will be true soon. When I turn toward the commandant's office, Rev doesn't move. "You're coming in with me to meet the commandant, right?"

He smiles, but stays where he is. "I think you can do this on your own."

"No, please don't go. Please stay with me. I don't think . . ." I look down, smoothing down the front of my tunic and playing with the stitching at the ends of the sleeves.

"You are one of the strongest recruits I've seen come through Denmark Military Academy. You can do this, Sam."

I watch him leave and then steel myself before knocking on the door. The first is too timid and I rap my knuckles on the wood again, more confidently this time, determined to show the new commandant how strong I am.

"Enter."

Standing behind the desk is the new commandant of Denmark Military Academy.

My father.

Slowly I close the door behind me, and when we are alone, I screw all military bearing. I run and throw my arms around him.

He grabs me with the one arm he has left, grunting as the weight of my body slams into him.

"Sam. Sammy. God, will you ever forgive me?"

I pull away because it's the last thing I ever expected to hear from him.

His uniform is too big for him now. He's lost weight in his face and his muscles are soft from lack of use. The sleeve for his left arm, useless now, is pinned up neatly at the shoulder.

"Daddy . . . ," I whisper.

"I've made a hell of a lot of mistakes in my life, Sam." His face looks like it's crumbling. "After—" He gestures to his missing arm. "After this, I realized what was important. I spent three weeks fighting like hell to get back to safety and back to you guys. Maybe if I'd gotten here sooner, we wouldn't be meeting like this." He brushes a tear from his face; it's the first time I've ever seen him appear vulnerable and I know I'm not going to be able to keep it together much longer. "But look at you. So strong. So brave. Your mother is so very proud of you. I'm proud, too, Sammy."

And once again, like so many times before, I dissolve into tears at my father's words. I cling to him until the tears stop falling, and then I cling to him some more.

After two hours, I finally find the strength to leave Dad's office. I thought I'd be walking back to the barracks on my own after spending so long with him, but Jonathan's still there. And Drill. My heart pounds but I don't care anymore. I'm as good as a cadet now. I run down the stairs and Drill opens his arms, waiting.

When Jonathan clears his throat, I pull away.

Drill doesn't smile, his military bearing strong and locked down, even though his eyes are sparkling. "Mac."

Jonathan smiles. "Like the new commandant?"

I take two steps, throwing my arms around Jonathan. "You knew?"

He nods, talking quietly. "Mom's in D.C. Walter Reed has a rehab wing."

"Thank you," I whisper into his ear. Dad's home, Mom's getting help. Maybe things are working out after all. "Thank you, Colonel."

He pulls away. "What did you call me?"

"Colonel. Getting you your rank back is the least I could do."

"You mean . . ." And then it's him reaching for me, pulling me in for a hug.

"Bekah's being invited back, too. They're drumming out everyone but Matthews tonight," I say when we're done with all the hugging. "General Matthews was in there—it was rigged from the beginning."

"I'm sorry, Sammy," Jonathan says.

"I'll deal with it next year. Tomorrow we get recognized."

Drill holds out an envelope to me.

"What's this?"

"Open it, McKenna. That's an order."

"Yes, Drill Sergeant."

The paper is thick and impressive. The black words scripted across the card invite me to attend the Recognition of Alpha Company recruits into Alpha Company proper. I can't believe it. My pulse quickens, but this time it's not from fear. "Is this for real?" I see from the grins on their faces that it is.

"There was never any doubt in Alpha's mind that you guys would make it through the year. They've been printed for weeks. Your recruit buddies are at the top of House Mountain now, but refused to be recognized until you were able to join them. If you want to go, we've got to go now."

"Back up there? I was just there two days ago," I whine.

Drill laughs. "Ready?"

I smile, throwing my arms around Jonathan once more.

"That's one hell of a dare you took on, Sammy."

"I didn't complete it, though, not really. I didn't get recognized on my own. Didn't pass the Worm Challenge on my own."

"As a McKenna, I proclaim the dare passed with flying colors. If anyone has any questions about it, send them to me, okay?" He laughs and spins me around before planting me back on the ground.

Drill parks his car on a fire road and we walk hand in hand the last mile up House Mountain. When we're almost at the top, he stops and turns toward me, dropping my hand. "I need to tell you something."

"Yeah?"

"I talked with your father on the phone yesterday. He told me not to tell," Drill says, holding his hands out in front of him to ward off an attack. "And your dad is still pretty damn scary."

"What did he need to talk to you about on the phone?" Could he have found out about us? The thought's ridiculous, but I can't help but wonder what he'd think of me crushing on my drill sergeant. The last thing I want is to let him down now.

"The normal cadet nomination process is being put aside for next year. He wants me to be cadet colonel."

"That's great!" I reach out for his hand and link our fingers together again. "I know you didn't want it, but you're going to be a great colonel."

He toes the ground with a combat boot, squeezing my hand before pulling away.

"It isn't great?"

He won't meet my eyes. I've never seen this unsure Drill before. Confident? Yes. Pissed? Definitely. But this insecurity? It doesn't suit him at all.

"Sure. It's great. It'll look great on my application to West Point and when I become an officer in the Army."

"But . . . ?"

He reaches his hand toward me, and I reach mine to his, our fingertips grazing each other's but not connecting, just like everything else with him this year. "But whatever this is . . . whatever we could be . . . it can't happen now. Not if I'm cadet colonel."

"You'll outrank me again."

"I will."

I break a little bit as the words tear at my heart. I want him to reach out once more, to feel his arms around me. I want the promise of his lips on me again. But he doesn't make the move. And neither do I. It doesn't matter when or where we would try to date, rank and duty would always get in the way.

He nods, knowing I've put it together. His eyes are sadder

than I've ever seen them. "Go on," he urges. "Your recruit buddies are waiting. I've got to meet up with Huff and the rest of the upperclass Alpha to get ready." He steps onto a side path that heads farther into the woods. He gives me one more sad smile, and it's all I can take. I have to turn away.

Nix, Ritchie, Kelly, Bekah, and all the others stand around the campfire they've built. Kelly smiles and waves me over.

The whole year I thought I had to be strong on my own here, but as I walk toward my company, knowing Dad's home, that my mom's going to be okay, that Jax is a kick-ass hacker, that Bekah's back on the DMA grounds, I realize that being strong can mean a lot of different things. Amos would have been proud I'd figured that out. I wish he had, too. Bekah breaks away from the group and meets me halfway.

"How'd you get here so fast?" I ask when I get close enough for my roommate to hear me.

"I was at Kelly's house, trying to figure out how to tell my parents I was going to go to jail. Your brother called when you started up here and Kelly's mom drove me up." Bekah gives me a tentative smile and I put my arm around her shoulders, squeezing. Together we walk to the campfire. When they see us coming, a cheer goes up from the guys who brought me out of hell, and I smile.

It takes a second to blink away the tears, to calm myself down, but it feels right, being up on this mountain with Alpha. I deserve this moment.

It doesn't matter what happens next year or even after that. We're Alpha. We're family.

And we've *earned* this.

P

S

acknowledgments

Did you guys know it takes a battalion to write a military school book? Well, it does. And there are hundreds of people who fall within its ranks. I know I'm forgetting people and I'll be eternally humiliated when I realize who you are. Consider yourselves thanked and appreciated appropriately now, in spite of my faulty memory. I am forever grateful for everyone who has walked in and out of my life and helped get me where I am today.

To my colonel, Jennifer Klonsky. You believed in this little soldier of a story when she was just a Worm. Your leadership made her the shining cadet she is today.

To my drill sergeant, Agent Awesome herself, Mandy Hubbard. You kicked my butt when I was slacking, you gave me encouragement when I wanted to give up. Sam wouldn't have made it past Hell Week if it weren't for you. She and I both want to thank you for not letting us quit.

To Admin Company, those behind-the-scenes people at HarperTeen who got this book into your hands and made it so pretty that even a tomboy like Sam would squee at the mere sight of it. Catherine Wallace, Ruiko Tokunaga, Melinda Weigel, Christina Colangelo, Rosanne Romanello, and the amazing sales force behind this book have made my words strong, fierce, and able to go into the world on their own. Thank you.

To my fellow Worms in the trenches of the publishing industry: each and every one of you has proven yourself willing and ready for the challenges. Thanks for all the buddy carries. I couldn't have gotten through this without you.

Brigid Kemmerer and Lee Bross—agency-sisters and incredible writers in your own rights. Thank you for taking the time to read, listen, speak, email me pep talks and pep pictures, and slap me across the Twitter face when I wasn't writing like I should have been.

Charity Thamaseb—I don't know how I was lucky enough to score a friend like you. You taught me how to find my voice and then listen to it, and you hooked me up with the best agent a girl could have.

Copil—You breathed life into the Society, my friend. There's not much more to say other than I miss you beyond words. Scotland has gained an incredible guy, even if you won't wear a kilt and think it's weird to be outside.

Jodi—knitter and pep-talker and no-bs-taker. You snorted and O.Oed and squeed at all the right moments. Even when you told me something I wrote sucked, you made me smile. You are the best cousin-by-marriage I have ever had. I wouldn't trade you for anything. Unless there were cupcakes involved. No, not even then.

Kristin Martin, Mandie Baxter, and John Hansen—the best CPs a girl could have. Your vision brought the DMA to life. Especially a certain, ahem, sweatpants scene, Mandie. That's all you, girlfriend. Never, never give up!

Martin—Holy hell, pigs are flying! Thank you for the positive thoughts, the positive words, the positive actions. You saw me through more than one bad day and sat with me countless times in our airport writing cave. Your unwavering belief in Sam's story and in my writing has changed me in ways I can't begin to explain.

Megan Crane—who made me realize, whether she knows it or not, that I could actually write a book.

Spence—You are the tattoo king. Thank you for spending hours tinkering with an idea I didn't know how to explain. You're the best!

Will the soldiers in Friend Company please stand up?

Alpha Company of Norwich University—my family and friends. It's been years, but I think of you often. I'm still amazed that I made it through. I'm smart enough to know that you all are the reason why. GTE.

Bekah—Thanks for letting me borrow your name. You are my first fan and gave me my first fan mail—in Spanish, even! I hope other people think my *libro* is *fantástico*, too.

Bre and Byron—Any mistakes in military structure, either at the DMA or in the military, are not from your lack of trying but from my severe inability to comprehend. Thanks for trying to explain something so complicated to a simpleton like me.

Joanna—You still owe me $25 for surviving the year. You know that, right?

The Millenium Rooks of Norwich University. This book wouldn't be here without you. *Essayons.*

Ollie and Tarascio, Rook brothers extraordinaire. Your guidance, memories, and understanding of military rank structure are worth more than all the Rook Books at the Wick.

Last, but certainly not least, may I present for Pass and Review, the soldiers of Family Company:

Bear—Thank you for not coming to get me the millions of times I called, in hysterics, begging to come home. I know it must have killed you. And I'm sorry. For the cuss words, for putting Sam through what I did. It's just . . . writing happy stories just isn't what I am meant to write. I hope you like Sam anyway. She's strong because of how you taught me to be strong.

Daddy—for giving me the courage, hope, and a belief in myself that only a father can give a daughter. I hope you're proud that, even though I've missed a few steps here and there, I'm finally dancing.

John and Gayle—You gave me your son, who taught me to be brave and reach for my dreams. I'm sorry I keep him half a world away from you, but I thank you from the bottom of my heart for the gift. I promise to cook dinner for once . . . just as soon as I'm done writing my next book.

Nan-Nan—Thanks for the early birthday present. So I almost died spending a night on the side of a hill during a lightning storm. Holding this book in your hands is proof that the near-death experience was worth it. I loved that birthday present more than any other.

Peggy—Thank you for the blanket under which I NANOWRIMO-ed most of the book. Your love kept me warm even when I had to put Sam through some serious . . . stuff.

Yames—Sam didn't have a sister, but maybe if she had, she would have believed in herself more. Thank you for seeing something in me that I still can't see sometimes. You make me believe in myself. Know what I'm talkin' aboot? Love you.

To S, X, and B—I know you're not in alphabetical order, and I know it'll probably bug me for the rest of my life, but I did have to save you for last. Because you let me be a crazy writer shut in a room while you guys played in a messy, neglected house or disappeared because Mommy just needed a few hours alone with the voices in her head. I couldn't have done any of this without you three ready to catch me if I stumbled. Every word in here is for you, because without you, there'd be no point.